THE TESTIMONY

James Smythe was born in London in 1980. Since completing a PhD at Cardiff University he has worked as a computer game writer/ narrative designer and currently teaches creative writing. He lives on the grounds of a boarding school in West Sussex. He can be found on Twitter @jpsmythe

Also by James Smythe

The Explorer

JAMES SMYTHE

The Testimony

blue door

Blue Door
An imprint of HarperCollinsPublishers
77–85 Fulham Palace Road,
Hammersmith, London W6 8JB

www.harpercollins.co.uk

This paperback edition 2013
1
First published in Great Britain by Blue Door 2012

A catalogue record for this book is
available from the British Library

ISBN: 978-0-00-746772-3

Set in Minion by Palimpsest Book Production Limited,
Falkirk, Stirlingshire

Printed and bound in Great Britain by
Clays Ltd, St Ives plc

MIX
Paper from
responsible sources
FSC www.fsc.org FSC™ C007454

Absence of Evidence is not Evidence of Absence.
Dr Carl Sagan
(on the potential existence of a deity,
or extraterrestrial life)

Absence of Evidence is not Evidence of Absence.
Donald Rumsfeld
(on the potential existence of weapons
of mass destruction in Iraq)

STATIC

Phil Gossard, sales executive, London

At first, we thought that the noise was just a radio. We didn't even think about how long it had been since we'd had a *real* radio anywhere near the office; it just struck us that it was the same noise, tuning it. We were sitting in the office eating our lunches; the sandwich man had done his daily delivery, and I had picked a ham roll. I *never* had ham. We didn't eat together, not usually, but we were trying it as something new, get the team together for a daily meal, something more social than just work. It promoted a sense of team-building that the management thought we were missing. At the talks, the meetings, they told us that we should learn to lean on each other more. This is a way to bring you all together, they told us. Three or four bites into the sandwich, I noticed it, niggling; like a radio, as I say, sitting at the back of the room. I asked the rest of them if they could hear it, and they couldn't at first, and then one of them did – Marcus, I think, from sales – so we followed the noise, tried to find where it was coming from. Is it speakers, from the computers? somebody asked, but it wasn't that. We thought it was louder as we went towards

1

the window, so we opened them. Where's it coming from? Marcus asked, but neither of us could tell because it sounded like it was coming from all around us. It seemed stupid to say it at the time, but it seemed like it was coming from inside my head; I didn't say that, and then the others started to hear it, one by one. The whole thing seemed to take a few minutes, I reckon – but it could have been less, could have been more – and when the static reached its loudest, Bill, our boss, decided to go downstairs, see if it was louder there. We watched him out of the windows, in the street with people from all the other offices, and they all just sort of stood there and listened. Within a couple more minutes everyone from the other offices was either out there as well or crowded round at their own windows, and we were all listening to it. And then it was gone.

Simon Dabnall, Member of Parliament, London

It's a rare day that you have silence in the House of Commons. There was some head of state in from one of the Eastern European nations, and that tended to make some of the back-benchers rowdy, make them show off. That's attention-grabbers for you. Some of the rabble liked to think that it might make their names stand out for future PM-related references. Sad, really. The visiting chap just sat and stared at the panelling. But it was a loud day anyway: something about the NHS (again), immigrants (again), terrorism controls in the heart of Staines (again), and most of the front-benchers were going at it cats and dogs. That pillock from Chester was waving his hands around as he shouted, like he was being pestered by a wasp, that way that he did, and nobody was listening to him. Then we heard the static – that's what we all agreed it sounded like, at first, like the sound of televisions in the middle of the night – and Chester stopped his flapping, and we listened. There's never any sound in the room that we don't know about – there were no crowds outside, no tours, and it's about as soundproofed as a room without real soundproofing can get – so we all looked around for the source, heads peeking up like we were meerkats.

When it was over – quick as it began, as if somebody just flicked a switch and turned the power off – we just sat there, and nobody said anything for the longest time, until the speaker told us to reconvene the following day. We all shuffled out onto the riverbank, seemingly along with everybody else on both sides of the river, and we just milled around. It's like a fire drill, somebody joked, but it wasn't *really* a joke. The tubes, the buses, nothing was running – everybody froze because this was an *event* – so we were all just stranded there.

Jacques Pasceau, linguistics expert, Marseilles

It was like you were trying to tune into the right frequency but you were wearing ear-muffs, that's how clear the noise was. We were working on a translation of something – me, Audrey, Patrice, David, Jolie – working on verbs, some dull shit like that for an undergrad class I was tutoring, and suddenly there it was, *Chhhhhhhhhhh*. I've never heard anything like it. I mean, people called it static, but I thought it was more like a growl, even. I said that out loud when it was finished and we were just talking about it over and over, and Audrey said that I was being stupid, but you know, I *wasn't*, not really.

Meredith Lieberstein, retiree, New York City

12th of April, life is normal. 13th of April, still normal. 14th of April, everything gets torn apart, or put back together, whichever way you want to think of it. We had only just woken up – Leonard's bladder, same as every night, tick tock – when it happened. I had the TV on, quietly, because I wasn't completely awake, and I thought it was coming from that at first, then they went to one of those *We Have A Fault* screens, and the noise didn't stop. When Leonard came back he flicked around through the channels, trying to find CNN – because that had never gone down, not that we could remember, or BBC World – but that was the same. *We Have A Fault.* How often do you need the news to tell you what's actually going on these days, anyway? The one time we needed it, and it was no help at all. Eventually one of them came back – Fox was first, I think, because I remember Leonard joking about there being a first time for everything – and they started telling us what we already knew, with no explanations. There has been an event, they said. Within minutes they were referring to the noise as static, though we thought it sounded more like paper being crumpled. Leonard was watching, flicking the channels, when we heard the beeping from outside, so I went out onto the fire stairs. Cars were logged up around the park, people out of them and walking around. You could see that they were scared, even from four floors up. Look at this, Leonard said, and I went back in to see the helicopter footage of the Brooklyn Bridge – those were the days when they constantly had the helicopters out, circling the city at night just *waiting* for something to happen, convinced that, sooner or later, they would be in the right place at the right time – and the bridge was chock-full of cars, some of them empty, some of them crashed (because the drivers had been fiddling with their radios or headsets, looking for the source of the static, I'd guess). This was – Fox News called it – a Community Event, capital C, capital E, like a ceasefire or an election or garden barbecues on the 4th of July.

Andrew Brubaker, White House Chief of Staff, Washington, DC

We were talking through POTUS' schedule, because something had to be added, visiting some library because he had said something about funding them – I don't know, small-time stuff. It was ten minutes to wheels up, cabin doors were sealed, press were all seated, and then we heard the static. When you're with the President of the United States sitting on Air Force One and you hear a noise like that? You assume it's an attack.

Piers Anderson, private military contractor, the Middle East

As a soldier, no matter what you're doing – sleeping, on a recce, whatever – you hear a noise you haven't heard before, you damn well listen. We were packing, and there was a hand-over at the camp happening. We'd been on recon, which was all we ever did in those days. It had been a couple of decades since we'd actually needed to be out there in any great number, but people – the people with the money and the power – were still scared. The Yanks were taking it over from us, which was a hell of a relief, let me tell you. We weren't having a party, exactly, but we were happy to be leaving, and then we heard the static. Somebody asked if it wasn't just the sand. We'd had storms a few days previous, and it was a bit easier to assume that it might be that than . . . well, whatever it was. I've seen the footage on the news now of people going crazy because of it, panicking, all that, but we just tried to get on with our jobs. We loaded the trucks, took them to the airfield. A random noise might have made us prick up our ears, but there was no way it was stopping us getting home, I'll tell you that for nothing. What did stop us coming home? Orders. We were barely on the plane when we were told that we weren't going anywhere, that we were to stay put until the government knew what the hell it was that made the noise. That meant that somebody somewhere was worried that it was terror-related, so we knew we'd be there for the long haul.

Tom Gibson, news anchor, New York City

I was putting my tie on again. We were at commercials, and I'd been watching it on the monitors the whole broadcast, mocking me, crooked across my shirt. I called for the floor manager to do it, but she was fumbling through so I snapped it away and used the picture coming off camera 2 to set it straight. When the static started we thought it was coming from the equipment, so my producer shouted up to the booth to check, but they said everything was functioning normally, but they could hear it as well, and they were soundproofed. It got louder and louder and then we realized that we were meant to have gone back on the air, so they played the filler screen while I got myself together. Somebody looked out of the windows, down at Times Square, and everybody was looking up. They all heard it, they said, so I made the decision to talk about it on air. We were the first to, first on with a report about what we would come to know as *The Broadcast*.

Isabella Dulli, nun, Vatican City

Part of our day was being a presence; being around with the people, walking around the City and spreading the word of God to them. Because that was why they were there, visiting us; to see the Holy Father and get his blessing, and to be so close to God, as those of us in service to Him were. The queues were always so long, at the ticket office, and we took it in turns to visit with the people as they waited, to talk with them of God's majesty. The day of the static, that was my day, my only one of the month, where I was attending the queues. The people started queuing in the very early hours, before the sun was even up, because the Tomb of St Peter was only open so very rarely. They wanted to see it so much, because it was so old. In the guestbook, they write that it smells holy, and that they can really feel Christ's presence there, the gaze of God Himself. I always laughed at that, because I said, You can feel His gaze everywhere, and they said, I know, but here *especially*. I enjoyed my days working around the Basilica, because everybody was always in awe. The morning of the static, I was so happy, ready for the day; I was down by the crowds, and they were asking me questions about my piety, about what it was like to be so close to God's love – It is a miracle, I would say, it is like no love that I have ever known before, and it is incomparable, original and beautiful and wonderful – and I was answering them as I always did. I was in a photograph with some gentlemen, come over from Germany, posing for them when I – we all – heard it. The tour guide that they had asked to take the photograph told us to say, Thanks be

7

to God, and then we heard it. The Germans said the phrase – I know, because I heard them, but they were so far away as to be blocked out, like they were in another room, shut away behind doors – but I didn't, because the static came, and everybody started panicking. All I could think was, Please, God, let this sound in our ears be a good thing.

Mark Kirkman, unemployed, Boston

I didn't hear it. I was in a bar, should have been in bed already, and everybody else stopped, listened, switched the music off. I tried really hard, once I worked out what was going on, but I just couldn't hear it.

Theodor Fyodorov, unemployed, Moscow

I was in bed, because Anastasia didn't have class. She had a bag of pot with her, so we did what we always did – put cartoons on, smoked pot in bed (I didn't have the heating on most of the time, not until it was so cold that the pipes would freeze if I didn't turn it on), and then I cooked breakfast, and we read books – she loved reading, loved reading all the English-language books, not even translated, showing off to me, because she knew I didn't read anything in Russian, let alone English. We were in bed when we heard the static, and it freaked her out at first, like a cat hearing a noise it doesn't expect; then she settled down, and we swapped cartoons for the news.

María Marcos Callas, housewife, Barcelona

We were staying in the city, for our anniversary. We always went back every five years or so, because it was where he proposed to me, in the Basilica, which was my favourite church. I had spent the morning praying by myself, as I did most mornings, and I was getting ready to finish before the service began. I prayed by myself because it was a way to truly get God to hear you through all of the other voices, you see – you pray so hard amongst a sea of ambivalence, and your prayer rises above the darkness – and then, all of a sudden, He started to speak to me, to us, to the world. We couldn't hear Him, of course, because He spoke in tongues, but it was His divine power. Romans chapter ten, verse seventeen: So Faith comes by hearing, and hearing comes as the Word of God. I sat there and wept, because I couldn't believe that He had chosen me, and then I saw that others had heard it, and I wept because it meant that we were all hearing Him, all of us, and we were all saved.

Dafni Haza, political speechwriter, Tel Aviv

I had just started my job that day, and one of the first tasks as part of my position was to issue a statement reassuring the people, letting them know that their government was looking into the situation. It was the same in every single country around the world; but I was new, and the people of Israel expected statements, so I wrote them. It wasn't an order. Part of the role involved thinking for myself, thinking on my feet, being pre-emptive. I had always been good with words. It was a particular skill of mine, to be able to phrase them the right way. My father used to say that I could sell *anything*, and that I should go into sales, into marketing; I agreed, but wanted to do something with those skills, something more than just *selling*. I wanted to go into politics, so that's what I worked for. Speech-writing was the way in: I was good at spinning things, making them sound good, or true. The static was there, everybody heard it, and everybody wanted to know what it was. It was my responsibility to give them an answer that came from the government itself, and reassurance was the government's watchword. That's the way that it works.

I had a team, and we had a press release being planned as soon as the television reports started asking what it was, and we realized that everybody heard it, it was a big deal – or it was going to be a big deal – and that we would have to deal with it. We didn't have time to even think about what it actually was. We had to just get on with our jobs.

Dhruv Rawat, doctor, Bankipore

I forget now why they were filming in the region before the static, but they had video cameras, full crews. All the children had run over to see what they were doing, standing by the catering tables – tables of food! In that heat! – and peering through, desperate to be on the camera. That was always the way, when the cameras were in town: all the children wanted to be in on it. They knew that they would probably never even see what they were being filmed for, but that didn't stop them. (Somebody, I forget who, said that the glare of the spotlight hits the people even on the streets of India, when they're already blinded by the sun. It must have been somebody intelligent, but I cannot for the life of me remember who.) I remember when I was a child, and the first time the television cameras came and filmed us all for the British news, and we didn't know what they were. That sounds like a lie, I know, but I was very young – only four or five, young enough to not know any better, and we did not have a television in my house, of course – and my friends and I did not believe that they could film us, put us on their screens as they did, show us what we looked like there. It was fascinating! People say, what moments made you decide to change your life? That was one for me, because they were so glamorous. There was one lady with them, wearing a long white skirt and a shirt that clung to her body like I had never seen, and a hat that was thick and white and nearly covered her entire face in shade. I went over to her, and she was the one who told us what they were doing there, and I thought, Some day I'll persuade them to film me. After that, my plan, of course, was to leave Bankipore and go somewhere else – of course, dreaming of Mumbai – and to be on camera. I never went, because nobody ever does. Instead, I worked hard at school, and then went to Bangalore and I became a doctor, and then I moved back to Bankipore, because I thought that I could do some good here. That is what all my doctor friends said, if they weren't going overseas; they were going home to do some good. Then, when the static happened and the cameras were there, I was the person standing closest to them, trying to see what they were there for. The woman talking to the camera, I recognized her from the international news television channel they showed in the hotel restaurant-bar – I lived out of hotels for a while. I was outside when the static happened, and the woman came over to me, saw that I was smartly dressed – I wore a shirt and tie to work every day, because it established a rule from the second I saw a patient, that I was a doctor, an authority – and she asked me if I heard the static as well; she wanted to check that it wasn't coming from their equipment. I told her, Yes, of course I did.

Is it a noise that's common here? she asked. A nearby factory or something? I said, No, I have never heard it before. I asked some of the children – who were over by my offices, by the wall, lined up as if they were waiting for their turn to be spoken to by the woman – and they said that they had not heard it before either. I am sorry, I told the woman. Will you say something about it on camera, just in case? she asked, and I said, Of course I will. She went back to her crew, who were all Indian as well, but they weren't local, because nobody from Bankipore had that sort of equipment (that I knew of), and they all came over, set up in front of me. What do you think it was? she asked me, and I said, seeing myself reflected in the camera lens, that I thought it was probably nothing, because we couldn't explain what it was. I am a man of science; there has to be an explanation for me to believe it, I said. Thank you, she said, and she moved on.

Elijah Said, prisoner on Death Row, Chicago

I was asleep when I first heard the static, in my cot. They called them cots, like we were babies. Lots of people in there didn't sleep, defiantly staying awake, rattling anything they could against the bars, or howling their way through the nights. They would try to make sure that nobody could forget who they were, or *where* they were. I am a murderer, their actions called out, you would do well to remember who it is that I am, what I am capable of. It is within me to commit horrors upon you, and for that reason, I do not sleep when you tell me to; I sleep on my own timescale. On the corridor, we didn't get exercise like the rest, didn't get library time. Our meals were visited upon us, delivered on trays, always hot, always neatly plated, our cutlery thin shards of blunt plastic that was counted back when we were finished with our meals. If we tried anything – and I did not, but I watched as others did, unrepentant in their drive for freedom, or revenge – the cutlery was removed completely, and the prisoner ate with their hands, like a primate, free yet ignorant. The guards would laugh as they spooned potato into their mouths, with the gravy dripping through their fingers; that's your punishment, they would say. No, I say: their punishment was both being there in the first place, behind those bars; and also would be delivered by Allah upon their death, a death that they entirely deserved for the crimes that they had committed toward their fellow man. They howled in the nights, dogs, desperate for their creator to put them out of their misery.

I could sleep through the catcalling, the constant abuse; but when a noise was unknown it would rouse me from even the deepest sleep. The static had us all on our feet, demanding to know what was happening. The guards ignored us, and left us alone. That was the first time I could remember the corridor being left unguarded; no matter how loud the shouts came for the next few minutes, the guards didn't return, and we were briefly free from their watch to do as we pleased within those confines; for my part, I was on my musalla, praying.

The guards returned after a few minutes, when I was still praying, and they put the lights on along the corridor, demanded that we turn out. They were on edge, frantic as mice. As always, I stood back, allowed them into my cell. As always, they invaded my privacy, their trust of my people so low that they felt no shame in their intrusions. They searched under my cot, in the metal basin they called a toilet, around my person. They searched my mat, which they were forbidden to do, and they provoked me, prodded me like I was cattle, all to get a reaction. You don't say much, do you? they asked, and I did not reply: No, I do not.

When they were gone, and the corridor was quiet again – a comparative quiet, a quiet that is still loud with shouting, but constant, our own personal take on the tranquil – my neighbour, a murderer by the name of Finkler, spoke to me. Hey, brother, he said, because he called everybody of colour that name – as if he were saying, I am one of you, the oppressed, the downtrodden, *we are in this together* – you know what that was? No, I replied. He carried on, even though the lights were now out, and the guards demanded silence from us: What d'you reckon it was, then? Allah will deliver answers, I said. He went quiet. Even in here he knew I could still kill him, if he didn't go at the hands of the state first.

WE'RE HAVING PROBLEMS

Phil Gossard, sales executive, London

As soon as the TV broadcasts came back online, we expected there to be answers. There weren't any. They actually only seemed to know as much as we did. In some ways, that was a relief, actually. I think some people expected the noise to be a signal, a warning. Some people thought it meant that we were being attacked, and who could blame them for thinking that? Biological, that was the biggest threat, but anything else, really. Nuclear, Semtex, we didn't care. We were all so on edge because it had been what, ten years since an attack? And there were constant whispers about terrorists holing themselves up, waiting for chances. I mean, there were rumours about everything, actually, especially about the new American president (that he was, despite his campaign promises, actually more anti-war than even Obama was, a couple of terms back) and about the threat from Iran. When it was done we left the windows and switched the telly on, and it had that *We're Having Problems* screen on the BBC – Aren't we just, I said out loud, but nobody laughed – and then a minute or so later it kicked back in. It wasn't a regular newsreader – they were

15

interrupting whatever had been on previously, so I suppose it was whoever they had to hand, dragged up from *Newsround* like it was work experience week – and then they reported what had happened, that we all heard something. They went to somebody outside BT Tower, asking for opinions. Everybody they spoke to was just confused. It was strange, actually; that corner is usually a flow of people moving between Tottenham Court Road and Oxford Street, but nobody was moving. They were just milling around, looking terrified or elated or whatever. Bemused, that's the word. Most of them looked bemused.

Bill hadn't come back from downstairs, so everybody started to look to me for answers. (I wasn't even second in command, but if in doubt ask marketing, right?) I didn't have a clue, so I told everybody to take the rest of the day off. Go home; see you tomorrow. Traffic'll be shitty, you should all get a head start. Nobody left though, not immediately. We went back to the windows and watched the streets, kept the news on in the background, and waited to see if anybody could work out what the noise was.

Peter Johns, biologist, Auckland

I remember thinking, Hang on, because the scientists'll announce something any second, tell us that they fucked up and that they've got it all under control. We was in this bar in Auckland and we missed the last boat back to the island because of the noise – I mean, who in their right mind is gonna get on a boat after hearing something like that? We didn't know what it was, so we waited. Trigger, my assistant, got behind the bar after the manager didn't want to serve us any more and just started pouring them out. The manager didn't even care; he was out in the street seeing if anybody knew what the heck was going on. We must have been in there drinking for a couple of hours before we even got so much as a whiff of an answer.

Andrew Brubaker, White House Chief of Staff, Washington, DC

Before the static had even stopped we had POTUS locked down in his office, and the service went over Air Force One top to bottom. They could do the whole plane (offices, press seats, cabin, hold, exterior) in two and half minutes. We cut off all comms to the aircraft – radio dark, they called it – and we sat still as they checked us a second time. I mean, totally still. Not even blinking. When they were sure that the noise didn't come from the aircraft they let us get up from our seats, start using some of the tech again. POTUS was on the phone to China as soon as the handset was passed to him, and he had the Russian PM holding, with calls to return to the Brits, the Germans, the Japanese. I heard him speaking to the Chinese President. I assure you, he was saying, this was nothing to do with us, it was a natural phenomenon, it was not an attack. It's a fine line, he said when he hung up, because those guys are ready to bite. They'll lash out as soon as we do. We step off the ledge first, they'll dive in after us.

When he was making the rest of his calls I told Kerry what was going on – she was the press secretary – and told her to keep the rumours under control. Does anybody know what the fuck is going on? I asked, and she said, Not a clue, so I told her to make something up. There's going to be a hell of a lot of confused people out there, and the last thing we need

17

is them reacting, so we're going to have to tell them something. The leaders of the free world couldn't just sit there and quietly wait for an explanation to fall into our laps; we had to make that explanation happen. You can't fly tonight, the service told us, so we got back into the cars and went back to the White House before anything else could happen. We were there within five minutes, and I was watching them fielding questions in the press room within seven.

Phil Gossard, sales executive, London

People slowly started filtering off – there was a thing somebody read on the internet about public transport being at a standstill, and we were all British, so that meant we should all rush and try to get on a bus as soon as possible – when the BBC started looking at different options for what it could be. They had an astronomer on from Oxford Uni, and he was saying that there was nothing in the sky. Couldn't it just be a sound from deep space? asked the presenter, like that was a thing we saw every day, and the astronomer said, No, it couldn't be, because there's nothing there. Nothing on any of the SETI equipment, we're getting nothing. It didn't come from space. Are you sure? the presenter asked, and he said, Ninety-nine point nine per cent. There's always a slight margin of error. So what could it be? they asked him, Could it be aliens? I remember this: he laughed a bit and said, At this point, anything's possible, right? He meant it as a joke, I think, but of course they took that as a yes and ran with it. Within minutes, every single news broadcast is saying that it could be aliens that caused the static. *Could be.*

Simon Dabnall, Member of Parliament,
London

I found myself in a McDonald's, if you can believe that, the one down by the Dali museum (and I remember thinking how appropriate that was). It was fit to burst with children and their somehow even more high-pitched parents; but it also had the huge television screens across the back wall that showed the news all day. I watched the reporters discussing the static, sticking their microphones in everybody's faces, trying to get opinions. They cut between them – some of them at the busier parts of W1, some of them in suburb areas, a very cold-looking man in Newcastle – and then they cut to one outside Westminster, talking about the close of session. It's clear, the girl said, that even the government isn't sure what to make of this curious state of affairs. No, they do not, I said to myself. (After that, the woman next to me moved her children along the bench slightly, putting her coat between myself and her daughter. She tutted. Tutted!) Then they cut to another reporter right outside where we were, microphone in the faces of the tourists, who seemed entirely confused by the whole thing. I put down my godawful coffee and went out there and watched the interviews. She kept looking over at me, as if she recognized me, but she didn't ask me anything. Sir, I heard her say to a burly Yank in sandals and a luridly floral shirt that gaped across his gut. Do you think that the static could be the first contact we have with another race? I'll be damned if I know, he said, but no; I would guess that it would be some sort of experiment by the government, that would be my guess. His whole family squeezed themselves into the shot to voice their opinions after him, and then all the other tourists who saw the cameras followed. *Savages.*

19

Andrew Brubaker, White House Chief of Staff, Washington, DC

I was speaking to the National Security Agency when the alien stuff started coming through on the wire, and the journalists at the back began shouting questions about it. Half of me wanted to step in, tell them that of course there weren't any fucking aliens, but the other half . . . I mean, look, there weren't aliens, clearly, but the alternative was far less palatable. We'd spent twenty years worrying about terrorism, about attacks, and all of a sudden there was this, and it would have been so easy for the press to panic about it more than they should have. As I say, we didn't have a fucking clue what it was, but it wasn't aliens, and we were crossing our fingers it wasn't anything worse. I told the press office to ignore all questions about that, just deny it, keep the cycle spinning for a while until we knew what it actually was. None of them believed it was aliens anyway; they just wanted something to fill column inches, same as we did.

I was heading down the corridor past the briefing room when a journalist from the *Post* stopped me, asked me how we would treat the static if it *was* a first-contact situation with an alien race. You really want me to answer that? I asked, and he did, so I said, We would treat it like we'd treat any other sort of first contact: with extreme fucking caution.

Ed Meany, research and development scientist, Virginia

We ran so many tests. I mean, we were into tests up to our asses, you have no idea. Picture this: there were seven individual departments of governmental science, and they each had sub-departments, three or four apiece. Each sub-department was running its own tests, so there were tests on background noise levels, radiation levels, NASA stuff, security stuff, tests to do with animals, asking people what they *thought* it could be. I mean, anything you can imagine, we were testing for it somewhere. There were only a couple of divisions not working on it, because they worked on the stuff nobody knew about – plausible deniability and all that jazz. We were sending out single-sentence press releases through the White House press office when we eliminated something from the running, just to try and get everything under control. Everything else was standing still. Two minutes after POTUS told us to start running the tests (even though we had already started, clearly, because we weren't the sort of assholes who waited for a go-order from somebody who had no idea what we were *actually* doing) there were statements put out to the press to calm the nation, urge the emergency services to keep going, to go to work as normal. We couldn't risk a shutdown of them, all of us knew that. So he asked everybody to keep going as normal, and I think most people did, that day. We did; the TV stations did, and I'm betting that every 7-Eleven was still selling Slushies.

Mark Kirkman, unemployed, Boston

I can't remember how long I sat in that bar and watched the TV. Hours, probably. Max, the barman, kept putting drinks in my hand, and I kept drinking them. I didn't say anything, that I didn't hear it, and we all just watched the news as it rolled in. They went on about the aliens for an hour, maybe more, and then finally they started asking, well, what else could it be? One of the early theories was something to do with cell phones, like that beep you get when you leave it on top of a speaker? But it didn't stick, and that became the news cycle. What is it, what is it, over and over. An hour later, every station was answering that question by sticking anybody with an even vaguely religious background on their shows.

Meredith Lieberstein, retiree, New York City

How to divide the world into three camps over a single hour: make them pick between science, fantasy and religion. Give them a situation, a hypothetical situation, then give them three possible reasons for it happening – could be aliens, could be God, could be something we made ourselves and just haven't worked out what yet – and ask them to choose. You choose the wrong one, the worst that happens is you choose again. So, we all took a stance, and there was a part of it that day – I'm not ashamed to tell you – that felt a bit like choosing between the side of the sane, and the side of . . . well, the *other*.

Phil Gossard, sales executive, London

There was a priest on the sofa with the BBC presenters saying that it was God speaking to us for the first time in two thousand years. (Since He first spoke to us through his son Jesus Christ, I think those were his exact words.) We can hear his voice, but of course we cannot comprehend it, he argued. The priest was old, set in his ways, you could tell. We can't comprehend it because He's speaking in tongues. Then he reeled off quotes from the Bible that seemed to back up his idea, if you squinted, and said that all good Christians should go to church and pray. If you believe, he said, you'll go, because that is how you can tell God exactly how much you love Him. He's made contact, the priest said; now it's your turn to answer back. That just killed it. Half the office had gone by that point, trying to beat the traffic and make it home for the day; that took most of the rest. Ten minutes later, people everywhere were flooding to their nearest church. And I mean that, it's not me being over-emphatic; the streets were clogged.

Meredith Lieberstein, retiree, New York City

Leonard wasn't a fickle man. He was a man of conviction; that's one of the things that I most liked about him, that most attracted me to him. He knew who he was. We saw the news reports about people flocking to their churches and synagogues or what have you, and he didn't even blink. And our closest synagogue was only minutes away, so it would have been all too easy for him to fall back on old habits.

We watched them on TV as they divided it up – and gosh, it seems like all we did that morning was watch things happening, when you really break it down. CNN had figure-heads from all major religions on within an hour, and they fought over what the static was. They didn't say it, because I suppose they couldn't, but it actually felt as if they were fighting about whose God it was. The Greek Orthodox priest kept nearly saying something, you could tell, then holding it back; he finally spat it out as the segment was coming to a close. What if it's Allah, he said, or somebody else, Ganesh, Buddha; just not whoever it is that you already worship? What if you've got it wrong? There was this look that went across them all, then, because I don't think that they had even considered that possibility. Typical, Leonard said. An hour spent in the presence of the maker, and already they're starting to wonder if they picked the right team.

Dafni Haza, political speechwriter, Tel Aviv

My husband called me so many times that day that I had to put my phone onto silent, and even then the sound of the vibrations against other things in my bag was irritating, so I hid it in a drawer and then forgot about it for a while. When he actually got hold of me he was frantic. What was that? he asked me, and I said that I didn't know. Why didn't you answer your phone? Because I'm busy, I told him. That was a common argument we had, because . . . There was a time that I was with somebody else, after I was married to him. Nobody else knew but the man and my husband, and it was only once, but the trust didn't come back. So he thought that I was seeing him again, or maybe somebody else, I don't know. He whined about it all the time. He didn't like that I had taken the new job, anyway. (The government in Tel Aviv is full of men, he said, when we argued about it; what he meant was, powerful men – the man I had cheated with was a powerful man, and it was a new theme, because when I had met Lev and fallen in love with him, he had been powerful too.) Look, he said, I just want to know what the static was. I'll tell you when we know something, I said, and he said, Come on, you know now, you're on the inside, you can tell me. I told you that I don't know, I said, but I do know that I have work to do. You'll tell me as soon as you find out more, okay? he asked, and I said, Fine. I love you, he said.

Jacques Pasceau, linguistics expert, Marseilles

It became this gospel, that it was the voice of God talking to us, you know? It was a definitive, apparently, because there was no other answer. We were watching the priests on the news, and the phone rang, and it was some Church-funded organization near Lyon, asking us to go and do some translation work for them. I asked them what they wanted us to translate, and the man said, Well, what He said to us, of course. I slammed the phone down, and Audrey said, What? What?, and I said, It was fucking static! You can't translate static! Audrey said I was cutting off my nose, blah blah blah, that we could get funding out of it, somehow, that it would help the university's reputation . . . I said to her, If you start going and working for these people and then you're wrong – if it *is* just static – then it's you that looks the imbecile.

I didn't ask her, because there were other people around, but I think she thought it actually *was* God, you know.

Audrey Clave, linguistics postgraduate
student, Marseilles

Jacques always acted like he was so much better than the rest of us, which is one of the reasons that I was so attracted to him. My mother used to joke that I only liked bad boys, and Jacques was as close to a bad boy as you got in the linguistics department of the University of Aix-Marseille, so it was only natural. We had only been on the same project for a few weeks, and we had only been seeing each other for days. I mean, really, we had kissed a few times, and other stuff, and then the static happened, and it was suddenly this big pressure cooker. People were going crazy outside – because you can't hear God without there being implications, right? And no matter how many times people say, It might not be God, it might not be God, there was no proof, no evidence either way, so people were always going to overreact and refuse to stay calm. They gave the rest of us a bad name, I think.

We were watching France 24, and there was footage of a riot happening near Notre Dame, because there were so many people trying to get in to pray there. There were too many people in the streets, and they were too on edge for anything to stay simmering. That's just the way it is with people. There had been so many riots over the years before it, so many people unhappy, and so much tension, because everything got worse after 9/11, you see, everything got so tense and kept on getting tenser and tenser, and that just meant that people were going to explode, sooner or later. You look at the riots in LA in the 1990s, in Seattle, in Athens, with the students, the ones in Egypt when they shut off their internet, the ones in London a couple of summers after they had the Olympics: you look at those; that's a boiling point, and people reached it, and they were scared. How long had it been since I had last gone to church? A year, maybe. So why shouldn't I have been scared as well?

We tried to stay focused, to get on with what we were doing before. (Now, I can't even remember what that was. Something . . . No, I can't remember.) We weren't all happy to be there, though; some people around the offices wanted to leave, some wanted to stay. I wanted to stay, because I knew that Jacques wasn't going to go anywhere, and I didn't want to leave him alone. If everything was going to be fine, then there was no reason that I wouldn't just stay there with him; and if everything *wasn't* fine, then I wanted to be right there as well.

Jacques Pasceau, linguistics expert, Marseilles

Some of us wanted to run away there and then – which made me so angry, because there was nothing to run from in the first place – but I persuaded them all to spend the night there, or that we should prepare to spend the night. The trains and buses weren't running properly, and I only had my bike, so I couldn't exactly give everybody a lift home. What we – David and I – decided was that we needed to have some booze there, have a bit of a party, so we offered to go and get supplies. Nobody was going to make it home that evening; Audrey lived in Aix, David was from Avignon, Patrice was from Carpentras, I think, so it was pretty much out of the question. David and I told the others that we would go to the supermarket, get some stuff – Be the hunters, Audrey said – and we left the other three in the offices.

Everything on the way to the supermarket was closed, which must have been because of the static. It was a Monday, there was no reason for anything to be shut, and the supermarket was 24 hours anyway, so we thought it would be fine. When we got there though, there weren't any members of staff around, and the front door had been opened – David noticed it – forced back, we reckoned. The place was full – if you weren't at church you were shopping, right? – and everybody was just grabbing at the meats and fish, and those aisles were pretty bare, so we headed straight for the tinned stuff, baked beans and soups and tins of olives and anchovies – anything that we could eat cold, basically – and then ran to the wine, got what we could. We weren't fussy – it was to get pissed, not worry about the quality of the grape – so we took the German shit, the Rieslings, the Blue Nun, the sweet stuff that nobody else wanted. I found some German 'champagne' and showed it to David, and we both laughed but we took it anyway, because it was free, and it would do the job.

Then we heard people screaming by the front and there was this guy with an enormous white beard, down to his chest, and he was waving this old rifle around, that looked like it was an antique, even. Oh my God! David shouted (and we found that pretty funny when we left, and thought about it). The old man was threatening to shoot people unless they left the supermarket – You will all repent! he kept shouting – so we took that as our cue to run. The glass by the wine had been smashed along the front of the shop, so we picked the trolley up, lifted it over, and we started to run with it up the street. The guy saw us and chased after us – he was barefoot, and he cut himself over the glass, and I shouted back, Stop and fix yourself! and then he screamed, Take this! and we both stopped and braced ourselves, because we thought he was going to shoot at us. (I don't know why we stopped running; seems pretty stupid, thinking about it now.) But he didn't fire; he threw the gun at us instead, at our feet, and I went and picked it up, put it in the trolley. You never know, I said. When we had made it to the top of the hill I took it out to look at it, stared down the barrel, made *pew-pew* noises. We opened a box of the wine, started guzzling it as we walked back – much slower than the walk there – and when we got in

David took the gun to hide it before Audrey saw it, because she would have totally freaked out.

Andrew Brubaker, White House Chief of Staff, Washington, DC

We had a statement prepared that POTUS was going to go on air with. It was the fourth or fifth draft, maybe, and we *never* wrote that many. We were a two-draft administration – the writing staff getting one out, then I made changes, sometimes POTUS changed a word or two. That was usually it, but this one, POTUS insisted on going over everything himself. And it kept changing. The first draft was about how we didn't have the right answers but we had our best men working on it; the second was about how the answer might not be the important thing, and maybe the *question* that it raised was what mattered; the third draft was about speculation being a dangerous thing (and that was aimed at both the press and every other country across the entire god-damned world); the fourth draft was just begging people to keep themselves under control. We had to face the rioting head on, we knew that. What we heard – the static, whatever – was still there, but suddenly we, as an administration, didn't care as much what it was, because reports were coming in from LA, from Texas, from Chicago, reports about the people of America becoming restless.

You know, actually, that's not true. They were restless *before* the static happened. We'd spent nearly twenty years going no lower than a Yellow alert level. That is, by definition, telling the people that there's a *Significant Risk of Terrorist Attacks*. We went up to Orange for almost every holiday, it felt like, and that was *High Risk*. We even hit Red once, near the end of Obama's first term, when we had intel about a much larger attack that never happened, something to do with our relationship with Iran. That wasn't the only alert: every few years somebody stepped forward with a car bomb and a promise, threatening something worse, and they did their damage – sometimes only emotional, because we were fragile, as a nation – and we never heard from them again. We got coded messages, grainy cell-phone footage of somebody that they tried to make the new Bin Laden, but nothing ever stuck. All it did was make half the people nervous, the other half complacent. So, yeah, the natives were restless to begin with, and we didn't have an excuse or an explanation for the static, not even close. POTUS' statement was the best we could manage, asking people to stay calm, to try and get back to normality. He asked that the people going to worship stayed as civil as possible, and remembered that everybody had their own ways of worship, we were a multicultural society, you know the sort of thing. He said, If you think that there's a chance you could be involved in a riotous act – I absolutely cringed, because we should have caught that word, stopped it sounding like he was talking about a fucking party – just walk away, and let the authorities deal with it. It was those riots we were most worried about, because they were starting up as reports of small groups breaking the front windows of shops, smashing up parked cars, but we *knew* how they ended.

When he had read the statement – straight down the line in the press briefing room, straight into Camera 1, just as he was trained to do – he took some questions, and one of the reporters asked him why he thought that people were rioting. We understand that hearing what we heard played with everybody's emotions, she said to him, but why do you think some people have turned to violence? Shouldn't we all be trying to get into God's good books?

That raised a laugh around the room from everybody but POTUS. The first thing is, he said, we don't know if it actually was a God, or indeed *what* it was. We'd be fools to jump to the conclusion that it's any sort of higher power; it's just as likely, if not *more* likely, to be something entirely explainable, and we've got our best people on it. I knew what was coming after that answer, so I made my way to the side of the room, tried to get somebody to get him off the podium, but it was too late. He was saying something about people and zealotry, and Jesus fucking Christ, that was going to hurt us, I knew, and then that same journalist asked the killer question, the one that we had danced around for so long. Mr President, she asked, do you believe in God? We had avoided it the whole way through the campaign, getting him to swear on Bibles and go to church and be a total hypocrite in service to his country – and we had the most right-wing running mate we could find, in bed with so many churches and anti-abortion clinics that it made most of us feel sick – but nobody had ever asked him outright. It was like *Scooby-Doo*; we would have gotten away with it if it hadn't been for that meddling journalist. Don't answer, I said, over and over, but he did, because he was the President, and Presidents always answered questions honestly in times of strife, right?

I am not a man of faith, he said, and then all you could see or hear were flashbulbs and shouts of follow-ups. Looking back now, it helped: it moved the news cycle on past the riots, just for a second.

Phil Gossard, sales executive, London

When I finally left work I knew that the only way I'd make it home would be to walk. It was only a couple of miles as the crow flies, but London being London, walking that was going to be a trek. I kept trying to call Karen to see if she managed to pick up Jess from school but the phone lines were dead. I didn't know this then, but there's a lock that the government can put onto phone lines in states of emergency, like a terrorist attack, and that's what I think the person with access to the on/off button thought. But, it could have just been New Year's Eve syndrome, when the lines are clogged. No idea, and we never found out, of course.

There was a riot – although, it wasn't so much a riot when you saw it as a protest, a gathering, but every protest has the possibility of turning nasty at a moment's notice, that's what they said on the news – so I avoided the centre as much as I could. I clung to the river until I reached World's End, then cut north. Karen wasn't there when I got home, and there weren't any messages, so I started to make dinner, get it all ready to be cooked when they finally turned up.

What else do you do?

Meredith Lieberstein, retiree, New York City

Leonard was the sort of man who wanted to be a part of the action. He *hated* armchair pundits. I have to be out there, he said, so I let him go, because there was no way that I could stop him, not when he was in that sort of mood. He wanted to see what it was like out there, he told me. That wouldn't stop me worrying; didn't stop me worrying twenty years ago, wouldn't stop me worrying now. He liked to antagonize people as well, just having fun, but they didn't always see it that way. He came back soaking wet half an hour later. Where were you? I asked, and he smirked. I went to St Philip's, he said, and I spoke to some of the people there, and they put the fire extinguishers onto me. That damn smirk of his. I swear, he said, I didn't say *anything*. We both knew he was lying, of course, but I let it go, because that's why I loved him. I told him to take the sweater off so that I could wash it, but those white extinguisher-powder stains wouldn't shift. I always assumed that the stuff was washable, but apparently not. At least, not from cashmere, it wasn't.

Mei Hsüeh, professional gamer, Shanghai

We were raiding the tomb of the Night-King, one of the three Gods we hadn't yet taken down, because you needed a party of at least twelve, preferably twenty or so, and our guild wasn't one of the biggest, and most of the guild were from Europe, so getting together at the right time was a nightmare, because when I was on they were at work. I went professional a few years ago anyway, because I had some amazing instanced weapons, some armour, and I was forging my own stuff which I could sell to the noobs for an insane mark-up – like, the sort of price my old economics teacher would have been so proud of me for – so I was full-time online, never having to leave Barleycorn.

(Outside of it all: I had an apartment, and cupboards full of ramen noodles, which my mother hated, because she said I should eat Chinese noodles, and a fridge full of bottles of Mountain Dew and Red Bull, imported from this shop in the

Bund. I had a 3gb fibre-optic line, which was the best I could get in my apartment, but I wanted an upgrade, so was thinking of going wireless, but hadn't.)

We were mid-raid when we heard the static for the first time, and we didn't know what to think – we did think it was something in-game, and they had been doing these events, heralding the arrival of the next expansion, and this new enemy, this dragon called The Redeemer – so we just got on after it finished. Some people said it was everywhere, and that was fine, because the dungeons weren't going to raid themselves.

Dhruv Rawat, doctor, Bankipore

My biggest case that day, I remember, was a man with a swollen foot, so swollen he could barely even walk on it. I pricked it and it was swollen with yellow pus, so I sent him to the hospital, but he told me he wouldn't go, that he didn't have the time. Can you not do something for me here? he asked, so I did what I could, drained some of it, wrapped it up, sent him on his way. It's infected, I told him, you have to take care of it, you have to go to a hospital. Okay, okay, he said, I will. After I saw to him I went back to my hotel, and to the restaurant. Mostly, in those days, I didn't eat meat, and their menu had more vegetable dishes than most, so it suited me. I was eating my dinner when I heard a woman's voice; it was the news reporter from before. Hello again, she said, you're staying here as well, or just eating? No, I said, I'm staying here. I thought you lived here, she said. I do, I told her, but I don't have a place. It's a long story. I love it here, she said, which I thought must have been a lie, because there wasn't very much to love, not really; the mountains, sure, and the cricket club, but she would never have been allowed in there – mostly that was for the richer men from Patna, though they had offered me membership when they heard that I had moved into the area, because they liked doctors. The people are so *genuine*. She said it with real conviction, and I suddenly had to believe her. I asked her why she was there, what she was filming for, and she told me, but I can't remember now. I'm Adele, she said, and I introduced myself, and we shook hands over the table. That's when we heard the static for the second time, and I carried on eating, and she watched me as if that was more interesting than the noise itself.

Elijah Said, prisoner on Death Row, Chicago

Even as everybody else scrabbled around in the mud, searching for the cause of the static, I was reading a letter informing me of the date of my impending death. The letter was delivered at its scheduled time, because all of these things had a schedule: when I would be told; when I would be given my time with friends and family; when I would be led to the chair. Usually, such an envelope brought a hush upon the corridor; the prisoner was led to the imminent room with the counsellor, and that only meant one thing, and the corridor would fall silent. Not so for my envelope, as only seconds after it was handed to me, the static began again. There was no counsellor. My clock remained ticking; I prayed to Allah as I read the date, the words that committed me for my past indiscretions.

Andrew Brubaker, White House Chief of Staff, Washington, DC

POTUS shouted over the static, Find out what the fuck this is, so I called Meany in R and D, even as it was still going on. We were in a car headed back toward Andrews, to get on the flight that we had abandoned only hours before, and the driver turned around instinctively, because he knew that we weren't going anywhere. We'd had some intel from a source that it was – and I stress, intel is rarely accurate, *never* 100 per cent accurate, and frequently completely wrong, because it's spun out of gossip and rumour itself, for the most part – but we'd had intel that it was some sort of weapon. I had that on a piece of paper handed to me as I got into the car, and I was expecting a briefing on it on the plane, so I knew next to nothing. Meany's name was on the report, so I called him as soon as it started. Tell me this isn't a weapon, I said, and he said, Sir, listen; this sounds like a warm-up. Bear in mind, I've got Meany in one ear, the damn static inside my head, so I'm shouting. It's not warming up, it's here, now, because I can hear it. Are you measuring this, taking readings, finding out where the fuck it's coming from? Yeah, but there's nothing, sir, he said. We've got oscilloscopes and digital audio stuff, and nothing's getting picked up, but we can all hear it. And it's happened twice now, so that might indicate that it's warming up, or that the first time was a warm-up. I don't know.

None of us knew. In the FBI – I came from the FBI, FBI to secret service desk job to politics, like that was a normal route – there's a rule about serial killers. First time they kill it's to see how it felt, or because it was an accident. The second kill was because they found something in the first that they liked, and they wanted to see if they could recreate that feeling, that high. It can still be a coincidence, and it's not quite a pattern.

I heard POTUS on the phone to the First Lady, checking on her and the kids, and then . . . We know it wasn't static now, right? It was that garbled, fragmented noise that you get when you drive out of a tunnel with the car radio on, as it becomes clearer, picks up the signal again. It suddenly went from noise to words. *My Children*, it said, and then faded back into the static as quickly as it came. Our driver, I forget his name, he looked like he was going to hurl. Pull over, I screamed at him, and he did. The agents in the vehicles flanking us ran from their cars, swarmed ours, and I threw open my door. Get him to the White House, I said, and then I saw POTUS, and he looked absolutely terrified. I'd seen this man face down talks about nuclear disarmament, negotiate peace treaties, win an election, for God's sake, and he always looked calm. That was how he was going to be remembered, we always said during the campaign: the calm President, the cool one, the collected one.

In the FBI, it was one kill for a mistake, two because they liked it. We used to sit in the offices and pray that a third body never turned up, because if it did . . . Well, then you've got a real problem on your hands.

THE FIRST *BROADCAST*

Mark Kirkman, unemployed, Boston

I was getting ready to leave the bar – it was still open, daylight
outside, or it just hadn't shut, maybe, because Max was just
as interested in watching the TV as the rest of us – when *The
Broadcast* came, the *My Children* message. I didn't know about
it at first; I noticed that everybody in the bar suddenly went
completely silent, and then I saw it on the TV, as the hosts
did exactly the same. Can you hear this? one of them asked.
Oh my God, can you hear this? Everybody had that same
vacant look on their faces, and I was out of the loop again. I
still didn't hear a thing, and then it was over.

**Simon Dabnall, Member of Parliament,
London**

That first day, we changed, as people. I am all too well aware
how terribly melodramatic that sounds, but it's a truth.
Whatever it was that spoke to us during that first *Broadcast*,
everybody – or nearly everybody, I always forget about those
few that didn't hear it – but nearly everybody was joined in

something common. Regardless of the truth, it joined us for those brief moments that we were listening to it. If there was any doubt in the minds of the religious, that opening gambit, *My Children* . . . it was powerful.

I was hanging around on the South Bank when it happened. It was just starting to rain, and all of a sudden we heard it, and as soon as it finished, there was this cheer, as if we had finally won the World Cup or something, coming from St Paul's. I couldn't even begin to head over there, because the streets were so busy, and everybody started rushing that way, as if they were trying to make up for all those years that they spent not praying. I stayed where I was, because I'm rational; because *My Children* could be the call of any one of billions of parents, not necessarily a deity.

I mean, maybe we'd just tapped into somebody's angry mother, for a second?

Audrey Clave, linguistics postgraduate student, Marseilles

As soon as we heard the static start up again, I tried to write down every detail that I could hear, that I could pick out from it. I tried to write down the phonetics of the static, you see, to try and see if there was anything in it, running them by Patrice as they came out, to see if he agreed with them. He was off his game, I thought, but he did it, helped me out, and by the time that the voice spoke the page was full of noises and sounds, and then we heard *My Children*, and I wrote that down as well, and then it ended. We didn't say anything for ages, not for the longest time, and then I realized that we had the punch line, finally; and maybe the stuff before it, the noises, the static, that was the joke, or the puzzle? I got the team around, said that we had to work on it, but all I really wanted to do was to call my parents (but I knew that they would be at church). It took us a minute or so before somebody remarked that the words were in English. We all understood English perfectly, so I didn't really notice it, but it was English words that I'd written on the page, and English words that *The Broadcast* spoke. So then it became, well, why was it in English? Where did it come from?

Jacques Pasceau, linguistics expert, Marseilles

I laughed, and said that if it was English, it clearly wasn't God, because He would speak in, I don't know, Aramaic, probably, or something that we didn't understand. (Or, even better, something that everybody in the whole world understood, their own language, like a magic trick.) Audrey snorted at that, because she *wanted* to believe that it was God so badly. Maybe it's because most of the people who pray to Him now speak English? she said. So He chose that language to meet the majority of the people.

The most spoken language is Mandarin, I said, Why didn't He choose that? Well, maybe He's not Buddha, Audrey said. Maybe He's actually our God?

Dominick Volker, drug dealer, Johannesburg

I was in the back of a car being taken to, I don't know, one of the Jo'burg kêrel houses or other, I forget which. I had been caught taking my money from one of my dealers in Lavender Hill – well out of my usual area, but he had a lot on him, so

I had to go down there – and they were taking me off, hoping to pin something on me afterwards. It wouldn't stick, so I wasn't worried. There was too much chaos that day for anything to stick.

We passed this group of bergies on the side of the road and the kêrel locks the doors – locks his doors, because all of a sudden he's afraid! Rough area, this, he says, and I don't answer. Not talking? You some sort of mompie? No, I tell him, I just don't want to talk to you, eh? Then he gets a call and pulls over down the road, outside a house, and he comes back two minutes later with this grinning fucking kont, stinking of dagga. This guy laughs as he gets in the back next to me. He does that click thing with his teeth. Fuck's sake, I say, do I have to sit next to this one? The policeman tells me to shut it, and he starts off again. We're two minutes down the road – the guy next to me hasn't stopped smiling the entire time – and then we all start to hear the static again. I thought this was over, the stoner says, and then it gets louder. The guy in front pulls over, stops the engine, and we all just listen, and then we hear it. God. Then the kêrel unlocks his door, gets out, and just walks off, leaving me and this fucking reefer-stinking loser just sitting there, doors locked, right down the road from them fucking bergies. It's a bloody miracle we made it out alive.

Dhruv Rawat, doctor, Bankipore

It was first thing in the morning, which was my busiest time, because everybody came before they went to work. Lots of the jobs started early and ended earlier, so I was always busy, it seemed. This one day there wasn't a queue, which was rare, or so it seemed; I never had a chance to actually look outside to see, but there was always somebody at the door as soon as one patient had left, always another waiting to tell me about their illnesses. That morning I had the man with the bad foot back in, and he had put it up on my table. I took care of it, he said, I swear to you, I swear. You didn't, I said to him, because if you had, you wouldn't be back here. Did you go to the hospital? I asked. No, he said. The parts where I had cut it, tested it, drained it, they were black around the holes; The flesh has turned necrotic, I told him. What does that mean? It means that you have to have it cut off; not the foot, just the dead flesh, before it spreads. You'll have to go to the hospital right now; I'll take you there myself if you can't walk or drive. No, he said, no, it's fine. You cut the dead flesh off yourself. I trust you. I told him that I wasn't equipped, but he insisted, pointing at the scalpel that was in the medical kit on my desk. You can use that, I have a strong pain threshold, I can take it. I had lifted the scalpel, and I was dangling it over his foot – because I knew this man, and I knew that he wouldn't leave until he was satisfied, or he would leave and he would hobble around on his rotting foot until it was forcibly removed from his body, which would be the eventual outcome – and then *The Broadcast* happened. I sat there with the scalpel against his skin and listened to it, and he went quiet as well, for a while. When it was done he said, Well? Are you going to cut it off then? I will, I told him, just later. I went out onto the street to see what was going on – because it was inconceivable that it was in my head, no matter what it *felt* like – and it was . . . It was like a fly, buzzing around. Everybody was looking around for it, looking up in the sky to see if there would be something there to give them answers.

Isabella Dulli, nun, Vatican City

After the static, because they didn't know what it was, they stopped the tourists from going into the Basilica, and certainly from going down into the tomb. It is so fragile; they only let 200 people in every month, that is why it gets so busy, why the tourists are so desperate to see it when we do let them, why they queue all night, sometimes, travel from hundreds of miles away. The tour guides took them away from the queue, told them to head up to the square, that they would have to come back. Most of them said it was fine; some of them complained. There's no way you can come in, because it might be unstable. Then, we didn't know if it was just from the building, or the electrics. I went down into the Basilica anyway, because I had been looking forward to it for days. It smelled so old, still, even with all the cleaning that they did, for pres- ervation. It smelled of stone and dust, and there were very few places I loved more in the world, partly because of that very smell. I went down into the darkness – because the lights are so dim, it is always dark in the tomb, and there are always guides, because the ground is still unstable, like a building site in so many ways – and I knelt in front of the tomb itself to pray to the father of our church. I wasn't praying for anything at all; only praying as I always did, out of love. Then I heard it, His voice, so strong through the darkness, but not the darkness of the tomb, the darkness of my heart, of the world; it was not frightening, or threatening. It was just all that I could hear. I thought of all of the faithful written about through history who He spoke to, His voice so strong; and I thought, and me. I was joining those whom He loved the most, who He was so close to as to spread His word directly, to fortify belief and to set His awe in the minds of His people. I cried in the darkness; my tears patted the stone of the tomb, and I was so happy right then, knowing that this was the happiest moment of my life; everything built up to that, and I would never be alone again. It was me and my God, and we were together.

Tom Gibson, news anchor, New York City

As senior anchor I had certain privileges. I got to pull rank on shifts, and as mine came to an end, after a very long day, *My Children* hit, and I decided that I wasn't going anywhere. As soon as we heard what *The Broadcast* was saying, I knew that this could be the biggest news story of all time.

Meredith Lieberstein, retiree, New York City

The priests on the news after that first *Broadcast* looked so smug. There is nothing worse than a smug priest, Leonard said. He got so angry with one of them – I told you so, I said this was the case, the priest kept saying to the reporter; This is the Lord come back to speak to us – that he threw a tangerine at the television. It split all over the screen, burst like a water bomb. He cleaned it down – his temper never lasted for more than a single, regrettable second – but the apartment smelt of it all day, of that sharp citrus smell. It's nice when it comes from a scented air freshener; it's horrid to live with it all day when it's not, so sweet and bitter and *real*.

Leonard and I used to be Jews. We're Ex-jews, he would say whenever anybody asked, Capital E, lower-case j, as if that hammered home his point: *I've got my own emphasis for these things.* He liked having things in his life and then renouncing them, that was another of his things. (I've realized recently, thinking about it, how many *things* he used to have.) We stopped being Jews in the late Nineties, not long after we first started seeing each other. He had just left his first wife, an awful woman called Estelle, and we found each other in a bar one night. We spent hours talking about everything and anything, and that pattern stuck. On our fourth date we got onto religion, and discovered that we felt the same way – disheartened, mostly – and that was that. We woke up the next day and decided to not bother any more. We already both used to celebrate Christmas more than we did Hanukkah, so it didn't affect us there, and all the other stuff, it just felt natural to ignore it. We did that until the end of the next decade, when Leonard got his cancer, and then I started to think about it, to wonder. *He* never did, of course; cancer was a fight, and it could be beaten by hard work and perspiration, as far as Leonard was concerned, but I didn't feel that way. It was diagnosed in the late stages, and the doctor told us that if he operated the next day, Leonard might be lucky. *Might be lucky*, he said. That's a chance of a chance, outside odds at best, I figured. I had to drive home to fetch Leonard his pyjamas and a book, and on the way I passed the synagogue on Willet, so I stopped the car and waited until the next service started. I remembered every part of it – it was so ingrained, even after over a decade of not thinking about it even *once* – as if it were deeper than memory, like it was a part of my DNA, even – and

I prayed for Leonard to get better. I prayed for an extra edge over the *Might be lucky*. And he *was* lucky. They cut the cancer out, they did radiotherapy, he was sick for a while, weak as the old man that he never wanted to be, and then he started to get better. I don't know what saved him, whether it was the luck, the doctors, the prayer, but something did. I carried on going to synagogue, once a month, maybe less, and Leonard stayed healthy. That felt like a fair deal, and I never told Leonard. Every relationship has its secrets.

After he threw the tangerine he kept on shouting at the TV. It doesn't mean anything, he kept saying. It means sweet f-a! It's a voice, could have come from anywhere. The priests were sure that it was God making contact. In the book of Revelation, it says that our God will return to us, speak to us again. This is simply Him making good on His promise. Sanctimonious pricks! Leonard kept shouting. They're acting like this is definitive proof!

I didn't say it, of course, but I wanted to ask him how he was so positive that it *wasn't*.

Hameed Yusuf Ahmed, imam, Leeds

Here's the thing: it doesn't matter where you were when you heard it. It doesn't. What does matter is how you dealt with it afterwards, how you reacted, if you panicked; or if you got on with your life, your responsibilities. I wasn't asleep during the static before, because I was leading prayers already. How did we react? We got on with it. God is present every day; that's why we pray to Him, because He is there. If He wasn't there, we wouldn't pray, you see? It's easy. When the static came, I was in the mosque, half past four, just as it was nearly light – and I mean that, it was that red sky outside, that sort of colour where the sky looks like blood in water – and we were praying. We carried on after it, because if it was God speaking to us – that was what the televisions said, what they all wanted us to believe – if it was, He would make it clear. We had jobs, duties; you cannot be distracted by a noise, just a noise and nothing more. Now, *The Broadcast*, that was different. Again, we were at prayer. This could be a trend, I thought when we heard the static for the second time, before the voice came through, this could be a trend. I carried on leading the prayer, because that was what we did. When we heard the voice, that was the first time in over twenty years that I broke prayer. It was only because there were others praying who panicked before I did, standing up, leaving. That level of disruption, none of us could ignore it. Please, be calm, I said – the first words I ever broke outside the prayer, can you fathom that? To instil a sense of calm? – but that didn't help. I mean, the people might have trusted me to guide them when they were in control, but I think that was the hard part about *The Broadcast* for some: the lack of that control. To have something so rigid – a life, a *belief* – and to see, to feel it slipping away as soon as you hear something that you cannot explain . . . I finished the prayer, but so many left while I spoke I couldn't even count, so I kept my eyes shut; I didn't need them to know what I was doing, what I was saying.

I was in the offices afterwards. We called them offices, but they were just a room at the back of the mosque where I kept my papers, some books, had meetings with some of the community. If they needed guidance, that's where they would see me. The room itself was awful, a little white-walled box

47

with peeling paint, because it didn't warrant upkeep. I called
it the library, because it sounded better, and because there
were shelves with books upon them, and all the books offered
more than the rest of the room, the rest of the mosque – than
the entirety of my knowledge: His teachings written forever,
indelible, because words never die, never lose their meaning.
Everything I taught, everything I am, it comes from those
books, from those teachings. When I die, all that I am and all
that I think dies with me; the teachings live on. You ask yourself
what should be the most important of those, then: me, or
those books. I was to stay in the library all day, because that
was when the Muslim people of Leeds needed their council
the most; it suited me, because I opened my books and read
them. There was no television in the library so I didn't know
what was going on outside – how much they were making it
about God, or about the Christian God – but I *did* know that
I had a full diary of appointments, and none of them arrived
for the meeting, so I continually sat and read my books. There
was always more to learn. I led a prayer a couple of hours
afterwards, and then I got myself ready to go home, locked
the office. When I got outside I saw him for the first time,
young boy, only eighteen, nineteen, maybe even younger. He
had that fur around his face, not like anything you could call
a beard or a moustache, but he was growing it. Perseverance
in the face of adversity; always made me happy. Assalamu
alaikum, I said. Can I help? He said, I don't know; maybe, I
don't know. You want to have a talk? I asked. He nodded, so
I unlocked everything again – this is what we do – and we
went back to the library.

He sat in the chair I usually sit in, which was strange, to

begin with; but he wasn't to know. I didn't recognize him, which wasn't such a surprise, because he was younger, and it was getting harder and harder to persuade young people to actually come and be a part of their community. Actually, no, persuade is the wrong word, because it's not like that. Not enough families were actually *involving* their young. There shouldn't have had to be persuading. He sat in the chair I usually used – I am hesitant to call it *my chair*, because it wasn't mine, but that's how I thought of it, because it fitted me, because I sat in it every single day – and rubbed his hands together. Who's your father? I asked him. My father? Why do you want to know? It's important, I said; maybe I know him, because I can't place your face. That's right, he said, I'm not from here. I'm staying here for the week, he said, with a friend. (I forget what it was like, having religion when I was his age. Did I have it? I'm sure I must have, because it was everything to my father. He was an imam in Algeria, if you can believe that, and he came to England when I was only a few weeks old. That changed him, because in Algeria it was just his life; here, it was an uphill struggle, he used to say. God wants you to prove your love, and there is no better place, he said. He fought for this, and then he died. He – I have to be careful about how I say this, because it's so easily taken the wrong way – he seemed to get a second wind for the fight after September 11th, even though he was so old, his breath failing him. Some days he could barely speak through his breathing, and he still attended every prayer, still staunchly defended our rights. He was in his element. He hated what was done, hated everything about it – I have never seen him so angry as I did in those days after it happened – but he wanted to challenge

49

misconceptions. Is that wrong? He wanted to show that not everybody is capable of what those people did. I was already on my path, but his belief – which was stronger than any love he had, for better or for worse – was inspiring. I read to him from the Qur'an as he died, and I will never have any regrets for that.) Listen, he said, this is not my mosque, right? I've come to you because I can't go there. Why can't you talk to your friends and family, your own imam? I asked him, and he shook his head. He won't understand, none of them will. Won't understand what? I hadn't sat down the whole time, waiting for my own chair; I sat opposite, because it felt important. This was my fault, he said. This voice, the static. He was crying, shaking; I put my hand out to him, took his hand in mine. Don't be a fool, I said, we don't even know what it is. I committed zina, he said, right at the time of the first static. You had intercourse? I said, and he nodded. That's who I came to see, he said, still crying, a girl. And you think that you made this happen? I would have smiled if zina wasn't important, if this wasn't something that seemed to matter so much to him. (And I was pleased that it did mean so much, even if it took something as strange as *The Broadcast* to make it so.)

You haven't seen what they're saying? he asked. On the news and everything, they're all saying it's God, *actually* God. They don't know, I said, but he shook his head. No, no, you don't understand, they sound like they *do* know. It's God, and He's here because we sinned too much, and I was the last sin, the last straw. And I said, God inspires those who love Him to sound convinced, because it's what they believe. But if it is God, a sin like zina won't be reason for you to be punished. He dried his eyes. But that's what we've always been told, he said, my father told me. People tell others a lot of things for their benefits, I said. But this? We'll wait and see how this works out, okay?

Peter Johns, biologist, Auckland

Those mentals you see living on the streets, with their thinking that they had a direct line to God, or saying that they were hearing voices? Suddenly, we were all in that same damn boat.

UNRAVELLING

Dafni Haza, political speechwriter, Tel Aviv

Lev called again as soon as it finished, when we were left reeling in the office, attempting to work out what on earth the noise was, the voice was. Somebody told us that it was worldwide, because it was on the news, and I told one of the assistants – who had been working for the government for longer than I had, and knew his way around the ropes a little bit more – to get somebody in the Prime Minister's office on the telephone, to tell us what was happening. Lev's call, I ignored. I cancelled it. He could wait. (He left a message, crying, telling me to call, saying that he was worried, but I didn't think he was worried about *The Broadcast*, more about what I might have been getting up to.) We had a constant stream of information leaving the office, all coming from the government itself, and we vetted it for language. That was most of our job. But it completely stopped, no messages, no nothing, which meant that one of the other assistants had the press on the telephone, begging him for information. We have to tell the people something, the woman from the news station was shouting – we could all hear her voice carried through the telephone line, echoing out of the handset

– so you have to tell me something. I could see the assistant getting upset, so I went over to him, stood next to him to let him know I would take the call. You have to tell the people, or there will be problems, the woman on the other end of the phone shouted, and the assistant, as I reached for the handset, said, We'll tell you as soon as we know anything ourselves, okay? That was the news story for the next half an hour, how the government, sat there in Tel Aviv, were ignorant, or unwilling to help, or unwilling to provide answers. It wasn't the assistant's fault; this wasn't exactly a situation we were knowledgeable about.

Audrey Clave, linguistics postgraduate student, Marseilles

We got so drunk by the end of it all, even though I was saying we should work. I don't think I have ever been that drunk in all my life, honestly. People kept coming in from the concourse outside, other grad students, members of the faculty, random strangers, all saying that we should go outside. We're having a party, they kept saying, and I kept saying, I have to work on this, because it's important, blah blah blah – they didn't listen.

Jacques Pasceau, linguistics expert, Marseilles

I told Audrey that she was being boring. She said, Jacques, this is important, and I said, So is making the most of today! Enjoy it!

Audrey Clave, linguistics postgraduate student, Marseilles

I was trying to get on with the work at hand, trying to make sure we had everything covered. I – Look, I believe in God. I believed in God then, so much, because I was *sure* that it was Him speaking to us. So I wanted to work out what the static was, because if it was important, a message, another language, maybe, that would be crucial. So we kept working, but Jacques kept filling up my glass, and I thought, what harm would a little wine do? We started saying the stuff, the phonetics, out loud, seeing if they resembled anything, and then we recorded us saying the noises, sped it up, slowed it down, tried to see if the software matched anything to any languages, that sort of thing, but nothing was happening. People kept coming in, as I say, and asking us to party, and then other people were coming in and asking us to go and pray with them, but we stayed inside, doing the work (apart from Jacques, who was drinking really heavily). Then somebody ran in, told us to come outside, and we said, No, no, we're busy, and they said, There's somebody on the roof. So we all went outside and looked, and there was, and we saw him – it was a man, but we didn't know him, probably a student in another department – as he fell. It was awful. I asked a girl there why he did it, and she said, I don't know, he just kept saying, Sorry, sorry, apologizing for something, and then he jumped. They call it jumping; it's not jumping, not when you just step off like that.

We all took that badly, but Patrice dealt with it the worst. He was already looking a bit ill before it happened, and then he just started crying. Oh my God, he kept saying, so we got David to watch him, check he was alright (David was huge, built like Andre the Giant or something, so we knew Patrice would be alright if he went off on one), and we tried to get back on with the work. I was so drunk by then it was pointless, and we pretty much went back and passed out, I think.

Meredith Lieberstein, retiree, New York City

The first suicide that I saw about was on the news, mentioned not because it was noteworthy, but because it happened just out of shot in Times Square. The reporter was conducting interviews in the crowd – and most of the mob at that point was religious, most of them there because it was a way of congregating, as people tended to do at times of stress, I suppose – and it was like New Year's Eve, only without that horrible cheap glitter-ball; then somebody off-camera screamed, and the camera flipped just in time to catch the body hit the pavement. The reporter kept saying, Oh, oh, oh, shocked, so Leonard muted it. As if we need to hear that, he said.

Ten minutes later, he read on the internet that it might not have been a one-off case, and then, over the next hour, hundreds of reports started coming in that other people had followed suit. It wasn't coincidental; it was a fact of circumstance. People had found proof for something that they either wanted or didn't want, and they acted on it in a way that they thought was appropriate. Apparently a lot of inmates killed themselves, thinking that they had no chance for retribution. That was strange, because they should have waited, to see if there were going to be any more messages; stranger still, though, were the people who killed themselves because they were *happy* that God spoke to them. Leonard found somebody's blog where they had left a post saying, essentially, I'm going to be with Our Father! Because, if there's a God, there must be a Heaven, and if there's a Heaven, it must be a better place.

Only, that wasn't like anything that we *knew*, of course. We didn't know anything. We knew that we all heard the words *My Children* in our heads, and whilst some of us might have chosen to believe that it was God speaking to us, we didn't have any proof. And with the ones trying to avoid, I don't know, The Rapture, maybe, it must have just been a catalyst. Guilt can make you do funny things; with those people, it set them unravelling.

Elijah Said, prisoner on Death Row, Chicago

The Broadcast invaded my dreams. In my dream-state I was a child, back with my mother, my father, but knowing then what I know now: how she would die, the man that he would become, the purpose he would feel in his heart, watched over by a loving God that he did not yet know existed. My father played with me in the street, throwing a baseball that looked like the moon; he promised me the world. I told him to not lie to me; and then I heard the voice. It creaked in as part of my father's speech, at first: *My Children*, he said to me, and I was ready to protest, to say that I was their only child, unless – are there more secrets? Then I realized that I was awake, that I was on my cot, as always. I got out of bed, dressed myself, ignored the rest of the prisoners. What was their time? Mine was limited. Let us out, some of them shouted, we're innocent. None of us were innocent, not on this corridor. You did not get to the corridor by being innocent.

What d'you reckon? Finkler stuck his hands through the bars of my cell, reaching across from his, flapping his hand like a flag alerting me to his presence. I mean, holy crow, he said, how in the hell did we all hear that? You think it was God? He seemed almost completely unaware of who I was, how little I related to him. He would snort through my prayers, when he bothered to hear them, and yet here he was, hand of friendship extended. Sounded like God, he said. I did not reply. I would ignore him, and he would retreat. He carried on talking: If it was God, do you think He'll forgive us? I've never contemplated that part, you know? That we're here, and we were going to die, sure, but I always assumed there was nothing after, nothing at all, just blackness, you know? I'm sure that I heard him smirk at that, a private joke, however unintentional. I was a rarity on the corridor, a prisoner that they couldn't pigeonhole. I had education, which so many here did not; the crime I was here for wasn't thoughtless, or without reason and logic. I was the spearhead of a sacrifice, which many did not try to understand, or did not care to. They saw me as just another man of colour, a brute, a thug: they offered me drugs, or expected that I had access to them; they assumed that I was willing to fight them, which I was, but not on their whims. Finkler persisted. I mean, sheesh, God! Wonder if He spoke to everybody or just us guys? Maybe He's been on our side all along; maybe He knows I'm innocent. Finkler had killed six women over a twenty-year period: they caught him burying the seventh alive. His guilt was without question.

The alarms rang out, even in the corridor, where we were completely locked down. When our cells opened it was at the behest of armed guards, guns pointed at us. Those who are lost have nothing to lose, the governor said of us. The alarms seemed louder than we had ever heard them. Somebody's kicking up a fuss, Finkler said, must have made a break for it. Or they're fighting. I didn't try to see. I sat on my cot and prayed, again, that I might see some way through this. Shit, Finkler said – and what I wouldn't have given for him to shut his mouth – maybe they'll stay our sentences, because, you know, God's here! They won't stay our sentences, I said to him, breaking my silence. Our sentences are not just in this world. Oh, sure, he said, but, you know, I'd rather face *that* one in forty years, when it's actually my time. He fell quiet. In another life, I would have ended Finkler's life in a heartbeat. Here, now, he sounded sad, the tragically hopeful murderer, rapist. He pleaded for pity and forgiveness, because his crime was thoughtless, driven by lust and desire, not the betterment of his people. He and I were nothing alike.

Mei Hsüeh, professional gamer, Shanghai

I was Teolis, my Dark Elf Necromancer (level 83, about two years' worth of playtime), and the first dungeon we were hitting was in the Northern Lands. So, we dressed for snow – they rolled that out in the last update, having to adapt your armour for the environment – and I travelled up there on Hector, my winged horse. I gave Te'lest a ride. He was our guild's best tank, a huge Orc, built to withstand whatever punishment could be thrown at him. We were trying to assemble the guild together, because we'd arranged the time a few days before, but most of them weren't online. Fifteen out of thirty were offline, so we said we would wait. There's a goblin newsreader in the Northern Lands who reads real-world stories out like he's a town crier, and he was saying about the riots. He was the first person I remember seeing using the words *The Broadcast*, and at first I didn't even know it wasn't an in-game thing, and then I saw other people using it – this troll was trying to find somebody with the skills to carve it into his hammer, and another guy was making armour with it printed on the back – and I realized it was outside as well. I thought about logging off, and then all fifteen arrived, which was enough to do the first dungeon, easy, so we rolled off, and I forgot about it for a while.

Phil Gossard, sales executive, London

Karen and Jess got home ridiculously late because the roads, Karen said, were at a standstill with people parking outside churches. Not at the side of the road, either, she said, but right there in the middle of the road, if that was all they could find. You should have just ploughed through them, I said, show them who's really boss. I didn't mean that; it was a thoughtless thing to say. We stayed up and watched TV all night, and I tried to explain to Jess what *The Broadcast* could be if it wasn't God. All her friends said that it was. She went to a church-affiliated school, and that was all they were talking about. Eventually I said that she had to go to bed, and that caused a tantrum, but she had school the next day. Can't I stay home? she asked, and I said that she couldn't. She hated school at the best of times. She was born with a vascular birthmark on her face, across her cheek, her nose, meeting her top lip on the left side. It got paler as she got older, but it was there all the same. She had a rough time of it with the other kids.

I went up to check on her ten minutes later, when they

were cutting away to yet more talking heads, an easy way to fill the time. She was kneeling by the side of her bed, and I'd never seen her do that before. I'm praying, she said, and I asked her what for, and she said, I think I'm going to ask for a dog. I told her that God didn't work like that. Fine, she said, I'll pray that school is cancelled tomorrow. I think that's more his sort of thing, I replied.

Audrey Clave, linguistics postgraduate student, Marseilles

Jacques and I ended up sleeping in this room off the language labs, somebody's office, one that they gave to a professor with a title but not a real job, one of the codgers. There wasn't really anything in the room; it was more like a big cupboard when you stood in it, with an empty desk and a cactus (because it couldn't die) and some books on the shelves, all covered in dust. There was a rug on the floor, Turkish, it looked like, expensive, and it had barely been used. I should take that for our office, I said, and then Jacques moved the furniture over up against the window and we locked the door and lay down. That was the first night we slept together, had sex, whatever. Afterwards we were going to sleep, and I had just shut my eyes when we got woken up by David banging on the door. Open up, he shouted. It's Patrice, he's gone, and I don't know where. We got dressed and Jacques ran with him to the green in the middle of the main buildings, to see if he was there or if anybody had seen him leaving. I went out the front to get some cigarettes from the machine – I could taste them on Jacques, and I suddenly missed them, that taste – and there were people out there staring up at the roof, just like with the guy before. Patrice was on the parapet, I could see his legs dangling. The building wasn't exactly tall, only five storeys, but it was old, high ceilings, and he was just sitting there. He didn't seem to be moving. I ran upstairs, praying to God that he would be there when I got to him, and he was. Don't jump, I said. I just want to sit and talk, and he nodded and said that was fine, but he had been crying, and he looked so sick that I wondered if he had taken something, but I didn't want to ask, not then.

He offered me a cigarette, like he could tell somehow that I wanted one, even though I hadn't smoked in nearly six months, and I coughed my way through the first few drags, shuffling along the ledge with him. I didn't look down. We didn't talk as we smoked; we sat and swung our legs. When I had put mine out, smoked only halfway, because that was all I could manage, I asked him what he was doing. He lit a second one, which I thought was a good sign, and he said, Maybe, if I pray really hard, He might accept me back. Back? I asked him. What do you mean, Back? You haven't gone anywhere. Besides, eh, it might not be Him. It might be anything. You want to be praying to a bunch of aliens? But I must have sounded fake to him, because I sounded fake to myself. I was sure that it was God. Come back inside with me, I said, we'll go and have a coffee and talk this out, and he nodded, we both stood up, and he just stepped off the roof. I heard the crowd scream, but I didn't look down, because I didn't want to see that. I ran downstairs, I don't remember screaming or crying, but apparently I was, and by the time I got there this one guy, a stoner I recognized because he was always sitting on the benches outside the offices, told me that Patrice was the third person he'd seen that day do it. I sat there and waited for the police with Jacques and David, who found me when they heard the crowd scream, but the police didn't come until the next day, they were so busy.

HOW IT FELT TO BE SPECIAL

Andrew Brubaker, White House Chief of Staff, Washington, DC

I kept asking Meany for updates on his theory about *The Broadcast*. If it's a threat, we need to know. We're doing research, he kept telling me, we're working on it. Sometimes, that isn't enough. We had all been awake for God-knows how many hours and we were all feeling it. POTUS had it worst: he was doing interviews, press ops, reassurances. And his reassurances had to sound real; the rest of us got to sit in the war room – we called it The Danger Room, POTUS' special name for it, a joke, almost – and we got to say exactly how nervous we actually were. You factor in the stress, the tiredness gets that much worse. We had eye drops to help us function, and coffee. We even had a girl from the assistants' pool do a run to the Starbucks.

There were whispers from sources – the same source that said it was a weapon, that the voice was some sort of weapon being used against us – that somebody was gearing up for another attack, as well. We didn't have any more than that, other than that the rumour came from a source in Iran, so we moved the satellites to watch the countryside around there, covered Iraq, the Russian borders, China as best we could. If they see this, we'll have hell to pay, one of the Joint Chiefs said, and I told them it was fine. I'd rather that than the alternative. We watched China move some of their troops along their borders; they had people stationed along the borders with Tajikistan, Kyrgyzstan, Kazakhstan and then – and these were the real worries – India and Pakistan. It was when you saw nuclear powers edging toward each other, that was when you started to worry. Somebody in the room asked why they were moving – What have they got to gain from that? he asked – and I said, They're just nervous. They're probably worried that it's a weapon. Just like we are, he said. POTUS didn't say anything.

I didn't think it was an attack, and neither did he; and if it wasn't, that left very few options. Something we did by accident. Aliens. God. It was insane to even be contemplating those last two options, but we were both pretty sure it wasn't an attack.

Ed Meany, research and development scientist, Virginia

I spoke to the President for the first time that night – the first and the last time, if memory serves – because *he* wanted to know if I'd worked it out yet. It wasn't enough that I was reporting to Andrew Brubaker every ten minutes with the zero updates we'd managed, but he wanted to check that I was working properly. I guess a phone call from the President is meant to scare you, make you leap to action. Truth be told, we weren't any closer because it was the most pointless exercise we'd ever worked on.

There was no signal measuring on any of our equipment when we *could* hear *The Broadcast*, and given that it had stopped, there wasn't even anything for us to *not* be able to measure. He wanted me to be able to say, definitively, that it either was or wasn't God. I couldn't. What's that philosophy quote? If God wasn't real we would have had to invent him?

Dhruv Rawat, doctor, Bankipore

Adele had dinner with me again; she was so upset about *The Broadcast*, and I told her that it was fine. At home, she said, they're saying that it has to be the voice of God – that or aliens. She smiled when she said that, because it was so preposterous. But God, she said – and this gave her an even bigger smile – I mean, can you imagine? We had been eating this dish local to the area, and to the hotel, I think; it was mostly spiced potato and rice, in this sauce with okra, beans, tomato, paneer, but it wasn't spiced, not even slightly. I remember because I ate so much of it I felt ill, and sat back in my seat, patting my stomach. That made Adele laugh. There was a television on in the bar at the back, with the news showing the bombs in America. (It's reactionaries, the barman was saying, they always act after something else has started a battle.) You have to remember, I said to Adele, all of your people think that our Gods are vastly different. She smiled, as if she – she wanted to tell me that she already knew that, I think. Oh yes, of course; but this – I mean, we don't know what it is, but it could be the answer for all of us, couldn't it? This could end war, it could solve all our problems, put everybody on a level playing field. This could be proof, Dhruv; aren't you excited?

I said, I think there's only reason to be excited for proof if you wanted proof in the first place. For me, I've always known God is with us, because of *all* of this. That's the difference. But proof, she said, not belief or faith, actual *evidence*. They're totally different things. I know, I understand, I replied, but this isn't evidence of anything: it's just a voice. It might help those starved of their own self-belief, but for us, we shouldn't need it. Sure, there's that mystery of what it was, but it wasn't God. Besides, I said, as a joke, which of the Hindu Gods would it be without the others? We finished dinner and that seemed to have been that. When it was over, she thanked me for a nice evening, went to her hotel room, and left me sitting at the dinner table on my own. She had charged the whole bill to her hotel room before I could have a chance to pay.

Isabella Dulli, nun, Vatican City

I don't know how long I stayed down there. It's so quiet down there; there is only you and the smell of the stone. Some people say that it smells of death, but they don't mean that so negatively. They mean, it smells like you're closer to Him, to His kingdom. I don't know how long I was there for – most of that day, because I was completely alone with Him, and I revelled in Him for that time. I was special. That was how it felt to be special. And I was waiting, more than that, in case He was not finished. *My Children* . . . It is such an invocation, and it sounded as if He was going to tell me something about the children. I was going to be party to something special.

I hadn't decided if I was going to tell anybody else what had happened to me when I went back to the Basilica, and then the Basilica was empty. I went into the square, and that was empty too; it was only just getting dark, and all that I could hear was the sound of horns on the streets outside, where the taxis and buses were. At the gate, the police were waiting, keeping people out. What's going on? I asked, and they told me to get back inside. The people at the gate looked so scared, frantic. Let us in, Sister! they shouted. You have to tell them to let us in! What's happening? I asked the guard again, and he looked at me as if I was insane, pulling his whole head backwards. Are you mad? he said, and then he and his friend both laughed at me. You heard it, of course they're going crazy outside. All the tourists have been told to leave the City, or they would tear the place apart! I knew straight away, of course, but I asked the policeman what everybody heard, and he laughed again. The voice of God, he said, you remember that happening, yeah? I walked away – the people behind the gates, in the street, were calling to me still: Sister, Sister, give us a blessing, help us to tell our Lord of our love!

I didn't know where to go; I felt so sick, and I couldn't bear to see anybody else who had been blessed – or who heard the voice – so I went back into the Basilica. Then I heard them, coming in through the far entrance, laughing and praising him, Hallelujah, Hallelujah. I went down to the tomb again, and for some reason the lights were off, the guide lights, so I was in the darkness completely. I knew the tomb so well that I didn't need anything to show me where to go, and I found myself on the floor of the tomb, trying to breathe in through the closeness of the air. I asked Him why, because I needed to know, but there, when He could have answered me, His most devout, He chose silence, and I could only hear my voice echoing back at me for the longest time as the world celebrated how close they were to Him, finally.

Elijah Said, prisoner on Death Row, Chicago

We heard the guards talking at the end of the corridor, saying that there had been a problem in a block that we had never heard of. Neither Finkler nor I were old-timers. We'd been here less than six months, both of us, and the amount of talk about the rest of the prison flew by. You ignored it; no need to learn the ropes when that same rope would eventually hang you. The guards saw us listening and told us that it was time for our showers; it wasn't close to that, but the noise of the water deafened all else. They switched them on, told us to strip, prodded us – myself, Finkler, a thug from New York who called himself Bronx, a man who smothered his wife and children while they slept, name of Thaddeus – into the shower room. The water ran hot always, and we were forced to stand inside it, directly under the faucets so that they soaked our faces. They couldn't be sure we were washing properly, they said, and this was the only way: scalding our skin. Finkler turned thick pink, like a lobster; he complained about the heat. Thaddeus wept. Bronx kissed his teeth and turned, and called Thaddeus a whiny bitch, and laughed at him. Nobody spoke to me, or looked at me. These people were not dangerous; they fashioned themselves as threats, either by accident or intentionally, but they were nothing. We stood under the faucets and watched as the guards – two of them, Johannsen and another one I didn't recognize – spoke in the corridor. I heard Bronx whisper something, out of his faucet, closer to me.

We can take 'em, he said, rush over, I'll take one, you take the other. This panic, we could be out of this fucking place. Bronx was a rapper (though nobody could lay claim to having heard his music); he had shot three people from a moving car, caught by a traffic camera. Come on son, he said, we can get out of here. No, I said. He laughed, rocked backwards – he fashioned himself like some African chief, his laugh belly-deep, a false man to his very core – and grabbed my shoulder. No shit, he said, you like it here, eh? I washed myself. You fine with staying here, dying in this place? Shit, man, you crazier than Finkler. He nudged toward Thaddeus; I knew before they even whispered to each other that the family-killer would join in with the plan; he didn't cry over his family, he cried over *himself*. There's two types of pity in prison: self, and for what you did. You have self-pity, my father used to tell me, you can't have any self-respect. Thaddeus was nothing but self-pity, a ball of it. Next thing I knew, he was running toward one guard, Bronx toward the other. They barrelled into them, slamming them against the wall. The guard I didn't know the name of was quick; he shouted, reached down for his stick, but Bronx was faster, clubbed him across the face with his forearm. Come on, he shouted to me, you can get the fuck out of here. Solidarity in colour. I turned away, took a towel, dried myself and returned to my cell. What the fuck? Bronx shouted. You won't make it, I said, but he didn't listen, and the three of them ran down the corridor.

Only one who returned – ten minutes later, cowering, shakier than when he left – was Finkler, and he didn't say what happened to Bronx and Thaddeus, and I didn't care to ask.

Simon Dabnall, Member of Parliament, London

The Cabinet was called in that morning, dragged out of our beds at some unholy hour and forced to wearily make our way back to the city. I was Minister of State for Business, Innovation and Skills, which sounds exactly as dull as it was in reality. It was a position that I didn't ask for, but when they offered me a place on the Cabinet I said Yes. I had been in the party for nearly twenty years; it made sense, I think, to them. I was the elder statesman, which is a ghastly thought, so I sat there and read the reports that my staffers had made for me, and I took extra pay for my troubles. I had, in a previous life, worked in the City. Apparently, this meant I should govern the finances of businesses the country over, I don't know. Regardless, I was called in, and I obeyed the paymasters to a T. I don't remember if we discussed the practicalities of giving everybody a day off, a religious holiday. I'm sure that it must have come up. My assistant only bothered to make it in because I promised her a rise if she did.

We were meeting in Downing Street, so I was told, and it wasn't until after the gate checks that they said the meeting was in 12, not 10. Everybody was already in the room apart from the PM and the Deputy, and it was like a bloody mothers' meeting in there, all talking at the same time, all doing whatever the heck they liked. Thomson, the pillock in charge of education, was even over by the window, cranked open, fag in hand. Smoking! In a Cabinet meeting! I asked where the PM was, and that seemed to be a point of contention. Nobody knew, exactly. I've heard a rumour, Thomson said, that he's done a runner. After a few minutes the Deputy PM turned up, asked us to sit down, confirmed it. Somebody saw him in Brighton, he said, and we've found his suit and his wallet on a beach. Somebody saw a man of his rough description waddling into the sea earlier today, wading out, then not

70

coming back. Is he mental? Thomson asked; Has he gone completely bloody barking? Barely blame him, I thought. Has the press got this yet? somebody asked, and the Deputy shook his head. I'll be making a statement in a couple of hours. And you'll be standing in for him, I'm assuming? That was Thomson who asked, because he always hated the Deputy PM. I will. Rabble rabble rabble, went the room, and then Thomson lit another fag, and walked out. Three or four more of the Cabinet followed him, either trying to calm him down or just, I don't know, to get out of the room. I didn't say a word. I rarely do, I confess, because people tend to tune out when I speak, even when it's about something important. We abandoned the session before most people were even having their breakfast, saying we'd reconvene later that day. Strangest walk down Downing Street I'd ever had, leaving there.

I decided to get the train home. Some of them were running again, or trying to; the stations were hideously understaffed, the barriers open, the ticket booths empty, but some drivers had turned up. On the board at the front, where delays get noted, some wag had written *The End Is Nigh!*, and they had drawn a smiley face underneath. I have no idea why, but the platform was almost completely empty. It was eight o'clock in the morning on a Tuesday, and nobody was going to work. Madness. I stood on the platform for twenty minutes or so before a train popped up on the board, read through a copy of *The Times* that somebody had left there – little more than a pamphlet really, no interviews, cut and pasted from their website, but bless them for trying with everything that was going on. I got myself a Curly-Wurly from the machine, as I hadn't had time for breakfast, and was sitting watching the rats when this man started talking to me. I hadn't noticed him before; he was scruffy, but only as much as most people have the *potential* to be, I suppose: a few days of unshaven chin, some scuffed shoes, greasy, scraped-back hair. I wonder if the rats heard Him as well, he said, and I laughed. God only knows, I replied, expecting some sort of follow-up, but he went silent. Fine, I thought, you started the conversation; it's your right to finish it. A minute passed, then he sat down. They're acting just the same as always, he said, meaning the rats again, and I agreed. Maybe they've got it right and we've got it wrong, I said. We're running around and panicking, they're just getting on with it. He scowled at me. I'll bet they don't even understand what God means, he said.

Before *The Broadcast* I would have described myself as a faded agnostic – faded, mostly, because I rarely thought about what I believed or didn't. Once I thought that I had a tumour so I prayed that it wasn't, and it wasn't; it was a cyst, just a lump. Of course, through that I found out what was *really* wrong with me, and that led me towards a potentially abbreviated lifetime of pills and medicaments, so horses for courses. Either way, the praying didn't do me any favours. I didn't have the patience to listen to preaching before *The Broadcast*, and I certainly didn't have the patience after it. I didn't think that it was God. I didn't know what it was. I was part of that enormous percentage of the population that was just wholly confused. Regardless, I smiled and nodded, because it felt like a time to be polite, and the scruff began fidgeting. You know when you see shoplifters, and you can tell that they're shoplifters because of the way that they glance, all nerves and false confidence? So when the train started approaching I got up, walked down a way towards the map on the wall, even though I knew full well where I was going. When the train stopped I kept walking down a few carriages away from him, and I sat opposite the only other person in the carriage, an Asian girl – Japanese, I think. She smiled politely, and I smiled back, and it was friendly and quiet and I was away from him. Phew, relief, et cetera.

We were four or five stops along when I heard the door at the end of the carriage click, and the man stepped through, so I put my head down, tried to ignore him, but the Japanese girl, bless her cotton socks, smiled at him. He started speaking to her, rambling on about retribution and penance. He's here among us, he said, even though it was patently clear that she didn't understand what he was saying. Then he said something about eternal rest, about sending us all to eternal rest and I thought, What if he's got a knife? What will I do? I was ready to, I don't know, throw myself at him or something, at least try to wrestle him to the ground, but he stopped, turned back towards the door. Soon, we will all be dead, he said, and he opened the door again and stepped out, and to one side between the carriages. I screamed, I'm sure, and so did the girl, and we heard his body as it smacked against the glass windows, pinballing between the carriage and the wall.

We pulled into the station and the girl threw herself through the doors onto the platform. I followed her out, checked she was okay, but she suddenly seemed terrified of me, as if I was going to turn on her, as if we hadn't both been in the same predicament. Clearly, I was the crazy man's accomplice. I was home half an hour later, and I spent the day watching the news wondering if they would mention him, but they didn't.

Of course they didn't; he was just another one of the many. A week previous and I wouldn't have been able to escape hearing about him, at least for the first couple of hours after he died.

Hameed Yusuf Ahmed, imam, Leeds

I kept thinking about the boy – he didn't even tell me his name, in case I went back to his imam in Birmingham (or wherever) and told them about him, I suspect – all through the day, the night. Samia had prepared dinner for us, as always, and we spoke about our day. We didn't have any children. I told her about the boy, and she made noises. He should have known better, she said. I know, I know, I told her. But he didn't. He came to me, and we should be glad of that. He really thought that he made *The Broadcast* happen? Yes, I said, he was convinced.

When we were both sitting down, Samia asked me what I thought it was. Really, what did you think? What do you think it was? By that point I had seen a newspaper on the way home, seen the theories, but I didn't know what it was. I told Samia that, and she seemed disappointed. I thought you might have had an idea. I have ideas, I said, I have ideas that it was satellites, or something wrong with the radio, like the scientists are all saying. You don't think it could be God, then? No, I said, and nobody in their right mind would. We ate in silence, and I worried that she wanted more from me, an answer. To what? I don't know. We went to bed, and I slept, and I had the most vivid dream.

In my dream, God – my God, Allah, the sustainer, the one who guides – was real, tangible, a person. I cannot remember what He looked like; I forgot that as soon as I woke, but I knew that I had seen Him. The rest of the dream . . . I couldn't remember the rest. I remembered seeing God, and that was enough. I woke up before Samia, made my way downstairs in the darkness, put the television on. I had almost forgotten that we were all in this together; the newsreaders reminded me. I sat at the kitchen table and read my book. Samia appeared after a while, told me that I was running late. You need to get dressed, she said. I didn't tell her about the dream, because of what it could mean, seeing God like that. I couldn't tell her that I had put a form to Him, or that I had had the dream at all. She would have asked what it meant, if it came from prophecy or the devil, and I did not know. I said the prayers with the rest of the believers – we were less than half our usual number, though I can't now say for sure that it was because of *The Broadcast*, and not just me miscounting, or worrying too much – and then went to go back home, to eat, to ready myself for the rest of the day. The people didn't leave; they waited outside the library-office for me, suddenly full of questions, so I went straight to them. That was my role; that was why God chose me. I was of those who knew that praying to Him came above all else.

Phil Gossard, sales executive, London

We were just about to leave the house when somebody rang about Jess' school, on a round robin, saying that they were shut for the day. The school was attached to a convent, and the nuns were too preoccupied to even think about teaching. Jess was chuffed. I think my prayer worked, she said, and I told her that it was a distinct possibility, even though I was *sure* that it wasn't. I'll definitely pray for a dog tonight, she said. Fine, I told her, you do that. My offices were shut for the day as well – a personal day for all, the email from head office said – so Jess begged Karen to take the day off so that we could all do something. I can't, she said, because hospitals don't shut down just because everybody suddenly thinks they've got religion. Jess and I spent the morning on the sofa watching terrible daytime TV; one of those talk shows was asking if people's relationships had changed because of *The Broadcast*. It was – and this isn't surprising, I suppose, but – it was everywhere.

Dafni Haza, political speechwriter, Tel Aviv

I didn't sleep; none of us did. And I wish that I could have said I spent some time deliberating over what it was, but I didn't do that, either. We had a constant stream of telephone calls from all sides, and I had to have conversations with people at every stage of government to get the message in our first governmental address correct. They hired me for my ability to write the words that they would want to be heard saying, but even then they had their own ideas to the point where I discovered I was nothing more than a transcriber, tidying their phrases into slightly tidier ones. Nobody in the office had any time for thinking for themselves, because it was all so frantic. Then I had a call from the Prime Minister.

The Prime Minister was a terrifying woman, but strong, and you had to respect her for that. When she was chosen to lead it was under this veil of friendliness and light, because that's the image the Knesset gave out; but in international waters she was terrifying. It's what the country needed, apparently. She will sort out the problems in the West Bank, we were told, and she'll stabilize international relations. Those were the promises, and whether she kept them or not, she was who the Knesset elected, and we chose who was in control of the Knesset, so we were . . . I don't want to say, to blame, because that sounds negative, but we made a choice, as a people; we were responsible. She was known as a leader who didn't take chances, and who was opinionated and strong in discussion, and who was not swayed by the thought of war. And her office called me, and told me that we needed to have a meeting. This was to be one of the first tasks of my new role; my predecessor had told me that he hadn't had cause to meet with the Prime Minister once in his two years in this role.

I was taken by car to her offices, even though they were only ten streets away and I could have walked it – I was used to walking everywhere, that was how I stayed fit – and then scanned through security, made to take off my shoes, empty my pockets and my handbag. They made me turn my telephone on, to prove that it was real, and I saw that I had seven messages when I did, which meant Lev was getting impatient with me. I would have hell when I got home, I knew that, but some things were more important. The Prime Minster's office was painted entirely white, with a wooden desk, pictures – both of family, and religious – on the wall behind her, but nothing else. She wore her hair not unlike mine, though she was blonde, dyed but perfectly so, so that you couldn't tell, even from her eyebrows. So, you're the writer? she asked. She smoked a cigarette, and indoors, no less, even though her party reinforced the smoking ban in Israel. I am, I told her, and I was going to say something else – something kind and respectful, regardless of whether I felt that respect for her – but she interrupted me. Here's a telephone number, she said, straight to me. I want to be able to get you directly, none of this going through middlemen and assistants, okay? There's going to need to be a connection between us, a dialogue, so the message doesn't get diluted. Are you okay with that?

That sounds fine, I said, so I just call you directly? Any time; you need to know the message, you talk to me, and we'll put it out there. She gave me a telephone, a mobile, government issue. Only I have that number, she said, so that I can always reach you. For now, just tell the people that we're working on it, that we'll have answers very soon. You know the problems: this can't become about religion, not here, because that will make everything so much worse. Okay? Okay, I said, and then she put her head down and started writing something. After a few seconds it was clear that it wasn't for me, so I backed out, and I waited outside the door. I kept thinking about the messages that Lev had left for me, and told myself I would call him when I had the chance – *if* I had the chance.

THE SPARROWS ARE FLYING

Tom Gibson, news anchor, New York City

At four in the morning we had a roundtable, representatives from all major faiths. The point was to find an order, a structure. We were under instructions from the government – stepping in in a way that I hadn't seen them do since we left Iraq – to represent as many faiths as we could get our hands on. There was unrest in lots of the communities, people who didn't necessarily worship the same deities as everybody else – let alone speak English – and we had to make sure that everybody was catered for. Only problem was, that was one hell of a lot of people, and we had to give them all a slot. Fine. But before they went on air, they all had to sit in a room together and wait their turn. It was all okay – even civil, I'd say – until the atheist guy, some scientist from MIT who wrote some books, had his fifteen minutes, until he started yamming on and on about how stupid everybody else was being. I can't believe, he kept saying at the start of his sentences: I can't believe that you people think this could be real; I can't believe that you're all so lonely as to believe that God exists, and wants to speak to you; I can't believe that you're falling for this. The

79

priests and rabbis and guys in headdresses, they argued blind with him after a while, but then they were arguing with each other, because they had cases for why it was their God, why it wasn't Christianity's. Eventually the atheist started getting really annoyed, shouted at the Catholic priest. I can't believe that you think some man in the clouds is just going to start speaking to us all, and the priest said, Explain what it was then, if it wasn't that.

That was the crux of the argument. There was no other explanation, nothing at all; the Catholic guy sat back and smiled, just like he *knew* that he was right. That was when I was called out of the room, and we were told that there was something happening uptown, and that I should get ready to get back on the air.

Andrew Brubaker, White House Chief of Staff, Washington, DC

I had five minutes free, so Livvy came by and I sat down with her in the gardens and we ate a sandwich she brought along, sharing it. That was nice. I hadn't even finished when my phone rang, and the pass that they used – *The Sparrows Are Flying* – meant that I had no choice but to drop it, shout goodbye to her, run inside. The code meant that we had a serious threat. By the time I made it into The Danger Room, it wasn't just a threat: it was confirmed, going to happen, and we had to accept that.

The *New York Times* had printed this article in the morning that we should all, collectively, put an end to war. We don't need to fight any more, the editorial said, because this is it; proof. Every war has been caused by religion, they wrote (which isn't strictly true, but difficult to argue with). We can end this, because there's no need to fight any more. It was idealistic nonsense written by idiots. Religion might have started off the conflicts in Afghanistan, Iraq, Palestine, but *we* never involved ourselves for religious purposes. People could throw a lot at our motives in the past – oil, money, power – but we, America, hadn't ever gone to war in the name of God. It had been hundreds of years since the crusades, nearly thousands, but people didn't forget, apparently. I can't say for sure that the article was a catalyst, but it ended with a line about *Our God*, meaning America, meaning Christianity, and that was the biggest issue we had: where to attribute *The Broadcast* to. Or who, maybe. It was English-speaking, and the accent hard to pin down, but it sounded . . . It sounded like one of *us*.

That was POTUS' first proper terrorist threat, as well. I had been at the White House for the tail years of the Obama administration, I had seen these before, but one this big hadn't happened yet during this presidency. The threat had come in as being for a targeted attack on New York, and we had word that a device had been left on the corner of 59th and 5th. We didn't get that info until seconds before it went off; there wasn't any time for POTUS to even ask what he should do. It was designed to hit foot-tall traffic, tourists, people on their way home. It wasn't a huge strike; early reports had casualties in the sub-triple-figures category, but that was only because there were far fewer people on the streets than usual. On an average day it would have hit thousands, potentially. More. POTUS was devastated that we didn't get to it in time. I reassured him; we were given a warning that there *was* a bomb, not an opportunity to do anything about it, and the two were vastly different.

Mark Kirkman, unemployed, Boston

The bomb was reported live. It wasn't like some terrorist attacks, where it's all whispers until they get footage; Fox, CBS, NBC, they all had people on the streets with cameras. They all filmed the smoke, they all got as close as safety or the police would let them. Honestly? For a second, it just felt good having something else to talk about. I know that's an awful thing to say, but I had spent every minute since that first static wondering why I didn't hear it, and this . . . It was something that I could relate to. I used to live in New York City, before I moved to Des Moines. I had worked there, and every bit of it had memories. And the bomb itself, I got that; I had been a street cop for a few years, back before the office job, before I knew what I wanted to actually do. I had worked bombsites, standing there, keeping the crowds back. I recognized the faces of the guys working the scene, in the background of all the footage. I was back in the bar, because I didn't have anywhere else to be, but this time everybody was asking me questions, about protocol, procedure. Would they have known it was gonna blow? Max asked me. I don't know, I said. How did it get through? Why didn't they catch it? That was the biggest question; the next was about who was responsible, and I didn't have an answer for either.

I hadn't said anything about not hearing *The Broadcast*. I didn't know what it meant, and nobody else would know either. Most people assumed that it was God, and I suspect that they wouldn't have been thrilled that I didn't hear him.

I kept asking myself, if it *was* God, what did that mean? I'm not a bad person; I've never ruined anybody's life. Mostly, I've stayed quiet, to myself. I had one vice, and it was nowhere near as bad as those some people who had heard *The Broadcast* were walking around with. I kept quiet about that, and concentrated on the bomb, and that filled about two hours, then the news cycle began flitting between the two: on the one hand we have a specialist telling us what the presence of a God might do to our evolution as a species, our progress; on the other, we have the shocking footage of the inside of the Apple Store, the hole in New York that left numerous people dead, footage of the smoke, the rubble, the bodies. The news channels flitted between the two as if it was a tennis match.

Andrew Brubaker, White House Chief of Staff, Washington, DC

We had POTUS ready to speak to the nation within the hour. I wrote the speech for him, because it had to be ready to go direct to air: we, America, have to stay strong until we have answers. The grotesque act of terrorism toward us will not go unpunished, and right now, we're closing in on the perpetrators. We'll do our best to keep you safe, America.

Meredith Lieberstein, retiree, New York City

Leonard was furious, watching the President give that speech. They're going to attack somebody, he said, they're going to attack somebody, you just watch. I made him go to bed early that night, because he was so on edge, and he was making me irritable, but I couldn't sleep because he wouldn't stop grinding his teeth.

Mei Hsüeh, professional gamer, Shanghai

We went down to fourteen when we lost a Goblin Wizard called Stryfe, because he said there was something happening in New York, something about the emergency services. He was lucky we weren't on a role-playing server. On those games, you even mention a real-world place, you can get banned, or at least shouted out of town. He quit halfway through killing the dragon, leaving us one healer down, but we weren't angry with him. He told us that there was a bomb or something before he quit, so we knew what was going on a few minutes before the news channels even did.

Andrew Brubaker, White House Chief of Staff, Washington, DC

The most important thing is to keep control. In a situation where you could just lose it, where it's ready to slip away at a moment's notice, you cling on and pray. Straight after his TV statement we were in The Danger Room asking if there were any more coming; we had every informant we knew reporting in with what they knew. We have to know who's responsible, POTUS kept saying, because this cannot go unpunished. He sat at the table as we all told him what we knew, and he acted like the sort of President you see on TV, gritting his teeth, his hands in fists on the table. Calm down, I told him. You can't do anything if you're this stressed. Somebody asked if we should get the Vice President along. Does he know about what happened? I asked, and they said that he did. Well, that's good enough, I told them. Last thing we needed was him storming the hallways; that would have sent POTUS' blood pressure through the damn roof.

We knew a lot about the attacks, because of the delivery, the trigger we found at the scene, the body. I call it a body; it was shreds of skin burned into the flame-retardant belt that the IED had been strapped to. DNA markers told us that the attacker was from Iran, or the region; we just needed to know who he was working for. Over the few years before Iran had become more of a problem, or their people had, the amount of smaller attacks attributed to cells started in the country had grown exponentially. Nothing serious – car bombs here and there, more threats than actual successful attacks – but Iran, they were the buzzword. Twenty years ago it was all Iraq and Afghanistan; now it was Iran. We didn't announce where he came from. People were making assumptions, and they were assuming correctly, but assumptions were still far less dangerous than them actually knowing.

We had moved up to Orange alert as a reaction, without us having to even make an announcement when we heard *The Broadcast*, just in case. Then the bomb went off in Nevada, and the ones in Omaha and Baltimore, and before we could even breathe we kicked it up to Red. (But as the press pointed out, we'd *never* been at anything less than Yellow, not since we introduced the scale back at the start of the century, so it shouldn't be a shock that we were so willing to move on it.)

Ed Meany, research and development scientist, Virginia

We all had friends in the Nevada office; most of us used to work with guys who were stationed there. We didn't know what they were working on, but as soon as it blew we were told that we weren't to say a word to anybody about it. We were all under the heaviest NDAs that ever existed anyway, so it wasn't like any of us were in the habit of casually speaking to the press. If anything leaked out of that administration, it was meant to. The rest of the stuff? It never made it to the public. When we saw POTUS making a statement a few minutes later, he said that the Nevada office was a basic science lab; he didn't mention the links with the army it had. He might not have even known; so much was run without going through POTUS, so that he had plausible deniability. I mean, Jesus, stuff was run through with Brubaker's knowledge, if it had the right clearance. Sometimes, everybody had to be kept in the dark. Even then, when everything was in danger of going to shit, the most important thing was that we kept our secrets in place.

Andrew Brubaker, White House Chief of Staff, Washington, DC

We lost a town hall in Baltimore, a (mercifully near-empty) mall in Houston, injuries not deaths. And we lost a research facility in Nevada, so there were clean-up crews sent in to deal with that. Why those targets? We had no idea. The MO was different at each one, as well; if they didn't all hit at the same time we'd have questioned whether they were even related.

One of the joint chiefs suggested that whoever did the attack – meaning, the organization rather than the individuals – that they had been waiting for this, or that they were all in place already, waiting for *something*. If they were responsible for *The Broadcast*, he said, this was superbly orchestrated; if they weren't, it was just incredible. We'll worry about those, he said, and he put a staffer on it. They'll need clean-up crews; you've got bigger things on your plate. I did.

We're at Homeland Security Level Red, POTUS told the people, which means that there is a severe threat of terror upon our great nation. Our freedom is being threatened, but the terrorists will not hold us down. Until we have caught these criminals, we will not rest. He announced that the terror level changing meant that all forms of public transport were to be locked down; that all municipal and public buildings were to be shut, with the exception of emergency service buildings; that houses and private property could be subject to police and army checks without need for warrants. We request that you stay in your homes, he said, and if you see anything suspicious, report it to the local authorities. We know you're exercising your right to religion, but we request that, for your own safety, you keep your prayers at home rather than in the church. Get a good night's sleep, America, he said.

Then we heard *The Broadcast* again and we knew that there wasn't a chance of anything he asked actually happening.

Jesús Santiago, preacher, New Mexico

When I went to unlock the church doors there was already a crowd outside. I did not have the building open for worshipping on Mondays, only on Tuesday, Wednesday, all the other days of the week. There were forty people, maybe, waiting, all the usual congregation, so I told Juanita to calm them down, park the car at the back and then go and talk to them, keep them patient. Enough, enough, I told the crowd. You have been very patient, so I will open the church in a few moments. It was so hot outside – a hundred degrees, the man on the television said – so they were sweating, fanning themselves, drinking water. Inside, the building was air-conditioned. They would have to wait for this, slightly, as I had to pack up the office in the boxes that I took over the night before; this was going to be my final sermon.

I never meant to lie to people, I kept telling Juanita. It was never my intention to cause pain, or disrupt their lives. All I wanted was to give them something, eh? Something that they could *keep* and hold close to their hearts. Religion, worshipping God, before *The Broadcast* it was something that people did because it was there, or because they wanted to feel better about themselves; like, Somebody is watching me, I am doing this for *Him*. I made that more real for them. My pappi, my father, also named Jesús, from the day I was born he told me that we were descended from the family of Christ. He showed me maps and drawings that *his* pappi showed him, drawings of our family tree, how He travelled across His lands, across Europe, across the sea to South America, and He married a woman, and they had children together, and their children had children, and so on, and that led to me. When I was growing up, that is what I knew to be true. When he died, pappi told me that it was all a lie, that he invented it all for the sake of his church; but by then I had my own church, and I had a congregation, and they knew when they looked at me that they were closer to God than they were the days before. And the money! They donated money, to run the church, to show how much their faith was worth, and I became accustomed to it. Juanita and the children, they always wanted more, more clothes, a bigger house, so I kept it up. It was not a lie; it was the way things were.

When *The Broadcast* came, I knew that it was over. If they have the real thing, they do not need a phoney to make them feel better, so I knew that they would turn against me, sooner or later. I came in to get the money that I left – it was in notes, all of it, and I kept it under the floor of the altar, the safest place in the city, because nobody would dare to damage an altar, nobody, not in this city. I put the money into bags, and when I was done I took them to the car, put them in the trunk, came back and opened the doors. We're ready for you, I said, come in and worship Him on this, the best day of your lives! They came inside, and there were so many of them that they were in every seat, standing in every space they could, standing even in the doorways, until I pushed some of them back. We have to have the doors shut, I said, because otherwise the air conditioning will not work. I think that they understood.

When we were doing a blessing, near the end of the service – an old lady who could not walk, but believed that by touching me she would be cured by the Lord, listening to all of her prayers – the doors opened, and in walked Jorge Delgado, who never liked me, never came to church. He pushed through the crowd, until he was in the aisle. Nobody wanted to stand next to him, because he was dripping with sweat, and he looked ill. Jesús, he shouted, and everybody turned to look at him. Jesús, what do you have to say about this? I greeted him: Hello,

89

Jorge, welcome to this celebration. Jesús, what do you have to say about hearing your great-great-grandpappi, eh? What do you have to say now? Jorge never believed me, always said that I was a fraud, and I knew that this would be one of those times. Sit down, I said, and we can talk when this is over, but he didn't. It was the morning, not even twelve yet, and he was drunk. His shirt was yellow around the neck. Eh, fuck you, Jesús. You've been taking these people's money for years, and now they can ask God themselves, they can ask Him if He even saw so much as a penny of it. Let's watch you sweat now, Jesús. He pushed some people along one of the aisles, made them cram in more, sat down and put his feet up on the bench in front. I tried to ignore him, but he was there for the rest of the service, smiling at me. He looked like a wolf, I kept thinking.

When it was over – There will be no collection today, I announced, go home and just pray to our Father that we might hear from Him again soon – all the congregation left. You're so lucky, one of them said to me, that you can be so close to Him, we are all so jealous. I know, I said, I am the luckiest man alive. When they were all gone, it was just Juanita and I and Jorge, who didn't move. I told Juanita to wait in the car. You send her away, Jorge said, we need to talk man to man. Very sensible man, you are, which makes sense, because you have got perfect *genetics*, eh?

As soon as Juanita was gone, Jorge came over to me. His breath smelt of marijuana and alcohol, and the rest of his body smelt of sweat, like he hadn't bathed in days. You are a fraud, Jesús. You're a fraud, and I know it, because God would never have a relation like you. You give me back my mother's money, and I will leave you alone. (His mother used to come to church, before she died; she was one of the biggest benefactors, and was much loved by the community. When she died, she left Jorge with nothing.) You give me every single bit of that money and I will not tell the news channels what a fraud you are. Of course, this made me laugh, because he had no evidence, no proof, so we were in the same situation, his word against mine. Jorge, I said, your mother's money went to help the needy; it is not here any more, and so you cannot have it. I am sorry, but she loved you very much. God damn it, Jesús, he shouted, I want that money. There is nothing more important to me than getting that off you, and I will *die* before I see you leave here! Do not be a fool, I said; the devil reasons like a man, but God? He thinks of eternity. I stole that line from a film, and it made him think, for a second, before he hit me. He threw his fists at me, over and over, but I am not a fighter; I could not defend myself. He dragged me to the altar, screaming, Where is it? Where is it? but I would not say. He gave up after a while and left me there on the floor. I cannot remember much; Juanita said that my face was terrible, but the cuts were all in the flesh, all just on the skin. She watched Jorge leave the church and kick the wall as he left. I'll be back, he kept shouting. Eventually she came inside, helped me to the car, got the money, and we left that afternoon. We didn't lock the church, because at least that way the community could use it, and she had to drive, because I could not see. We collected the children from their school, and we drove toward the East Coast, where Juanita's sister lived, and we could start again.

The bombs started going off as we were driving, and we stopped and spoke about it. Do we go there? she asked, Won't it be too unsafe? I said, No, we'll be fine; nobody will think of attacking Virginia. It's not New York, I said. Besides, God will protect us. Thirty minutes later we heard about the next bomb, and the next, and we turned around because Juanita told me that if we didn't, she was going to open the car door and just get out there in the middle of the road, and we headed south, toward the border, back where we had sworn we would never go.

THE SECOND *BROADCAST*

Simon Dabnall, Member of Parliament,
London

I had been on the tube and going to London Zoo on the morning
that Princess Diana died. I remember that I had a friend down
to stay from Manchester, only for the weekend, and we had been
planning the trip for weeks. We didn't hear about her death until
we were on the train, when I saw it on the front of a newspaper
that the man across from us was reading. Then we noticed the
crying women at the other end of the train, and the driver made
an announcement that, in way of tribute, London Zoo was closed
for the day. No doubt the hippos wanted to wear black and curse
at their gods for taking her, when she was still so young.
Everybody remembered where they were when they heard the
news, just as people used to say was the case when they heard
that JFK had been murdered.

When I heard *The Broadcast* properly for the second time,
I was in a cab on my way to my offices. The driver had put
Radio 2 on, because he wanted to listen to the news, about
the bombs in America, and he kept asking me what I thought
about hearing God speak to us. I was telling him that I didn't

necessarily believe that it was God – like some mad empiricist, I needed evidence, not guesswork and hearsay – and he was exasperated, almost argumentative, and then the static came back in. I wondered for a second if it was just the radio, then remembered that we were entirely digital. It tuned in faster than it did before, the words coming in then slipping away again. The driver stopped the car, pulled over at the side of the road, got out and stood by the door. I'm sorry, he said, I need to stop. He stood there crying, and I listened to the newsreaders react, terrified, elated.

Do Not Be Afraid, the voice said.

My Children; Do Not Be Afraid.

Dafni Haza, political speechwriter, Tel Aviv

The voice was somehow more tangible the second time, but still, there's no way to put a finger on it, or to say what it even sounded like. The closest thing I can describe it as is that voice in your head that you hear when you tell yourselves to do something, or to not, that moral niggle. It was that, but different. I don't know.

Anyway, when we heard it the second time, I knew the public reaction would be worse still, or at least harder to deal with; especially in Jerusalem, because of the pilgrimages. We had a difficult time anyway, managing the people who came to us for their religious outlet, journeying from Bethlehem to Jerusalem, then driving to Nazareth; we knew that they would cause us more problems, and we had already put out statements urging them to return to their hotels and stay there until we knew what *The Broadcast* was. As soon as it told everybody *Do Not Be Afraid* we knew we would have more problems. It's like a mother telling her children that they can't have a treat: it's only ever going to cause tantrums. And the American situation was tenuous at best: everybody knew that they were looking at Iran as responsible for the bombings, which meant they were looking at them for answers about *The Broadcast* as well. Wasn't it conceivable, the Prime Minister asked me when she called after it happened, that they somehow engineered *The Broadcast* to give them an excuse for everything else that happened? When I got off the phone from her, I saw that Lev had called again, and then we started hearing about violence on our side of the West Bank, worse than it had been; they said that there were bomb threats being called in, that the PLO had taken that chance to make their move. Ever since we agreed on terms about how to divide the land it had been a threat, that their more extremist side would show its face. And we were so close to reaching peace – or something that resembled peace, after so many decades of it being hellish – that any sort of extremism was likely to ruin it all. As soon as we saw that on the news, I had another call from the Prime Minister, and we wrote a statement that tried to distance our government from any potential retaliation. I said to the Prime Minister, why are you talking to me directly? I'm just a speech-writer, and she said, the Head of Communications has just quit, so you're what I've got.

I'll take the job, I said. Of course I'll take the job.

Dominick Volker, drug dealer, Johannesburg

Ag, that fucking place was a nightmare. I was out working, trying to collect from some of my dealers. I would sell to students, and they would sell it on for me, but I needed people to work the rough districts. I mean, nobody was going to fuck with me, but that doesn't mean I wanted to be there. And then, just as I was getting nervous, the second *Broadcast* happened, and I thought, for a second, it was speaking to me, you get me? *Do Not Be Afraid*, like a heads-up that I would be alright.

Phil Gossard, sales executive, London

It happened again when we were back in the office. Three days after it first came into our lives, and we had stuff to catch up on; or, more realistically, prepare for, because the US branch wouldn't open again for days, so we had to cover them. Jess' school was still closed, though we still weren't sure why. Karen had joked that the nuns were planning terrorist counter-attacks. They're too busy building false habits from Semtex, she said. We weren't even close to being as locked down as the US, though. Everything there that couldn't be vigilantly defended, it seemed, was just closed, hang the consequences. There was something different about their government's reaction, though, to whenever this happened before. I remember when I was a teenager, when 9/11 happened, and they were so aggressive, so bull-headed. And that's not a criticism; it's what they needed. Here, they just seemed resigned, like they were almost disappointed that it was so small, that there wasn't more in the way of noise and fury. There were no planes crashing into buildings; this was grass-roots stuff at its finest.

The sandwich man came, because these things repeat themselves, foreshadow themselves, the universe giving you constant hints of what's to come if you know what to look for; I had a ploughman's. I was sitting down about to eat – it was only just gone eleven, but I hadn't eaten any breakfast because of having to sort out sending Jess to a friend's house – and then it – He, It – spoke again through the static. It felt like a goodbye, to me. Most people didn't agree, but I thought that it definitely felt like a goodbye, or the first stages of one. It felt like one of those conversations you have with a girlfriend, when they sit you down and say that you need to talk. It felt like that, and everybody knows what that actually means, when you have that conversation.

Some of the other people in the office started crying. I didn't understand that; I didn't feel that way at all. Same with watching the people in the other offices. I went to the window just like we did that first time, watched them running down the street towards the tube station or the car park, frantic, like there was some real sense of urgency. What do we have to be afraid of? I asked, out loud, to nobody in particular. Some of the people in the street looked up at me, then their faces changed, whatever-they-were to scared, terrified. What's wrong? I asked. He's going to fall! one of them said, and for a second I thought that it was something prophetic and knowing; but they weren't talking about me. They were talking about the roof, above my head, where Bill was; and they watched as he stepped off, plummeted past the window. I had been leaning out, to get a better look – because I didn't know it was Bill before he did it – and I didn't have time to get out of the way completely. He clipped my hand as he went, thudding onto a car below. Its alarm didn't go off; he just smacked the roof, sank into it face down, arms outstretched, as if it were his bed. Some people ran over but it was already obvious that he was dead. The rest of the office cleared out, some quietly, some in tears, and they left me there on my own to shut down their systems for them, log them all out. When it was all done I sat in the office and finished the sandwich, because I was so hungry, and I rubbed at my hand where it had collided with Bill. It was bruising, dark purple and blue and angry.

Dhruv Rawat, doctor, Bankipore

I was lying in bed, because I had the day off. It was my day off the rota, and I had nothing to do, so I lay there and thought about the talk I had with Adele – which felt more like a fight, like an argument between friends than a conversation, and I was angry with myself for speaking the way that I did, for not vocalizing my thoughts better – when the second *Broadcast* happened, and we were told to *not be afraid*. I didn't react, because I wasn't afraid in the first place. I lay there and thought about how the rest of the world would take this; and then the telephone at the side of my bed rang. I picked it up, and the receptionist told me to wait, that I had a call from another room. Adele, I said when the line clicked, are you alright? She sounded terrified. He says, *Don't be afraid* (and she was already paraphrasing it, making it sound less than it did), but of course that'll make us scared, of course it will. She spoke so fast, I could barely make out the words. I mean, what are we meant to do with that? I asked her her room number and she said, No, tell me yours, I'll come to your room. Mine's a state. Two minutes later I heard her tapping on the door, and I answered it. I had pulled a shirt on as well as the pyjama trousers I sleep in and had not yet changed out of; she was in the same clothes that she had worn the day before, as if she hadn't even been to bed. I had tried to make my bed, but failed; I was terrible at those practical things. She didn't even seem to notice.

I've called my parents, she said, and my sister; they're fine, but they say it's mayhem back at home. (She was from Manchester, in England.) I wish that I could go back, to be with them; or bring them out here, show them how calm it is. She laughed, I remember her laughing – a lot – during that conversation. I mean, you're barely reacting, she said, you're all acting like, I don't know, like this is just a fly buzzing around, and it's there and you can't ignore it, but it's not worth getting stressed about. I didn't say anything. But it is worth getting stressed about, even if you don't believe that it's God, because there's something that we all heard, Dhruv, and we all heard it at the same time. Isn't that news? Isn't that important? Yes, of course it is, I said, for sure it is. I didn't know what she wanted me to say. I should go, she said, I need to get some sleep. I don't know what I'll do tomorrow; I'll have to talk to the producers back in the UK, see if we're putting a hold on filming. She stood by the door, hand on the handle, ready to leave. I should call them, I suppose. Sure, I said, perhaps you could do some filming here for them, you know, about *The Broadcast*. That made her laugh, and I asked why, what was funny about it. The news is full of people running around and bombs, and you think they want footage of you people standing around, trying to get on camera and not really having opinions on this stuff? Come on, Dhruv. She was crying; she let herself out.

Hameed Yusuf Ahmed, imam, Leeds

One man from the community was having doubts. Actually, no, they were all having doubts, it seemed, but this one man

99

was almost vigilant about them, expressing himself in ways that went against almost everything we taught about how God should be treated. I have always wondered if our God is the only God, he said to me, which was an admission that I had never heard before. He said, I have always thought, what if we're wrong? I recognized him, but again, I didn't know his name, and he didn't introduce himself; he assumed that I knew already. Talking to him then, I realized that I didn't know everything. I was never that big-headed, to think that I did; but even locally, my community, those people who I should have been guiding, they were having doubts. The people coming into my office before him had all told me similar things, or expressed them; they were worried about what *The Broadcast* meant, and they might not have said it in those words, but they wanted to know what happened if it was a God. He is Allah, the one, I told them, from scripture; He knows your heart. They wanted validation; they doubted everything. This is what happens when your leaders don't have absolute conviction; when faith isn't enough. Many of them suggested that it could have been Allah speaking to us; I listened but didn't speak, because that went against all I had taught them. If it was, they said, why would He have spoken in English? Surely He would use Arabic, or maybe a language even older?

The man who was having doubts was talking to me about them in the frankest way possible. What if we've all been wrong, have you ever considered that? What if it's not about age, or who was there first, or whose laws make the most sense; what if the Christians were right all along? Or, what if, I don't know, it's actually about who shouted loudest? There are more Christians than there are members of Islam, right? I didn't know what to say to that, so I cleared my throat, and then the static came again, and we all heard *The Broadcast* for the second time.

Do not be afraid? the man asked when it was finished. How am I not meant to *be afraid*? He turned to me, looked me right in the eyes – I didn't realize it until then, but he hadn't been looking at me, not right at me until that moment – and he said, You, this is your job: reassure me. What is this? You know it doesn't work like that, I told him. I am not the voice of God, nor do I have a link to Him. I am only here to guide you in His ways. So what does He say about this? he asked me. He got up, opened the door, shouted to the rest of the people waiting, who were talking to themselves already, unable to talk about anything other than *The Broadcast*. What does our God say about this? he yelled. What does He say we should be doing now?

I did not have an answer.

Audrey Clave, linguistics postgraduate student, Marseilles

Patrice's father was a priest, and he insisted on having the funeral the day after Patrice died, first thing in the morning. We got up and drove down there to his church, but it was just us and a few relatives that we were never introduced to. It wasn't until halfway through the service that we realized that either his parents didn't know that he was gay, or that they didn't want to know, because it wasn't mentioned, and nobody said anything about his life or his friends or even the sort of person that he was. His father just looked ashamed the whole

101

way through, reading the bits about God's love for us all, and loss. He didn't talk about Patrice; he spoke about God. Fucking hell, Jacques said afterwards, what a pig that man was. I defended him, because he was just coping with Patrice's death. We all were, and he was dealing with it the only way he knew how.

Afterward we stood in the graveyard and Jacques sang some of The Smiths as a joke – *A dreaded sunny day, so I'll meet you at the cemetery gates!* – but nobody laughed; and we told stories about Patrice, about what we liked about him, that sort of thing. We were watching them burying him in the distance – they used a little digger to pick up and dump the soil, can you believe that? – when we heard *The Broadcast*. When it was over we sat on the ground and watched the digger quietly until Jacques broke the mood, reaching over and grabbing me.

Audrey's afraid, I reckon, he said, and then he started singing 'Girl Afraid', another Smiths song. He knew all the words for some reason, so we just let him finish, his voice sounding wrong pronouncing the English words, this imitation, almost. Girl afraid, he sang, where do His intentions lay? Or does He even have any?

Isabella Dulli, nun, Vatican City

Do Not Be Afraid, the voice said, and that was when I realized that it could not be God; or, it could not be *my* God. My God would understand that we were not afraid, that we would bask in His light. The darkness was my own place for worship, away from the crowds outside. I could hear them, through the gates – the guards must have let them in, because we were to be a pilgrimage, and the only way that they could have held the masses back was with violence, and they would never have gone that far. I could hear them singing hymns, all in English, because they were tourists, and how could they know? *Do not be afraid, for if you really love me, I will always be with you, rejoice, rejoice, rejoice.* They were so happy, I could hear their voices through the walls of the tomb, vibrating through the Basilica. He is not your God, I said, and I heard myself say it for the first time, even though I had been thinking it; in the darkness, it came back at me, my voice but so distant, and I believed it. Before, He spoke to missionaries, or to those blessed. He spoke to those who loved Him or those who despised Him, but never like this. This was not our God, and I had to believe that. I recited His words to Him in that tomb, knowing that He had to be watching and listening to me, in this time when the world had gone insane: Do not have any other gods before me. You shall not make for yourself an idol, whether in the form of anything that is in heaven above, or that is on the earth beneath, or that is in the water under the earth. You shall not bow down to them or worship them; for I, the Lord your God, am a jealous God, punishing children for the iniquity of parents, to the third and the fourth generation of those who reject me, but showing steadfast love to the thousandth generation of those who love me and keep my commandments.

Hameed Yusuf Ahmed, imam, Leeds

Samia bit her nails all night; I went out to pray before bed, and she chose to stay at home. I feel ill, she said, but she was lying; she was lazy sometimes, and we both knew it. I chose to ignore it. When I got back she acted like everything was normal, like she hadn't been thinking of the questions she wanted to ask the whole time that I was gone, even though I knew that she had. Like I say, I chose to ignore it. She wasn't subtle. I sat on the sofa and she threw the questions at me, casually: what were the people asking you today, what do they think it was, what do you think about it, what does it mean? She was stretching towards the questions I really didn't want her to ask, and I pushed them away, batted them back. I don't want to talk about it, I said to her. God will talk to us all in time, let us know His will.

She had always found it hard, this life. I knew it, and she knew it, but it was yet another part of our lives that we chose to ignore, because that felt like it made it all better.

Elijah Said, prisoner on Death Row, Chicago

The new guard in charge of our corridor was called Cole, and he liked to think of himself as a hard-ass. That was his phrase when he introduced himself that day, before the second *Broadcast*, and he slammed his fists together as he said it, clenched, the knuckles cracking. He went down the corridor and spoke to Finkler and myself individually, keeping his voice hush-quiet so that the other prisoner couldn't hear. Finkler was so loud that I heard every part of his side of the conversation; it was nothing, just words. Then he came to me, acting like Finkler had told him secrets. Finkler didn't know any to tell. You're one of them Fruits? he said, laughing. They enjoyed that; mocking a role, a title, a calling, a purpose. I know all about you guys, all about you. I know all about you. His voice was ruddy, reedy, stained with years of cigarette smoke. Finkler's conversation had been gentle, amenable; he was suggesting that it was something other than it was. He came right up to the bars, speaking quietly. You and them Islamic brothers of yours killed all my people, right? Hijacking planes, planting bombs, hiding in caves. Sure, I know you people. I moved to the bars, grabbed his head in one motion, pulled his face to the metal. You don't know anything, I said. We are nothing like those murderers; we are innocents, and true. I dropped him – he had been on the tips of his feet when I held his head – and he rushed backwards, gasping for air. He shouted something, but I cannot remember what it was, and then we heard it. *Do Not Be Afraid.*

Shit, shit, Cole said, what is that? It was as if he had forgotten about the first *Broadcast*. Was that you? He panicked, moved down to Finkler's cell. Did you hear that, Finkler? Of course I did, oh wow, I mean, we all did, right? That's what they say? Everybody hears it, everybody hears the voice of God, that's what the papers say? He sounded almost sanctimonious in his pleasure. Holy shit, Cole said. It's amazing, isn't it? I could hear Finkler grinning.

Katy Kasher, high school student, Orlando

Have you ever heard of The Holy Land? It was this theme park down the road from the House of Mouse in Orlando, and they tried to compete, but it was no frigging contest. They had a room where you could see evolution – you started in the Garden of Eden, where humans lived with dinosaurs – and a ride that took you through the plagues from the Old Testament, like a ghost train. And they had this show twice a day, like the Main Street Parade but *infinitely* more gay, where some douche dressed up as Jesus, walked through the crowd and did a mock crucifixion on these huge polystyrene rocks, and you could watch the show while you did rock-climbing up the wall carved out to be the face of Jesus, like Mount Rushmore. We used to go three or four times a year, all the family, because Mom and Dad thought it would bring us all closer together. All us kids, me and my cousins, we just wanted to go to Disney instead, or Universal, because the Holy Land didn't even have those giant turkey legs, or churros, or anything. *The Broadcast* came again on Grammy's birthday, and Mom had us up at stupid o'clock – seriously, it was still totally dark outside – just to drive up there, get there super-early. We were putting everything into the car when it happened, and Mom and Dad stopped, looked up, smiling, and then she turned to me and said, Wasn't that wonderful? And I was all, Wasn't *what* wonderful? I hadn't heard it the first time, because I was asleep, we thought; this time, I think I ruined her day.

Mei Hsüeh, professional gamer, Shanghai

We all heard it outside the game, of course, but then, five minutes after the second *Broadcast*, somebody – had to be one of the mods – set up something to play in-game, which was hilarious. I mean, we were still worried about what it meant, but it was totally relevant to *then*.

Andrew Brubaker, White House Chief of Staff, Washington, DC

We were in The Danger Room, getting opinions on the best way to fight back against the bombings. Over the few hours previous we'd pieced together that they were from a terror cell we had pinpointed as working out of Iran, with rumoured ties to their government, but their government denied everything. They would, one of the joint chiefs said. We were talking about tactical strikes, targeted at training camps that we knew existed, zero civilian casualties. They were purely designed to show that we weren't fucking around, and we had them ready to go. I mean, literally, POTUS said the word, they'd be launched from carriers in the Mediterranean, just off the coast of Turkey. POTUS needed reassuring, because he'd never done one of these before. We'd gotten to the point where some of the weapons we had were so exact that they were like an acne solution: you find a spot, you nuke that spot, the rest of the skin is clear. It wasn't like the old days of towers of rubble and burning bodies, and the chance that they could go wrong. It's a science, I said to him. Estimated casualties based on sat knowledge were in the low triple digits, and if the government turned over the heads of the faction, that would be it. War over.

The Broadcast came in just like before and we all heard it, clear as day. This time we got the signifiers, in the speech; it was all in English, with an accent we couldn't pin down. POTUS was devastated. What does it mean? he asked the room, but none of us had an answer. We have to make a statement, I said, try and keep things under control. Jesus, Drew, he said, I just need to know what this means before I say anything. I need to think. Fine, I said to him – and I was snappy, because we didn't have time for him to pussy out – I'll tell you what it means: it means that there's suddenly going to be a whole lot of very, very angry people out there that this happened again, and that it was only in English; it means you're going to have US citizens suddenly asking what there is to be afraid of, and they're all so on edge you're going to have to reassure them that everything's fine, even when you know it isn't; and it means that you're going to have to step the fuck up and lead this country, because we're in trouble, here.

He stopped crying. Alright, he said, alright.

HOIST THAT RAG

Theodor Fyodorov, unemployed, Moscow

The day after *The Broadcast*, Moscow fell apart in protest, the people wanting to know answers. There were many, many questions, and they had them written on their boards, and they chanted them in the streets. They wanted to know why we didn't hear it in Russian (because not everybody spoke English, and some of the people – most of the people – didn't even understand), and they wanted to know what there was that we should or shouldn't be afraid of. They wanted to know why the church had not made a statement yet about *The Broadcast*, about what we should think of it. It was all over the television, the streets full of people marching toward the Cathedral of Christ the Saviour, so when I woke up I told Anastasia that I wanted to get a better look, to go down and join them. Do you really care about this? she asked, and I said No, but that I wanted to see. I always like knowing what makes people tick, I said. She said that she wanted breakfast before she joined me, so I went by myself.

I used to live in Tula, but Anastasia got an apartment near Taganskya, which is right in the middle of the city, so I decided to move here, and move in with her. I didn't know the city well, still, even though I had been there for weeks, so I decided to just go with the crowd. Everybody was walking so slowly because there were so many people, and it was like an army, left right, left right. After a while I saw some people I recognized, some of Anastasia's friends from university, and they told me that the crowd was going to demand answers from the Patriarch right there and then. He has to tell us what's going on, they said, you should come and help us. I explained that I didn't have an interest – I didn't believe in God back then – but that I would go anyway. I want to see what happens, I told them. Anastasia joined us a few minutes after that, and we marched. The crowd sang songs that I knew almost all of the words to, because there were versions with swearwords used at football matches, and we moved slowly, so slowly, but we kept going.

The television called this a riot, but it wasn't like any riot that I had ever seen. The atmosphere was amazing, so friendly and happy, and everybody was so happy to be alive. I remember years and years ago there were riots in Manezh Square, seeing them on the TV, the burning cars, the hooligans, and they were nothing like this. This was so civil all the way. All I saw was people of all ages, in a spirit of camaraderie, a celebration of good news, they thought. We are not alone! some of them kept shouting; Through this all, we are not alone! Then, after a while, we started to get word that some of the people in the crowd, the ringleaders, they wanted to take the church back. Take it back from who? Anastasia's friends asked. Take it from the church? I said that they should ignore that gossip. It's probably Chinese whispers, I said, and then a man in front corrected me. No, he said, they want to take it back from the Orthodoxy, because they have lied to us for so long. What happens after that? I asked him. What's left after that? Whatever comes next, he said.

The good spirits – the singing, the shuffling – carried on until we stopped suddenly. More whispers came through that we had been stopped by the police, and then others came through saying that the front of the crowd – which we couldn't see – had reached the Cathedral, and that this was all that we would see. Anastasia's feet were starting to hurt her, and Marcela and Alexei, her friends, decided that they wanted a drink, so they went into a shop we passed and bought a bottle of schnapps, because it was cheap. Other people got bottles as well, and they kept us going for the next hour. We couldn't go forward, because we were still, and we couldn't go backwards, because the streets were full behind us, so we drank and sang. We stayed there for another hour, and then people behind us started drifting off, and we realized that we weren't getting through to the front. Whispers came from the other end then, that something had happened at the Cathedral, that the police were there. Where's this coming from? we asked the whisperers, and they said it was from the television, so we agreed to meet back at Anastasia's place to watch it. By the time I got there, pushing through the crowd, I had been split up from the others, and Ana was already there (because she's so small, I think, which made it easier for her to slip through the people). You have to see this, she said before I had even taken my coat off. We sat and watched the footage of the Patriarch bleeding on the steps of the Cathedral, and the police rushing toward the man who shot him, and that man then shooting himself in the face. He had a sign with him that read *God Doesn't Care What We Do*, and the news cameras kept focusing in on it, showing us the sign over and over even as his blood started to soak across the pavement and into the white cardboard. The crowd were heaving, pushing forwards, even when the police were smacking at them, telling them to stay back, and then another man, so angry, screaming, threw a bottle of *something* with a rag in the top, set on fire, and it smashed all over the church. The paint was a lacquer, and it went up like it was oil. Anastasia couldn't stop crying, so I tried to turn over the channel but the same image was everywhere, so I just told her to shut her eyes tightly.

Dominick Volker, drug dealer, Johannesburg

By the time I got back to my old lady – she hated it when I called her that, because she said, I'm not old, I'm only twenty-six, and that made me laugh – she was already on the pipe. I told you, I said, don't fucking do that stuff, I don't want our kid to end up like a bloody retard. I worked hard to get us this, I said, don't fuck it up now. We had a nice house, in a nice district, well away from the rest, because I made enough money to keep it there. She didn't have to work, and we had two dogs, because that was what she wanted. She was pregnant, so big she was nearly bursting. She had wanted a baby for fucking ever, and I kept having to tell her she would fuck it up if she kept smoking, but she didn't listen, so I had to do better rules. Nothing harder than pot, you hear? I hear, she had said, but I didn't always believe her, because sometimes I wasn't home for days, so I didn't know what she would be getting up to. I asked her if she had been watching television, if she knew what was going on; Ag no, she said, nobody's got a clue. She left it fifteen minutes or so before sparking up again, and I told her not to, but she ignored me. Poor fucking baby will be coughing up his lungs in there, I said.

She said, shouldn't you be out selling? But I didn't think people would be buying, not that day, not in my usual markets. They've got something better today, eh? I said.

Dhruv Rawat, doctor, Bankipore

I was up very early, even though I had so little sleep – I remember looking at my clock when I couldn't sleep, getting upset with myself about it, turning over and over. The hotel didn't have air conditioning, so my room was very hot, and that made me more uncomfortable. That's another thing that I missed about Bangalore: the air conditioning. They had started putting it everywhere, something that my hometown was pitifully far behind in regards to. I bathed, made my prayers, did not eat breakfast. I was at work so early that I managed all of the week's paperwork before I even had my first patient, which was the man with the foot again. He had wrapped it up in his own bandage, which was little more than a tea-towel; it wasn't bleeding any more, and the wound was pink where the skin was getting better. It worked, he said, look, it's getting much better. Good, good, I said. You're an excellent doctor, he told me; I will tell your father how good you are at this. He stood up, ready to leave, and I asked him, Have you thought about *The Broadcast* like they are everywhere else in the world? What? he asked. Sorry, I said, I'm just wondering. Have you thought about what it was – who it was, maybe, I don't know – that we all heard?

Well, yes, of course, he said. I have wondered if it was a form of God, somehow. That's what all the English and the Americans believe, I think. You wondered that? I asked, and he said, again, Of course I did. Because who is to say that it wasn't? What about the Vedas? I asked him, and he shrugged. If it is Brahma, somehow, thinking we should be spoken to – and don't you think that sounds stupid just to say it? – but if it is Brahma, I don't think it will matter that I wondered *if* it was. And if it isn't, well, it probably isn't real anyway.

Meredith Lieberstein, retiree, New York City

We woke up to the news that New York was under a curfew of sorts. It wasn't *called* a curfew, that wasn't how it was sold to us, but Leonard said that's what it was. We're requesting that you stay in your homes where possible, he read off the website. Requesting? You wait, they'll turn it into an order before you can even blink, he said. There were little riots, panic-fuelled and disorganized, but for the most part people seemed happy staying in. They don't want to even let people go to churches, Leonard said, because they're worried that large groups of people like that equal some sort of target. That was Leonard; when they let you go to church he mocked you for wanting it, and when you couldn't he wanted to stand up for your rights. He was a complicated man.

Regardless, people were panicking all over the country, all over the *world*. It was so ambiguous, *The Broadcast*, so open to interpretation. If you believed in God – and people did, far more readily than they had in the months before *The Broadcast*, that's for sure – if you believed, then there was the question of what we should be afraid of. Most believers wrote it off as saying that we shouldn't be scared of *The Broadcast*, of God's presence, and they found comfort and solace in that. Some didn't, and wondered if this wasn't telling us in advance not to be afraid, not to be afraid of what was to come. And then those of us who didn't believe, who were sitting on the fence or just plain stubborn, we were asking where it came from, still. We were saying, Well, there must be a scientific explanation for this, because there *always* is, because it's *never* so ridiculous that you have to just make a wild leap into fantasy.

But then, we lived in New York. We were down the road from the bomb-site, only a ten-minute walk, and we could smell the ash on the air, so we were afraid almost constantly, and we *wanted* reassurance that we knew we couldn't have. Leonard knew that it wasn't God, but I . . . I didn't.

Andrew Brubaker, White House Chief of Staff, Washington, DC

The Broadcast was one of those situations where everybody heard what they wanted to hear. It was a Barnum statement. You ever hear that? The circus leader, P. T. Barnum, he used to have this theory about generic statements being taken over by people, hearing what they want to hear. That's how cold readings work: they throw stuff out there, and as long as they hoist that rag into the air with enough conviction, the people it's targeted at will believe it and read into it whatever it is that they're looking for. It's like horoscopes: they're generic, but people believe them. For most people that was fine; for our enemies, that was an invitation.

Ed Meany, research and development scientist,
Virginia

I met up with Sam Tate, one of the guys I'd been to college with. He worked in R and D, special projects, weapons and weaponization, stuff that I didn't know about and didn't want to, and he asked to have a coffee with me, talk through something. He looked nervous. They've told me I'm going on site somewhere, he said, and they've asked me to – I put my fingers in my ears. I don't want to know, I told him. Alright, he said, so we sat in silence for the rest of the drink. When we were done I asked if he was alright about the Nevada bombing. I knew that he had friends out there, that he'd worked out there for a while. Yeah, he said, I hated working there. You really hated working there? I asked, and he said, You have no idea; at least now I'll never have to think about it again, will I?

Andrew Brubaker, White House Chief of Staff,
Washington, DC

We pulled some staff from the DC office, told them to make their way to Ohio, to the silo there. We weren't ready to launch them, not even close, and they hadn't been tested, but we wanted them there in case. It never hurt, we reasoned, to have every eventuality covered. Of course, as soon as you start thinking *Nuclear*, it's there the whole time, in every conversation that you have. But we were a long way from that.

Where we *were* was having conversations with the Supreme Leader of Iran about handing over the groups that he claimed didn't even exist. We've got intelligence reports that name names, we said; he kept denying it. At this point, he said to POTUS, why wouldn't we give them up to you? You know that we'll be forced to retaliate, POTUS said. Believe me, Mr President, the Supreme Leader said, we do not want that. We had been off the phone for five minutes when reports came in of more bombings: a church in Reseda, a supermarket in Seattle. Fuck them, POTUS said, and we got back on the phone, told the Supreme Leader that we were going to tactically strike targets that we believed were associated with the terror cell. We didn't take it to Congress; we didn't tell the UN our intentions. We just did it. We hit three camps along the Iran/Afghanistan borders, places that we had heard were amassing weapons, training soldiers. It was going to be a game of Battleships, and we would win, and we would keep our hands clean because they struck first. We hit those camps and then waited; if they retaliated, we'd retaliate harder.

That afternoon we found a video on the internet, claiming to be made by a terror cell that our intelligence reports had previously linked to Iran, taking responsibility for the bombings. There was no face there, no Bin Laden or Hussein to get angry at, just a shot of one of the camps burning, flattened, almost, and a voice speaking, telling us that until we admitted that the voice heard around the world was an American hoax they would maintain attacks on American soil. Repent and you will be spared.

Dafni Haza, political speechwriter, Tel Aviv

Everybody knew about Iran, the threat it posed. For a while, when everything settled down in the so-called Middle East a decade or so before, it was all the international press seemed to talk about. America – in fact, no, the whole world – had been worrying for years about the potential that they had to attack, because it seemed that no amount of sanctions could stop them, or stop their people. When I was a little girl it had all been about Iraq. Now Iraq was a gentle ally, neutered in the eyes of the world, and their brother – who had been there for so long, biding his time, it seemed – became the real threat, only he did nothing. Rumours had surrounded them for over a decade that they were building weapons, but those same rumours surrounded us, even; there was something about Iran. Israel, of course, was estranged anyway, so as a people, as a government, we weren't concerned when the Americans began their bombing. But it seemed rash, I think. When we saw the footage on the televisions, of the bomb-sites, then the terrorist cell video that appeared after it, it all became very real. Even those wars before, decades of conflict in this part of the world, they seemed like they would be brushed away, because this – the potential of this – was so much worse.

Piers Anderson, private military contractor, the Middle East

We were hundreds and hundreds of miles away, still in Turkey, so we didn't see a thing, but it only took ten minutes before we knew about it on the TV, and only a few minutes after that word started trickling in that it was the Americans that had launched their attack. Are we at war? we asked the suit in charge of the mission, and he said that he didn't have a clue whether *we* were, but the Americans almost certainly were. Are they ever not? he asked.

Phil Gossard, sales executive, London

I watched the footage of the Yank missiles – or, rather, of the aftermath of them, the satellite footage of smoking craters, then the video of the terrorist taken from the internet, or the supposed terrorist. It didn't seem real enough; that a terrorist would just use YouTube? That seemed wrong, somehow. That was on every news station within a few minutes, but the presenters weren't giving it a chance, not actually listening to what it was saying; like they were telling us, This *isn't* a lie, that *was* the voice of our God. The biggest issue, and nobody was actually talking about it, it felt like, was who was actually right. We all were; none of us were. We didn't know if it was God, aliens, technology, V'ger . . . Could have been anything. *The Times* said that, post-*The Broadcast*, 92 per cent of British citizens polled believed in the presence of a higher power. But that raised issues in itself, because there was no way that 92 per cent of the British population were Christians. There were Muslims and Hindus and Jews and Buddhists, so who the hell was actually right? The papers were going with the Christian God, and Christianity was the largest religion in the world, so most would be fine with that. But those people who *weren't* Christian . . . Who was to say that they were wrong, that everything they believed was wrong?

My hand wasn't getting better from where it had hit Bill as he fell. I wondered if there was a broken bone, maybe; the bruise ran right across the back of it. Karen wanted to get me in for X-rays but I told her to not worry about it. We had always agreed to keep her medical opinion out of the marriage; it made her a hypochondriac in some cases, made her shrug off real problems in others. I could still move my fingers so I knew it wasn't totally ruinous, and it felt better, even as it looked worse. It'll heal, I told her.

Mei Hsüeh, professional gamer, Shanghai

They started cutting off internet in some countries, trying to – this was the theory – constrain the flow of information. China was one of the first, and most of the people I knew went, but I got my internet from a private pipe, which cost me more, but was worth it – especially then, because everybody else lost all contact to anything that wasn't government-controlled. So many people disappeared from the servers, but there were enough still going – most of the Americans, the Europeans. (I guess the local servers were emptier, particularly for places like China and Korea, but I didn't touch those – the people who played on them were so snobby.) I still had mine, because my line came from a company who weren't government-controlled, which was amazingly lucky, really. They filtered everything, and I picked them because they used proxy servers, hid it all from the government, so I got to stay online. Our guild was down to twelve all of a sudden, which meant we had just enough to do another dungeon, but only barely. It would be close.

Katy Kasher, high school student, Orlando

My Dad was a pilot, flew for Delta a few years back, then after that some smaller airlines, mostly doing shuttles between states, that kind of thing. He was grounded because the airports were all shut, and that made him angry. I think he was trying to forget that I hadn't heard *The Broadcast*, whereas it was all

Mom would talk about. She was full-on that it was the voice of God, and that because I didn't hear it, He was testing me. She called up the local priest, and he came right over as soon as he heard why.

Mom told him that she was worried I had the devil in me or whatever, but he said that he was sure God had just decided that I wasn't ready to hear from Him yet. She'll hear as soon as she opens her heart to the Lord, he said, even though I was sitting right there with them. She just needs time; everybody will hear His call that wants to. (He didn't ask if I wanted to, but I believed in God, so yeah, sure I wanted to, of course I did.) Mom then asked if there were others he had heard about, like me. (I think she wanted to lure us all into a Hot Topic and lock the doors or something.) He said that I was it, which made her look so sad. The priest kept smiling at me, which was a, pretty creepy, and b, made me keep thinking of that bit in the *Exorcist* remake from a couple of years back, where he talks to the girl and is all *The Power Of Christ Compels You*.

Dhruv Rawat, doctor, Bankipore

Later that afternoon, after I had watched the news about the missiles, I went to find Adele, because I wanted to apologize. I was not completely sure that it was my fault she was angry – what she had said came out of anger, that much was certain, and I assumed that it was because she was here and her family was there, and she was alone here (apart from her crew, who were as much strangers as anybody else, and me, who . . . We were still strangers. I didn't even know her entire name). So it made sense that she was angry. In those situations, I always liked to apologize first; it showed strength of character. I went to the hotel and asked for her room number, because I didn't know it, and they called her on the telephone, but she wasn't there, or she didn't answer. Can you tell me her room? I asked. I need to speak to her, and you'll be closed maybe by the time she returns. I knew the girl on the reception desk – she was a cousin of one of my old friends, though he had left and moved to Malaysia, and I don't think she remembered me from the time we had met – and I gave her my best smile. Sure, she said. She wrote the number down on a piece of paper. I went straight upstairs, tried knocking on the door, but there was no answer, so I went and sat with the newspaper – I wanted to read everything about the rest of the world, because it was so easy to forget when nobody was worried about it – and I watched on the news about America's actions, which they were treating as the start of World War 3, accusing everybody of everything. I waited all night, and then I knocked on her door again, when she would have been going to bed, so surely would have been in, but there was no answer.

In the middle of the night I had a telephone call; it was Adele. She was crying, and drunk, I think. How can you be so laid back about this? How is this not just tearing you apart? All of you, you're so fucking desperate, and yet this, you just let it be, as if it doesn't even matter to you? Why don't you even care? I told her, I do care, of course I care; it's just, if this is all a plan of – you would say God – then we should just wait and see what it means to us all. Worrying about it means nothing, don't you agree? She was absolutely silent. I'm so sorry for earlier, I said, for what I said. I should have been more understanding. And for this, I'm sorry: you shouldn't have to be alone through all of this. What do you mean? she asked. I don't understand what you mean. I mean, all I am saying is that if you don't want to be alone, you don't have to be. I think that's why none of us are as scared as you are, maybe; because we're never alone. I don't know what you're saying, Adele told me, and she hung up the telephone. I tried to call her back again, but there was no answer, so I went to her room for the third time that day, knocked on the door. Adele, I said, it's Dhruv, please let me in. I want to explain. This has all turned out differently than I wanted.

She didn't open the door. I went back to my room, turned off the light again, and I watched the telephone in case she called me back and wanted to accept my apology (for something that I did not do wrong in the first place).

THINGS FALLING APART

Simon Dabnall, Member of Parliament, London

Petty bureaucracy reigned. The Deputy PM, elevated to power by virtue of resignation, decided that we needed to address the situation with the US, with where we stood. We haven't been attacked, he said, and we don't know all the facts. It was casual government at its finest, as he danced around and tried to be as non-committal as possible, but the message was clear: we weren't going to help them. Frankly, I was relieved, because the Americans were getting into it so quickly that I didn't know how long it would be before they were ankle deep with no way out. Usually these things – the process of terrorist attacks, of threats of retaliation, of that actually escalating to action – they took weeks. This time it could be counted in hours, and that put us all in a very dangerous situation indeed. There's a real worry that we'll actually manage to hold the country together in all this chaos, the Deputy PM said, so there's no point in shitting in the bed just because we don't want to go to sleep. (Some of the back-benchers laughed at that like naughty school-children, which only served to remind me, once again, how old I was.) We spoke about it, but there was a consensus: America was, for the time being, on their own with this one.

And then there was the matter of the Church of England to deal with. Before *The Broadcast*, of course, Church and State were constitutionally separated (unless something required them to be curiously conjoined, in which case we treated them as one and the same). But in this case they were very much kept in their own paddocks. People spoke about the potential God being Christian, but what they really meant was that he was Catholic, or some derivation thereof. The C of E, for all its faults, was in a bit of a pickle. If it *was* God and he *was* the Catholic chap, their main source of funding – being the people of England and her provinces – was in serious danger of disappearing. Why invest in a company that's failing, where the product has been proven faulty and the CEO was only invented 600 years ago to help clear up a messy divorce?

I cried out of an afternoon sitting listening to archbishops selling their stock in favour of lunch, by myself, from the McDonald's down by the Thames, a guilty pleasure of mine that I never tired of, and I had just noticed that the Wheel wasn't turning when my telephone rang. It was Waitrose in Putney; my sister was there, collapsed at the till. She's drunk, the man said, and I think she's had an accident. He said that last part quietly, hushed. I didn't know what he expected me to do about that; he was the one surrounded by shelves full of cleaning products.

By the time I arrived Dotty was propped up on a chair at the side, under the telephone station. Come on old girl, I said, and that set her off crying. She wept the whole cab ride back, and I had to give the driver extra money to stop him worrying about her throwing up on his seats. He kept staring at us in the mirror, though, which I hate. When we got back I put her to bed, but she wouldn't stay lying down. What the hell is the matter with you? I asked her, and she said, I just can't deal with it, Sim. What? With *this*, she said, with *it*. She waved her hands above her head, then opened the top of her shirt to show me a crucifix on a gold chain, one of those overly detailed ones with the miniature body of Christ, tiny nails through His hands, tiny crown of thorns on His head. Lovely detailing. I never knew that He was real, she said, and she pulled the cross off her neck. I've done such things, so many things that He said we shouldn't do. I didn't dare ask any more, so I put her to bed again, told her I'd be back.

I phoned Clive from the living room. Clive was her husband, and I wanted to know why on earth he wasn't called, or if he had been called, why he didn't get out to help her. He said that he didn't have a clue that she was there. I thought she was at home all day, he said. Well, I told him, you really should come back here, because she's a danger to herself like this. She needs to be looked after. He asked me to wait for him, so I said that I would. It took him nearly two hours to get back, even though he only worked in Hammersmith, only across the bridge, and when he walked in he absolutely stank of whisky.

Andrew Brubaker, White House Chief of Staff, Washington, DC

I was doing a conference, detailing the strikes we had made, talking about the fact that we were certain of a swift end to the conflict. I said something like, When the terror cells and the nations involved in harbouring the criminals involved come to their senses, see the opposition facing them, we're confident that this will all be over swiftly; and the reporter from *The Times* piped up, interrupted – which wasn't done, not in the press room, not during a statement – and asked me why we were even at war. We were attacked, our freedom was attacked, I said, and he said, Sure, but by what we can only assume are religious zealots. Why did the US retaliate against Iran? This guy thought he had something, and I wanted to prove to him that he didn't, so I answered. The government of Iran refused to hand over the criminals responsible when we requested them, and we had warned them that if they didn't, we would be forced to retaliate, and then we did. Yeah, and I understand that, he said, but did you have evidence that the government even had the criminals? Did you have actual proof? Because we've been doing this with Iran for years now, haven't we? Assuming things? Was this just another case of the US government jumping to conclusions? I didn't say anything, because I didn't have an answer. He continued: Because, the terrorists, they were probably just jumping to conclusions as well, after *The Broadcast*. They probably just panicked, just scared that their entire belief system might be crumbling. It's not totally unfair to think it could have been some sort of attack on them, right?

That was where I chose to end the press conference, because he was right. He was completely right, but we were too far gone for that sort of logic. As soon as I was out of the room I heard that the British had decided to refuse our call for solidarity, and that we were having issues with other members

127

of the UN, countries who didn't agree with our decision to jump in as quickly as we did. I prayed to whatever it was that spoke to us then that Iran didn't fight back any more, that they gave us the terrorists, and that we could just end it all as quickly as it started.

Meredith Lieberstein, retiree, New York City

Leonard was so angry when the news started showing the British Deputy Prime Minister – apparently they were having some trouble with the real one, disappeared somewhere, the newsreaders said – when they showed him saying that the UK didn't support our President's decision to attack Iran. Leonard was so, so angry. I can't believe that we asked for their help, he shouted, this situation shouldn't have even existed! How dare we beg other people to get into this mess with us!

New York was different to the rest of the US anyway, because we have a thing about terrorism. We band together in times of national stress; it's what makes us unique, and that always appealed to Leonard, that New Yorkers had this built-in sense of a sort of *protective morality*. They'll all know this is wrong, he said to me. I should organize something to show the government what we think of them. We were all too aware of the protests – which had turned to riots across the globe, as the situation in Moscow had shown – but Leonard wanted to make this one different. He went onto his blog – he kept a political blog, which I gather quite a few people used to read – and he started planning. As far as I was concerned it was a good project for him, something to keep him busy.

I snuck out and went to the synagogue. It was so busy that I couldn't actually get in for the service, so I had to join the queue to get into the next one along. Apparently they were going to start doing blessings on the lawns of Central Park, just to fit everybody in, as if it were some sort of rock festival, and the rabbis were playing guitars with their teeth.

Isabella Dulli, nun, Vatican City

Nobody missed me when I was down in the tomb, and it wasn't until somebody came down to pray to St Peter that they realized I was there. The lights came on and woke me up. I was sleeping in the dirt on the floor, so close to Him, trying to get closer. Sister Dulli, are you okay? It was one of the Cardinals, one I didn't really know, but he knew my name. He was Spanish, I think, and he spoke to me in creaky Italian that I had to strain to understand. Let me help you up. He was older than I was, and frailer; I think I remember that he had ill health, something to do with his breathing. He wheezed, certainly, all that dead air down in the tomb. He tried to let me use him to pull myself to my feet, but I did most of the work myself, truth be told. How long have you been down here? He seemed genuinely concerned. Not long, I said. He didn't ask why I was there; when I was upright he leaned back against one of the guard railings that we put up to keep the tourists back It's amazing, isn't it? To think that this is all validated now.

What do you mean? I asked him, and he smiled. Well, you know. People say you're insane for believing this. The last few years, you know how it's been. Harder to follow Him, eh? The Cardinal must have seen my face then, whatever I looked like. It wasn't harder for you, I understand. Faith is all subjective, eh? You didn't believe? I asked. He shook his head. No, no, I did. Something is lost in the translation, I think. I believed, but there was always a worry, a wonder. A question, eh? He smiled, because he thought that this was normal, but I wanted to shake him, tell him that I never questioned it. And *The Broadcast*, it wasn't validation, it was a lie. Evidence isn't a voice in the darkness, I said, you can't really believe that it is. No, he said, of course not, of course not. We both stood in and looked at the tomb, at the other graves that they unearthed over the years, until I couldn't stand it any more. I need to get fresh air, I said. He nodded. It's a wonderful day, he said. I didn't reply.

Outside, the light was so much brighter than I expected, and it took me a few seconds there, in the Basilica itself, to get accustomed. It was so busy, people crowding like they did in the queues outside, like they did when there was a mass or the Pope's birthday, or even a new Pope's address, when they spoke to the people for the first time and told them that they were God's chosen one, His representative here, His heart, His voice. I couldn't see for them for the first few seconds before they parted briefly, and the light from behind the Baldaccino was so bright. Everybody was singing hymns again, but it all dropped away. They listened for the voice, for that blunt reassurance; I saw the light of the Lord, and that was all I needed. I fell to my knees and wept; they crowded me, putting their arms around me. We know, they said, it's a miracle, a miracle. You don't know, I told them, don't tell me what you think you know.

Audrey Clave, linguistics postgraduate student, Marseilles

France was in really good shape, actually. Before *The Broadcast* we were sort of a joke, I think, sitting in the middle of Europe, just bloated and holding all these other places together, like a hub. And as people, we have a reputation. But we only had a couple of days of looting and the suicides, no different to everywhere else, and then we recovered and settled down. We didn't have the panic that the Americans had, shutting down all their transport links, shutting schools and malls; we just got on with it. Jacques and I decided that we should go on a date, because I couldn't stop thinking about Patrice, thinking about if I could have stopped him. You need cheering up, Jacques said, we should go and get some dinner. He knew just the place, apparently, down in L'Estaque, past the port itself, right by the seafront. We got a table by the window – business was slow everywhere still, that much hadn't recovered, so we got one of the best tables easily – and we watched some of the ships, the fishermen off as if this all never happened, and we ate mussels and fries and drank this strong pear cider that Jacques loved. We spoke about *The Broadcast*, because it was still so *there*, and so important. Jacques liked to debate about it, talk about the possibilities, what it could mean. We were totally hung up on the Americans attacking Iran that evening, the conversation being about America's ownership – Jacques' word – of *The Broadcast*. In many ways, he said, it's like they're actually saying that they own this version of God, you know? That's typical of them, steam-rolling over everything.

There was a man behind us having dinner with his wife, and they were both stinking drunk when we arrived, not even started eating yet. Halfway through the meal she stopped drinking but he carried on, and I had to watch them the whole time whilst I tried to eat, watch him as he gulped at his wine, as he slopped cream sauce over his shirt. Our dessert had just arrived when he leaned over toward us. His wife tried to stop him, shooing him off, Don't say anything, that sort of thing, but he leant in as far as his chair would let him. Hey, he said, so Jacques turned to look at him. Hey, you think everybody here will get into heaven? I don't know, Jacques said. We'll have to wait and see. Hey, no, listen, the man said; What I mean is, you think even you niggers will get in? You think that God will have a vetting policy, maybe, stop you getting in before you fuck all our women up there as well? He was looking at me when he said that, and that made Jacques even angrier. Shut up, Jacques told him. He gave him a chance. Hey, I know, the fat drunk said, why not just end it all now, see if you get in, and then you can let all your other brothers know, yeah? So Jacques stood up and punched him first, threw his fist into the man's face before the manager ran over with a waiter and they pulled them off each other, pushed them both onto the street. I went to watch but the fat drunk's wife didn't bother.

I'd never seen an actual fight before. In the movies it's all speed and repetition, thumping a face over and over, but in real life it's much slower. After just two or three punches and some things that looked like kicks but didn't connect both of them were slower, panting, but Jacques was clearly winning (if it could be called that). I wondered if I shouldn't be cheering him on, you know? Eventually he just stopped, left the fat drunk on the floor. You're not worth it, Jacques said, and he spat on the man, this big ball of blood. He had lost a tooth, and his mouth sounded mushy when he talked. No cabs stopped, probably because of the blood, so we waited for a bus back. We sat on the back seats and I put antibacterial gel on his cuts, kept them clean.

When we got back to his place he took a shower, and I watched him through the open door with his head tilted back, mouth hanging open, the water running in and then dribbling out again, red from his gums. When he got out he told me how bad it was. I've lost some teeth, he said. How many? I don't know, a few. Three or four. I'll go and see the dentist tomorrow. On the television there was a drama about *The Broadcast*, the fastest that I had ever seen a programme made, about this man who was doubting God and then heard it and then turned his life around, stopped him from killing himself. It was awful, but it said *Based On A True Story* at the start, and I thought, Jesus, isn't everything, almost? In bed, Jacques kissed me and I forgot about the holes in his mouth, and I suddenly got that metal taste on my tongue, so I told him that I was tired and that I had to go to sleep. I just lay there feeling sick, because all I could taste was his blood.

Andrew Brubaker, White House Chief of Staff, Washington, DC

I woke up to the news that we'd had another warning; that there was a school right here in DC with a bomb planted. We hadn't closed schools, because they were off limits, as far as we were concerned. It wasn't a game, exactly, but there were rules with this sort of thing.

I mean, Jesus Christ. Who fucking blows up a school? Who thinks that's *fair*?

Samantha Neumark, primary school teacher,
Washington, DC

Only half the class was in, because the kids' parents were so worried about possibilities, or they had the days off themselves. Lots of people couldn't get to work when the trains stopped running, and I think they liked the excuse, so they kept their kids at home. I lived five minutes away, and that was walking, so I didn't *have* any excuse, and a lot of the kids were just as local. We were concentrating on reading, working through a book together, all these fairy tales but updated to be about more modern concerns, so Jack and Jill went up the hill to fetch a *bottle* of water from the shop there, that kind of thing. We were reading that together, slowly, so we picked that up where we left off. I didn't notice the extra car in the lot, because nobody would ever notice that sort of thing, even though afterward, the police insisted that I would have seen it as I walked in. I didn't notice it, it was a car, parked with fifteen, twenty others. We were halfway through the class, and Jennifer Pritchard was reading, and I was about to pass the reading over to Jon Bayliss when the building shook. I remember that I went under my desk as fast as I could, because I grew up in California, and we were quake-trained. We knew, the room shakes, you get under a table or in the frame of a doorway, just do it. I didn't even think. When I was under I shouted out to the kids to do the same, because by that point I couldn't even stick my head up to see what was happening; the digiboard had fallen down on top of my desk, and I could hear windows smashing, and children screaming, and I couldn't do anything. Even when the shaking stopped I could hear the screaming still, and everything got hot, and I knew that we were on fire somewhere, probably the hallway. Shout to me, I screamed, tell me if you're hurt or alright, but all I got back was screaming.

My classroom was the other end of the building to the lot, so we got off the best, or the least-bad, that's a better way to put it. I managed to kick the board away after a few minutes, because I knew that if I didn't I could die there, when the flames hit the desk. I didn't stop to look at the bodies in my room. There weren't as many as there had been kids, so I assumed that some of them made it out, but there were a few. I didn't stop. Is that awful? I think that I knew they were dead already, and I wanted to get out. Is that awful?

The exit was next to my classroom, out the back, onto the playground, and the rest of the kids from the school were there on the grass at the back, lying on their backs, some of them coughing, some of them completely still. I knew that I should go over and help them but I couldn't; I sat on a bench at the side and coughed and cried until the paramedics asked if I was alright. I told them that I wasn't, so they took me to their ambulance out the side, on the road, away from all those kids. Is that awful? I just couldn't stand to be there with them.

Andrew Brubaker, White House Chief of Staff, Washington, DC

The official response was that a terror cell, fuelled by hatred, had decided to take out their anger on our country. We didn't sell it as a retaliation for what we had done, because we had attacked their training camps, and we knew that there was a chance that those camps had kids in them, had mothers, whole families. They're not civilian areas, they're training camps; we didn't bomb cities or villages or hospitals or schools. There's always a chance that people will be in them that you wouldn't want to kill, but they're training camps, and you just have to live with that chance. But we didn't do *anything* to their families and children on purpose, and they did. Stuff like that? It really helps you to reinforce that you know what side you're on. We decided that we weren't going to sit around and wait for it to come to us; we weren't going to let them make another strike.

It was like a new motto: We're America, and you really shouldn't fuck with us.

Dominick Volker, drug dealer, Johannesburg

One of the prats who works for me turned up at the house. He rang the doorbell, so I asked on the intercom who it was, he said, It's Mick, so I let him in. He was a student, bit of a stropper, but better than some of the tsotsis I worked with from the rougher bits of the city. I knew he wouldn't be there to cause me any grief, at least. What's the problem? I asked him over the intercom. (I was only half-listening because of the news, with the kiddie school being bombed.) There's a fucking riot, he said, over in Yeoville. Alright, I said, I'm coming, I'll drive us. He looked a fucking state. I hadn't seen him in weeks, and he was using, I could tell. He had to make a payment soon, and I knew as soon as I saw him he wasn't going to make it, so I thought, what a fucking prat for coming to see me. We got into my car, because it was a trek to Yeoville, and we were in the seats when he suddenly pulled a gun out, stuck it in my belly. Right, he said, where do you keep your supply? Ha ha! I laughed at him. Nê? This is really how you want to play this? You want to have a stick-up, right? I mean, I could tell he wasn't going to hold it on, because he was sweating, kept glancing over my shoulder. You can drive us there, he said, and I said, don't be so fucking stupid. I said drive! he shouted, so I did. Alright, you're the boss, I said. You're the boss, boss.

I drove around the block a few times, and he didn't even seem to realize, then when we came to some robots I drove slowly until they went red, pulled up and waited. I grabbed his head, slammed it down onto the dashboard, punched him in the nose two or three times, until I saw blood, grabbed his gun, held it into his gut and pulled the trigger. It sounded like a car exhaust, you know? And there was never crime where we lived – as I said, it was a nice area. There, you motherfucker, I said, there's your fucking stash. Hope you fucking rot. I opened his door and pushed him out, leaving him in the road. It was quiet, nobody saw me. When I got home I looked on the news to see if there really was something happening in Yeoville or not, but they didn't say anything, and they didn't mention that kont dealer, because nobody would have given even half a shit about him. My old lady asked what had happened, so I told her that he was just confused, wanted some advice on something. She didn't care; she was just being polite, I reckon.

Dhruv Rawat, doctor, Bankipore

The girl from the reception desk ran to find me when they found Adele's body in her bedroom, because her camera crew had come in again – I remember now, she was making a documentary on the railway, because they were putting new trains out, and that was something that we – our country – was famous for, the people hanging off the backs of trains, packed into the carriages, and the poverty of the trains, what it meant to be packed in like that, crushed up against yourself – and they couldn't get her to open her bedroom door. It felt like an age since I had tried to get her to. I had even started telling myself that she had left Bankipore completely, because the girl on reception, when I had asked that morning, didn't even think that she had been out of her room at all. So when they came to fetch me, I was surprised.

There's a woman and she needs a doctor, the porters shouted, you have to come and save her! I ran up the stairs behind them, before I even knew it was Adele, and they had already moved her from the floor where they found her – I knew this because of the vomit on the carpet, barely visible when I first went into the room because it was so pale – and then I realized that I was in her room, the room I had knocked on the door of so many times over the past couple of days. I checked her body, but she had been dead for hours. You can tell as soon as you see one, because of the eyes, the temperature of the body, the way it lies there – this is one of the first things that they teach you in medical school, because in Bangalore they show you a dead body on your first day so that you're prepared for anything, so that you know what you will have to deal with – and I could tell that it was pointless trying with Adele. But, still, it's what is expected of a doctor. The camera crew stood at the back of the room, lined up along the wall, and watched me as I went through the motions of feeling her wrist, looking at her eyes. She's dead, I said; they left me to pull the bed-sheet away from the mattress, where it was tightly tucked in, and covered her body and face. You should call for an ambulance, I said to the porters. Can't you do it? one of them asked. They'll listen to you.

Fine, yes, I said, I'll do it. I called them from the lobby, because I didn't want to be near her, and then I went to the bar and drank juice. After a while the camera crew sat with me. Haven't you got somewhere to be? I asked them, and they said that they didn't, that their time had been paid for already. They ordered drinks as well and sat with me, and it felt like hours before any of us spoke.

Mark Kirkman, unemployed, Boston

Cable television kept me sane. Everybody else seemed to be getting on with their lives – these new lives, in the wake of their sudden exposure to whatever it was – and I was stuck with mine being exactly as it was. I couldn't face going out to drink, so I got some from the shop and sat there with the TV flicking through repeats of old baseball game highlights, episodes of sitcoms, food channel shows, with the beers in my hand or in the freezer.

Later that day, drunk, I found the chip I got given a year before, that I then ignored when I fell off the wagon again, and I wondered if I couldn't find a meeting, try to pick up where I left off. I was looking for the nearest one, on the net, when I realized that it would be full of people talking about how *The Broadcast* reaffirmed their belief in what they were doing, so instead I forgot about it, and decided to just stay as I was.

Katy Kasher, high school student, Orlando

Mom had grounded me even though I didn't actually do anything wrong. She was so scared about what it meant, that I didn't hear *The Broadcast*, and she and my dad wanted to spend all their time either in church or praying, anyway. I thought she'd drag me along to church, try to get me healed, but I think she was ashamed. I had the internet, though, so I spent my time trying to find anything about people who didn't hear *The Broadcast*. I figured that I couldn't be the only one, and it took me ages to find anybody else, then I found this site, just some blog where somebody was asking if there was anybody else who hadn't heard it, and it said to leave a comment, so I did, with my email address. She got back to me, like, a minute later, maybe.

Ally Weyland, lawyer, Edinburgh

I put the thing up on the web in the middle of the night, thinking, Well, it'll take a few days for it to spread around Google, so I won't hear anything for ages, but it fucking exploded, and I had hundreds of comments, which . . . God, I was so excited. Because I'd been thinking that I was all on my own there, for a while. Then I read the comments, and my God, that was an eye-opener. They were all from these religious whackos, saying, Oh, you'll burn in hell, Oh, why doesn't God love you, what did you do, Oh, guess we won't be seeing you in heaven, all that sort of shite. It was like somebody took my spam filter and swapped cock references for ones to religion. I read through hundreds of them, and all just to find the one response I was after – the one that I needed,

I reckon, to stop me from going completely batshit – from Katy, this girl in Orlando. Her email was amazing: Hello, I think I'm like you because I didn't hear it either, everything here's falling apart, here's my Facebook page. She seemed like a sweet girl. I have no idea how I would have dealt with it when I was her age, feeling that alone. And it was really very trusting of her, maybe even stupidly so; I could have been anybody, and if any of those wankers thinking I should die because I didn't hear *The Broadcast*, if any of them got a hold of her, fuck knows what they would do.

We swapped emails back and forth a bit, so I could check she wasn't just another crazy, and then she sent me her phone number, so I called her and we swapped stories. I didn't even know if you were real, she said. I assured her I was, and we chatted for ages and ages, about what it felt like, about the craziness of our parents – hers were proper Crazy Christians, mine were Catholic, and both our mothers had spent the last few days sellotaped to the pews in their churches. I was scared it was just me, she said. Me too, I told her, but this is better, because now we can just be scared together, eh? I gave her my details, told her I'd stay in touch, that she should call me if she wanted. About ten minutes after I hung up I saw this thing on the TV about the Mormons, and I wondered what the chances were of finding two other people who didn't hear it in one day, because they had to be pretty fucking slim.

Joseph Jessop, farmer, Colorado City

My father, when he was alive, had been a tremendous man: full of vim, vigour, and he was righteous. He was the model for fatherhood, how I wanted to be for my children. I only ended up with the one child, in the end, though not from want of trying. I was my father's first-born, so I had his name, a name that I gave to my own son as well. It's the way that the line works. My second wife Eleanor always said that I was born to be a father; unfortunately, I was unable to give her the children that she desired, which meant we never grew as close as I would have liked, certainly not as close as Jennifer and I were. We had little Joseph – Joe – and that really sealed our marriage. I still wondered why I had been struck with the infertility, after my first child, but Ervil Smith, the Prophet, told me to wait. He was the conduit to God, the voice of our people, able to speak to God, to gain His counsel on matters that affected us all. When we first heard *The Broadcast*, it was Ervil Smith who told us that it was God's way of testing the rest of the world, providing them with the opportunity to come and seek us out, to seek out the true way to His path. He said that we shouldn't be afraid, and then *The Broadcast* returned, told us the same thing, and we all believed. Only, Joe didn't hear God's words.

We had always known that those who didn't believe in the Lord would not be saved; that heaven was reserved solely for those people who trusted in the true word of the Lord Jesus Christ, His Father, and the Prophet Joseph Smith (who I was, myself, named for). When I was a younger man, my father had taken me to a mall in Tuscon, and we had spoken to anybody willing to listen to us about the word of the Prophet, no matter their religion: Christian, Jew, Church of the Latter-Day Saints. We had asked them why they believed as they did, and mostly they said, Well, it's what we were taught to believe. My father told me that this was indoctrination; that they were swayed by older voices than ours telling them the way. If they'll believe their parents, and their parents' parents, surely they'll believe the words of the true Prophet? So I went around and asked them to listen to the word of the true God, to be saved, but they turned me away. On the way back home that evening my father explained that they were just scared, afraid to hear the truth, and that it wasn't their fault. It's the will of God that they don't hear Him, he told me, because God only speaks to those who He wants in His kingdom. That's why we have the Godless. When the reckoning comes, they'll learn and try to repent their ways, but we will have spent our lives earning our guarantees into His heaven, at His side. So when Joe couldn't hear the voice, I didn't know what that meant, but I knew that Ervil would; or that God would, and Ervil could ask Him.

I waited outside his office to see him for over an hour, because I wanted to speak to him at the first possible opportunity. Emma-Louise, his first wife, made me lemonade while I waited, spoke to me about my family, asked how we all were, and I did the same for her. She was one of eight wives, so it took her longer, but that was fine, because it kept my mind off the conversation that I knew was coming. Ervil didn't like being asked to commune with the Lord, unless it was of highest importance. Eventually he opened his office door, invited me in. He wasn't fully dressed; his tie hung around his neck, and he was buttoning his cuffs when I entered. Are you sure? I asked, and he waved my concern away. You've seen me swimming in the lake, Joseph; I'm sure you can stomach me doing up my tie in front of you. Everything fine in the shop? he asked, and I told him that it was. Excellent news, he said, but that means that there must be another issue. He smiled, cocked his head, and I wondered if he knew already, if this was his way of testing me. It's Joseph, my son, I said. Young Joe. Still no reaction from him. When we heard God speak, he didn't hear it.

Ervil sat bolt forward as if I had scored him. He heard nothing? His whole manner changed, kindly to fractious, friendly to formal. I wondered if you would confer with the Lord about this, to find out if there's a special reason for this, I asked. He got up from his chair and paced the back of the room. I hated it when he paced. I'll speak to him, he said, I'll do it now. Meet me with the boy in ten minutes outside the front of this building, when we'll have an answer to what we should do for your family. I fetched Joe from eating his breakfast, cleaned his face for him. He wasn't much of a talker, but I told him to be on his best behaviour. Whatever the Prophet says to you, you tell him how much you love God, you hear? He nodded. You're going to be fine, I told him.

The Prophet was already outside his house when we got there, but he didn't say anything as we approached, just stood there like a cowboy, braced. God says that He knows of your boy, he told us. He says that, by not hearing His divine words, he is an abomination of His creation. He says that I am to punish the boy. Joe hid behind my legs, and I told Ervil that he had to be sure about this. It's punishment, Joseph, he said, and then the boy *will* hear the words of the Lord. This is God's word, Joseph. Do you really want to go against God's word? He reached around my body, grabbed at the nape of my son's neck, threw him down onto the soil, sending puffs of dust up all around us. You will learn from this punishment, boy, he said, you will learn that there is a true Father, and when He speaks to you, you will listen. Jennifer had to hold me back, but a crowd was swelling, people on their way to work, or just milling around, and they left a circle around Ervil and Joe, like it was some sort of dance. Get up, boy, Ervil said. He was crying the whole time, that's important, sobbing and snivelling, snot running down his face. Ervil slapped him. Stop crying, boy, and take this like a man. Another slap, another, and this one made Joe fall down again. God told me to lash the boy! shouted Ervil, ever the showman. He had a box with him, a case, that I didn't see until that moment, and he opened it and pulled out a bullwhip, thick and tarred and cracked from tip to tassel. I stepped in. You will not use that on my son, I said, and that made the Prophet angry. You're questioning the word of God? he asked. Maybe you need some as well. He snapped it backwards – it flew out, must have been two whole body-lengths of a man – then forward, in a swoop, and the tail drew itself across my legs. Your son has a demon in him! Ervil shouted. God would have me strike the demon out! He raised the whip again, to strike at Joe this time, and I grabbed it, stopped him. Leave my son alone, I said. He bared his teeth, so I pushed him backwards, to keep space between us.

He's only a child, I said, loud enough that the crowd would hear us, he doesn't have a demon. You would question God's word this blatantly? asked Ervil, and I replied that God had spoken to us all, and that it was obvious to me now that none of this – of Colorado City, of the book of Mormon, of Ervil's speaking to God – none of it was real. Ervil acted as if he had received an arrow to his heart. You must have a devil in you as well, Joseph Jessop, so I will whip it out for you. He swung for me and I stepped forward again, punched him in his eye, and he flopped backwards like he was made out of straw. We're leaving, I said, because this is no way to treat a child. It's no way.

Jennifer and I packed the car, got Joe on the back seat. She sat with him, to comfort him, and I drove. We barely had any money, very few clothes; most of what we had was shared, or traded. We asked Eleanor if she wanted to come, and she said that she did not; and because we hadn't had any children, there was nothing to make her. So I wished her well, and we drove away from Colorado City. We stopped in a diner on the outskirts of one of the nearby towns, ate food quietly. They had a television on in the background, and when I went to use the washroom I noticed an advertisement for a show, saying that they wanted to hear from people whose lives had been changed because of what they were all calling *The Broadcast*. They were willing to pay handsomely, the lady on the promotion said, so I noted the telephone number and called them from the payphone right outside the diner. They said that they wanted to see us in California as soon as we could drive there. I said that we could be there by the following morning, if I drove through the night.

Angelica Role, television presenter, Los Angeles

The post-*Broadcast* times represented my highest ratings period since we pulled out of Iraq five years ago. Then we had a two-week Coming Home! celebration, interviews and video journals and reuniting families live on air, and the ratings were a solid 3, going to a 4.2 in the Female 25-to-40 bracket, a 4.6 in the Female 40-plus. Those were Oprah-retirement numbers, and we knew – we *thought* – that we wouldn't see numbers like that again, then *The Broadcast* happened. We had a week of solid reaction pieces booked, mostly people talking about where they were, what they were doing, what they felt *The Broadcast* had been telling them, talking about the suicides, the aftermath, we had atheists spinning it, we had everything; but we needed something extra-special to end the week on. The easiest people to get on the show were experts, because they wanted to talk about what they knew, or thought they knew, and there was only so much religious posturing that an audience could take. Nobody liked to watch people argue about their beliefs; they wanted gossip and villains. You want the viewer to feel better about themselves, and feel sorry for somebody else; that's where you hit the golden ratio, the midway point between feeling smug and piteous. So I had the researchers working twenty-four-seven to find somebody who had a different spin on it all, something that might get the numbers up a teensy bit higher than they already were, and on the Thursday night the Jessops fell into our lap.

It was perfect, really: a religion that most people didn't understand, faded in recent years but still there, little more than a cult; a villain, in Ervil Smith, the leader of the place, a deranged old figurehead; a hero in the Jessop family, running away because the youngest boy was in danger, abandoning their belief system in favour of what is *right*; and, last but not least, a boy who . . . You know, I was about to write that he had something almost supernatural about him, because he *didn't* hear the voice of God. That's so strange. But he didn't, and that was something completely different. He gave us every one of our tick-boxes and more, so I wiped the slate for the Friday show, completely blocked it out for them, and we started running advertisements the evening before about it. Tomorrow, on *The Role Call*, we'll show you something you've never seen: the boy that God forgot.

SECOND COMINGS AND DRAGONS

Piers Anderson, private military contractor, the Middle East

We stayed in Bodrum for that week, keeping as low a profile as possible, packed into a hotel near the airport while they worked out what to do with us. It was one of the bonuses of not working for the army in a traditional sense: you got to stay in hotels, because there was actually a budget assigned to your excursion. When word came through that they wanted us to move, we were on the road within half an hour, because that's the way we did it; we got bonuses for being prompt, for getting to destinations on time, for other aspects, mostly casualty- or control-related. We were accompanying some of the regular army boys, and it was sad to see their APCs, which weren't much more than vans with benches in the back. We were in fully reinforced hummers for this part; we had air conditioning. It bred resentment between them and us, but we couldn't help that; if they were in our position, they'd have done the same. We headed to Yüksekova, tiny place, where we made camp just on the outskirts (on land covered in so much

149

dry bloody brush that it would have gone up in seconds if you so much as broke a glass there), and the whole time the villagers stood watching us. One of them offered to bring us food, so we said alright, and we got these awful dog-on-a-stick type things, gave us all the shits. Last thing you want when there's not even any bloody bushes around the place; squatting over sand's one of the most ignominious things you can suffer. We got a field kitchen set up, put some tents up for the sleepers, spoke to some of the locals – we were always nice, always friendly, because that didn't cost anything – and we waited. The army boys had already moved on, headed right into Iran on whatever their mission was, but we were held back. That was another perk of being with a private military contractor: you got to bide your time, because you weren't as expendable. Sad fact, but a true one. If you died, somebody somewhere lost money. If an army boy dies, it's a casualty of war, a name on a plaque near a statue; PMC lads were a far more costly expense.

Turkey was a trick, of course, because the Muslim thing ran through there as well. You could see it in their Prime Minister's face on the telly when he pledged his allegiance to the rest of Europe, asking himself what mattered more: a possibility of religious sanity, or the delicate fragility of the European Alliance? So he gave us permission to use the country as we pleased, and the British government got their boys here, another five or six of us PMCs, all in case this situation exploded in the West's face. They were worried about Iran – or Iraq, or even Pakistan, at a push – reacting badly to *The Broadcast*, so we waited to see what would happen. Don't think they counted on the Yanks throwing their weight around the way they did, and that made our orders shift slightly: if Iran looked like it was going to launch something, we were to step in. If the Americans looked like they were going to launch something? We ran like fuck. We had to sit and wait until something happened, so we did. We played cricket on the dusty fields – dust so bad you couldn't see the ball coming towards you if the ball was too fast, so we had to do it underarm, slowly – and we played football with the kids from the village, but they were vicious little fuckers, slicing your feet out from under you at a moment's notice. One of them, Urkhan, was a shover, and he didn't care if he went down with you, as long as you didn't score. The ground was so rocky it'd tear chunks out of your knees, but they all escaped unscathed, because the skin on their knees was so scarred and hard already, from years of playing there. We spent post-match sitting on the side pouring iodine over ours. Urkhan wanted to be a waiter, to move to Istanbul, so he was learning English, one of the few that could understand us. When we got our orders to move out, to head into Iran, we told him, told him to thank the rest of the village for their hospitality. Don't die, he said, and he grinned like the scar-riddled little shit that he was.

Andrew Brubaker, White House Chief of Staff, Washington, DC

We managed to intercept a bomb in the Rockefeller Center, and that was really the last one we were willing to let through the cracks. POTUS wanted to know how it was happening, how we hadn't stopped the terrorists making it into the country. The best we had was that they had been there all along, sitting, waiting. They might even have been born here,

I said, and that terrified him. The acceptable face of terrorism was the stereotype. They flew over on a plane, C4 packed into their turbans; the thought that they could be here already was far worse. Why are they doing this? he asked, and again, I didn't know. If I knew we'd have been able to end it all much sooner, but I didn't, so we couldn't.

I've never had issues with decision-making. It's easy: you make a decision, you stand by it, and you *refuse* to let that decision define you. That was Obama's mistake, W's mistake, Clinton's mistake. They let their indecision define them, define their presidency, and that was something that we wanted to avoid. So I could feel as guilty as I wanted about what we did, what we ordered, but we had to live with it and work from that point forward rather than worrying if it was the right choice in the first place. The UN was stepping in, asking us to wait it out, saying that we were stepping over our jurisdiction, but there's a point comes where decorum and diplomacy become moot. We had terrorist threats against our people, and there was only one language that those people understood.

I did an interview with the *Harvard News* that morning, because it had been on the books for months, and because we wanted to present the White House as being completely together, completely in charge. We brought the girl into the Oval Office, sat her down, let her marvel at the seal, the chairs, they all did, and then she had five minutes with me. We had POTUS stick his head around the door at the end of the interview, call me away – they loved that, like pulling a rabbit from a hat – and that was meant to be the end, leave them on a high note. When he had disappeared, she didn't seem impressed, so I called her on it. I voted for the other guy, she said. We all pick a side, I told her, and sometimes we pick what's best, even though we might not like it, right? She wrote that down in her book, and I let her. Seemed like that would be the least of my worries over the next few days. Weeks. Hopefully not longer.

POTUS and I were running through his speech – more televised speeches in this week than he had given in the rest of his first year in office, somebody joked, but that wasn't actually a joke – when we had word that there had been another bomb, in Boston, and that only served to reinforce that what we were doing was right. When we were done I called the staffers into the press office, closed the doors to everybody else, told them what was happening. Some of them cried, because they felt complicit, I suppose. Take the next hour off, I said, have a coffee, a donut, and try to relax, because it's going to be crazy around here for the foreseeable. And don't leak this, I said, knowing that somebody would, and that we actually wanted them to. That's the point: you tell the kids not to do something, they push their luck. We needed it leaked, because then we got to come in and tell the world that it wasn't as bad as it first sounded.

When the press room was cleared I sat there by myself for a few minutes. I don't remember what I was thinking about.

Phil Gossard, sales executive, London

Our interim boss – dragged over from HR, only because she knew everybody's names – shouted at us to be quiet, that the US President was on the TV making a statement. We watched it, then Marcus from sales said, Well, we're all fucked.

Dafni Haza, political speechwriter, Tel Aviv

I called Lev back, and he answered and started screaming at me, saying that he was alone, and that I was ignoring him. Lev, I don't have time, I said. I don't have time for *this*. He said, I'm coming down there, and I told him not to, but he came anyway. I watched him pull up, and I telephoned him, told him that I didn't want to see him. You will see me, he said, or we are *over*. This is my job, I told him, and he said, Sure, like the last time you had a job. Fuck you, I told him. I never swore at him. Fuck you. Don't you dare, he said, you come and see me. I hung up the telephone, took the battery out, threw it out of the window at him, and then I told security that he was a threat, that he was making threats to me. I'm in the office with *her*, I told the security officer, and I watched from the window as they dragged him down the street, hands behind his back. Straight after that, my work phone rang.

We're going to the television studios to make a statement, the Prime Minister said, I need you to come with me, write it for me in the car. When I got back upstairs to fetch my things, the televisions were showing the American President's statement again, and I didn't have time to watch the whole thing, but they were looping the content underneath the screen so quickly that I could barely keep up.

Meredith Lieberstein, retiree, New York City

I thought that Leonard was going to keel over, and that would be the end of him. The President – Leonard spat when I said his name for the rest of the day, comically, almost – announced that we were going to take Iran away from the hands of the

154

terrorists in charge, because they were a threat to our liberty. Our liberty! Leonard shouted, over and over, Oh, because *our* liberty matters, but theirs doesn't?

It wasn't like with Saddam all those years ago. Our problems with Iran came from the threat, that vaguest of notions; they had weapons, we were sure, but they maintained that they didn't. Way back when, they signed the treaties along with everybody else, but we were sure that they were – at the very least – doing research. Every time we had another threat, another bomb, another suggestion that they – as a *power* – were getting stronger, we worried more. But, on this occasion, we were doing something baseless. The government of Iran weren't despots, they weren't ordering attacks, there wasn't a problem with them, that we could see, apart from their lack of cooperation (we were told) with handing over terrorist cells to our government. They were a proper government, and we were going to throw the full might of our military forces at them to get them to roll over and concede. It's unjust, Leonard said, and if they weren't attacking us before, they damn well better had now. That's more than this damned government deserves.

Tom Gibson, news anchor, New York City

We cut to the conference as it was on, then spent the next hour dissecting it, then every part of the cycle for the rest of the day, almost, was repeats of it. We've given the Supreme Leader one more chance to hand over the murderers to our government, and then we're going to be forced to take action, the President had said. And it was hard, because of the bombs – especially the one at the school, that was brutal – so it was

155

hard to disagree with what he was saying, with going to war, essentially, even though there was something about it that just seemed . . . hasty.

Simon Dabnall, Member of Parliament, London

We had another conversation about it, but the Cabinet was in agreement: we were not touching that with the world's biggest ruddy barge-pole. We agreed that we should try to reason with the Americans, call them off, as it were, maybe even stick our noses into negotiations between Iran and the US, if we could get them talking, but in terms of the army? We weren't touching it. We would offer no support, no help. We had troops on the ground in Iran, we were told, a few hundred of Her Majesty's and a few PMCs, and we would be using them to help evacuate areas in danger, hospitals, schools, anywhere we could, but they weren't going to engage. They were overseers, there with the Iranian government's permission; but they weren't going to be our soldiers. This conflict? It wasn't our battle.

Piers Anderson, private military contractor, the Middle East

We swapped the Hummers for vans, unmarked beige troop-carriers, because we were told to keep as low a profile as possible. The trip from Turkey to Tabriz was a hundred miles, maybe a bit more, but it wasn't all main roads, so we knew it'd take a while. It's less sandy than you'd think, even though the stuff gets everywhere, parts of your body that never even see water in a shower. It never swirls in the wind; it just sits there, like dust in sunlight. Our orders were to get to Tabriz, which was one of the sites most likely to be attacked, we were told. It was a hotbed of political activity, camps all around the local towns surrounding, and we were Tabriz's cover. We didn't know what the Americans' first move would be, so we just did as we were told: get there, wait, if something happens, help the people where they needed it.

There was really only one road, can you believe that? One road at least that wasn't just tread-laden sand and dirt. The van drive ended up taking even longer than we expected, nearly a full cycle of the light, and we didn't stop. We're under instructions, the driver said when I asked him to, so the men ended up pissing out of the back flap, their piss dribbling along the road behind us as we went. It looked like we were leaking fuel. When we arrived we were shown to the camp. It was night, and we were running totally dark. We heard that there were American troops a hundred miles to the south, out of any potential blast zones, and we knew that we were safe from them – although with the rumours flying around the men at the time, they weren't nearly as assured of that – but the Iranians . . . We didn't know. We worked out that we weren't *officially* there, anyway – we weren't allowed calls home, we weren't allowed to visit the towns. Halfway through the night we got woken by this scream right above us, then bangs in the distance, and then the sky lit up.

Tom Gibson, news anchor, New York City

We had word that we shouldn't cut to our stocks and trading segment like usual, that we should keep running the news, and then, five after eight, word trickled in that something was going on in Iran. We tried to get hold of our correspondents, the guys we used to usually go to, but there wasn't anything; and then it came like a flood, all the information in one go. There had been an attack on Tehran; it came from US carriers off the Persian Gulf, but we didn't know the size of the attack, the payload et cetera. We couldn't get a line into the country for what felt like hours, and when we finally did – somebody in the south, so far away from Tehran and actual civilization that they knew even less than us – we already knew that we were in the shit.

Piers Anderson, private military contractor, the Middle East

We watched the bomb in the distance. It started with a flash, and then there was a bang, like a lightning storm down the road, the sky bursting, and it did it again and again; tiny explosions. The sky kept flicking on and off, like a dark room with a flashing un-set clock in it, and then we saw smoke billowing upwards, and then another explosion. This one started small and grew, and the smoke that was already up there – and I hadn't thought about this, but we were a hundred miles away, so how high must that smoke have been? – that smoke flew away, dispersed, as if somebody had just blown it away, and a tower of greyness rocketed upwards in its place. This was like all those videos you see, films, TV shows when you know that something nuclear has just happened: a mush-room cloud, and they call it that because that's what it looks like. Somebody better with words than me might have a different way of selling it to you. It was nearly beautiful; the sky bright behind it, like some weird version of daylight that came from the ground rather than the sun. It wasn't for a minute or two that I realized that the light must have been the city burning.

Andrew Brubaker, White House Chief of Staff, Washington, DC

The first missile that we sent – an AGM 175, codenamed Fester – was a success. We had expected that, but there was always a danger that it would be shot down before it hit. It wasn't. The damage was catastrophic, we were told. That was a poor choice of words. It wasn't a catastrophe; that suggested that it was an accident. The second series of strikes – smaller payloads, codenamed Gomez, Morticia, Pugsley – hit their targets then, the major army bases, the nuclear plant at Bushehr, and within half an hour we had the Supreme Leader begging for a phone call. We officially accepted their surrender at a quarter to midnight, only four hours after we started the assault, and that would go down in history as the second shortest war of all time. That night, I didn't sleep yet again, even though I tried to.

Piers Anderson, private military contractor, the Middle East

We were told to get out of the area as fast we could, that there was actually nothing we could do. Nobody had a clue what the size of the payload was, so we didn't know the blast radius, or how far the fallout would hit. We crammed into the trucks and drove back towards Turkey. We left the town to fend for itself, because we didn't know what was coming, and we were on the clock. The British government had thought that we'd be playing with a land invasion, maybe; they evidently weren't expecting the fireworks. We went back the way we came in, only this time the locals were all outside, just watching the sky. You couldn't see the blast from there, but the sky was clear enough that the storm effect, of something going on, you could see that. And the air felt warmer, anyway. I know that it wasn't, but it felt it. One of them asked the translator why their television wasn't working, and he told them that Tehran had exploded, and the chap just nodded. As if, that's expected. As if, Oh, yes, we were waiting for that to happen.

Dafni Haza, political speechwriter, Tel Aviv

We were on our way to the studio in Jerusalem when the rumours about the missile went out, when we all knew that something was going to be hit, and then we saw that Tehran had been attacked, and that changed what the message had to be. It suddenly became about, How do we get across a reassurance to our people when this is happening? The Prime Minister spoke to the Palestinian Prime Minster about it when I was writing the script, as the cameramen did light tests, and the Palestinians agreed to support us in their speech as we would support them in ours. When she had hung up, the Prime Minister joined me at the table. They don't know anything about the PLO threats, she said. They say that, but they've said that ever since we divided the West Bank up, and they've had countless opportunities to stop the antagonism, so . . . She dismissed it, waved her hand. What have we got?

I was talking her through my first draft when we heard that

the missiles had struck, and that changed everything. As I say, it put a hold on what we were doing, where we were with the statement; we had to rewrite everything. By the time the Palestinian leaders arrived they had their own ideas, their own communications people, and we spoke about it, what it meant to have somewhere so close – geographically, of course – being so damaged, and we knew that we would have to reassure the people of Israel and Palestine that not only would our countries be fine in the wake of *The Broadcast* – which was still an unanswered question, still such a worry, the meaning of it – but fine in the face of impending war in the region also. Because that threat was always present, always hanging over our heads. The sword of Damocles, the press said when we announced the divide. It's a temporary solution, when there are still so many displaced citizens, and now they're displaced on both sides of the conflict. We waited to see how Iran reacted, because we knew – the Prime Minister said as much – that we had to play this one carefully. I know, I said, I'll write something precise, perfect.

Andrew Brubaker, White House Chief of Staff, Washington, DC

The British Deputy PM was so angry he looked like he was going to cry. That was the worst I've ever seen a head of state, acting or not. We had him on a video call in The Danger Room. POTUS dealt with him perfectly: wait until they're threatening you in that way, he said, wait until you have thousands of dead bodies on your nation's soil, then tell me that you wouldn't have done the same. They fought it out, but what was he going to do? We couldn't take the strike back, and the Iranian government had already stepped down. It was the trigger; suddenly everybody else was scared of us, it seemed. Overnight, we became the foremost power in the world again, and the British Deputy PM, for all his shouting, was still the false ruler of a tiny island in the sea. He asked POTUS what he thought God would make of it all – everything went back to God, same as it always did – and POTUS said that if He was real, and if He'd had any issue with it, He would have stopped it happening. I remember, he said something like, God said that we shouldn't be afraid, but how can we not be when you're pushing the button?

When the call ended, POTUS was upset. I didn't want to be a wartime president, he said. I've got a degree in socio-economics. I know, I told him, but you play the hand you're dealt. After that, every country who even vaguely considered us a threat – or themselves a threat – called us up to pay their respects, or try to find out if they were next.

Dafni Haza, political speechwriter, Tel Aviv

We discovered that Iran had surrendered by watching the news. The Prime Minister said that she wanted to talk to the American President, so some of her people went about setting up the telephone call, and I wrote the speech as I listened to her go through security protocols, jumping through hoops. I was at a table a few feet away when the call connected, and she said something that I didn't hear to her security guards, and I was asked to leave the room. I sat outside, finished the draft, and waited for her to need me back in the room. I didn't even think about Lev: all I could think about was when I could get into the room.

Andrew Brubaker, White House Chief of Staff, Washington, DC

The joint chiefs told POTUS to stay quiet, to not give anything away. He reassured each person that he spoke to that there was no need for concern, that our actions are only ever based on evidence and concern for the well-being of our nation and its citizens. That seemed to subdue most of them.

Dafni Haza, political speechwriter, Tel Aviv

The Prime Minister came out to speak to me after she got off the telephone. She smiled, asked if I had written the speech yet, which I had. It just needs your approval. She read it in front of me and smiled. This seems fine, she said. I'll make some changes myself. You've done excellent work. I stood up, and she said, Oh, I think it's better that you don't come into the room with us. You should go home, see your husband, relax. It's been a long day. My husband is gone, I said, and I didn't explain what that meant, and she didn't ask. I can stay here in case you need me. She smiled, like she expected me to say more. I would love the job full-time, I said, after this. It's what I've always wanted. You've been an inspiration. I'll stay with you, and I'll write if you need it, or whatever else.

After this, she said, I am going home. I'm making my statement and handing in my resignation, and I am going home to see my husband and my children. You have children? No, I said. You ever want them? No, I said. She shook my hand, such a firm handshake, like my father's. They're a blessing. Thank you for your good work.

I went to a restaurant that had a television, showing the

speech she made. She didn't use many of my words. One of the men in the restaurant said she was a bitch, blamed her for the trouble. Bitch, he said, she got us into this. And listen to what she says, how she talks, like some aggressive man. She should be softer. You sound like my husband, I told him. He laughed, looked at me up and down. Lucky man, he said. I called him a pig and left the bar.

Mei Hsüeh, professional gamer, Shanghai

The internet is like a microcosm, and online games aren't any different. We all spoke about the US announcement, some of us in character, some breaking totally, but we all had opinions. Some of the people were getting aggressive – racist, even – in their agreement with the retaliatory attacks, so the mods bumped them from the server, gave them a time out. But most of us were civil, trying to work out what it all meant. An orc I didn't recognize ran into the dungeon and said, That's World War 3, then, but then I pointed out the countries involved had technically been at war for as long as any of us could remember, so this was, really, just a continuation of that.

Jacques Pasceau, linguistics expert, Marseilles

All we could do was watch the footage of Iran, of what the US was doing to them. Audrey and I watched it at my place, first, and then went into work. David was already there, working already, writing something down, and I said, Good morning, but he didn't really bat an eyelid. Yo, David! I shouted, and then he looked at me, his eyes all red and teary. What's wrong? I asked, and he said, You people, you're just taking this as fine? I asked him what he meant, and he said, This, speaking to God, bombs, missiles, wars . . . You're not running around like fucking headless chickens? Nobody thinks that this is the end of days?

Some people think that, I said, some of the newspapers are joking, calling it Revelation, like the book. This is nothing like the book, David said; that was more like second comings and dragons. This is . . . He didn't finish the sentence, so I told him that I thought it was showing off. Showing off? he replied, Who is He showing off to? We're fucking tiny compared to Him, we're nothing! Why the fuck would He think that He needed to show off? We're all going to die, he said, all of us, and there's nothing that we can do.

I took Audrey out for coffee that day. She spent the morning looking at her notes, not really working. We had pretty much given up. I'm thinking about emailing those people who didn't hear Him, you know, she said. Maybe that's a clue. She was clutching at straws. When we got back to my apartment there was a message to call the university admin staff, so I did, and they told me that David had died, killed himself, in the lab. David, in the lab, with the hunting rifle (that we got from the crazy man back at the start of this, that I brought back here for no reason at all other than because). I told Audrey what happened, that we needed to get dressed and go to work. Jesus, she said, as she cried, that's two of them dead, now, both because of this fucking miracle. I know, I said, and I ran my tongue into the hole in my smile and tasted that thick bitterness that you only get when it's your own blood.

DIRECT FEED

Isabella Dulli, nun, Vatican City

Even as word started coming through to Vatican City about what was happening – there were so many people there, I can't even begin to tell you – it was already being written off by so many as righteous and just. Our God has stepped forward and filled us with His love, and we must spread that love through any means. The Holy Father did an address from his balcony – I didn't see it, because I was in my quarters, lying on my bed, but I could hear it, everybody heard it, as if it were trying to outmatch *The Broadcast* itself.

And He said unto them: go ye into the world, and preach the Gospel to every creature. Go therefore and make disciples of all the nations, baptizing them in the name of the Father and of the Son and of the Holy Spirit, teaching them to observe all things that I have commanded you; and lo, I am with you always, even to the end of the age. The Pope preached these words from his balcony, and the crowd heard them as validation for the sins of the world. I cried to our Lord to help us, to instruct us; but again, there was no reply.

Dhruv Rawat, doctor, Bankipore

I handed in my notice at the clinic – which really only meant saying I was leaving, as they did not fight for me to stay, because they were preoccupied by that point. I got on the train, which was filthy and busy, and our stereotype was absolutely reinforced, and I thought about Adele and her camera crew, and how she had to take them around to see things that were worth filming, things that they would already have known everything about. She was talking to them about what she needed, and they had to follow her around and listen to her. She could have interviewed them, but they had to be quiet and point their camera at what she saw, and let her report it even if it was not true. They told me, We had to see what *she* saw, and not what *we* saw; they were very different things. That's always the way, though, isn't it? I said. Look now, at the people on the television. (They were talking about the missiles, about what America was going to do to the world; they had people on the street in cities crying about their losses, rubbing their eyes, tears on their faces.) They're acting up for this, aren't they? It's all they ever do, now.

In my new hotel in Bangalore – which was empty, I was the only guest for some reason – I watched the news. On the BBC they spoke about Adele, only a mention, because she was, they said, a dear friend. They showed a picture of her when she was much younger, standing outside a grey, concrete building, the walls slick, as if it had been raining just before, and they said that she had been in India, putting together a report on the state of our transport system going into another decade without upgrading or changing it. In that sentence they told us the entire point of her report, and rendered anything she might have found useless, because suddenly the world knew, once again, that we had failed to do what had been promised. Adele's efforts were for nothing, but I don't think that I cared about it, because it didn't stop me sleeping, and I didn't see her face, and the news reporters didn't mention her again because there was so much more happening.

Ally Weyland, lawyer, Edinburgh

The same day as the bombs footage was everywhere, so were the Jessops. The clips of them on that awful *Role Call* chat show – talking about the whipping incident, about being Mormons, about the son's autism, how they fled – were all over YouTube, even despite the war stuff going on everywhere else. There's a certain group of people who don't care about the news; they care about the pop culture entertainment shite, and the two are very different. It was that lot I had to thank for seeing about Joseph and his son as fast as I did. It was the worst, seeing them portrayed so horrifically. The show was obviously recorded before the Americans attacked Tehran, so they didn't even mention that stuff; they did nothing but talk about the fact that – in the words of the TV people – *God ignored Joe Jessop*. They didn't fuss over what else *The Broadcast* might have been. They just assumed it was God, and the audience were all happy to go along with that. There was a woman at the front, and the camera kept focusing in on her; she had a rosary around her neck, one of those with big fake-ruby stones on a chain, and she clutched at it all the way through Joe's interview, as he said what he didn't hear. The clips of him would have been the main news story, but they were bumped for the stuff in Tehran – and rightfully so – but I kept thinking, if it had been a bigger story, we might have found hundreds of people in the same boat. As it was, the news buried it. Or, no, rather, *nearly* buried it. There was Mark, as well.

Mark Kirkman, unemployed, Boston

I decided that I didn't want to watch the news, so I flicked the channels to find anything else. That's when I saw the Jessops: the kid terrified, crying, all these women in the audience pawing at him, and that awful fucking host standing back, watching it all, not stepping in. When the show ended they flashed a number up on the screen, and the voice-over man asked that anybody else who didn't hear the voice of God come forward, talk about their experiences. There was a toll-free number, and I wrote it down. I figured that it was my best chance of meeting other people in the same situation.

Phil Gossard, sales executive, London

I remember that my hand was getting better; I could use it more, certainly, even though the bruise was still there. It didn't hurt me to hold my spoon as I ate my cereal, and it didn't hurt me to drive. Karen was working constant shifts, it felt like, because they were understaffed. It's taking three times as long as it should to get people through, she told me. The day before, all the X-ray department were gone, so they were relying on nurses to run the scans, and that slowed them exponentially. She asked me to run her into work, so I obliged. Aside from *The Broadcast*, and the fact that the Americans had lost their marbles, it felt like we might start getting back

169

to normal sooner or later. Karen asked me to a wait a few minutes – she'd left some changes of uniform at work, wanted me to take them home for her, get them in the wash – so I stood in the waiting room and paced slightly as she went off to get them.

Dhruv Rawat, doctor, Bankipore

It was not hard to find a job, because some people had abandoned their places. I called my old professor and he knew somebody, and they had me at work that afternoon, because they were understaffed. My pay was ridiculously low, because it was a temporary wage, but it didn't matter, because it was a job, and I was back in a proper city again. They filled my temporary appointment calendar with their waiting lists, and my days became full, and I could look at the plan for my temporary future there, and see it all laid out.

Tom Gibson, news anchor, New York City

There was a process that had to be followed when the station received something potentially serious, like a threat, or information that could jeopardize a case. People speak about the press like it's the devil, but, really, we just did what we could. If the press didn't do it, somebody else would, but that didn't mean we were without morals. If we received a piece of information about a story that we didn't know, if the story was a murder case or something, we would check with the police that it wasn't something they were withholding from the public before we aired it. It's fine to let the people know who's out there being bad, but not at the risk of them not being caught.

Or, worse still, at the risk of people getting hurt. If we got something more serious, there was a process where we called the cops, the heads of the network, lawyers. We didn't just air any old shit; that would be idiotic.

The DVD came in before the post, even; it was there when I turned up for the morning shift, addressed to me. It had been scanned by security so they knew it wasn't a bomb or anything, and I watched it in make-up as they got me ready. I was only two or three sentences into the video when I told one of the runners to call Jack Roscoe, who was the station head, and to call for the detective we always spoke to about those things, and we all assembled in the viewing room (which was this almost cinema we had, for screenings). I told the guys who were anchoring before me to fill in, and myself and the rest of the news team, along with three guys from the NYPD, two from the FBI and what amounted to most of the board of directors, sat and watched it like it was some red-carpet premiere.

Phil Gossard, sales executive, London

I was getting a chocolate bar from the machine in the waiting room when it came on the TV – previously they'd been showing one of the awful morning shows, so I hadn't been paying it any attention – and they said it was direct feed video from the US, where the clip had just been handed in to a news station. It was that terrorist, the one we never found out the name of, sitting by himself in a room in a cave just talking. The message seemed clear enough: it was a promise that we were all going to die.

(Incidentally, if you ever get the chance to be in a hospital waiting room – a hospital room where everybody is already worrying about what's wrong with them, wondering why they haven't been seen yet, hoping that the person sitting opposite them isn't contagious – when they announce that there's a biological agent been released by terrorists, turn it down. Just get out of there. It turned to chaos within minutes, and it took until the police turned up to put a lid on it. Karen came back with her bags of clothes minutes later, fought through the crowd to get them to me, and told me not to wait up.)

Tom Gibson, news anchor, New York City

The guy in the video was a typical . . . He looked a certain *type*, you know? He was dressed in black, long grey beard, black turban, older. His eyes were doing that thing of being pitted, like they'd actually dropped in his face. We didn't know who he was – the FBI ran their face-check software, nothing came up – but he spoke like we did, like he didn't need an introduction. He spoke directly to the camera – if I didn't know better I would swear that he was media-trained, because he never took his eyes off the lens – and there was already a translation on the bottom of the picture, where they had put subtitles on for us. It was, as far as these things went, a professional job. It was filmed in HD, which was a step up from the usual terror video, and some of the guys in the booth reckoned it was made with Final Cut Pro. He claimed responsibility for the bombs we'd had, for the blowing up of that school, and said that it wasn't over. We are preparing an attack stronger, more devastating, than anything you have ever seen, he said, and we will make you pay with weapons that you've never imagined. We will punish every false believer in your lands, and you will tremble before us. Nobody will be saved, the terrorist said. You made your God tell you to not be afraid; instead, we will give you that of which you are most afraid. There was a debate about whether we should air the tape at all; the FBI guys were adamant that it was a bluff, a hoax. They can't attack on that scale. We've got eyes everywhere, and some slip through, and that's what happened today. But more than this? Every city? Nah, they said, not a chance. That's fairy tales. It always happens, people claiming responsibility for stuff they didn't do. We'll sit on it and wait.

We didn't want to cause panic, so we discussed it in the viewing room, decided to keep it under our hats. Then we heard that other networks had the video as well, and it was on the air right at that moment, which pretty much meant that any chance we had of keeping it under control was out the window. From that point it was damage limitation; working out ways to minimize panic, to keep the public calm, and to reassure them that, should such an agent be released, their safety and preservation was our number-one concern. People think we're all about, Get it on the air, get it on the air!, but the reality is that there's bigger stuff to worry about, sometimes. Sometimes we could actually help, soothe the beast by delivering the information in the right way.

Of course, nobody gave a shit what we said. They were always going to panic. There was no control there.

Andrew Brubaker, White House Chief of Staff, Washington, DC

We immediately sealed off the White House, got our best scientists – Meany sent a bunch over – to start scanning for anything that might make it through. Nobody got in or out of the building's security gates. We were on lock-down, only as a precaution. At that moment, we didn't have a clue if this secret magic gas even existed or not, but it was better – for us – to be safe than sorry. We kept getting figures about the death tolls in Iran, and we were doing fine until somebody discovered that, with one of the blasts, we misjudged, and we took out an area that wasn't doing anybody any harm: a hospital, some residential streets. We were talking about ways to spin it – we had the idea to mock up footage of Iranian soldiers, maybe, retaliating, keep the Iranians on the back foot – when the news broke to the press. We just had to ride it out.

Piers Anderson, private military contractor, the Middle East

We ended up camping in this fox-hole we made on the Turkish borders, because we couldn't make it any further. The Americans were all along the borders, so we were waiting for HQ to give us a new pick-up destination. We knew they were flying planes regularly, getting people out; we just had to wait our turn. One of the lads started having a little panic, a little fit, and it was a pretty hairy one, so we sedated him. (Sedated him the good old-fashioned way, that is: swift fist to the side of the jaw, knock him out for a little while.) We got word from one of the locals that people had made it out of Tehran, and then they passed us as they tried to get anywhere. One man had a car full of people, and he stopped near us, fell out of the door, looking more ill than anybody I've ever known, kept saying something over and over. The translator told us that he was talking about the bodies in the roads. By the time we woke up – or by the time it got light, because none of us slept, apart from knocked-out Dennis, who got nearly four hours – the man was dead himself, still on the side of the road. Nobody wanted to touch his body so they left him there. By the time we got back to base camp they still didn't have an ETA on when we would be leaving, so we sat and waited for the plane to come.

Simon Dabnall, Member of Parliament, London

Jesus Harry Corbett, what were we going to do with the Americans? I'd never seen protests like it. The one in Washington, DC was bigger than any papal announcement, state funeral, coronation; bigger than them all combined, I'd guess. They estimated the number being five million people protesting in the US alone when they started. I think it was much, much more, but of course they were going to play it down. And there were protests everywhere, but nothing like the ones on American soil. On that day, of course, the war – if you could even call it that – was over, but the threat remained, both from the American government, and the unnamed terrorist in the video. Regardless, this was a crowd filled to bursting with anger, larger than any police force could hope to contain, especially given that the public services – police, hospitals, fire – were still suffering from losses factored in after *The Broadcast*, the God-squad claiming their victims in every church across the world. They rushed and drove back everything in their way – cars, police, soldiers, horses, a *tank*

175

– and it looked like there wasn't going to be any way to stop their numbers swelling.

As the day went on a message started coming out from some of the US groups, demanding the removal of their President, that he be put on trial for war crimes. In the UK we crossed our fingers, because it looked like they might actually have a point.

Andrew Brubaker, White House Chief of Staff, Washington, DC

We called the National Guard into action, sending units to as many of the riots as we could, and what we got was about 60 per cent of them willing to do their jobs. The rest just didn't turn up for work. The UN told us to withdraw from Iran; we told them that we wouldn't be doing it, that they were welcome to send in peace-keepers to help us out, but that without us policing it, the chances of Iranian insurgents gaining access to their weapons – their nukes, we meant, because we damn well knew that there were silos, and that they had had those silos for nearly a decade – the chances of them trying to blow us up were very high indeed.

The news stations started speculating that POTUS would step down, but there wasn't a chance of that. He was voted in to keep the United States safe, and he did just that. He would have to answer to Congress, we knew – especially because they weren't consulted before we attacked, and there'd be hell to pay for that – and our approval rating would be zapped, but we had another three years to worry about wrenching that up; and we would, once people saw that what we did was for the best.

Meredith Lieberstein, retiree, New York City

I didn't hear from Leonard all day. He said that I should stay home, make sure to record him if he ended up on the news, but he didn't. There were far too many people for that to happen, and his protest was just a drop against the sheer scale of some of the others. I kept checking his blog, updating people as to where he was, but most of New York was a sea of signs and chants that day, so there was no way that anybody was going to find anybody else. And the videos of them on the internet! Every possible cause you can think of, somebody somewhere was marching for it. For every Leonard there was somebody screaming for the death of any and all of what they called Sand-niggers. It was grotesque, it really was.

I didn't actually think about that terrorist's threat all day, not really, not until one news report not long before I went to bed, where some woman in the crowd shouted something about how, if we left Iran now, they might not release the weapon in the video. I didn't even think about it until then, that it was a threat that people were really taking seriously. Poor thing looked terrified, I remember. Of course, they kept saying, on the news, that there was no such weapon; they had specialists on, people in the know, and they all laughed at the prospect. A week before, though, and all those scientists would have been laughing at the concept of God, so what did they know?

Leonard managed to get a phone call through to me eventually, to tell me that he wasn't going to be home. The networks were jammed tight, and it seemed like I couldn't use my cell all day, but he managed to get through just as I was starting to worry. They're probably jamming the calls, he said, ever the conspiracy theorist, to stop us organizing ourselves. Probably, I agreed, but I didn't actually think that was true. We're going to stay on the far side of Central Park, he said, and we're going to pick this up again tomorrow, and we won't stop until we've got what we want. I didn't ask what it was that they actually wanted, because I was a realist, and I knew that they didn't have a cat's chance of actually getting it. When he had hung up I sat in the living room and said some prayers, to nobody in particular – I didn't know which God I was praying to, certainly – but I said them, and hoped that that would be enough.

Theodor Fyodorov, unemployed, Moscow

Anastasia was out at the university, because she was insistent that our lives continued, went on as before, but, of course, I did nothing – she always said that was my problem. Everybody that I know watched the news that day, did nothing else *but* watch the news, especially if they still lived here. The government kept making statements to us, to reassure us, but I think that they were nervous. It wasn't that long ago that we were the biggest enemies of America, before the Arabs took over from us – I mean, I'm not saying we were the same threat, but my father always used to tell about the 1980s, and how it was hard for a while there. (There was a list of Hollywood films that he banned me from seeing, because he told me that the image of young Russians with guns, being so aggressive, would only run the risk of warping my mind.) The government kept telling us that we were fine, reinforcing our relationship with the United States – that was an exact phrase that was used, *reinforcing* – and saying that nothing would happen to us. When Anastasia got home, we said hello, like always, and I tried to ask her about her day, but she only wanted to watch the news as well. There were no classes, she said. The people at the university are starting to get restless, because the government aren't telling us anything about *The Broadcast*, about what they are. To which I said, Well, of course they're not, because they don't know. Do you really think there's anything they don't know? she replied. Or if not *our* government, then the Americans? And I had to admit, she had a point.

Mark Kirkman, unemployed, Boston

I was on the road heading toward LA when the footage of the terrorist hit the news, so I didn't actually manage to hear about it. It made me laugh, when I finally did, stopping to sleep after twelve hours of constant movement; I kept thinking about how I missed everything when it happened. I was perpetually playing catch-up.

Katy Kasher, high school student, Orlando

Even with everything going haywire all around us, Mom couldn't stop worrying about *The Broadcast*, or worrying about my not hearing it. I don't think that the two were separated for her. We were gonna have Grammy and Gramps staying with us, because they had an apartment right in the centre of Miami, and Mom was worrying about the protests there, so she sent Dad to go and pick them up, and Mom and I sat on the sofa and watched *The View* and waited for them. They were talking about the war, and then the blonde one – the religious one – said something about how we were forgetting that Christ told us not to be afraid, that maybe we should trust our government. The other women on there went mad at that – It wasn't Christ talking, We don't know what it was, that kind of thing – and then Mom turned to me, asked me if I'd been reading my Bible. She had given me a copy – a *second* copy, her copy, that she knew worked, like mine might have something broken with it, or might not be quite holy enough to have the right effect – and wanted me to pray with it at night, before bed. I have, I said (even though I hadn't), and then she said, I just want to know what it is that you did to affront Him, Katy. You're such a good girl, and then this? There are paedophiles and murderers and rapists out there – there are *terrorists* out there! – who heard Him speaking to us, and you didn't? What did you *do*?

I ran to my room and called Ally, but she wasn't there, so I locked my door and waited for her to call me back.

Isabella Dulli, nun, Vatican City

If there was one good thing about being in Vatican City when it happened, it was that there were no riots, no tension, not like there was everywhere else. Everywhere else, there was violence. When all the people are worshipping the same way, like they are drunk together and happy, singing, it's a better situation than the alternative.

BREAKDOWN

Simon Dabnall, Member of Parliament, London

The press referred to the incident as my having a breakdown, but it was actually the complete opposite: it was the clearest that my mind had been in years.

We had another emergency Cabinet meeting because of the hospital situation, and they told us about people falling ill, getting sick, dying. There were some men in lab coats delivering a report to us, but they didn't seem to have anything concrete. People are dying at an exponentially higher rate than in previous days or weeks, one of them said. What's causing it? somebody asked, and they said, It's a variety of things: some are dying from pre-existing conditions, cancers, diseases we knew that they had, and some have died of what we'd term natural causes. And the flu, the other lab coat said, some have died from complications arising from the flu. What do we do? the Deputy PM asked, and they suggested telling people to remain calm. We're doing tests, they said, and we don't know how long it'll be before we know what's happened. Could it be one of those animal flus, like we had at the start of the decade? somebody asked, and they shrugged. Could be, they said. When they had gone we discussed a curfew, to keep everybody under control; all the schools and businesses were shut anyway, so a curfew wasn't far off. If there *is* something we need to stop it spreading, was the general logic, and you can't argue with that. My mother's ill, and she won't last long, somebody said, so we really should think about ways that we can find out what this is. That was my breaking point, if memory serves. I stood up, and told them all that they were – and I rarely swear, but – fucking insane. We're paddling a leaky raft, I said, and it's clearly bloody sinking, so let's either patch it or just abandon ship, yes? They all looked blank then, and the Deputy PM said, Well, Simon, we're talking about ways to fix this, but we have to err on the side of caution. He smiled, as if that made it all alright.

Then I quit, I said. We've let the Americans bomb a country that hadn't done anything wrong; we've got riots and protests all over the country; people flooding to churches because they heard something speaking to them, something that might be scientifically plausible, or might actually be a fat man with a beard in the sky; and we're sitting here discussing the latest turn of events, that people are *dying* for no bloody good reason, and we're talking about it the same way that we fanny about discussing every other bloody thing that crosses our desks. We never get anywhere, with anything; we just bide our time until we have to make decisions. I think we've proven exactly how useless we are, so I quit. I walked out, down the stairs, shouted my resignation to the press and jumped into the first car I saw, told the driver to take me to my offices.

I told my assistant what I had done as I packed my boxes,

and she swore blue murder at me, because I had promised her a rise and now clearly wasn't going to deliver it. Go home and observe the impending curfew! I said, and she stormed off. I went home before the paps turned up, didn't put the news on. Instead I cooked a crispy duck from the freezer that I had been saving, finished reading a book on Orson Welles that I'd been putting off before because I never had the time.

Dhruv Rawat, doctor, Bankipore

The day was the longest I had in my planner, packed full of appointments. It always gets like this, the receptionist told me, which I think she meant to sound reassuring, but I took it there and then that she was telling me to leave; maybe she had a spurned lover who was the doctor that I replaced, and he wanted his job back. My appointment for before lunch – which didn't happen anyway, as lunch was always pushed back, and I ended up with room-temperature egg sandwiches from a machine that they had installed in the waiting rooms – was an emergency, it said, somebody who didn't live in Bangalore. I suppose that I shouldn't have been surprised to see the man with the foot, but I was: as I forgot (or tried to forget) about Adele, I forgot about everything else in Bankipore – the smell, the dirt, the hotel, the camera crew, my family. That patient, and his dying, necrotic foot.

He bundled into the room on crutches, dragging the foot behind him. Well now! he said, sounding almost happy to see me, this is a fortunate surprise! I said hello to him – I cannot remember his name now, another of the things that I forget – and he sat in the chair, lowering himself so clumsily. I stood and held my hands out as if I was going to help him sit, but I didn't, though I don't know why. I had touched so many people with worse illnesses over my life, but his foot . . . I could smell it through the bandage, through the air conditioning in the room, air conditioning which usually dragged every smell away apart from the strict stink of the disinfectant they used on the floors and surfaces. I tried to not vomit at the smell. Listen, the man said, my foot has got worse, you wouldn't believe it. What are you doing here? I asked him, and he said, My daughter lives here, she paid for me to get the train here and visit her while I was sick, because I can't walk well, you know. I saw that the bandage was the same one that I had put on him last; he noticed me looking at it. No, no, he said, sounding embarrassed, my daughter has washed the bandage you gave me, I have used antiseptic on the wound and kept it clean, like you said. He held his leg up, his foot out, as if he wanted me to take it. When I didn't – because, I can't tell you about the smell enough, how strong and revolting it was – he shrugged, crossed it over his good leg, started unwrapping the bandage. When it was done, I had never seen anything like it. I know it's bad, he said; he kept eye contact, his eyes red, and he didn't want to look at it. I'm sure it will be absolutely fine, I told him, there are very few problems like this that can't be fixed. I was lying. You'll need to go to the hospital, though; I can refer you. Can I call your daughter, get her to take you? No, he said, don't bother her, I'll go tomorrow morning. I can take you now, I said, you really should go, and I'll make sure you get seen straight away. No, no, he said, but I insisted. I called for a taxi, told the receptionist where I was going, to cancel my appointments for the afternoon. I gave him a clean

184

towel to wrap around his foot – I told him that it was because I wanted to keep it getting air, but really, I couldn't bear to touch the limb in order to wrap real bandages on it – and we got in the back of the car. The journey only took a few minutes, but neither of us spoke, so it seemed like an eternity.

The hospital wasn't busy at all, and they rushed the man through. What's his name? one of the nurses asked me when they were looking at him. I don't remember, I said. You're not family? No, no, I told her, I'm his doctor, at a clinic. I told her the name of the district I worked in and she nodded. Okay, we'll let you know how he is. I can't come through? I asked, but she shook her head. You can leave, or you can sit and wait. I chose to sit and wait. I telephoned the receptionist – Oh, you should stay there for the day, watch over him, she said, and I thought of her sneaking her lover back into my office, his old office, and letting him take on my workload – and then I put myself on those awful chairs in the corner of the room, near to the door through to the surgical wing so that the nurses wouldn't forget that I was there. Once, the same nurse walked past me and smiled, and I said, I told him to come and see you days and days ago, before it got this bad, but he wouldn't listen to me; what can you do? She didn't answer me.

Night came, and I asked them again, How is the man I came in with? He's in surgery, the nurse told me. What for, what are they doing to him? I don't know, she said. I'll try and find somebody to let you know. But she didn't, so I ended up lying on those chairs and trying to go to sleep.

**Audrey Clave, linguistics postgraduate
student, Marseilles**

David's funeral was very different to Patrice's, first of all
because it nearly didn't happen. The churches were so busy
that they said it would be weeks and weeks before they even
thought about it, and the hospital wouldn't keep the body in
the morgue for long. It'll need to be disposed of, they said,
we're too busy, too many bodies. They broke it down to something that basic; no room here, move along. David's parents
wouldn't stop crying. We want to bury our son! they said, so
we went to one of the private cemeteries, negotiated a price
for a space. Jacques went to pick up his body by himself,
driving David's parents' car. I offered to go, but he said that
I should stay with them.

**Jacques Pasceau, linguistics expert,
Marseilles**

I stood over his body and tried to tell myself that it wasn't
my fault, that he would have killed himself anyway, found
a way to; but that gun. I kept seeing it, seeing the guy holding
it up, the crazy guy with the beard, and then me taking it,
because I thought it was, what? Funny? When I moved
David's body I had to do it by myself, put it on a trolley
and wheel it to the car and bundle the black sack onto the
back seat like I was a grave-robber, and the whole drive back
I kept thinking that if I looked in the rear-view mirror he
would be sitting there, hole in his face, begging me to stop
it from ever happening.

Audrey Clave, linguistics postgraduate student, Marseilles

We buried him without any sort of religious service. He has come to us, proven Himself to us, and then David did this? We can't do this in God's name, in His light. We dug the hole and we put his body in, without a coffin, just in the ground. This is probably illegal, Jacques said, and he was right, I think, but it didn't matter. What mattered was that David was laid to rest. Even though they didn't want it, I said a prayer as we threw the soil on, only whispered it, so nobody heard me saying it. Jolie came down with us, read something – she and David had a thing a while back, didn't turn to anything, but she knew what he liked. She read a poem he used to love by Claude Royet-Journoud. It was a poem that sounded like it wasn't meant to be read, you know? Of course, we didn't even know he liked poetry in the first place. When the service was over, or when we were finished, Jacques stormed off. I chased after him but he had disappeared.

Jacques Pasceau, linguistics expert, Marseilles

The last line of the poem was something about the body being a life-sentence in the future, like, being alive would be a crime; and that pissed me off, that Jolie chose that to send David away with, that she didn't choose something that honoured his *life* more. I don't fucking know, I stormed off, and I was in the woods down from the graveyard when I realized that the space between my teeth was bleeding again. The day before it had been getting better, and then, all of a sudden, I started to taste the blood again, as if I was sucking on a cent.

187

Peter Johns, biologist, Auckland

My assistant, Terry – Trigger, we called him – he found the eggs. I have rotten insomnia – I just don't sleep. They say I'm losing sleep, but that isn't true. It's not like that; I can't find it to begin with. My wife's a saint, putting up with me like this. It spreads, the insomnia, to narcolepsy, just falling asleep, nodding off when you'll be doing something else. My body, the docs said, just decided when it needed to sleep, and it happened when it happened. We were – me and Trig – out on a drive-around and we parked up when he saw me passed out next to him. Of course, I don't remember squat, but this is what he told me. So when I'm asleep he wanders off, he's checking out a nest we know about – the Tieke, beautiful bird, only a few of them left, so we nurture them where we can – and he sees some eggs in the nest, none of the birds there. When he gets back he notes it down, like we do with all the unattended nests, in case they don't come back and we have to step in, and we head back. That evening, on the way home – Trig's driving again, I didn't trust myself some days – he says, Wait, let's check out the nest, and the eggs are still there, but there's no birds around, so he suggests that we take them, stick them in the incubator. Where the bloody hell has their mum got to? Trig asked, because they weren't abandoners. Some birds? Couldn't trust them to stay ten minutes after the eggs have popped, but the Tieke, they were nesters. Must have left, I said, maybe they're scared of being bombed, eh? She'll be back. But, as I said, we couldn't afford to take those things for granted, right? So we climb up, take them out of the nest, put them in one of the boxes we've got, and we got them back to the labs, put them in the incubators.

Hameed Yusuf Ahmed, imam, Leeds

Another day of endless queues of people asking for me to give them some sort of validation. They had seen the priests on television reassuring their parishioners, followers, *flock*, that they were listening to their own particular God, a Christian God, telling them that He was there to help them; they all asked me the same questions, and I told them all that I didn't have an answer for them. I don't even think that mattered, I don't think they expected a truth; they just wanted reassurance that they weren't on their own. I was important to them; they wanted to know that I was just as confused as they were. I reassured them in my beliefs, and they left, and that should have been enough. It wasn't, of course; they went back to their homes and they were just as confused as they were before they spoke to me. Fortitude of faith, I told them, believe in your God, that He will make everything as it should be. Remember, we are told to not question His faith. Remember this.

Samia was in the queue, along with all the rest. I saw her when there were four or five people in front of her; she waved at me, softly, so she didn't draw attention. When it was her time, she sat in front of me professionally, folded her hands in her lap. What's so important it couldn't wait? I asked her. I'll be home in a couple of hours. I wanted to address you in the same manner that everybody else does, she said, and I want actual answers. She pulled out a list of questions – the same questions as she had asked me before, written down so that she didn't forget any – and started reading them out. You tell me when you've got an answer to one of them, she said, stop me from reading them out and answer it, because I don't think that you do.

189

I feel like you're accusing me of something, I said, and I don't like that. This isn't the time for us to have an argument; my community needs me. She snorted at that, like a dragon. I need you, she said. I have questions, and you should be answering them. I want to know if you even think that our God – Allah – if you even think that He's real, because I'm not so sure. Don't say that, I said, but I don't know if she heard me, because I think my voice was too quiet. This is no way to live, in the darkness like this, not even knowing, she told me. We do know, I said, of course we know. We don't, Hameed. She looked so sad. We don't know anything.

Benedict Tabu Tshisekedi, militia, Democratic Republic of Congo

After the second time we heard it, the white people seemed convinced that it was their God, somehow talking to them through the magic of their minds. He had opened a channel to them, and given them hysteria. They had brought with them a map when they first arrived, a map that they spread out on the ground and showed us, not only in terms of the world itself, but also their individual countries, and they tried to teach us to pronounce their place names – Jämtland, Norrköping, Sjælland – and when we could not, or when some of the youngsters asked more questions about places that they had already heard the names of (What is America like? I want to visit America!), they got restless, and put the map away. Another time, they said. That was a week before *The Broadcast*, when they arrived in their convoy of jeeps.

The day before the static, another jeep arrived, with two more white men and a black man. The black man was armed, with a gun that none of us recognized. We played like boys, and asked to see it, and he held it out and showed it to us from a distance. He was American, the only one who wasn't the same colour as the skin on the bellies of our goats. He held the gun out and said, There, you can see it, and one of us, Peter, asked if he could hold it, but the American said that he could not. I know what you boys are like, he said. By that point, we were already eating the food that the white people had brought with them, and we were helping to build the school that they wanted to make with us. When we've built it, they said, we can start to teach you in it, and then when you leave here you will be prepared for the outside world. We can give you an education, and that's a gift that every child should be given. We did not say this, but we were not children. The children of the village stood behind their mothers' legs and were scared of the white men; we puffed out our chests and took strides just as long as they did, our feet falling into the same marks in the sand, our sandal prints filling the holes of the prints made by their heavy boots. We wore sandals and shorts and shirts when we saw them, unlike the children, who stayed naked as they cowered. We had spent the week before the black American came building the school, because our fathers were not in the village, and we were the protectors. The white men offered no threat, but they brought materials to make the buildings, and our mothers seemed happy with the thought of what they could do, and Father Saul – who was the priest that had lived with us for over a year by that point, come down to us from Darfur, far north, bringing with him the word and teaching of the Lord Jesus Christ – said that we should listen to them. They're only here for your benefit, he said. It was Saul that named us – he is responsible for me being named Benedict, which was not my name before he arrived with God eight years before, and it was Saul that ensured that we could all speak English, because it was the language of the future, he said – so we listened to him. He established the church that we used, which was also his house, and he was the one who shook hands with the white men when they arrived, introduced us, told us to not be scared. They acted like old friends, but they never spoke about how they knew each other, if they did at all. Saul is the one who told us that a schooling would be how we could move to America! So when the American came, we wanted to know first about his gun – which was much cleaner than our guns, and the bullets felt so heavy compared to what we were used to – and then we wanted to know how he came to live in America. I was born there, he said, which we could not believe. How did your father and mother come to live in America? we asked, and he said, They were born there as well. When he arrived, we had already built much of the building for the school – there were thirty of us, who the white men called boys, but we knew we were the men of the village, and we worked fast.

That evening, the American slept inside the school we had built; when we said prayers together, all of us, even the white men mumbling through the words we knew from heart but that they struggled to learn, he kept his mouth shut, and he did not say Amen, even though he then ate the food with us. Father Saul had told us that this was a crime against God, and that He would punish you in His kingdom, so when the American did it we did not say anything, but when he was asleep we spoke about how it would have repercussions. I didn't really sleep that night: I stayed up and watched my mother and my sisters sleep instead, and occasionally looked at the American in the shell of the schoolhouse, because he awoke in the early hours of the morning, and I wanted to see what he would do. I did not trust him, and his gun would be able to take on ten of ours.

In the morning, I was awake early, because it was my job to walk to the well, make sure that we had water. Father Saul had been responsible for the well being as good as it was; soon after he arrived, he had some people come down to look at it. They brought a machine with them to dig deeper into the ground, and from that point the water was cleaner. When my father left with the other fathers, it became my job to do the water in the mornings. Other boys became farmers as they became men – we had seven different animals, and then farming cereals, which was the other source of food. I fetched water, which was risky, because sometimes there were complications, and other people wanted the water from us. I was fetching the water late when I heard it – because I had been awake, and because we were all awake until late in the night, and then it was a long walk to the water, and a longer one back, or it felt like, carrying it. I was walking back when I heard the static for the first time, and I thought that it was something coming across the land between me and the village. We always had animals, so I thought that it could be that, and it wasn't until I got back with the water – less than usual, because I ran slightly, I was excited and nervous to make it home – and everybody had heard it. We asked the white men what it was. Was it a helicopter? asked Anthony, one of my

193

friends. Maybe, they said. They spent the rest of the day playing with the radio in their jeep, and thinking it was that. We could tell, because they tuned the static in on it over and over, even though it sounded different. When it happened again, they even stopped talking to us, and the project – to build the school – was put on hold for the day. We'll come to it tomorrow, they said, and they got into their jeep and complained that their telephones weren't working properly.

Two of them left to go and make a telephone call, and two of them stayed behind, with the American. They didn't really talk to us, and our mothers said, Pretend that they are not even here for the day, we have so much to do. They all moved into the school, and we didn't even eat dinner with them that night.

The first *Broadcast* happened the next day. We were sitting on the floor – only half the men of the village were there, the rest were off doing the jobs that their fathers had done before they had left – and we were watching our mothers making food, preparing lunch. Some of the boys had caught a huge bird, and we had all pulled its feathers off, and the women were getting the meat from its bones. Then we heard the voice, and Father Saul began to weep. What was that? Anthony asked. What was that voice? It was God, Father Saul said. That was the voice of the Lord our God, speaking to us, His faithful soldiers. Why did He speak to us? I asked, and Father Saul said, Because we have spent time with Him, devoted to Him. Because we are faithful, and we exist for Him. Father Saul was a good man. He tried to spend time with us, teaching us the ways of the good Christian, educating us – he was our school before the promise of the school – and trying to help us with the future. This was his goal, he would always say, to help us find our way towards the future. We should pray, he said, and he started, and we all joined in. The two white men and the American stood away from us and watched us, and kept looking in the direction that their friends had driven, every few minutes glancing down the track. We prayed all day, and Father Saul tried to involve the white men. He is the God of all of us, he said, you can pray alongside us. We are okay, they said, we have work to do, but all they seemed to be doing was looking at maps and walking around with a telephone – Anthony told me that it worked from something in the sky, as high as the stars, but he was a fantasist – and getting angry with each other. I asked them eventually why they were so angry, why they did not rejoice as we did. We just want to know where our friends are, one of them told me – the more friendly of the two – so I said, Well, God will be keeping them safe. The other one of them, the one who looked at us less, who always seemed distracted, he said, Don't be fucking ridiculous! He said it with so much anger that the American even stepped forward. He did not raise his gun, but he stepped forward to listen, but I said nothing more.

By the night it was clear, I think, that the other white men were lost, or had decided to stay in Mwanza for longer; when we all went to sleep that evening, we could hear the white men arguing with the American about how long it would take them to walk it. He said it would be two days, maybe – we knew that it would be more like three, and suspected that he knew this also – and they said that on the next morning they would leave. When we woke up they were packing their things, still looking down the road every few minutes. The American came to me and asked if he could accompany me to the well, as they needed to fill their canteens. I told him that he could, and we walked off together. He was very tall, and wide. When I told him this, he said that he used to play American football. Like soccer? I asked, which was a sport that Father Saul had introduced to us. Nah, different. You play with your hands, and you run, and you tackle people. He showed me a tackle, how it would happen, barging his shoulder into my side, but he didn't knock me over; I think he was worried about how thin I was, because he kept saying, You should eat more. We got to the well and I showed him how to get the water, and then we walked back, and I asked if I could hold his gun. Sure, he said, but only you, only here. I looked down the sight and I could see so far, animals in the distance. I could shoot one, I said, and he said, You could, but that wouldn't be fair. It's all about fair: don't shoot what can't shoot back, that's a rule to live by. As we walked again I asked him if he was happy that we heard the voice of the Lord, and he said, Sure, if that's what it was. What else could it be? He said, I'm waiting until I get home, and I can work that one out for myself.

By the time we were home – because we were late, as I walked slowly so that I could talk to the American more – everybody was wondering where we were, and the white men were getting nervous. We have to leave, they said. They were putting their bags on their backs when we heard the second *Broadcast*. Father Saul called us all into the middle of the village when it was done and led us in prayer again. We are not afraid, Lord! he said, but the white men didn't seem to agree with him. They spoke in their own language – it sounded like they were confused, slipping over the English words that we knew, making them sound almost like singing – and then barked at the American, telling him that they had to leave. He said, We should wait, because I don't know what that is. We'll go without you, they said, and he said, Fine, I'll wait for the others. They'll come back. The angry white man, the one with no patience, he ran over and grabbed at the water packs, and then reached for the American's gun. We'll need this, he said. The American laughed. You're not taking the gun, he said. Give us the fucking weapon, the angry white man shouted. We paid for you to be here, and then they wrestled over it. It looked dangerous, until Father Saul stepped in and picked up one of our guns from one of the boys and shot the angry white man in the foot, and the man fell backwards, onto the floor, crying out. What is wrong with you people? Father Saul asked – his English was better than the rest of us, because he was much older, and he had been speaking it for many, many years, and when he spoke with authority it sounded like a king or a president – and then he went over to the white men and told them that God had spoken, and that they would do well to listen. Have you not thought: all this violence here, and yet He still speaks to us? This is a magic, this is what we needed most, and you will flee from it? You are cowards, and God will punish the meek.

For the rest of the day, the white men looked after each other, watched by the American, though he stopped at dinner and joined us, and prayed, even. In fact, I think the white man who wasn't shot prayed as well, which means the only one that didn't was the one who lay on the floor in pain, writhing, trying to keep the ground-dirt from going into his wound, which, Father Saul said, was his penance.

THE LAST *BROADCAST*

Simon Dabnall, Member of Parliament, London

One of the nicest things about being British is that you're up before the Americans. I'm sure they would argue that it's good for them, that they get to see developments through for longer than we do, but that's predicated on the events starting in their time-zones. In terms of the day-to-day, the calendar, they spend the day chasing us with news stories, catching up as they go. The day of the last *Broadcast*, they were all asleep just as we were heading towards our mid-morning snacks, just as I was sitting in my house wondering where to go with my life. We were the smart bear, full of porridge, and they were grumpy Goldilocks, roused from her bed. When we heard it we were already watching our television sets, watching the scenes of destruction from around the world, how the protests in America had continued through the night, and we were already aghast; so when the news that we were suddenly abandoned – if, proviso, it *was* God, blah blah blah – when that came through, we were braced for it, I think.

Phil Gossard, sales executive, London

Jess and I were at the supermarket, shopping for food. I had been promoted to Head Chef until Karen got home, a role I fucking hated. And Jess was sick of beans or sardines on toast, so we had to shop. We were at the cash-point outside, queuing. The credit card readers were all down – apparently it was a nationwide thing, some sort of glitch, the people who usually sorted that stuff out being understaffed (like almost every-where else) – so we were all getting wads of cash to do our shopping with. All of a sudden Jess started acting weird, bending over a lot, hiding her face, so I noticed – of course, because kids think that they're being subtle when, really, they're anything but – and I asked what was wrong. Nothing, she said, so I looked around, and there was another kid, about Jess' age, with her dad, fetching a trolley. Jess looked up, hair over her face – over her birthmark, pointedly – and then looked at the cash-point. How long now? she asked. When they'd gone past I asked Jess what that was about. That was Tanya, she said (Tanya being the worst bully in Jess' school, a ten-year-old girl that Karen and I quickly learnt was a complete – pardon my French – a complete cunt when it came to our daughter). Right, I said, I want to talk to her father, so I marched out of the line and into the shop, Jess crying as I went, begging me to not say anything, but how could I stay quiet?

We found them by the salad ingredients. Excuse me, I said, civility, politeness. He asked if he could help; I explained who I was, who my daughter was, what his Tanya was doing. He shook his head. That's not how we've heard it, he said. We've heard that it's Jess here who's doing the bullying. You really think she's capable of that? I asked. She's been bullied her whole life. He stood closer to me, raised his voice. People were looking. My daughter's got bruises across her legs where Jess here has kicked her. She's a nasty piece of work, and you need to sort her out. I didn't know what to say to that, so I hit him, swung my hand into his cheek, my bruised hand. It clicked, and he spat blood, and he stood there swaying. I had this horrible flash to those kung-fu films where a man gets killed by one punch, and I worried, for a second, and then he snapped out of it. He was about to hit me back – and I was about to let him, because I was pretty horrified at myself, actually – when we heard *The Broadcast*, and that stopped us fighting. If it *was* God, the last thing I wanted to be doing when He was watching us was being stuck in the middle of a fight.

Audrey Clave, linguistics postgraduate student, Marseilles

I was cleaning my teeth when we heard *The Broadcast* for the final time; *Goodbye*, He said. Just that, nothing more, and then it was gone, the static, everything, and the world felt so much quieter, I just cannot even begin to tell you.

My Children. Do Not Be Afraid. Goodbye.

María Marcos Callas, housewife, Barcelona

I was in church. We were back home, and I went to church every day, just as I always had, nothing changing just because He had spoken to us; everything was the same. I was in church, and I was praying, moving around the stations of the cross, giving Him everything, and then He announced that we were to be alone, all alone. That He no longer wanted to watch over us. I know, I know, ever since, people have suggested that He was simply saying that we've developed enough that we no longer need Him, like a mother pushing their child away when they leave their teenage years; but I didn't feel that. I just felt that we had let Him down, terribly let Him down, and that He was so ashamed He just couldn't bear to stay any more.

Theodor Fyodorov, unemployed, Moscow

We heard it, and Anastasia worried that there would be another riot in the streets. I told her not to worry, that the police force – who were a constant presence since the first one – would hold anybody back who tried to, and she said, Oh, you really think that the police will actually be working still? After hearing that? I said, don't be silly, this will calm down, but, of course, it didn't.

Mei Hsüeh, professional gamer, Shanghai

That final *Broadcast* cleared everybody for a few seconds. Doesn't matter how many people it looks like are standing around talking in a game, if they aren't at their keyboards they're not there at all. It's just empty avatars, and for every single person gathered on my server, that was what we were, while we picked ourselves up and tried to work out what was going on. Wasn't just online they were quiet, though; I took my headphones off and I couldn't hear anything from anywhere.

Dhruv Rawat, doctor, Bankipore

I woke up to the nurse shaking my arm, saying, Doctor, Doctor. I forgot where I was, even, until I felt the rim of the chair in my back. I'm sorry, I didn't mean to sleep, I said. We thought you should know that he's awake, the nurse said, but not for long. You can say hello, if you like. Wish him well. I will, I said, and I followed her down the hall. I was desperate for the toilet, but there wasn't a chance to go before I saw him lying on his bed. He looked like he had been carved, or that there was a trap door in his bed and that's where half of his lower body was, because there was only one leg that I could see. The other ended in a blunt lump at his thigh, and it twitched as he faced the wall away from it, trying not to look. He didn't greet me, so I said hello first. Doctor, he said, they said that you stayed the night, I am so grateful. I am so sorry, I said, have they called your daughter? He nodded. She's on her way, apparently. I don't know how this happened, he said, and then we heard the last *Broadcast*. What? he asked when it was finished, what does that mean? He moved his whole body like a cat that you've put on its back, wriggling to put itself right again, moving the stump where his leg had been violently up and down. What was that?

It was the voice, I said, you know, they call it *The Broadcast*, we spoke about it before. No, he said, that was so angry, so upset. (And even after everything else I read about it, he was the only person to think that it had any emotion in the voice. In fact, most people just heard it as monotonous, unfeeling, apart from that man with his missing leg.) I have to leave here, he said, this is the worst place to be. No, you need to stay, the nurse said, and I repeated her words exactly. But this is Shiva! he shouted, Don't you see? Don't you see that? They sedated him, and in the corridor I watched the other people panic and cry, unaware of what or who had left them, but feeling suddenly alone anyway. I think you should go, the nurse said, as if I was to blame for all of this, so I did. I stood outside the hospital and realized that I didn't know his name, so I couldn't call and check up on him, but then realized they would know who I was talking about when I mentioned him, the man with the necrotic foot who had to have his leg amputated. I went back to the surgery but it was closed, with no sign why. I assumed that *The Broadcast* had an effect. In my hotel room, I sat in my underwear near the air conditioner and pretended that the outside heat didn't exist.

Tom Gibson, news anchor, New York City

Just as you're in danger of forgetting about something it comes right back into view – and that sounds incredible now, to think that we could ever *not* be concentrating on something as pivotal and life-changing as *The Broadcast*. We didn't have time to breathe in the studio, just had to roll with it, keep selling *The Broadcast* as something that could be anything, we still didn't know. But what we did know was that it would change everything, that the issues we had with the protests were just the cusp of what was coming. And if it was God, there were two theories: that He was testing us, to see how strong our faith was; or that He had watched us tear ourselves apart over the days before, and wanted nothing more to do with us.

I really, really hoped that it wasn't God, because I had a feeling that it could only make things even worse than they already were.

Dafni Haza, political speechwriter, Tel Aviv

I was back at home by the time of the last *Broadcast*. There wasn't any word from Lev, nothing from the security officers, so I assumed he had been taken somewhere. I could have called up some contacts, found him. Instead, I watched everything on the television, and I drank, even though I didn't need to, even though the television was crazy enough. I slept, eventually, on our bed, still in my clothes. I told myself that I had to stay dressed in case the Prime Minister called, in case she needed me for something.

Mark Kirkman, unemployed, Boston

The Role Call had put me up in a hotel, and I was in the bar, by myself. It takes a certain sort of person to sit in a bar in a strange hotel and drink themselves near-sick; it takes a person who wants to be noticed or stopped, or both, because the prices are the same in your room. You want company but you don't make an effort to talk to anybody. You sit with the other people in the same situation. I realized quickly, though, that I wasn't in the same boat as those guys, because they heard *The Broadcast* when it came back for the final time, and I didn't. They sat there and their jaws dropped, and the Japanese man next to me started crying, and the music got switched off and everybody seemed completely shell-shocked, but I carried on drinking until I worked out what *The Broadcast* had said, and then I drank some more.

Katy Kasher, high school student, Orlando

Mom called me into the living room where she was sitting on the floor like she was a kid, and she asked me if I heard it. I should have lied, but I didn't think quick enough. Heard what? I asked, and that sent her off, hitting me on my arms. You weren't listening, she said, you didn't listen and now He's gone, and you'll never hear His glory, and you'll be all alone. I went to my room, packed my bag and climbed out of my window.

Simon Dabnall, Member of Parliament, London

It was just all so melodramatic.

Peter Johns, biologist, Auckland

It had only been a few hours since we felt that we were back in again, back to what we did best. I checked the fences, the cameras we had set up around some of the nests, to check they were all okay – we used to joke it was like *Jurassic Park*, you remember that movie? – and Trig went to check the incubators. Then *The Broadcast* hit, and I heard a bang from the back room, so I called out, check he was alright. I'm fine, he said, little shit just bit me, is all. One of the birds had hatched in the night, and it was sitting there, pleased as all heck with itself. Trig's hand was swollen and red from the bite – those little things can't half nip – so I told him to wash it, antiseptic, all that. We don't want it turning nasty, I said.

Hameed Yusuf Ahmed, imam, Leeds

Samia was inconsolable. I didn't know whether to stay with her or go to help the community. In the end, I took her with me, and sat her in my office as she tried to catch her breath.

Elijah Said, prisoner on Death Row, Chicago

When we heard the final *Broadcast*, Finkler acted like it was the end of the world. I heard him crying, shouting out, asking why, begging God to stay with him. He beat the walls, and I felt it through every part of my cell, all the furniture shaking from where it was fixed to the wall. I was on my cot and I felt it, and I heard the bars rattle in their fittings. Cole was at his table reading something, and he didn't seem to react at all, didn't put the magazine down, kept reading, staring at the page. Finkler started shouting my name, asking me why God had left. Brother, why has He left us? he asked. I refused to answer him. In the distance, the alarm was ringing again, but this time nobody seemed concerned with that.

Cole rose from his chair, put down the magazine. Fuck it, he said, fuck it. He walked to my cell door, opened the box and keyed the code. The door opened – he heaved it, all his strength – and he walked on. What is this? I asked him, but he didn't answer. He opened Finkler's door next, then walked on, down the corridor that I last saw Bronx and Thaddeus go down and never return from. That way led to genpop, to the fields, the workshops, the exit. The other way – where the lights were kept off, because they didn't want us staring – went to the chambers, and the viewing room, and the imminent room. I walked to the now-open doorway and watched as Cole kept walking. Where's he going? Finkler asked. Again, I said nothing. He got up from his own cot, walked into the corridor – keeping one foot behind him, in his cell, in case this turned out to be a trap – and then repeated the question. He repeated everything; back when I was a teacher, we would have noticed him, singled him out for attention; before I had the call from Allah to do His work. Brother, he asked me, you think we can leave? I saw it, in his eyes. He turned to look at me, and he was happy, excited, optimistic. Through everything, I had never seen him optimistic, even the way he acted, so blinkered and oblivious. Should we leave?

You shouldn't go anywhere, I told him, you should stay here and wait for order to be restored. The disappointment in his face. What if this is God's way of telling us what He wants? What if He told that guard to let us out? We should listen, right? We should listen? His back foot had left his cell; his decision had already been made. Sit down, I told him, using my best voice, my deepest, most commanding voice; it failed me. He turned and ran down the corridor, a rabbit fleeing a hunter. I sat back down on my cot and waited for order to be restored; I was here for a reason, and that reason did not change because a coward chose to open a door.

Andrew Brubaker, White House Chief of Staff, Washington, DC

I wasn't asleep when we heard it. I never fucking slept, it felt like. It sounded like a period, POTUS said, and I agreed. That was it, the end. (Of course, if it *wasn't* God, it was just a random word, right? But I thought that it probably was God. I didn't have a clue what else it could be.) We were right, because that was the last time we ever heard it, so . . .

POTUS asked to speak to Meany straight after it, so we called him on the phones – POTUS wanted to bring him physically in, see him in person, but we were still locked down – and POTUS asked him what *The Broadcast* was again. Last chance, Meany, he said, and Meany took the longest pause I've ever heard somebody take with a President, then said, It's not actually a broadcast, not as we understand it; it's not coming from anywhere, we can't pick it up. There's nothing there, absolutely nothing there. Based on the readings we've got, it didn't even exist. Besides, he said, if it's really gone for good, what does it matter now?

Ed Meany, research and development scientist, Virginia

After I got off the call I was sure that I was going to be fired, but I wasn't. I was left to get on with whatever I wanted, which at that point meant trying to find a trace of something – anything – that might indicate the origins of *The Broadcast*. I'm a stereotypical scientist: I need facts, not some story to give me justification. Somebody wondered whether it wasn't voices from stuff we had broadcast ourselves, TV shows, music, the stuff that they say on the ISS or on space missions; maybe it was that stuff, bouncing off satellites. That theory at least sounded plausible, even if it didn't explain how the voices bounced down to earth and inside our heads. Another of my researchers remembered this film he saw when he was a kid about some aliens who learned how to talk by watching American TV shows. Could be them, he said, which was ridiculous, but nearly as plausible as the populist alternative.

Jacques Pasceau, linguistics expert, Marseilles

Audrey and I were getting on just fine, really; she had pretty much moved into my apartment, because I lived so close to the university, and we ate all our meals together, though mostly that was in the office. Or, she ate *her* meals, because I wasn't really eating because my teeth still hadn't been fixed as all the dentists in the area decided that it wasn't worth them working, with the protests and everything going on around them, and the wound was so fresh that I could only taste blood almost constantly, so it tainted everything I ate.

After the final *Broadcast*, we were talking about what we thought it all meant. We didn't talk about anything else, I don't think. She wasn't over Patrice's death, David's death. It was all too much. She was eating a pastry, or pretending to, picking at it; I had a bowl of cereal that I didn't touch (because I hated seeing the milk left over on the spoon with my blood in it, like some sickly syrup). We were already in the lab, with our notes on the board at the back, same as every day. We tried not to think about what David did in there. I think He's just letting us know more about Him, Audrey said, like He's just showing us what He can do. We know what He can do, I said, if it was Him; He spoke to everybody in the world at the same time! Not everybody, she said, He missed some people out, like that boy in America. Well, then, I said, we have a whole book of things He apparently did, remember? With the plagues and the floods and the resurrections? She didn't say anything, but I wanted to provoke her. It was good to get a reaction. It's not God, anyway, I told her. She huffed. I hated the way she used to huff. God is just a trick of the light, I said, cheap tricks and magic. Whatever, she said, I'm impressed.

RECKONING

Ally Weyland, lawyer, Edinburgh

I stayed up all night watching the news, because I couldn't sleep, because I still didn't know what it meant, not hearing it. Sometime just after midnight – this was on the BBC News Channel – they started talking about how British hospitals were totally understaffed, that the initial *Broadcasts* had stopped some people going to work, and that those places were machines: you remove a few cogs, they get backed up. The presenter said something about how, in the wake of the protests – though she called them riots, there was some real confusion those days about exactly what they were – there were far more people in the hospital than usual, that we should stay at home from hospitals unless it was absolutely urgent. Then, around three in the morning, the American news played their second video of that terrorist, and it was like it all just collapsed even more than it already had, if that was even possible.

Tom Gibson, news anchor, New York City

We had hundreds of thousands – millions even, people were saying, without any real means of doing a proper head-count,

210

bar computer software guesstimates and sending people out to literally count heads – hundreds of thousands of people camping in the parks of NYC, camping out all over the States; just as many people, if not even more, making spur-of-the-moment pilgrimages to churches, to pray to Him to stay with us post-*Broadcast*; and we had thirty of us in the station, running everything. A full-slate day, you'd have a crew of fifty, maybe more, taking care of all the little jobs. The news had exploded with stuff from all over the country, things that were related but not; hospitals were full because people were fighting, getting themselves in trouble post-*Broadcast*, for example, and schools were all shut. Public transport had been down for days now, and that was making its own waves outwards, financial problems; the airlines were making statements, threatening to sue for loss of revenue, the trains edging toward the same conclusion, and we kept getting emailed videos from people trapped all round the world, US citizens unable to get home. There was too much news, and there can *never* be too much news. Then, same as before, a DVD appeared in the mail, unmarked, unlabelled, no traces of anything on the envelope other than an NYC postmark. The FBI didn't even bother telling us to hold it this time, because they knew it would be everywhere else again, and they'd be showing it as soon as they found it.

It opened like it did before, that same terrorist – we felt safe to call him that, in lieu of a name – sitting in that same cave, on the same chair, wearing the same black robes – though there's been debate about whether it *was* a cave, whether it wasn't a studio, but I can tell you, it was a fucking cave, from the echo in his voice – and he sat there and spoke about how we were trying to trick him. You say that your God is dead, but he has never existed. We have unleashed a fury into your air to make you all suffer for your ignorance, and you will bow your heads and beg for mercy, and know who is the true God, when this is over. *We have unleashed*, past tense now. Even the FBI guys looked scared.

Ed Meany, research and development scientist, Virginia

POTUS had us checking the air straight away, moving all our teams away from researching *The Broadcast* and onto another completely futile branch of research. We didn't find anything in the air around DC, not in our labs, not in the White House. And that means we didn't find pathogens, viruses, bacteria, toxins, nothing radioactive (apart from the standard low-level stuff where you would expect to find it). The President was ready to completely lock the country down, do everything you'd expect during what *should* have been the worst attack we'd (probably ever) seen, and he asked us to judge what it was, to tell him how dangerous it was, and we had nothing for him. If it's been released, it's not been released in DC, I said, so he ordered me to put together teams all across the country, start testing everywhere (which, of course, we were already doing, but their results were taking longer). They started trickling in, one by one, same results as we had in DC; there was nothing in the air, nothing anywhere. Just like *The Broadcast*, it didn't exist.

Andrew Brubaker, White House Chief of Staff, Washington, DC

POTUS kept saying, We have to find out what this thing is, and where this cave is, because I can fight this one. We asked people to stay indoors where possible – only *asked*, at that point, because we had a threat, but threats frequently happened, and rarely went to anything – and POTUS debated telling people that we were at Threat Level Black, scare them a bit more. There was no Threat Level Black, but, he figured, the people wouldn't know that; or it might reassure them, trick them into thinking that we were prepared for this sort of eventuality. There was probably a solid thirty minutes there where none of us mentioned *The Broadcast* because we were worrying about toxins and biological warfare.

Katy Kasher, high school student, Orlando

I completely forgot that there weren't any planes flying, so the airport floor was like some sort of *orgy* or something, people sprawled out asleep or eating or just resting, waiting until they put the planes back on. I went to the counter for one of the airlines, asked them if there was anything I could do, said that my mom and dad were in London, and I was left here, and they couldn't get home so I wanted to get to them because my Grams had just died, and they didn't look like they were buying it, so I started crying for them, and eventually one of them said, Hang on. She took me through the back part, sat me on a chair, went into a room without me, told me she'd be back. An hour later she was, and she told me to follow her, through the bits at the back of the airport that you never see. We've got you on a flight, she said. There are still planes running, mostly freight, but private planes can still fly – it's a loophole, she whispered – and there's one running staff back across to Heathrow later on today. We can get you on that, but there won't be any cabin service. It's fairly bare bones, she said. Yeah, because I cared.

Isabella Dulli, nun, Vatican City

The people cried as one; they shouted, called for Him – him, because it was not their God, despite their thoughts, could not be their God – called for Him to return to them. Do not leave us, they said, we have worked for you, we have prayed, we were promised our day of reckoning. You could hear their tears through every corridor of the City, every open space filled with them. The police called for them to depart, although even they didn't want to be keeping chaos. All of my order were called to prayer, but I denied them. Why won't you come? Mother Superior asked me, and I told her, It's because it is a false god, and there is no truth in its words. In the same way that a parent could never leave her child alone to suffer, so no God that we have worshipped so, that created us in such a way that we were in their own image, the perfect child; so no God could abandon His people in this way. She did not reply, nor did she force me to follow her. Instead of going to prayer, I packed a small trunk that I had been given for trips to undertake missionary work and left the City, walking out through the gates. All the people here to worship were in their own pain, and did not notice me leave, as if I were only a spirit, and out of their vision.

Phil Gossard, sales executive, London

It wasn't until the morning after *The Broadcast* – the last one – that Karen got home. It went fucking mental, she said, like I've never seen it. I'd still be there if I didn't have to have a shower, because some idiot threw up all over me. Her clothes had been washed, so she changed, and we talked about what

214

we'd heard as she did. I didn't even stop and think about it, she said. I mean, it wasn't God, right? So what was it? I don't know, I told her. It's easy to not be sure when something tests you; maybe it was God? She smiled at that. Have you been drinking? she asked.

Jess had some of her friends round, and they were praying in her room. Suddenly it had become a new thing, like the cycle of toys they all went through, or pretty-boy bands singing mushy pop songs. They sat in a circle and prayed. My mother, one of the girls said, says that we should pray for God to come back, and tell Him how much we appreciate Him. They did that, and I listened, then drove Karen back to work. When we got there the people were queuing out of the doors, literally onto the ambulance driveway, onto the pavements and the road. Holy shit, Karen said; I have no idea when I'll be back, alright?

Tom Gibson, news anchor, New York City

We picked up on the British hospitals story pretty quickly, put the feelers out to US hospitals, others around the world; every single one was reporting higher-than-usual cases. For most of them it wasn't something they saw as anything other than a burst brought on by stress, by people being in the streets, by hypochondria. We got people out to Mercy, to a few others in various cities, to see what was happening. Within a couple of hours we had a good idea of how busy they were; and only a few hours after that, they were twice as busy again. One of the correspondents put in her report, and, when she signed off, she said, It's clear that something here at St Mark's isn't right, and that was putting it mildly.

Mei Hsüeh, professional gamer, Shanghai

When people started dying we were down to eight of us, the core. There was me, Morgaena (Lycan Witch), Misty (Dark Elf Warrior), Kazmere (Goblin Caster), Bexoma (Goblin Rogue), Dreadclaw (Troll Warrior) and Snowfire (Undead Rogue). The Demon-God we were meant to be facing was called Droggs. He was a twelve-man raid at best, but we had been planning for weeks. You heard stories about people spending hours fighting him, days, even, because he was in stages, and once you passed some of them, there was no going back, even if you all died. So you stayed on it, plugging away. And some of us were worried about whether we could get ill or not, but I said, stay inside. What can happen if you stay inside?

Phil Gossard, sales executive, London

Karen's hospital was on the news, so we watched the report in case we saw her. We had the news on constantly, I remember, but we only turned the volume up when something important happened, and Karen being on TV was exactly that. She didn't say anything, she was just in the background, checking on people in the waiting room. There were people bleeding, clutching at wounds; people holding areas of their body, clearly in pain; and people coughing and sneezing, hacking away in the background. The report was flaky, not pinning this on anything, but even the reporter seemed concerned. They went back to her a few hours later and, by that point, her nose was streaming, her eyes red, and I knew that there was a real problem.

I tried to call Karen, but they were too busy to even answer the phone. I did it while they were on air, live at the hospital, and I was sure that I could even hear it ringing in the background as all the nurses tried to stop people from bleeding all over each other.

Ed Meany, research and development scientist, Virginia

One of the worst – busiest, I mean – hospitals in the country was George Washington, right on our doorstep, so I went down there with some of the Institute of Health guys, did as many tests as we physically knew how to run, even some that, frankly, we *knew* were a waste of time. We did air tests, random blood samples, random X-rays, looking for anything, searching the lungs, the throats, and we did all the tests in record time, and we still had nothing.

I reported back to Brubaker and POTUS, and categorically told them that there wasn't anything in the air, that there wasn't anything making people ill. It's coincidence, I told them.

Simon Dabnall, Member of Parliament, London

We managed to prove at least two stereotypes about the British that day: one, that we love to queue; the other that, given a situation where we can turn into louts, we damned well will. The protests were still happening, still clogging the streets, and the churches were still full, and then we had the hospitals to contend with. We had scientists doing readings, looking for biological agents, but they didn't find anything, so we – that is, the government – decided to write it off as hypochondria. All around the world we made that same decision, based on the same blank statement: that if there wasn't a gas or a poison in the air or in people's blood-work anywhere that we could find, there wasn't one, full stop.

If you can't measure it, it isn't there, right?

Ally Weyland, lawyer, Edinburgh

When I woke up, they were saying that all the hospitals were insanely busy, that was it, but I read around on the internet about it, and there were loads of sites saying that people were dying, that they had something fatal. Of course, that wasn't on the news, because they didn't want to panic people, I reckon, but it was there. Where there's illness, there's death; the two follow, hand in hand. About half eight that morning the government announced that all schools were to either be or stay closed, and only essential workplaces – public services, that sort of thing – were opening. They didn't say why, but it wasn't hard to guess. You get a terrorist warning about some sort of special new attack, and then there's something making people ill, making them sick? They've got to be related, that makes sense, and you can't pretend otherwise. On the internet people were saying, Oh, it's in the water, so I didn't have a shower that morning, and I only drank bottled water, even in my tea. Better safe than sorry, I figured.

I called the office to check that they weren't open – knew they wouldn't be, because most of them were too lazy to turn up even when we *were* operating normally – and then decided to pop out, get some eggs, treat myself to a fried egg sarnie for breakfast. I was pulling on my boots when there was a knock at the door, and there, on my doorstep, I find this tiny little American thing with a bad fringe and a T-shirt for a band that I'd never even heard of. I recognized her from her profile picture.

Katy, I said, what the fuck are you doing here?

Katy Kasher, high school student, Orlando

Ally looked different than in her picture: she was really stern in the picture, in a suit, but in real life she was in a sweat suit, trainers, and she had greasy hair. She invited me in, asked me how I got there – so I told her the story, how I spent all that time on a plane with some seriously peed-off flight attendants and pilots, and how none of them would say a word to me – and then worked out that my mom didn't know a thing about it. She didn't say she was going to, but she snuck off to use the bathroom and called her, told her where I was.

Ally Weyland, lawyer, Edinburgh

Mrs Kasher, I said, my name's Allison Weyland, and I'm a lawyer in Scotland, in the UK. Your daughter's just turned up here, on my doorstep. She flew here, I said, like an idiot. I don't have a daughter, she said, and I said, Oh, don't be so bloody melodramatic; she's here and she's upset. Tell her to call me when she's heard The Word, she said, and then she hung up. I didn't tell Katy that I'd called, because she would ask what her mother said, and I didn't want to tell her; not *that*, at least. Instead we sat in the living room and I put the TV on and made us some toast – the eggs would have to wait – and we watched as the newsreaders started to let it out that there was something terribly, terribly wrong.

Ed Meany, research and development scientist, Virginia

We didn't release the numbers that day, but they were getting crazier by the minute. We had fifteen bodies shipped in from across the country, helicoptered in so we could work on them at the same time, and we sliced them all open and tried to find out what happened to them, tried to find out why they died.

Meredith Lieberstein, retiree, New York City

Leonard was so proud when he got home from the second day of protesting, even though numbers were right down, people leaving for church or home or, worse, hospital. He'd heard rumours in the crowd that the people being ill was a government-driven exercise. It's designed to keep us in check, that's the rumour, he said. I made us dinner and we watched the news, because there was nothing else on, and I prayed in my head, thanking *whatever* was up there for making us healthy, for curing Leonard of his cancer years before, because those people at the hospitals looked so sick, and the relatives looked so worried.

Leonard had bruises all up his arms from people grabbing them, all over his chest from the people being in such a crush. It was like a party with nothing to celebrate, but we were all so happy to be there, to have done something. You don't see results from protests, he kept saying, but the repercussions! They'll know that we won't be silenced, that we won't end this. The buck stops with the government, he said. When we finally lay down – I told him that he had to get some sleep

– the rain had just started outside. Tomorrow, he said, I'm taking the day off, and we're going to go for a walk. They can all protest, and I'll be there in spirit, but I'm taking the day off.

When I woke, just as it got light, Leonard didn't. I turned over, shook him, but he didn't move, and he was absolutely cold. I sat with him until the alarm went off, and then I got up and made my cup of coffee as usual, and then I started making the phone calls. I didn't go back into the bedroom until the men came and took him away. I'm sorry, the man said with the clipboard. It isn't your fault, I said. We've had a lot of these tonight, he said. It's a hard time for people to deal with this all, right? Thank you, I said, though I don't think that was consoling in the slightest. I spent the day answering the phone, people asking for Leonard, people who didn't even know him. The *New York Times* called at one point, and asked if they could do an interview with him. He's dead, I said, he died this morning, and they paused, and then asked if they could do an article. He seemed like an interesting guy, they said – they called him 'guy', which he hated, but I didn't tell them that, because how were they to know? – and I told them that he was. Can it wait a week? I asked, and they said that they really needed it for the day after, so I said that the reporter should come and visit with me that afternoon. Everything moved so fast, those days.

When the reporter turned up he was far younger than he had sounded. He had a tiny little beard, beady eyes, and he wore a cap (though he did take it off when I answered the door, which I appreciated). Mrs Lieberstein? he asked, and I shook his hand. My mother was Mrs Lieberstein, I said. My

221

name is Meredith. Meredith, he repeated, and he wiped his shoes on the mat and then came through to the kitchen. Do you want a drink? Whatever you're having, he said, and so I poured us both iced tea. I'm sorry about your husband, he said, and then we spoke about Leonard. He put his recorder on the table and asked me questions and I just went on and on. I felt sorry for him, you know, because he really did just sit and listen to me ramble on, chew his ear off, and I don't know how much of it was actually usable. (I didn't read the article, though some of my friends told me that it was a very good piece.) I asked him if he wanted to see some photos and he did, so I got the laptop, talked him through some of them. I emailed him a couple to use for the story, and he finished his third glass of iced tea and said that he had to leave. On the doorstep he apologized again for Leonard's passing, and I said, Really, it wasn't your fault; God takes us when we're ready. And then we had a moment, where it sort of clicked that neither of us had thought about the implications of God in all this, in Leonard's death. Did He let him die? Did He choose to not save him? Does He even have that power? Or, actually, if it was Him saying Goodbye, is that why Leonard died? It had stopped raining as heavily by the time the reporter left, so I went for a walk in it, this must have been around four in the afternoon. I ended up in Central Park and I sat on a bench and watched the wildlife on a pond, and then I walked down toward 5th, looked at the wreckage of the bomb, which they were still struggling to clear up, walked down toward Times Square and just stood around waiting for it to get dark. The city looked beautiful at night, and I watched it all for hours, until well past midnight, until it was just drunk people stumbling along to their hotels. I was looking at the advertisements, at the sky, and I heard a crackle, and I held on for *The Broadcast* to tell us that God was sorry, that He wasn't going to abandon us. It was only lightning, though, and more fool me, because when the rain bucketed down and I had to rush to get cover under an awning, I realized that I didn't want it to be *The Broadcast* anyway; I wanted it to have been Leonard, back for one last message, back to say goodbye.

Mark Kirkman, unemployed, Boston

I think the producers forgot that I was there, in the hotel, on their business account. They either forgot or didn't care, because I wasn't thrown out, and neither were the Jessops. I met Joseph and his family my second day there, in the restaurant, at breakfast; I recognized them from their TV appearance, introduced myself. We ate together, told each other our stories, and then we spoke about what we thought it meant, that we didn't hear it. We watched the news as people got sick, as they tried guessing what was wrong with them, and the Monday morning, when we heard that we weren't going to be on the show at all – that the main stories had shifted again, and now the interest came from sick people, dying people, dead people – we spoke about what we could do to find more people like us. There must be more, we said. Anomalies like us never happened in tiny quantities, surely?

Joseph Jessop, farmer, Colorado City

Mark decided to ask the producers of *The Role Call* if they had any more names and numbers of people like him and

Joe, and that took him out all day. We spent the time in our suite watching cartoons, trying to stop Joe from getting too bored. Wasn't till he passed out in the afternoon that I managed to see the news, to see about just how many people were sick or dying, and I remember, I worried and worried that that could happen to us, to me and to Jennifer and to Joe.

Meredith Lieberstein, retiree, New York City

Some sycophantic relative, a cousin that I hadn't seen in years, had left a message on my answer machine, telling me how very sorry they were that Leonard had died. At the end of it, they said, Maybe now this'll start you praying again, praying to bring God back to us; so many years away from the fold, and look what happens. Now we're all abandoned, we need you more than ever, and you need us. Oh, shut up, I told the machine, and I didn't call her back, even though she left her number.

Piers Anderson, private military contractor, the Middle East

When we got back to England – we flew into City of London Airport, which had been cordoned off for us – we were escorted off the plane by people dressed like beekeepers, blood samples taken from each of the men, driven in black vans to a sports hall filled with beds, and we spent the entire day there without seeing a soul, helping ourselves to food from the field kitchens that were set up there. This was, we were told, standard practice after a mission: decontaminating us, checking our bloods. Then, before daybreak the next morning, we were woken up

and packed into vans by more beekeepers, ushered into decontamination rooms filled with shower-heads like sunflowers,
and then sprayed for twenty minutes with freezing cold water,
or something like water. Keep your mouths shut and your eyes
open, a man said over an intercom, as you never know where
enemy agents can get. One of the men made a joke about an
enemy agent getting up my arse, but none of us were really
in the mood for laughing, tell the truth. When the showers
were done the beekeepers showed us into white changing
rooms and gave us individual piles of laundry to put on, all
in pure white, like bed-sheets. You know why they make it
this colour, don't you? asked another of the men, and then
answered his own question: It's so that if you start coughing
up anything they can see it, see exactly where it went. It could
be contagious. They called me into a room with a giant mirror
and I answered questions to a beekeeper who introduced
himself as a scientist and spoke to me through a tinny speaker
in his suit. After the questions about the operation, about
where we were in proximity to the blast, about how long it
took us to clear the area, that sort of thing, he asked questions
about what we ate, where the food came from, where we slept.
What's this all about? I asked him, and he told me about the
deaths. People have started dying, he said, and we don't know
why. And you think it's related to the op in Iran? I asked, and
he shook his head, then contradicted himself. Yeah, he said,
some sort of retaliation. He checked my chest, my tongue, my
ears. You seem fine, he said. Just another few days and you'll
be able to go home.

PUSH THE SLATE

**Andrew Brubaker, White House Chief of Staff,
Washington, DC**

People become ridiculous. Stress makes sense depart, makes
the average man act in crazy ways. Rumours started wildly
spinning out of control about what was going on in the hospitals, and the crowds in the streets, still clinging onto their
protests even when they meant nothing, when they would
impact nothing, they started listening. The only thing more
dangerous than a crowd out for blood is one that's fearing for
their own life.

I was woken up by one of the security guys in my detail,
telling me that I had to get out of the building. I had slept in
the Lincoln Bedroom, because my eyes had been going, and
I knew that I was slower than I should have been. Livvy told
me to come home, when I called her, and I said that I couldn't,
but I promised to sleep, at the very least. Three hours I
managed, and then they dragged me out of bed, told me to
throw some clothes on, led me to the basement. There's been
a threat on the White House, they told me, and that was
normal – it was the highest-profile target in America, and we

received an average of three threats a week – but it hadn't come from terrorists this time. There's a group outside, and they're at the gates. We've got the police out there, but there's a lot of them. I didn't see it until we got to the safe-house, in Georgetown, and I finally managed to get to a TV, but they weren't joking about the numbers. The crowd was swollen, covering every bit of land they could, swarming the estate. They had pushed down the fence, and they were at the door, smashing the windows. The National Guard were on their way, or there already, but there were so many people in the crowd there was no way that this would end quietly.

The point of the safe-house was that nobody would know we were there, so the cars were sent away as soon as they dropped us off. The entire block was houses full of agents, so we were safe, we knew that much. POTUS and the First Lady were already in the house, already watching the footage. Was I really that bad a President? he asked, and I shook my head. (He was using the past tense then, and I knew he was going to quit after it was all over, whatever happened.) You were in a shitty situation, I told him, and you did what you had to do. In time, they'll remember that you protected them. I opened this, though, he said, I attacked them, and they retaliated, and now people are dying, and I am going to go to hell for what I did. He had been drinking pretty heavily. The First Lady was wringing her hands; I suggested that she went to check on their kid, and she got the hint. Look, I said to POTUS when we were alone, you did what was right. There's no shame in that. He was crying. I never believed in Him, he said, and then He turns up and everything ended up ruined. It took all of this, and Him leaving, before I realized that He was here all along, and that when I die, I won't be able to explain myself to Him, to explain that I was doing what was right. He's gone, Drew, and look at the mess I've made. You believe in Him now? I asked, and that made him cry harder. How can you not? he said. Just look at the evidence. Then he laughed at that, like it was a joke. But, you can't, he said, because there isn't any evidence, not a bit, not even a little bit. It's all about plausible deniability, right? That set him off laughing again, and then crying. I should sleep, he said, because this is all on me, now, right? All this shit is just all on me?

I let him go to his wife, and they cried together, and then they went to bed. Security posted themselves outside their bedroom door; I sat downstairs and watched the news and drank Kool-aid that somebody had made and put in the fridge, told one of the security guys to go and get me a bottle of scotch. He came back, I drank most of it, I passed out with the footage of the protestors climbing in through the White House windows still playing. I didn't wake up for a while, until I heard POTUS leaving his room, telling the man on his door he needed the bathroom. I heard him pat across the hallways, shut the bathroom door, and then went back to sleep. Next thing I knew I could hear the secret service guy beating on the door, shouting for him to open it, and then I heard the First Lady in the hallway. What's wrong? she asked, and then she shouted through the bathroom door. I got to the bottom of the stairs, told them to break it down, so they did, one kick to the handle. He was sitting on the toilet. Fucking inglorious way to be found. He's dead, the First Lady screamed, Oh my God, he's dead! I ran up myself, checked his body, and he was, cold and pale, his eyes open, slumped forward. I called

Meany, who spoke before I could tell him what had happened. Sir, the results have come back from bodies, he said, and there wasn't anything in their systems. They died of illnesses, cancer, or pneumonia, or internal bleeding, or heart attacks. Heart attacks? I asked, and he said, Yeah, a few of them, their hearts just gave up. There's nothing odd about any of this, apart from how many of them there are. You're going to have another one coming to you in the next few minutes, I said, and it'll be an urgent one. Why? Who died? he asked.

Tom Gibson, news anchor, New York City

Brubaker called us personally, which was odd, but we assumed it was an update on the riot. The White House was on fire, and the crews had only just turned up. We assumed that he wasn't there any more, so we were expecting an update on their safety, information about where they were, a statement, maybe. My producer took the call, hit me to get my attention as he listened, scribbled in the air for me to give him a pen. He wrote on his briefing sheet as he listened, big letters. *POTUS dead approx. 4:40AM, VP inducted later this morning.* I ran to the production office, told them to stop everything. Push the slate, I said; the President's dead.

Ed Meany, research and development scientist, Virginia

It's the strangest feeling in the world, seeing the most powerful man you would ever know reduced to skin, under green sheets as he waits for you to supervise opening him up, peeking around inside him, seeing what stopped making him tick.

Andrew Brubaker, White House Chief of Staff, Washington, DC

Ed Meany, research and development scientist, Virginia, called me three hours later to tell me that POTUS had a heart attack. There was some clotting around the arteries, he said, and so much adrenaline in his system. He just pushed himself too far. Same as the other heart attacks you've seen? I asked, and he said, No. I mean, some, sure, but one of them was an arrhythmia, a long-term problem, another was some sort of rupture in the walls. Find something that links them all together, I said, and he laughed, under his breath. Maybe it's like they've been saying on the TV, he said: these people only got ill when *The Broadcast* said Goodbye, right? So maybe it's that. We'll find out what it is, he said, to reassure me, I guess. If there's something in the air causing this, we can prove it, and then we can cure it. He didn't sound convinced, but I didn't push him.

Mei Hsüeh, professional gamer, Shanghai

It was the first suspicious death of an American President since the internet started, and it was barely noticed by the majority of people, because they all had other things going on. It came over the in-game chat as we hit the fifth stage of the fight against Droggs. He was in his second form: the elemental. I didn't even look away from the screen.

Dafni Haza, political speechwriter, Tel Aviv

When they announced that the American President was dead, I called the Prime Minister again, using my clearance, which still worked, somehow. I think maybe they hadn't had the time to update the protocols, or they didn't care. She's not here, I was told, she's not in her office. Will she be back? Is there a number I can call her on? She's not in the city, I was told, and you shouldn't be either. That's all the voice on the end of the phone said. What does that mean? I asked, but I think they had already hung up.

Mark Kirkman, unemployed, Boston

I had breakfast in my room, on a tray, because we – myself and the Jessops – had been told by the hotel that we were being kicked out. I hadn't packed, and I was throwing my things into my bag when I put the TV on, saw that they were already inducting the new guy. He made a speech, subtle and delicately written, that effectively laid the blame for everything on his predecessor's shoulders, and yet opened the door for further aggressive tactics. We all knew he was – for want of a better word – a warmonger. The President's death, leaving America in a war-time situation? It just gave the Vice President an excuse. We started this with blood on their hands, he said, and we'll end it the same way. This, that we will do, is right. They went to questions from the press, and the first journalist to stand up asked whether the President's death was related to the epidemic – her word – of deaths around the rest of the world. He dealt with the question well – We don't yet know the cause of any of those deaths, let alone the President's, though I'm sure we'll have the answer in due time, because our best men are working on it – and then fielded other, less interesting questions. When it was all done, flashes still blinking at the now-empty stage, they cut back to the studio, where that prick newsreader read numbers out from a sheet of paper. Three million, he said, and let it hang there before repeating it. Three million. That's the estimated number of sick or dead people in our nation's hospitals, as reported over the last twenty-four hours by our wonderful emergency servicemen and women. Three million. Over the rest of the world? Millions more.

Jacques Pasceau, linguistics expert, Marseilles

Audrey woke me up with coffee and juice and breads, though I wasn't going to eat them. My mouth was full of blood when I woke up, my pillow smeared with a patch of the stuff where my face had been. It was dried around my lips. I ran my tongue across the hole and felt how angry it was, but I didn't say anything to her about it. They're talking on the news about the epidemic, she said, how bad it's got. The President of America is dead! It's crazy, eh? Sure, I said. She bounced onto the end of the bed like it was Christmas. Some people think it's because God has gone, and they think we should all pray to Him to come back. What do you think? I think, I said, it's fucking crazy. He never left because He never existed in the first place, so you're wasting your time, hoping that He will come back, somehow make everything better. It's worth looking into, at least, she said, and I reminded her that we were linguists, not theologians. You think this is important, I told her, you talk to somebody who might actually care about it, yeah?

Audrey Clave, linguistics postgraduate student, Marseilles

Jacques was being a prick, telling me that I was stupid, that my opinions meant nothing. He barely spoke to me all day after that; he was such a fucking child, sometimes.

Mei Hsüeh, professional gamer, Shanghai

I died trying to get Droggs to leave his pit, which was the penultimate step of the battle, and I was getting another drink from the fridge when I heard the sirens outside, in the court-yard. I looked out the window and saw the firemen taking bodies down the stairs, five or six of them, all wrapped up in their own sheets. I went Away From Keyboard for a few minutes, watched them from the balcony. On the balcony above, I heard Mr Ts'ao moaning about his throat and his back. I went back online, where the rest of the guild were luring Droggs out with flame-bait. Seemed to be working.

María Marcos Callas, housewife, Barcelona

Since He left, we all got ill. We knew, of course, what that meant; that we needed His light to hold us together. We were created by His hand, so it only made sense that when we were out from His touch, we might suffer. The scientists on the television admitted it themselves; they found no evidence, no proof of the alleged terrorist's attack, so they were being forced to look to other avenues themselves. When in doubt of the truth, there He is, to show you the way.

Myself and the other people of my church decided that we were going to start having vigils to Him, in His glory, holding ourselves accountable for forcing Him to leave. Somebody has to be accountable, I told them all in an email, so we should step up on behalf of humanity and beg Him for forgiveness, that we might bathe in His almighty light. We sat in our church and we prayed, and all around the globe, hundreds of millions of followers did the same, and we prayed that He would return to us, heal us all, make us whole again. Over time, more and more of us got ill in the church, and occasionally, we lost one of the followers; but we stayed staunch and strong, the believers, we faithful, lucky few.

Benedict Tabu Tshisekedi, militia, Democratic Republic of Congo

We didn't see Father Saul after the last *Broadcast*, because he disappeared somewhere, only coming back hours and hours later, after the white man that he shot had died during the night. We crowded around him and asked him what it meant, that our God had said goodbye to us, and he said that he didn't know. It means . . . God has a plan for each of us, he said, which was something he always used to say when we were younger, and when we did not know that it meant he did not know the answer. He went and spoke to the American for a while, and then came back and looked around for a while, before asking me for my gun. I have to take this, he said – and he knew it was important to me, because it had been my father's, and was all that I had to remind me of him until he returned – and then he said goodbye to me, and walked off out of the village and down the road. The American told us that he had missionary work to do. He told me to tell you, Remember when he started here? He came from Darfur? Well, now he's gone somewhere else. I did not believe him, because we heard the gunshot a few minutes later, quiet, in the distance, but nothing else made that noise, and I knew that Father Saul had never shot an animal in his entire life, so it was not him hunting to survive.

Dafni Haza, political speechwriter, Tel Aviv

My work phone rang, and I had been drinking, but I answered. She needed me, finally: finally, I was a part of it again. Why do you enter politics in the first place? It's to become a leader, a ruler, to dictate policy and meaning and change lives. That's the goal. This was my chance. Hello, I said, expecting, I don't know, an apology, maybe. It was a recorded message. All government departments are being issued City Order 17, the voice said, an evacuation warning. Please leave Tel Aviv for a designated safe house. For more information, call this number et cetera. It wasn't meant for me, or it was an accident, because I still had the phone. I thought about driving into the city, to see the Prime Minister, because I wanted to be there when this went down, and when it picked itself up again afterwards. I didn't. I got down the road – driving Lev's car, some stupid American thing he insisted on because he liked big cars, big air-conditioned cars – and then turned around. My mother lived in Haifa. It wasn't far. I could pick myself up there.

Dominick Volker, drug dealer, Johannesburg

I tried to call for the ambulance as soon as Candy went into labour – she said, Oh shit Dom, it feels like it's coming, and that was the first we knew about it – but they didn't answer, of course, because nobody did. So I said, I can take you to the hospital, but she shouted, I don't think there's time, this little one is coming now! We knew what to do, sort of. I got towels, because they said that, and she said, It hurts like I'm being stabbed, so I gave her some morphine from the stash, thinking that would help her out. I sat on the floor of the living room – she said, I'm going to ruin this carpet, and I said, I don't give even half a shit, because this is more important, okay? – and I waited to catch it, telling her to push. It hurts so much, she said, so I gave her more morphine – not enough to hurt her, or the baby, but she shouldn't have been able to feel a fucking thing – and told her to push again. Don't remember how long it took, but I could see the baby. Ag fuck, I said, it's coming! Push! She didn't, and the baby didn't make any noise, even when I realized she was quiet and her eyes were rolled back. I grabbed the baby by the head, trying to get his shoulders to pull him out, but he wasn't moving either, and I couldn't do a fucking thing. I kept trying for a while, and then I had to stop, because he was bruised around his head, and I remember thinking, now, whatever happened, this wouldn't be right.

Meredith Lieberstein, retiree, New York City

I was a better sleeper than Leonard, when he had been alive. He always got up for the bathroom in the night, and then he would wake up as soon as it was light, and insist on turning the radio on, doing these exercises that he read about, designed to keep you living longer, keep you healthy. It's when the air's at the freshest, he would joke as he did it, and I would gradually wake up myself, by which point he would be done with the lunges and comedic tumbles that he used to signal the end of his act, and we would have breakfast.

That morning, when I woke up, it was to the birds and the light, and I had to switch the radio on myself. I lay there alone, on my side, and I listened to the announcer say that the number of people either dead or dying was rising, the estimates growing. The final numbers would be unfathomable, it seemed. We're all losing loved ones, he said, losing those that matter the most. He didn't say anything more, but you could hear it in his voice that he was mourning. He barely played any music at all – only the stuff like 'Imagine', sombre classics that barely felt like songs any more – and all I could think was, Leonard would have had such an issue trying to tumble to *this*.

Peter Johns, biologist, Auckland

Trigger called me out into the back room to show me his cut; the area around it was swollen and white, totally not the colour it should be. What the fuck happened? I asked him, and he shook. I dunno, he said, it was fine and then it just started hurting like a bugger. It wasn't even like a peck any more. It was red and puckered and bleeding, almost like lips, and he couldn't move it any more. Fucking hell, I said, we need to get you to a hospital. I'll be fine, he told me, I've just got the bot, that's all; get me some TCP, I'll be fine in the morning. (We kept a load of drugs, antiseptics, that sort of thing, on the island for the animals. Nothing major, but sometimes they got infections, and they were treatable by us, so we kept stuff for that. Neither of us was a trained vet, per se – we had visits from them, if they were needed – but we had skills and know-ledge, experience.) I helped him put it on the cut and he said, Come on, let's get on with the day. I went back to check on the Tieke eggs, see how the incubation was working out; the little bugger that snapped at him was sleeping on the side. That's all they did at first, but it looked healthy. It looks good, I shouted. Trig said that he was going to hose down the cages out the back – they needed cleaning properly every few weeks, washing and disinfecting – so I left him to it, did paperwork. After an hour or something I hadn't heard a peep so I went back, shouted his name, no reply. I found him by the taps, on the floor, soaking wet, eyes rolled back, like he was having a fit, so I slapped him, tried to get him to focus on me, took his pulse, picked him up, ran him to the boat, but by the time I got the engine started he was already dead.

Phil Gossard, sales executive, London

My hand *had* been getting better. Karen hadn't been home in . . . I don't know, days, probably; but I had been flexing it more and more, using it. The bruise had turned yellow, moving away from black, and it hurt less to touch. It hadn't been hurting at all when I didn't move it, which was a definite improvement; and then I woke up that morning and it was swollen, fingertips to wrist, like a cartoon where somebody had stuck an air hose under my fingernail, and there it was, an inflatable balloon-hand, multicoloured, red and black and yellow. I couldn't do anything with it, and I was poking it in the light of the kitchen windows when Jess came in, pulled a face. What happened? she asked, and I said, I have no idea. She looked at it closer, stuck her tongue out. Yuck, she said. Are you sick? I don't know, I said. I feel alright. But I didn't feel alright; I was sweaty, clammy, in that way you are hours before you come down with something.

I tried to call Karen, to ask her what I should do – it didn't look bad enough to warrant a hospital, not when there were so many people dying – but nobody at her hospital answered the phone, which wasn't a surprise, in retrospect.

Hameed Yusuf Ahmed, imam, Leeds

We lay in bed and watched about the hospitals on the television, which Samia had dragged in from the living room so that we could see it. I can't sleep without knowing what's happening, she said, which wasn't true, because she was asleep hours before I was, and there weren't any answers when she . . .

She said to me, before she went to sleep, Do you think it's because of us? Do you think we're the cause of this? What do you mean? I asked. Well, because we doubt. Do you think God has left us because we doubted Him, or because we, I don't know, because we believed in the wrong God? She started crying. Do you think we've brought this on ourselves? I held her, even though the thought of what she had said made me feel sick to my stomach, and told her that I didn't think so, that she shouldn't think such things. That sounds so stupid, even to hear it said aloud, I told her. She went to sleep not long after that, and I lay there and watched them wheeling bodies into hospitals, not knowing that there was no way to save them, or even what was killing them; and I watched Samia sleep from behind, the rise of her shoulders, the way her head barely moved as she breathed. I don't remember switching the television off; it was off when I woke up, hours later, feeling like I had barely slept at all. I got up first, because I always did, dressed myself, went to the kitchen, boiled water, squeezed lemon into it, drank it. When it was time to leave I thought about waking Samia to come with me, but thought better of it, thought that I should leave her to sleep. I was the only one at the mosque; I did the prayers as normal, because that was my role, even though the room was empty, and it was still dark outside. When I got home I made breakfast, and then went in to wake Samia. I don't know when she died; if it was before I went or after, seconds after she went to sleep or seconds before I shook her shoulder, kissed her cheek. She wasn't cold, I think; I'm sure I would remember it if she had been cold.

Simon Dabnall, Member of Parliament, London

Most of us humans have a shy acceptance of our lot in life; sure, there's always going to be those idiots who cause a mess and run around like they're on fire, but for the rest of us, we're human, we accept who we are, we get on with it. Still only days after we first heard *The Broadcast*, after suicides and violence and looting and riots and wars and protests, it took the threat of death sneaking up on you, just taking you without you having a chance to say or do anything about it, it took that threat to break the human race. I always said that I wanted a natural death, that I didn't care how it came as long as it was what was meant to happen; that I wanted to just drift off and that was that. Of course, I meant that I *wanted* to die in my sleep, surrounded by my loved ones. I said many things in my life, but then the reckoning – or whatever – came and I was forced to actually think about them. I realized how much of what I did, what I said, was actually about me. It wasn't selfish; it was just the way that we, as humans, are.

No, wait. The way that we *were*.

The Catholics, Christians – the combined religions, believing in *a* God, not necessarily the one they believed in a week before, but one who had been here and now, suddenly, was gone – were playing out the idea that it wasn't terrorists responsible for the deaths; that there wasn't some horrific biological agent, but it was actually a consequence of God's departure. People started latching onto it. There's no cure to this mystery terrorist biological agent? We can't even find it? It can't be real, they decided. They went through the Bible to find passages about how God's love keeps us alive, about how His strength saves us. We – the rational – know that the Bible isn't real; that the hymns that we sang, the prayers that we said, they all meant nothing, written by people in lieu of fictions and poetry, a target to aim our love at.

So you split the opinions of the many into two camps: those who think that the strange things that have been happening are coincidence, and those who think that they're examples of God's *something*. I remember seeing an interview with some atheists around the time of this, and thinking how broken they looked, how utterly useless. The interviewer asked about if they thought that the deaths were linked to *The Broadcast*, and one of them said, verbatim, How could they not be? This thing is more powerful than anything we've ever seen or even thought – how can they not be linked? God is letting everybody die as a way of proving Himself. Proving Himself? asked the interviewer. How can He be proving anything if He's left us, if people are dying because He's gone?

He's proved just how much we need him, stretched His muscles like a preening weightlifter, the atheist said – though, at that point, I don't think you could call him that any more; he seemed to believe as much as anybody.

BANGING ON DIALS

Andrew Brubaker, White House Chief of Staff, Washington, DC

We had lost control. I don't think it needs saying, not now, but back then we could have done with being told, because we thought that we were holding it together. We thought that, even though the people – protestors, religious, ill, dead – were huge in number, we still had authority, and we could wrench anything back if it slipped out of control. But then, everything moved so quickly.

Ed Meany, research and development scientist, Virginia

The body-count kept getting higher and higher, and we only had one explanation for why people were dying: they weren't getting *better*. Every injury, illness, sickness, disease, all of them suddenly became fatal, no matter whether they had been to start with. The common cold became the flu became pneumonia in a matter of hours, and it spread like colds did. It was quick. If you were near somebody who had it, you had a better chance of catching it than not. I argued blind with the other guys in the labs about this, saying that it was a proper epidemic, worse than any we'd seen before; if you had no way to fight off a cold, there was no way you weren't catching it. Everybody had low T-cell counts, like, bottom-of-the-scale low. If I was a TV doctor, I would make a leap to a conclusion: I'm sorry, miss, but your immune system has shut down, collapsed even, and you have weeks to live. But it was a theory, still, because we didn't have a reason, a cause, a way to explain why it was happening and how we might go about stopping it.

So I started taking medication, just in case. There were so many corpses in the labs, and we had masks and suits but still, couldn't hurt, I figured. I took the stuff they give to HIV patients, designed to boost their immune systems to stop them getting ill, stuff that fakes what your body should naturally be making. It seemed sensible, so I guzzled them. Work was pointless: everything just felt like we were turning valves or banging on dials for the sake of it.

Sam Tate called me later that afternoon, just to chat, he said, because he was so stressed, but there was something else. Have you found out what caused it yet? he asked, and I said that I didn't have a clue. It's completely untraceable? Completely, I said; if somebody did make this, they were fucking brilliant. I mean, it's like nothing that exists, Sam. He told me that he was at a silo – didn't say which one, and I didn't ask. Do you think they're going to launch something? I asked, and he said that he didn't know. I don't know how people can stand being responsible for that much damage, he said.

Tom Gibson, news anchor, New York City

We had people on the streets with cameras filming stock footage, and they were there when it all turned nasty. There was one group in New York who were protesting against the government, been there for days, camping out, unstructured, disorganized, pissed off; and another group of pro-God people, praying for their Lord to return, telling people to pray so that God would come back and save us all. They clashed by Central Park; it began with sloganeering, shouting words across at the other group, and then somebody said something that went too far and they sprang. They were like cats; a noise spooked them, and they leaped. They leaped toward each other, and that made it all turn nasty.

Mark Kirkman, unemployed, Boston

It spread across the US like a rash. I know that's a cliché, but it's what it was, and it itched, and people scratched it, because they were frustrated and wanted answers. The Jessops and I moved into a motel off the highway, and we ate food from the machine and tried to keep our heads down, because we didn't want any trouble. I had a telephone number given to me by the producers of *The Role Call*, sent in by somebody in the UK, and I called her from the phone in the room, premium rate. I can't talk for long, I said, but I just wanted to let you know that you weren't alone. Oh, I know I'm not, she said – her name was Ally, and she was Scottish, and I could barely understand her because of her accent, at first, but I got used to it – because I've got a visitor here from your neck of the woods, and she didn't hear *The Broadcast* either. Another one, I said, that's great. Aye, she said, and then there were four.

Ally Weyland, lawyer, Edinburgh

We agreed that he would call us every time they moved, let us know that they were alright. I don't know why we did that, because now, thinking about it, that sounds a bit crazy, checking up on these people we didn't know at all; but if there were only four of us in the whole world, we really should keep in touch, that was the logic. Katy still hadn't called home, and I hadn't told her what her mother said, so it sort of hung around the flat, stinking the place up while we didn't talk about it. But I could see her worrying about it, when we watched the news. When the riot-fight in New York happened, between the Christians and the whatever-they-weres, she worried then. And then the bombs; they made her worry even more. I mean, Christ, they made me shit my knickers, so God knows what they did to Katy.

Simon Dabnall, Member of Parliament, London

I couldn't find my tablets – at least, I couldn't find the open ones, still had a drawer of the damn things at home, but I am the sort of man who requires order amongst the chaos. In this instance, order meant using the currently open bottle, so I decided that I would head back to the office and collect them. They hadn't taken back my keys, so I knew that I wouldn't have an issue getting in. I parked on double-yellows – I was fairly certain that traffic wardens weren't being vigilant about parking violations at that point – and went in, got the bottle from my desk, and when I left, I realized that I had nothing to do. A sensible man would head home, pick up his life; I, on the other hand, decided to revisit the scene of the crime. I walked through the city again, towards Parliament. I didn't know what I wanted to find there, what I was hoping to get from my visit; there was a chance of seeing somebody that I knew, certainly, and a chance of seeing reporters, which might be fun. But, really, I was doing it because . . . Whingey Americans would call it *closure*, I suppose. *He needed closure.* I made it to the shadow of Big Ben, but couldn't bring myself to go in. Instead I sat on a bench at the edge of the river, and I found myself shaking, slightly. Not ill; just nervous.

Tom Gibson, news anchor, New York City

When the video came through – same way as the others, posted in New York City, nothing else to give it away – we aired it without watching it. That was irresponsible, but it had already been shown on CNN, and we were still worrying about ratings, about market share. It was the same man in the same cave, and he told us about his operatives. We have weakened you, he said, brought you to your knees. Now, we will execute you, he said. This will be your only warning. There wasn't anything about what the warning was for, or what was going to happen, to give us a chance to prevent it. It wasn't a warning: it was a boast. After this, you will know who is right and who is wrong, the man said, and then we heard an explosion, and we saw the smoke throwing itself into the sky.

Ally Weyland, lawyer, Edinburgh

We saw the news about the Statue of Liberty as soon as it happened, I reckon. That was one of those Holy shit! moments, where you really get the chills, when somebody does something awful. It wasn't awful like the bombing of that school had been, because it didn't actually hurt anybody, best we knew; but it was an institution, you know? Everybody got that, how much they loved that bloody statue.

Tom Gibson, news anchor, New York City

Lady Liberty didn't actually fall all the way: she slumped. Nobody was inside; the closure of public services meant that she had been shut for days. All this, said the FBI guys, was symbolic. You get that, right? We asked whether we shouldn't tell people to evacuate the city, because if there were more bombs, it would be safer. It causes panic if we flood the streets now, they said. We'll get the dogs. They cleared the area as fast as they could and we watched them tear in with their tanks and vans and dogs and start prowling the streets around the river, then running off in every direction from there, going to every nook and cranny. When they got back from the statue site a few hours later they sat us down to fill us in. The charges that had been placed were shabby, they said, half-assed, the sort of thing that looked thrown together. It was a professional job, the bomb guy told us, but it wasn't exactly super-terrorist stuff. It's nothing to *seriously* worry about, they said. Jesus.

Andrew Brubaker, White House Chief of Staff, Washington, DC

The Vice President of the United States was who we had. They always say, you can never pick your running mate; the people do it for you. You, the would-be President, are always going to have holes in your campaign, and you plug those holes with somebody who might make sense. They might be able to persuade you another way on a topic of discussion, they might have a solid military mind when you have none, they might be a mathematician when you have no head for numbers; but they're the other side of the coin. You run for office and you take somebody who might get you votes on the other side, because they're the way you win the majority. Most of one, some of the other. The VP and POTUS weren't friends – I don't remember ever seeing them together before we threw the VP's name into the hat on the trail – and they didn't exactly see eye-to-eye on the issues. The VP was on record as being pro-war during the Iraqi invasion, anti-abortion, pro-armament. He was an ex-soldier, three tours, and he was religious, super-, super-religious. He was, in terms of our administration, our plans for the future of the US, a liability, but that's what POTUS had needed on the ticket to win over some of the red states. He was closer to the red side of the fence, but that was what it took. I knew we'd be at war – a real war, not what it had been for the last fifteen years, not sitting in places holding your guns up in case somebody took a cell-phone out of their pants at the wrong time; a war where we would attack somebody to get some sort of resolution. We got back into the building a few hours after his induction, with the protestors cleared out, the army making walls around

248

the building. The Vice President sat in the Oval Office, with its broken windows and fire-damaged carpets, and we waited for him to make his move. I was there, but in a purely advisory capacity. The President had wanted my counsel on everything, my experience. This guy? He looked like he'd sooner charge in himself than sit back and listen to a liberal. We watched what was happening in New York and we waited. We have to catch these people, sir, I said. He waved me away. You'll see; the army'll deal with them, he said. And then Russian Hill happened.

Tom Gibson, news anchor, New York City

The video of that was emailed to us seconds after it happened, and we had it straight on the air, because it felt important. That's what news is, most of the time: what feels important. It's famous now: the clip of the shop-owner being dragged out of his shop, through the doors, the men kicking the doors off their hinges, then throwing him down as they set fire to the shop, throwing the petrol in through the windows, and making him watch as it burned. The one that started beating the crap out of the shopkeeper got arrested, I think, but the others got away with it. And the guy with the cell-phone who was filming it wasn't anything to do with the attack, but he didn't step in. He didn't exactly Hoo-rah when they did, but we still had emails from people saying he was complicit.

Andrew Brubaker, White House Chief of Staff, Washington, DC

Either the police didn't step in, and let that man get kicked

249

to death on the street, or they didn't get to the scene on time. They claimed the latter, but the footage showed a parked police car up the road, and there was so much noise they'd have definitely heard it, but they didn't do anything.

Tom Gibson, news anchor, New York City

I have – I *had* – a reputation, as being mercenary. I didn't like it, but that was the news. That's what it took. We got a report about the reported numbers of dead in the past twenty-four hours only a couple of minutes after the Russian Hill story played out, and I decided to not air them. I got one of the junior reporters to take over the broadcast and I phoned all the syndicates, got some of the runners and assistants to call all the other networks. That was the pull I had; direct phone lines. We all agreed to sit on the information until we had it confirmed; let the White House announce it, take the brunt. People shot the messenger, and we would be delivering the worst news possible.

Joseph Jessop, farmer, Colorado City

They showed the video on the television, the normal, daytime television. The man hosting the show said, This features some graphic images that viewers might find disturbing, and they showed the man being kicked. We had to cover Joe's eyes from that, then we switched the set off, went for a walk. Jennifer was sniffling, starting to get a cold, and I had seen on the television so many people who were ill from it, so I remembered how we used to fight colds back in Colorado City: you get out, you exercise, you work that cold away. It was a lovely sunny day, beautiful weather. When we got back, we saw that the government had announced an enforced curfew. We knocked on Mark's door, asked if he was watching, and he was. He looked so angry. When it's enforced, it's frighteningly close to martial law, he said, and I told him that I didn't know much about that. I kept thinking about that poor man in San Francisco. It'll keep people safe, though, I said. You want to come for food with us? I asked, and he agreed, but made sure when we got to the restaurant downstairs that he didn't sit next to Jennifer. Turned out they weren't serving food anyway, so we took some microwave mac and cheese from the shop and cooked it in our rooms, ate it off the saucers they'd put next to the coffee maker.

Andrew Brubaker, White House Chief of Staff, Washington, DC

The decision to impose the curfew wasn't made with my consultation. I turned my back and next thing I know, people are being *told* to stay indoors unless there was an emergency. The Vice President's press release mentioned that it would be enforced, if it needed to be; the press piled onto me when I walked past the bullpen, and asked me what that meant. I don't have a clue, I said, I'll tell you when he tells me.

Well, that was the wrong thing to say to anybody without the words *Off the record* in front of it; it was on the blogs within minutes, and that effectively shut me out of the Oval Office.

We're doing this to protect our nation, whatever their creed or colour; we're doing this to protect the *world*. There are terrorists and infidels and those who would see you come to harm, and we're facing the hardest time that we've ever seen. People are sick, people are dying, and the only way that we can keep you safe is by keeping those you love close to you. Stay in your homes, and we'll keep you updated. I watched him deliver the speech live, then asked for a few minutes. You can have one, he said, and I told him that I could be invaluable, that I had a lot to offer. No offence, he said, but what you've got to offer is what got us into this mess. Our God spoke to us, that was no accident, but you were too dainty in your response. If some Jihad-following rag-heads rally against Him, against His name? You don't fuck around with tactical strikes, son; you wipe those assholes out. He left me for a meeting with the heads of all the military divisions, the joint chiefs, some scientists, researchers from our missile programme, and I knew that this was going to get exponentially worse before it stood any chance of getting better.

Phil Gossard, sales executive, London

Jess was on the phone constantly, all morning, all through the afternoon. Her friends had heard all this gossip about the nuns from their school, how they'd gone on a pilgrimage or something, and they all found that hilarious. The phone wouldn't stop ringing; she'd hang up, it would ring again. My hand was buzzing. I kept holding it under cold water, because it made it less painful, made it seem slightly less swollen. On the news they kept talking about infections being fatal, about stuff maybe being in the air. If you have an open wound, the doctors on the news said, keep it clean, disinfected, wrap it in disinfected materials. I didn't have an open wound – apart from where the skin was starting to crack along the line of the fingernails, pushing them up, making them sensitive to touch – but I remembered when I was a child, on holiday with my parents, and I broke my foot. To get around the cast and let me go in the pool, my Dad put a condom around my entire foot to make it watertight.

Karen managed to phone in between Jess' frantic, giggling conversations, and I told her about my hand, underplayed it. It's just a bruise, I said. You should have let me check out the bone, she said, there's nothing I can do now. No, I told her, it's fine. She said that they had her in one of those suits, like she was working on the space station or something. They want to prevent us getting sick, she said, but I've got a bit of a cold, I think. My throat is sore. She sounded nervous, and I was nervous for her, but we didn't say it. Stay positive, I said; that was my concession. I am, she told me. As soon as she hung up I called my mum, because I had the chance to, and she answered in floods of tears, and I knew. I just *knew*.

LOSING

Phil Gossard, sales executive, London

I was getting ready to drive to my parents' house – I thought I should wear a suit for some reason, even though it wasn't like it was the funeral or anything, but I got it wrong, in my head – and Jess came in, gave me a hug. She didn't know my dad that well. We didn't really see them, because I was lazy, mostly, and because they didn't get on with Karen for some reason, I don't know, but we never really saw them. They lived so close, but we didn't see them. She wasn't too upset. We're going to see your grandmother, I told her, pack a bag. She didn't, so I ignored her – sometimes she could be stubborn, and she did things in her own time. I was gearing up to tell her to get a move on when she had another phone call, ran off for it. Get off the phone, I shouted, we have to go. She ignored me so I went into her room – I was fuming – and I took the handset. My hand was in so much pain, and she was . . . I took the handset, and I put it down. What the fuck is so important that you have to talk all day on that? I asked her, and she said, Well, one of the girls, her dad died this morning. Who? I asked, and she said, Tanya. I remembered her name;

Tanya was the girl who had been teasing Jess the most, the daughter of the man I had the fight with in the supermarket. I didn't say anything about that; I stayed quiet until she went to leave the room. Can I take the phone? she asked. I thought you didn't even like Tanya. I thought she bullied you. She did, Jess said. Doesn't mean I don't want to know what happened.

I knew that my hand was just waiting. I saw the stuff about people dying, and I saw my hand, black, rotting, it felt like, and I knew. It was inevitable.

Dhruv Rawat, doctor, Bankipore

I don't know why I didn't go outside when I saw that people were getting sick. I should have thought, I'm a doctor, I can help them, but I didn't. In fact, I did quite the opposite: I helped myself. I know that one of the main causes of sickness is germs, in the air, so I shut off my air conditioner and kept the windows shut. Out of my window I could see the clinic that had employed me – that was part of the reason for choosing the hotel that I did, because it was so close – and the people waiting outside, not yet frantic, but I knew that they would be. I should have helped them, I know, but I did not. I lay in my room and watched the television, watching the international news and seeing their reports about *The Broadcast*. They said, Here are some thoughts from around the world. There was a girl in America somewhere, another girl in England somewhere, a German man with long hair, and then me, right in the middle of the screen. I heard Adele's voice asking me what I thought it was, and I said that I didn't know, but that I was a doctor, and I needed facts. It was out of context, an old clip now, unrelated to who I was or what

255

was happening, but it ruined me. I took my clothes off in the heat and lay on the cold floor of the bathroom, feeling my back get stuck to the tiles because of the sweat.

I left the television on, and through that day and the next the situation got worse and worse, so I stayed in the room and didn't answer the door to anybody, and I ate the sandwiches and biscuits from the minibar, and occasionally looked at the clinic, at the people outside it trying to get in, and then not trying to leave.

Simon Dabnall, Member of Parliament, London

I watched a woman fall into the river, off the Vauxhall Bridge, down near the Tate. I don't know if she fell or jumped, actually, but it wasn't far enough to kill anybody, and all you'd get was an awful swim in water that hadn't ever been clean, as far as I was aware. (Oh, no, I tell a lie: they put cleaning agents in it for the Olympics. Apart from that, it was a brown quag.) She fell in, and she screamed from the water, and I stood on the side of the river and debated saving her. I could swim, I was there, but I didn't go for it. There was all this stuff about immune systems not working, and we still didn't know what was actually going on with that. I didn't offer my help; I wasn't ill yet, and I didn't want to risk it, frankly. I knew that there was a better-than-average chance that, if there was something worth catching, I'd catch it. Most people had an immune system to be destroyed; mine was, as they say, already *compromised*. There was, I reasoned, a better chance that I'd pop it than most, and I was fine with that; because it's easy to come to terms with when you know it's going to happen sooner or later. For me, it's nearly always been the case that it would be sooner. She didn't die; a man who saw her leaped in from the edge, grabbed her, dragged her to the bank. Everybody rushed over to check she was alright, but I stayed back.

I had the phone call as I watched a woman from the crowd doing mouth-to-mouth on her. It was Clive, my brother-in-law, and he asked if I was sitting down, as if that actually made difficult news easier to hear outside of bloody *Eastenders*. Yes, Clive, I said. What's Dotty done now? She's dead, he told me. I assumed for a second that it was like everybody else, a virus or the flu, some terrorist after-effect, like with so many other people over the last few days, but no: this was suicide, delivered with a sharp knife in their bathtub while Clive was out. I found her when I got home, he said. I've called a funeral home, but there's nobody there, or at the police. Do you want to come round? he asked, and I said, Honestly, Clive, I really don't. I don't want to see her. He wasn't crying, which I didn't blame him for; she put him through a lot. He sounded so shaky, though. What are you doing with her body? I asked him, and he said that he didn't know. I don't know if we'll find anywhere to bury her, not now, he said. Are you sure that you don't want to come and see her? he asked, and I could hear that he wanted me to, so I said that I would. I didn't do it because I felt I owed it to them; I just thought that I would regret it if I didn't.

Audrey Clave, linguistics postgraduate student, Marseilles

I couldn't stop looking at Jacques' mouth, because it wouldn't stop bleeding. Also, and I didn't tell him this, but it had started to smell, like when somebody hasn't cleaned their teeth in days, or weeks. It was bad breath but worse, you know? It should heal alright, I kept telling him, because it's the mouth, and that's what they say, right? That it heals really quickly, faster than any other part of the body. He wouldn't talk about it. There are more important things than my mouth, he said. He told me to fuck off when I said he should try and see somebody, go to a hospital, maybe. You've seen what's happening in those places, he said, you haven't got a chance in hell of making me go there. You'd go if you cared about me, I said, if you cared about us. Fuck you, Aud, he replied.

I let him cool down, then asked him what was wrong. You really fucking think that this is God? he asked, and I didn't reply, because I knew what I believed, and what he didn't want me to believe. It was better to stay quiet. I mean, I knew you were naive, but thinking it's really God? That's just retarded.

The end, I suppose. That was when our thing, whatever it had been, that was when it all ended between us.

Phil Gossard, sales executive, London

I had to drag Jess off the phone, using threats of stuff her mother and I could do to her – we would ground her, we would take her phone privileges, we would make her do the washing up, that sort of thing, only gentle threats, but they usually seemed to work – and eventually we made it into the car. I put her in the back, and I checked her seat-belt, because that's what you do, as a responsible parent. I tried to call Karen again, to tell her what had happened to my dad, but there was still no answer, so I rang her mobile – which I knew would be off – and told her we were going to Canterbury, that we'd be back the next day. I thought that the traffic would be worse than it was, but the streets were dead. They were quiet. So we drove. I had Radio 4 on, and they were doing special reports on Africa, and some woman was saying that we had forgotten about those worse off than ourselves. We have a responsibility, she said, and they reeled off numbers of predicted deceased in areas where there were no medicines, and it was terrifying, the sort of numbers that put genocides to shame. This weapon has killed more than any war in the past, more than any drought, and we step in to stop those; why have we not stepped in to help here? There was a counterpoint, of course, that we had enough problems here at home, that we had to fix those. Besides, the counterpoint man said, how do you fight something that you can't understand, much less find? The woman arguing for Africa then said, You think it's God, don't you? and the man said, If the shoe fits, and the whole argument became about that then, about deciphering *The Broadcast*. Eventually the presenter stepped in: Either way, he said, we're fighting things we can't see. I remember that moment, that line, because my hand spasmed, stopped working, the pain going right up my arm, and I slammed it against the steering wheel to try and get feeling back into it, but that made the wheel shudder and the car hit a kerb. We were only a mile from the house.

I was fine; that's the irony of the crash, because I didn't even have my belt on. It hurt too much to get my hand to do it, so I didn't bother. I didn't have a scratch on me, not a single one. Just Jess. She hit her head on something, or snapped her neck when we hit the lamppost, the paramedic told me. He couldn't tell. We won't know until somebody more qualified looks over her, he said. I waited nine hours for him to show up, nine hours that I spent sitting on a wall near the car, alone, because I was told by the flustered woman at 999 to not move her, and to leave the car. When he left – without her body, because they had been instructed to not take any back to the hospitals, because they suddenly weren't important – I called my mum, and told her what had happened. She wailed, for Jess, for my dad, for all of us. I tried to call Karen, let the phone at the nurse's station ring for what must have been twenty minutes before somebody answered. I don't know where she is, the woman who answered said, so I said, Well, can you tell her that her daughter's dead, and then I hung up. The car still worked, can you believe it? It still drove, because the crash was so tame, so pathetic, so I got back in with my dead daughter sitting behind me, still strapped in, and I drove her home.

Andrew Brubaker, White House Chief of Staff, Washington, DC

The Vice President called me into the Oval Office again, from my desk where I had been sitting and watching the news and working every single contact I had that might want to share anything that they knew, anything at all. POTUS' pictures had already gone from the office. I'm telling you because you deserve to know, he said, but we're releasing a statement now to the press giving the terrorists twelve hours to come forward, to tell us how to stop this. Why twelve? I asked, and he said, Because that's how long it'll take to prime the warheads we're gonna use if they don't. Twelve hours, or we point the missiles at the A-rabs, and I start reading out launch codes.

Ed Meany, research and development scientist, Virginia

The bodies we had in – and we were getting new ones all the time, because there's only so many tests you can run, and with a lot of the tests you need bodies closer to death – were coming up with crazy low T-cell counts across the board, thin blood, cell lysis, hep-low levels of white blood cells. We were pumping ourselves full of antiretrovirals, far above the doses that were recommended, and we all took injections of the stuff they give you before chemo to boost your immune systems. I took vitamins as well; handfuls of them. Everybody coming into the building was scanned, sprayed, made to wear sterile suits. We didn't know what was causing it, but they all had severely compromised immune systems – like nothing we'd ever seen before – so we at least had something we could try to cure.

Brubaker turned up, refused to strip for the decon hose-down, so we told him to get in a suit and wrote it off. It's hard to say no to a man like him. He asked us what we'd found, so I told him. There's nothing in the air, I said. There's this – I hesitated, but I called it a disease – there's this disease that's tearing through people, but it doesn't leave a trace. Where did it come from? he asked, as if we had a fucking map. We don't know, I said, because we can't find it. Natural? he asked, and I said, No, this is man-made; it has to be. It's really unbeliev-ably cutting edge; we've never seen anything this amazing. I mean, we *cannot* find it. This is proper top-secret, years-from-now research. How was it delivered? (He was sweating, which meant that he was worried about this for bigger reasons than just the disease itself.) We don't know, I said. Best guess? Airborne. It's too fast for anything else. And I'd think it has an insane range. We had prepared a box of drugs for him and the high-level staff to take; This stuff will stop you getting ill, we think. Take some yourself, give some to the Vice President. What is it? he asked. It's the stuff they give to people about to undergo serious chemo or long-term operations, boost your immune system beyond belief. It's medicine, I told him.

He was going to leave when I reminded him about *The Broadcast*. Don't you want to know where we are on that? I asked, and he smiled. You still don't know where it came from, what it was? No, I said. We're working on it, but it's practically impossible without a signal, without something to trace. He nodded. I don't know why we're still paying you all, he shouted as he went into the decontamination room. It was rhetorical, I think.

Andrew Brubaker, White House Chief of Staff, Washington, DC

I didn't want them to think that I was powerless. I knew we were losing everything, but that power, from my job, my position, was something that was *mine*.

Jacques Pasceau, linguistics expert, Marseilles

I decided that I was going to go to see my sister. It would let me get away from Audrey, because I knew that she would take the break-up badly. She was that sort of girl. My sister lived in Avignon, but I wasn't going to just sit around and wait for *whatever* to happen. The news was a constant block of death, of people – reporters – stationed outside hospitals, coughing and spluttering. Audrey said that I should get my teeth seen to, because she was worried that it could be related to whatever was making these people ill. They're getting infections from their wounds, I told her as I left, this isn't infected. It's just bleeding. Besides, I said, if you pray to your God about it, surely He'll save me on your behalf?

I put my leathers on, my helmet, got the bike out of the garage, and I was all ready to go when I noticed that another of my teeth, one of the canines, was loose. I wiggled at it with my tongue – I was so used to the taste of my own blood by that point that I didn't even notice it – and it just slid out, easy as that. I spat it onto the floor, onto the concrete.

Simon Dabnall, Member of Parliament, London

Dotty looked awful, grey and old and devastated. She smelled already, like the whiff you get from empty wheelie bins, and her arms were wrapped in burgundy towels. Clive had covered her body in a bed-sheet, presumably to preserve her dignity, and mine; but it hadn't helped, as the water had soaked through, and it was clinging to her naked body, leaving nothing to the imagination. It took me a second to realize that the towels were dyed from her wrists, that they had been off-white before Clive (I assume) put them there. You shouldn't have her just sitting here, I said to Clive. I know, he told me, but the ambulances say that they can't be here today, maybe not even tomorrow. How are you? I asked him, and he said that he was fine. Bit of a cough, he said, then he actually coughed, as if to illustrate the point. They've been saying on the news that any symptom, no matter how small, might be a sign of whatever this is that's killing people. I listened as Clive's throat dryly slapped itself around, and I thought about how neither of us was going to be long for the world. I'm sorry, old girl, I said to my sister's body, but you might just be better off out of it.

Elijah Said, prisoner on Death Row, Chicago

The alarms didn't stop, and food wasn't served as it should have been. I slept on the cot when night came, pulling the bars shut myself, but they wouldn't lock. The next morning everything was silent, and the lights were off all throughout the block. I opened my cell door, walked to the shower room, checked that; checked the other cells; looked out of the windows in the hallway to genpop, to see the lights on through the rest of the prison. They were timed, I knew, so that didn't mean anything. We were in the older wing; everything was still manual. There, they could lock the place down in seconds. I walked to the door that adjoined us, found it locked: they kept it locked sometimes, but Cole had opened it; it must have shut after Finkler left. I banged on the door, to let them know that I was there, but there was no reply. The other end of the corridor: the imminent room first, with its plain table and chairs, and its window looking out over toward the river, to give you your last taste of freedom, of blue skies and green lawns and muddy water; then the observation gallery, black plastic chairs, boxes of pale white tissues; and the chamber itself, a chair in a room, a medical cupboard at the back wall, leather straps, a telephone. I picked it up, listened as it rang at the other end, but nobody answered. I waited by it, tried it again, and then went back to my cell and sat, and waited.

Ally Weyland, lawyer, Edinburgh

Katy came into my room and told me that she had been watching the news. There's so many people dead now, and they're not giving numbers out or anything. You want to call home? I asked her, and she nodded. I couldn't stop her, even though it might upset her, if her mother reacted half as nastily as she did when I rang. I gave her the handset, told her the code for calling the States, left her to it. Five minutes later, when I'm elbow-deep in washing up, she comes back in, red eyes, clenched fists. There wasn't an answer, she said. No answer from the house or their mobiles. They're probably in church, I said to her, but she knew what I was actually thinking. I'll try later, she said. I tried to call my mother then, because we hadn't spoken in a couple of days, but there was no answer from her either, even though I let it ring and ring and ring, and she never really went out anywhere. We both thought the worst, so we sat in the living room and ate digestives. The phone rang then and we both leapt up, but it was Mark, not a parent; they were moving on, he said. We're not sure where, but Joseph's gone to rent a mobile home, drive back toward the East Coast. I took the phone into my bedroom and we chatted for ages, because he seemed like a nice guy, and I needed somebody to talk to.

Mark Kirkman, unemployed, Boston

My parents were already dead, long before this; listening to Ally talk about hers, about Katy's, I was glad – relieved – that they never lived to see this.

Andrew Brubaker, White House Chief of Staff, Washington, DC

As soon as I got back to the White House I shut myself in my office, opened the pills, swallowed some down dry. I called Livvy and told her to stay in the house until she heard from me. You're not feeling ill, are you? I asked, and she said that she felt fine. Good, I said, don't go out anywhere. Just stay there, and I'll be back soon enough to get you.

What's happening? she asked. I think it's all about to get worse, I told her. Worse? She sounded like she didn't believe me, and, thinking about it, I don't see why she would have. Worse? It was as bad as it could get, surely?

Mark Kirkman, unemployed, Boston

It's a lot easier to not worry about your loved ones when you don't have many to worry about. I had spoken to Ally for ages, long enough to distract me. Joseph had gone for the RV, one big enough that we could put my bike in the storage container at the rear, but we weren't leaving until the next morning, and that meant I had solid time by myself. I sat in my room and stared at the minibar and wondered if my liver would catch up with everybody else. Eventually I opened a bottle, and I drank, and then I slept.

When I woke up, Joseph was shaking me. You were out for the count, there, he said, and he tried to pretend that there wasn't a bottle on my bedside table. I thought you should see this. The Vice President was being interviewed on Fox News. We have our top scientists working on this problem, and we're assured that there will be a cure imminently, he was saying. I could tell he was lying; he was awful at it. He leant in closer. We can't let terror win, he said. We can't let this overpower us. To that end, we're going to be pursuing further tactical strikes against those countries in the Middle East that we believe could have information as to the whereabouts of the madmen responsible for this attack. When they attacked us before, when they planted bombs, we started putting pressure on them. It's time to apply that pressure. He sat back, smiled. People of America, I know you didn't select me as your President, but I will do the job entrusted to me to the best of my ability. Pray for me, America; pray for me, as your President.

Andrew Brubaker, White House Chief of Staff, Washington, DC

You said we had twelve hours. *They* do, he said, but this was my way of lighting a fire under their asses. We're priming the strikes now, because it's important that we're prompt. I'm the President; when I say something's gonna happen at a time, it's damned well gonna happen. I called him a motherfucker, and I left, because we both knew I was fired anyway. There was no point arguing with him. I went to my office, threw my personal stuff into a bag, took my pills and left. I handed my security card in at the desk, and that was that.

Meredith Lieberstein, retiree, New York City

I prayed – actually prayed, out loud, on my own in the apartment – that what killed Leonard was his old age, his heart, some remnant of his cancer from years before. All I wanted was that it was something tangible, not like the people on the news, mourning in community, in denial about what had happened.

They were in denial about what might have killed their loved ones, refusing to believe that it could be a biological attack, or that it could even be our sudden lack of God; that was worrying, because denial, as a stage of grief, came before anger, and there were so many people in denial that I dreaded to think what would happen if they all moved onto stage two at the same time.

Hameed Yusuf Ahmed, imam, Leeds

I stayed inside for days, after they took Samia away. I didn't open the mosque; the only time I went down to it was when they tried to burn the place to the ground.

I had a phone call, and I wasn't answering the phone, because it was terrified Muslims I didn't know the name of, all asking me for advice, asking what they should do. I don't know, I told the first few, then I just stopped answering. I don't know why I answered it that time – I forgot, almost, picked it up, said Hello, and the man on the other end of the line told me that the mosque was burning. I stood at my window and watched it, three streets away, as it smoked; as the night grew orange around it, like a halo; as the fire brigade turned up, doused it, and then it smoked again. I knew that every part of it – the rooms, the walls, the books in the library, all of their words – would be gone. I didn't bother to look at it, or ask how it happened, because I already knew; it was a lost cause in every way. I thought about *The Broadcast*, and how they happened, and how each one coincided with somebody expressing their lack of faith; and I told myself that it was just that, coincidence. Nothing – nobody, no entity, whatever name they went by – could be that cruel, that *pointed*.

I stayed inside because I felt so weak and limp there was absolutely nothing else that I could do.

WAY DOWN IN THE HOLE

Joseph Jessop, farmer, Colorado City

We had decided to ignore the curfew, because it seemed so pointless, so token, Mark said. It seems like something that they wish they could enforce, but we've got no reason to stay here. We left LA that morning, and stopped at an Applebee's for breakfast, because it was one of the few places open. Truth be told, I loved the food, but Mark made a face when I suggested it. Still, as I said, it was one of the only places open. This was round about when we started noticing shops being shut, or worse: abandoned, some of them, and looters had taken their fill. (We were just as guilty as most, when we passed a gas station later that day and Mark said we should fill up. There was nobody there at the counter, so we helped ourselves, right to the brim. This stuff'll be rare in a week, he said, talking about the fuel, and I hadn't even thought about that part, so we filled plastic fuel canisters up as well, loaded them into the luggage hold.) We paid for the Applebee's, though; we sat in a booth and we ordered. The owners were ignoring the curfew as well, they said. Don't know how we'd live if we didn't, the man who served us said, and there's a healthy chunk of you guys who feel the same, am I right? I was worried about Jennifer, because she was croaky, her throat ragged, and none of us said anything, but we knew she was ill. And I was worried about myself, as well, because I could feel it when I breathed through my nose, that sense of it being bunged up. Mark was fine, and Joe didn't seem to have anything wrong with him; he was rattling on like normal, which I was grateful for. We ate eggs and bacon and Joe had pancakes with syrup, and we were getting ready to leave, to get back on the road, when Mark noticed that there was something different on the TV. It was an advertisement, only rather than being thirty seconds it took the whole block of them, beginning to end.

Nobody knows what *The Broadcast* means, the voice-over said, as they showed images of pretty fields, of idyllic cities, all like you'd see from a film. Nobody knows what it means; apart from the faithful, apart from the true believers. *The Broadcast* was God speaking to us, testing us. Our hospitals are filled with the dying, as was foretold; those who don't believe in His shining majesty will not be saved. *The Broadcast* wasn't a *Goodbye*: it was God's way of letting us know that He was listening to our prayers. The video changed to showing that famous painting, the one on the ceiling of that chapel in Italy, of God and the angels and Adam, touching fingers, you know the one. We're still listening, the voice-over said, why not come to one of our services and let God know that you are too? The advert was paid for by a society called the Church of the One True God, who we hadn't heard of before.

Mark got angry with it; he watched not to curse in front of Joe, but we could tell he was furious. That's totally irresponsible, he said, that's not how we should be talking about this, but I didn't know how we should, if not that way. I listened to Jennifer cough and I thought, Well, if it could save her, save us, it would be irresponsible to not at least try.

Mei Hsüeh, professional gamer, Shanghai

I screamed when we finally killed Droggs, because that was one of the last missions I had to do. I couldn't believe that we did it with only eight of us, because that should have been impossible. I was so happy I screamed, and then I heard banging on the ceiling. It was Mrs Ts'ao. Are you okay? she screeched, and I said, Oh, I'm fine, I'm fine! I'm glad you aren't dead! she said. Me too! I replied. Mr Ts'ao was still coughing, though. She seemed more worried about me than him.

We celebrated in-game, taking Droggs' skull back to Barleycorn on a spike, because that was a perk of killing him; you could mount it in public. Only, it was so quiet there. Usually, when somebody mounts Droggs' head, there's a crowd. We did it all by ourselves. I had to take a screenshot to prove we'd even done it.

Phil Gossard, sales executive, London

I didn't know where else to put Jess, so I put her on her bed, laid her down on top of the duvet. Her eyes were already shut, and there was a second where I forgot what had happened, seeing her there. I had woken her up the morning of the crash, and she'd been there, same pose.

I tried to call Karen again but there was no reply, even when I put the phone on speaker and let it ring and ring and ring for what must have been hours. I sat in the kitchen and thought about Jess, up there on the bed, and I rubbed at my hand, still in that fucking condom, because the pain was right up my arm, in my shoulder, the base of my neck, and I didn't know what that meant. Come on, Karen, I said. Pick up the phone.

Audrey Clave, linguistics postgraduate student, Marseilles

I was crying, trying to call Jacques' mobile, get him to come back, but he wasn't answering. I didn't know where he was, because his flat was just the same as when I was last in it, no clues. I thought he might have left me a note but he didn't; his bike was gone, so I knew it wasn't somewhere close. I sat on the sofa and waited, and I noticed that all the photos he had on his walls, they all had him in there somewhere. Egotistical bastard.

The flyer came through his letterbox after it became dark, when I decided that I was going to spend the night there. It was just a photocopied piece of paper, a quarter of an average sheet, and it was only black and white, with a picture of Christ, superimposed in front of a church. Come to Him, the note said, and you can pray to have your soul saved. Come and let God know you were listening to Him. The meeting was at the Catholic church in La Montade, only a few minutes from Jacques' place, so I thought, What harm can it do?

Simon Dabnall, Member of Parliament, London

I had never been a religious person. I don't think that came across in my day-to-day, but I couldn't really get along with the way that they treated certain people. In fact, there you go; I wasn't a church person. People assumed that meant that you weren't religious, but it wasn't necessarily always the case. I didn't know if there was a God, but if there was – this was the big 'if', of course, before *The Broadcast*, if that provided any sort of actual proof – if there was, I hoped that He wasn't the one that they told us about in school. (It was, at heart, an intolerance thing.) But I did know that I didn't want to sit in my house and die; I wanted to be out in London, in the city that, for all its – and my – sins, I loved. I went walking, and found myself – by chance, or whatever it was that I approximated as being chance – at the Abbey in Ealing, a gargantuan sand-coloured building, sharp parapets and spires, deeply dug grooves running the height of it, tucked away on residential roads, absolutely hidden from the world. I never understood why it was so hidden, away from the centre of the town. The only thing attached is a school, and then houses as far as you can see. And that day I don't know what I expected, but there were crowds there, running out of the doors and down to the bottom of the hill, almost to town. It was like a concert, people clamouring to get to the front, and I didn't really know why I was there. They were blinkered, leading each other in prayer, the Our Father rolling off their tongues like they had never said anything else. A woman was convulsing by a tree, her husband propping her up; she threw up on herself and her husband shouted that she was taken by the spirit. It was nothing to do with our current situation, as the woman was clearly ill, dying, most probably; but that's us, right? That's humanity. Able to adapt at a moment's notice, to take something and run with it. She must be channelling His spirit! shouted another woman, this one infinitely more shrewish, and if I didn't know better I would have thought that this was a scam, some nineteenth-century thing where they then give her a medicine and sell it to the poor idiots in the crowd with too much money and not enough self-control or intelligence to know otherwise. If I didn't know better. In reality, people crowded around her and stared, and then she pulled herself together, said something about how great God was (it was off the cuff, almost, God is so powerful, like that, just tossed out) and everybody around her acted like that was – no pun intended – some sort of gospel. She wandered down the road and collapsed, but the crowd didn't see that part.

We are here, somebody shouted through a loud-hailer, though I couldn't see them, to worship the Lord God, our One True God. Almost everybody shouted Amen back, me included, the Pavlov's dog of a Catholic upbringing. This was a new religion that claimed the world in days, hours, swallowed all the old ones, united in worshipping something that still wasn't there, no matter how much they wanted it to be. And the worst part of it all was that I didn't believe it, but I was there, for some reason, and I was praying with everybody else, and I was thinking about God constantly as I snugly slotted into that crowd. I looked at all those people, standing there, being filled with this sense of unity and I wondered if this was all a scam, if somehow somebody had found a way to beam a false message into our heads, fill us with false hope, lead us down dark alleys, make people die. If there's a God, then surely there can also be a Devil? But that Yin and Yang, it doesn't work like that; because everybody assumed that if there was a God, He was good. They wanted Him – *we* wanted this thing that was happening, everything that was going to happen – to be happening for a good reason, I suppose, and to be happening because it would, in the end, make us all stronger.

Ally Weyland, lawyer, Edinburgh

Suddenly, the Church of the One True God was everywhere. They were just the Christians sticking a new name on, letting the C of E have a big shebang with the Catholics, ready to embrace all those Jews and Muslims who agreed that they were in the wrong and wanted a piece of the bearded, white-robed God. It was like the Crusades, only without the violence, them just swallowing up whole countries in what seemed like hours. Their advert suddenly made it onto the telly, and there were flyers through the door, loud-hailers in the streets. Katy asked if we should go along, see what it was all about, but I told her it probably wasn't worth it. We didn't hear *The Broadcast*, after all; I'd expect they wouldn't take kindly if we told them. We wouldn't have to tell them, she said, but she didn't fight it. Last thing I wanted was to stick myself around that many people, that many chances to catch whatever it was that was seeing people off. It's just me and thee, chicken, I said. And Mark and Joe, she corrected me. Aye, sorry, I replied, and Mark and Joe.

As if by magic the phone rang, and it was him, Mark. I expected parents – actually, no, I *hoped* for one of the parents, not expected, because I expected, by that point, the worst – but I was pleased to hear from him. He sounded stressed.

Mark Kirkman, unemployed, Boston

Joseph insisted on stopping the van when we passed this church off the freeway, one of those big white sheds that seemed custom built with the express purpose of raising money. They weren't getting in, because nobody was, not at that point; the crowd stretched back to the side of the freeway itself, all of them looking tired and hungry, some of them ill. Jennifer wasn't looking well herself, I noticed, and Joseph had been coughing. I called Ally when they were caught in watching the praying – or taking part, I didn't really see – and told her that I was worried about them. She made a joke – Because they've gone to church? – and I laughed. No, I said, they're ill. They're not dying, not yet, but you've seen how it goes. I know, she said. How's Katy? I asked, and she said, She's alright. She misses her parents, she's only young. They'll open up flights soon enough, I said, they'll have to. Would you come back here with her, in case? Dunno, she said, depends on if you'd be coming to Florida to meet up with us. That sounded like an invitation, I said. It was.

Mei Hsüeh, professional gamer, Shanghai

The power went the next morning. Don't know if the government cut it, or if it was a glitch or whatever, but it went just as we started another dungeon, right before the endgame. I was so angry, because I didn't even get to camp my character, so I didn't know what I lost. I could have lost hours of work. I didn't know. I went onto the balcony to ask if anybody else had lost power, and Mrs Ts'ao was already out there. Hello, I said, good morning. You've lost power? She nodded. We have a gas cooker, she said, you have to come up here and we'll make you breakfast. Okay, I said.

Mr Ts'ao was angry at the television, because of the power. Have you been watching the news? he asked, We have, and the world, pah! What a state it's in. They were trying to watch international news, as the Chinese services were – his words – full of lies about what was happening. I told them that I was watching it online, following it in my game. Can you still get that? he asked, and I said that I needed power, but then I remembered my old laptop. I ran down and grabbed it, and had to tweak the graphics to get it to run properly, but then I was in. I went to the crier in the Northern Lands and the three of us stood around and listened as the funny little dwarf read out all the stories as they happened.

Andrew Brubaker, White House Chief of Staff, Washington, DC

There was going to be a funeral for the President at St Matthew's, just like there was for JFK. He should have been remembered, but he wouldn't be, at least not outside history lessons where they discussed those Presidents who made crucial errors in their administration. There were barricades established, even though, with the curfew, there wouldn't be much in the way of a crowd, and the few security guards outside the church didn't care whether I had my pass or not; they recognized me, ushered me through. The coffin was at the front, closed; I said what I had to say in front of it, kneeling because it felt right, rather than because I felt any sense of . . . respect to the place, to God. POTUS and I had worked together for years; a few years of being acquaintances, nearly three solid years working on his campaign, the year we spent in office. I owed him an apology, I thought, because I advised him. He'd be remembered for the decisions, but I was just as culpable. His wife wasn't there; I didn't ask after her, because I was scared of what she'd say if she saw me. She would blame me as well, I assumed. There were only hours until the missiles were going to launch, and I didn't want to hedge my bets with being in DC, so I called Livvy, told her to pack the car up with stuff.

As I was leaving I asked one of the morticians what time the service was starting. No service, he said, not a religious one. Where are the priests? I asked – because, as much as POTUS wasn't a believer, it was customary; having been sworn in on the Bible, you left the same way – and he said, They're all at church. Not this church? No, he said, the Church of the One True God. They're using St Patrick's. Right, sure, I said. I didn't even know who they were, that's how quickly they sprung up.

Dafni Haza, political speechwriter, Tel Aviv

Haifa was much quieter than Tel Aviv, and my mother was thrilled to see me. She didn't ask about Lev, because she had always hated him. Instead she made me tea, and I told her about my time in office. I'll use that, I told her, with whatever I do next. We saw on the television about all the people who were dying, more and more, and we counted our blessings, such as they were. I could tell that my mother wanted to go to synagogue, but she didn't labour the point, and only left for it when I was asleep.

Katy Kasher, high school student, Orlando

Ally told me about her conversation with Mark, about how he said he'd meet us in Florida if we made it back over there, and I told her I wanted to go. All I could think was how my mom and I had argued, and I didn't want *something* to have happened to her after that. I asked Ally if we could go. You don't have work, I said, and I'll put your tickets on my mom's credit card. She said we couldn't, that there weren't any flights. They weren't flying before, and I got here, I said. Not much chance of that happening again, she said.

Ally Weyland, lawyer, Edinburgh

I'm too fucking soft, that's my bloody problem. Far, far too soft.

Katy Kasher, high school student, Orlando

I was crying, trying to call my mom and dad again, and Ally came in. Look, we'll go to the airport and see, she said. Better than sitting here twiddling our thumbs, right? I called home again, left Ally's cell-phone number on the answer machine and we left the house. The streets were almost completely empty.

Meredith Lieberstein, retiree, New York City

I ended up on 5th, outside St Thomas', me and forty thousand other people, according to somebody in the crowd. Nobody was bothering to move us on; the much-vaunted curfew had turned out to be a dud. Somebody in the crowd, speaking so loudly that I could hear them but couldn't even see them, said that it was just the government's way of covering themselves. If they've told us to stay in, and there's a bomb, they're not to blame, he said. He sounded dense, but it was a theory that Leonard would have fully supported.

I had a spot next to a store, one of those clothes places where the front porch is made like a beach hut, with a surfboard and dark wooden walls, and there was a lady standing with me, drunk, I think; slurring her words, certainly. I really want to go to bed, she said, and I said, Well, why don't you, then? And then she pointed her finger at me and said, I know your type. I ignored that and told her to swap places with me, so that she could rest against the window. She swore at me, and then pushed me aside, and screwed herself up into a ball on the floor. She was a snorer as well, started right up. Shouldn't you wake her up? asked a man, and I said, No, she's drunk, let her sleep it off. Sure, he said, okay, and then they finally opened the doors to the church – we didn't even know that they were shut, we were just there, so far back that we couldn't see them if we tried – and the whole crowd moved forward in this big chunk, and all of a sudden I was a few shops down, in front of a bakery, and I couldn't see the woman any more. I tried to shout back, to tell people to wake her up, but of course nobody was listening to me, they just marched forward. All I could think was, I hope that nobody tramples on her, I really do.

I had been staring at stale cupcakes in the window of that damned bakery for a few hours when we finally moved again, and I ended up in front of the next shop, and there, bright as day, was Leonard's first wife, Estelle. I never liked Estelle, not least because of the stories that Leonard told me about her

281

(about her cheating, how she used to just bitch about people behind their backs, the things that she'd say, the debts that she ran up (that we were still paying after they divorced!), her general attitude), and she hadn't phoned me after he died, even though I called her, left a message, told Jacob, their son, what had happened. I'm surprised to see you here, she said, I would have thought that you'd be sitting shiva. Well, I'm not, I said, I'm here. At a Christian church, no less, she said, and that smile just spread itself across her face like butter, just like Leonard used to say it did. I don't see you sitting shiva either, I said, and she said, Well, no, he lost that privilege when he left me for you. And this isn't Christian, I said; the Church of the One True God is non-denominational, so they say. That made her snort. What about Jacob? I asked, and she said, Well, I didn't expect him to turn up. She leant in closer, which put us nose-to-nose, and I could smell her lipstick, and she said, He never liked you, so I would think he's mourning in his own way. Oh, do try to not be such a bitch, I said, and she made a shocked noise, a little burst of yelp. What did you call me? People tried to turn in the crowd to look, and so I said, louder than I usually speak, Don't play that card, Estelle, and then she said, totally out of the blue, Did they ever discover why Leonard died? Because, the way I reckon it, it was just before all those other people started dying. Will there be an enquiry, do you think? I turned my back on her and tried as hard as I could to not cry, but all I could hear for the next five minutes was her telling the people around her in the crowd that I stole her husband from her, and now I was here calling her a bitch, and I wasn't even honouring his memory in the proper Jewish way, and I felt like just shouting out,

Well, what does it matter if I don't follow Jewish rules, there is no Jewish any more! But I didn't, because I know that would have made the tears come out harder still, and then she would have won.

I didn't wait to see what the people in the church would have to say for themselves; nothing would have made up for what I lost, I suspect.

Ally Weyland, lawyer, Edinburgh

The airport was chocka, unsurprisingly, people desperately waiting for them to put planes back on. That's always the way with airports, I reckon: they have to let you in in case you've got a flight, even when everything's locked down. Besides, where else were the people going to go? We spent hours there with all those other people, as they coughed and choked their way into the air conditioning. If we weren't ill before we're going to catch it now, Katy said, and I said, Maybe we're immune. Hadn't thought of it till that point, really, but I texted Mark about it, see what he thought. He texted back with a *No clue*, and told me that the Jessops were at a church, and he was sulking by the van.

Katy called home again a few times, but there wasn't anything, and that set her off crying, really, really bad crying. I hugged her and lied to her, all that stuff you're meant to do, but I was actually jealous; because I'd have loved to have just cried, but I had to be the strong one.

Phil Gossard, sales executive, London

On the news they started reading a list of hospitals that were shutting across London. There weren't many, but enough. Karen's was on the list, and they didn't give a reason for the closures. They sold it like they were too busy to take other people, but I assumed that it was something else, probably. I assumed but hoped that it wasn't. I sat by the phone and wished that it wasn't ringing because it was so busy, but I knew – when I kept picking it up, listening to the dead dial-tone – that it wasn't the case.

Joseph Jessop, farmer, Colorado City

Seemed like the church was running three or four different sermons, because we ended up listening to a man who wasn't a priest, just a convert since *The Broadcast*, dressed like a stereotypical preacher in this bright white suit. The illness we're all feeling, it's because God is punishing us, he said, because we didn't listen to Him enough. That can all change, and *should* all change! We have a platform to tell Him all about our love, and we should use it. He looked so tired, the man did, and I was tired myself, from the drive, from having to have Joe up on my shoulders so that he could see. His throat was creaking as he spoke. We know that He's listening, because we heard Him speak; tell Him of your love! The preacher stood down, and a woman ran onto the stage, one of those fat, wealthy types. She held her hands up. Praise the Lord! she shouted, I used to only be concerned with myself, and now I know that there is somebody else there, I intend to change my ways. Now I know that I can be saved, I want to ask you, Lord, to not abandon us. We have so much to learn from you.

The crowd went through getting up, saying something nice or pleading or begging, even, that God come back. There wasn't very much praying got done, just lots of talk about saving ill ones, or knowing that dead relatives passed on because it was God's will. Everybody seemed so sickly, like Jennifer was, like I knew I was. Then the preacher pointed to Joe, called him up. Young man, you must have a story, he said, tell us why you're here. I didn't want to go, but everybody turned, looked at us. What's your story, little fella? No, he doesn't want to speak, I said, and then somebody shouted out, It's the kid from the television, the one who didn't hear *The Broadcast*. The crowd weren't nasty – I had worried that they would turn on us, chase us out, pitchforks and hollering – but they kept asking us questions. Is he scared? asked the preacher, and I said, No, what should he be scared of? Well, of hell, said the fat woman, because he's got to be heading that way if the Lord didn't even see fit to speak to the boy. It's because you came from that *commune*, she said, like it was a nudist colony, like we committed grand sins there. It says, in the Bible, about sins. Oh, for God's sake, I said, and they gasped, as if taking His name in vain suddenly rendered me the Devil itself. Why aren't you begging forgiveness? they asked Joe, directing the questions at him, but he was such a little kid, how could he answer? He started crying, gasping for air the way that kids do, so Jennifer picked him up. Shame on you, she yelled, and that got Mark's attention. Come on, he shouted, let's get out of here.

He drove the next leg and we tried to calm Joe down. He didn't really understand too much of what happened, but he got enough to think that they hated him. Kids are perceptive, Mark said, and I guess he was probably right. We stopped a few hours later, at an Ihop, hoping to find something to eat, but the place was shut, abandoned, it looked like, even though the lights were all on and the door was open. Mark went in to check the place out, came back and told us that the burners were all on. Somebody was here, he said, and they must have left; we should eat.

Mark Kirkman, unemployed, Boston

I didn't tell them about the dead guy in the back room; the manager, it looked like. He wasn't killed or anything. He had just died. His right eye was bloodshot, his tongue lolling out of his mouth. I don't know anything about disease, sickness, whatever, but my few years on the force – coupled with even more years of sitting on my sofa and watching bad medical dramas – told me that it wasn't murder. I shut the door to the back office so that Joe didn't accidentally see the body and went back down, told them to head on in. I can fry a mean egg, I said.

(There was a second, when we were just sitting down to eat, that I thought I heard a noise from the back. It was just the grill cooling down, the way that they do, clicking like a car radiator, but I thought that it was the manager for a second, that it was the beginning of the zombie uprising. When I worked out what it was I started laughing, trying to hide it with mouthfuls of egg. What's wrong? Joseph asked, and I had to tell him that it was just the situation, that it was everything. You have to laugh, right? I asked, but I don't think that persuaded him.)

Elijah Said, prisoner on Death Row, Chicago

Still hours – days – after it happened, nobody came. I lay on my cot and watched the ceiling. I didn't think about *The Broadcast*; it seemed so long ago already. I slept and dreamt, of my childhood; everything in my life I purged myself of, pushed aside – Janelle, Clarice, our home, my job; and of Allah, calling to me. When I awoke I was alone, still, in the darkness. I opened the cage, as that is what it was, and I made my way to the chamber. Inside the medicine box – marked with the red cross, the sign of health, of safety, of we-will-make-you-well-again – I found a syringe in a black box, sealed. I assumed that this was how they would kill me; how they would send me to my maker, make me pay for what I did. I sat myself in the chair that they would have used, pulled my shirt off, took the leather and strapped it to my arm, tightening it until the veins lurched to the surface of my arm. I took the syringe and looked around at the room that I would die in, knowing that it was to be the end, and I jammed the needle – thick, meant to break bone, it looks like, so that nothing can get in its way as it slides into you, ends you – into my vein, and I pushed the plunger. I had seen videos of people before, films, where they shake and shiver immediately; and they froth at the mouth, and beat at their heads, and scream for mercy. It is the end, and they barely have time to register it. I prepared myself, held the arms of the chair. I saw them: the people that I killed. I had been paid to kill, because I was a bad man, and they were worse. I saw myself, years before, abandoning my classrooms, my profession; leaving Janelle, because she did not understand; pulling on the uniform of the Fruit of Islam, because I had a mission; I saw myself abandoning everything that I ever loved, because the mission was never enough, can never be enough; I saw myself degraded, shallowed, unwhole, begging for work; and then I saw him, with his envelope of bills, and my family begging me to come home, and Allah *ashamed* of me; and I saw myself here, being logged, being oppressed, shoved, beaten, judged, condemned. I shook, and felt myself slip.

I fell to the floor, gasping; it hit every part of me, and for a second, yes, I felt like I was dying, but I did not. When I caught my breath, I saw that the syringe was adrenalin, always ready in case needed, a casual part of every prison medicine case; and I realized how stupid I had been, thinking that the stuff they would use to end my life – a cocktail, some of the people who went to the chamber before I did used to call it – thinking that they would leave that stuff there, that it wouldn't be kept under lock and key in a doctor's office somewhere out of reach. I thought about what else I could do – I was there to end my life, to cease from being what I had become – but even as I looked at the leather straps, the chair, the glass pane of the observation window, I realized that I was meant to die a certain way, in a manner passed upon me by a judgement greater than my own. I could not escape that.

I returned to my cell, pulling myself along the corridor until I reached my cot. I lay there and shut my eyes, but all I could feel was my heart, all I could hear was the beat of my blood around my body, rubbing vein against vein as they struggled to deal with what I had done to myself.

SWEATING IT OUT

Simon Dabnall, Member of Parliament,
London

We didn't have the faintest clue how bad it actually all was. In retrospect, the government did a better job than I gave them credit for at the time in terms of managing panic, managing expectations of what was happening, or going to happen. I assumed that they wouldn't even know where to start, when I left – not because I would hold that place together, but because I often displayed glimpses of morality that were painfully absent from many of my peers. So, damage limitation; they weren't giving out numbers of dead (or dying), they were giving constant reassurances that they were working on the problem, they were even suggesting that things were getting better. The hospitals that had closed were forgotten about in updates suddenly, and the presenters were caked in make-up so that, to the casual observer, you wouldn't notice that they were red-eyed and just as sickly as you were.

And, somehow, I still wasn't ill. I wasn't even sniffling. I walked to the centre of London – which was all I really remember happening those few days, if I'm honest, that walk to and fro, following the river, noticing how there were no boats moving on it, and when they weren't there it had an almost unsettlingly calm flow to it – and everything felt like it was coming towards an end. There was something in the air that felt like winding down; a taste, I can't explain it any more than that. If there had been another *Broadcast* that day I wouldn't have been surprised. I ended up walking up to Leicester Square from the river, up the Charing Cross road, along Oxford Street, down Regent's Street. It was the sort of walk I never did; I never went into that part of the city, not before *The Broadcast*, certainly; that was reserved for tourists, weekends with visiting relatives. It felt like six in the morning on a Sunday, it was so empty, and the shops were all shut. You could actually see the streets themselves, the architecture, the frontages of the buildings. The pavements, even; you never usually noticed pavements, and yet, there they were. I got to actually look up at the buildings, at their lines where they met the sky, see the cornices, the parapets. I stood outside Liberty's for an hour, maybe, just marvelling at it, at how anybody got away with building a doll's house in the middle of one of the busiest commercial districts in the world. How did it slip through the cracks? A real man wouldn't have cried at that, I suppose.

After that I was at a loss, so I headed down to the far end of Oxford Street, to see if this bar that I used to visit was open, or even still there, but it wasn't, and I wasn't surprised. I hadn't been there since my twenties, and I have no idea why I thought it might have survived. I saw the boundaries of Hyde Park, went in, and Speaker's Corner was there, just completely empty, so I took a spot, a nice open spot, and I stood there. There wasn't anybody else around – I must admit, I expected the crazies to keep their spaces, because this was finally a chance for their theories on aliens and gods and conspiracies by the KGB to be heard – but I was all alone. I started talking anyway, rambling along, because it helped for me to vent, to get everything out. I started talking about why I had quit and that spiralled into other subjects, rambling on and on. It felt good to be talking, at least.

Piers Anderson, private military contractor, the Middle East

We'd been inside the room for far too long, fifteen men sweating it out, worrying that they might have something because nobody came back, hungry and thirsty and stinking, because the showers were behind a closed, locked door. We had a buzzer, like a servant's bell, and it made people come to the window, see what we wanted. Then it just stopped working, stopped calling anybody to us. Some of the boys worried that it meant we were sick, but I told them that was bollocks. We were all fine, none of us were ill. (Course, we didn't know it then, but it was probably because of the decontamination and the shots and the quarantine that we were actually okay, that we didn't all kick it.) But they were antsy, and after too much time spent sitting on crappy beds with nothing to do, they were starting to talk about how to escape. Turns out it didn't take much: the door gave way after just a few kicks from Stevens' size 13s, and we were out into the labs. The guy who came when we pressed the buzzer was lying on the floor, not quite dead, but shivering, shaking, his sweat like an outline on the black marble floor underneath him. We called for an ambulance for him from the phone on his desk but nobody answered, so one of the boys – trained medic, good lad – said that he'd stay behind until he managed to get the poor guy more help. Don't know if he ever did or not.

London was deserted, or as close to deserted as a city that big can be. People were there, just not acting like they usually did, and doing everything slower. Seemed like every other house had police tape up, or a poster warning people to stay away. Cars, as well; there were far fewer cars. I went off from the rest of the boys, on my own, because I wanted some time to myself, to see what sort of a mess the place was in. I picked up a copy of *The Sun* (one of the few newspapers that made it to print, by the looks of it, all ten pages or whatever it was, like a bloody pamphlet), headed into the park, sat and read it cover to cover. There was no sport section, no TV listings, no letters or 'Dear Deirdre', no horoscope, no tits on Page 3; it was just telling us all what we already knew. The editor was having a giraffe, asking the UK to start ignoring all quarantines, returning to our daily lives: He will come back for us, was the quote, and when He does we will be ready for Him, with a country that has picked itself up and dusted itself off. I heard this guy shouting then, over at Speaker's Corner. He was the only one there, so I went over, sat opposite him, listened as he spoke about how we were losing our sense of ourselves just because we thought that God might be real. Aren't we? he asked me, and I said, I don't know, mate. You work in a hospital? I'd forgotten about the whites, so I told him no, told him that I was a soldier. You were in Iran? Yeah, I said, and he came down from the rock he'd been standing on, sat next to me. Aren't you angry, if there *is* a God, that He let you go out there? He didn't let us do anything, I told him, the PM ordered us to go, we went. Did you lose any friends? Yeah, I said, another unit was closer to the blasts. And you aren't angry, that He let that happen? If He *is* real? I didn't know what to say, so I did what I learnt from years of being a soldier: I kept schtum.

I'm sorry, he said, it's been a confusing few days, I'm trying to work it all out. He held out his hand. Simon Dabnall, he said, Member of Parliament. No, sorry, ex-Member of Parliament. Piers Anderson, I said, ex-soldier. Ex? he asked, and I said, Yeah; I think I've just quit.

Ally Weyland, lawyer, Edinburgh

I went to the loo, and when I got back I had a missed call on my mobile from my aunt. She answered when I called her back but she was in floods of tears, gasping back the air as she said Hello. She didn't even reel off her phone number like she usually did, so I just hung up, because . . . Well, you know. I think I knew what it meant. Funny thing was, she didn't even try to call back after that.

Tom Gibson, news anchor, New York City

Our numbers were down. Not viewers, staff. We were running the station on six of us, and one of the runners was starting to look vile, going yellow. I was alright, running off adrenaline. I had the constitution for it, one of those immune systems that kicks in when it's important and doesn't let up until I tell it to. We were reporting on what we could, and one of the few production staff said that they were jumping ship, heading to St Thomas'. Everybody seems to have gone there, she said, it's on the internet. We should go. I told her that I didn't want to, but she was persuasive, and . . . Other people have said this since: that the air changed, and it felt like we were heading toward an end. I could have just abandoned it all, gone out of the door and not looked back.

Actually, that's a lie. I would *always* have looked back.

Meredith Lieberstein, retiree, New York City

I went back home, cleaned my face off, made myself some breakfast – I didn't even know what time it was, but it was light by that point – and I sat at the kitchen table and wrote a letter to Leonard. It was a habit that I had, something I did when people died. I don't know how many times you had to do something for it to become a habit, but this one covered my mother and my father, some old friends, so Leonard got the same treatment. I don't remember the letter now, but it was mostly just how much I missed him. I wrote something about how I assumed that he wouldn't need me to tell him about the last few days, because he'll have been watching them, but I didn't know if I believed that, or if it was just something that I wrote to myself, instead, to make me feel better. I signed it and sealed it and put it in the cardboard box I kept in the closet, along with the other letters, and then made myself a coffee.

Tom Gibson, news anchor, New York City

It's when you're about to give up that everything comes together for you. I had a call from . . . I forget his name, the guy who took over as Chief of Staff from Brubaker. That place was, for a day, like a revolving door, one name out, another one in. He called the studio and the intern answered, and he whistled at me as I was talking about how empty Times Square was. I went to dead air but the call was worth it. They – we – were about to launch something at somebody. That's what they told me, that's what I knew.

Ed Meany, research and development scientist, Virginia

Sam called me for the last time, told me that they had started the launch sequence. It's not with the press yet, he said, but it will be. Jesus, I said, are you alright? No, he told me, no, I'm not alright. I keep looking at everything and I feel so responsible, Ed. Is there anything I can do? I asked, and he said no, that he'd be in touch when this was all over. That was the last time I spoke to him.

PAYLOADS

Andrew Brubaker, White House Chief of Staff, Washington, DC

I didn't hear the launch; I doubt that anybody outside of North Dakota did. Those things made a lot of smoke, but they were only as loud as a plane, and once they were in the air, you'd never know that they weren't just another commercial airliner, or crop-duster, slipping into the background of the sky. The missiles before, the first strikes on Tehran, they had been child's play. We named them after television show characters because it made it lighter for us, easier to process a codename that sounded innocuous, gentle. They would hurt, but they weren't harbingers. The big launch, the one that signalled the end of the twelve-hour warning period, was a Minuteman IV-C, the third iteration of a missile designed to hit five locations over a spread of miles, with full control of five MIRV warheads, each with a yield of just under 425 kilotons. It could travel just over 8,000 miles, and was leaving the US to head to Iran, where it would strike God-knows-what and God-knows-where. I only knew about the launch because Ed Meany called me seconds before it happened, asked me if there was anything to worry about. He still didn't know that I was off the grid, so he thought I might know more than him. I didn't. Olivia – Livvy, my wife – was already by the front door with the bags packed when I got back there. I gave her a handful of the pills from Meany, told her to take them – she wasn't ill, but there was nothing to say that she wouldn't end up dying on me, something I couldn't deal with – and we left. I threw my cellphone in the river as we drove, because if it was going to get worse, if it was all going to end, I didn't want to know any sooner than when it all did.

Ed Meany, research and development scientist, Virginia

All we could do was wait. We had to sit and wait as it flew through the air, watch the trajectory on a little screen, dotted lines instead of video.

I thought, as we all waited – I had nothing to do with the launch, you understand, but we were all departments of a whole – I thought, I'm sure we can come up with faster ways of making these things travel. You know, that was when I thought I'd still be doing R and D when this was all over.

Tom Gibson, news anchor, New York City

We couldn't find a single correspondent still working, either on the ground in Washington or wherever the missile might have left from. I held off, because I didn't know what to say. We didn't even know where it had been launched toward; the Vice President's threat had been aimed at Iran, but encompassed a large amount of the Middle East. I don't think he was picky.

297

Something was going to happen; that was about the best that I could offer. I put it out on the air, because I was told to, because there was no fucking chance of rumour control that day.

Andrew Brubaker, White House Chief of Staff, Washington, DC

I heard a rumour, months after this was all done, months and months, that the VP's wife had passed away an hour before the first missile was launched. She was only in her fifties, and there was no cause of death; that was the rumour, and it put her squarely in the Unexplained Deaths pile. She definitely died of something, we know that, because they had a shared funeral; but we didn't know exactly when. The rumour was, as I say, an hour before he launched the missiles. We think that's what tipped him over the edge; grief and religion and sudden, incomparable power apparently don't go well together. He had made the threat, and it was probably only that all along, but it forced him to follow through.

Mark Kirkman, unemployed, Boston

We had the radio on, and they announced that we had launched something. We're getting unsubstantiated, currently unverified reports, they said, and they didn't have evidence, just White House staffers unhappy and leaking whatever they could. They didn't say where it launched from, when it launched, where it was even headed – I mean, we knew, but we didn't *know* – but it didn't sound like a mistake, or like it would turn out to be bad information. I don't know why, but I was sure that the best thing we could do was pull the RV over to the side of the road and watch the sky in case we saw it. I didn't know whether I wanted it to be flying or not, or whether I wanted it to hit or not. There's a line between patriotic and idiotic, and I didn't know where it lay. Even if it was a biological agent released by terrorists that was tearing through us, it wasn't the fault of any other country, not directly. After a while of standing there I called Ally on her cell. We're at the airport, she said, We're still waiting to see if any planes are flying today. They won't be, I told her, and I told her about the nukes, and told her to get back home. You're safe there, I said, and this could get worse. Could? she asked. She was being sarcastic.

Ed Meany, research and development scientist, Virginia

Perhaps the strangest thing about nukes, even in this day and age, is that they still take hours to reach their target, that people still sit in a room and watch them soar, blip their way across screens. We've made them as powerful a weapon as we can imagine existing, and yet, even pushing them to Mach 4, they take well over a couple of hours to hit their targets. We only had commercial television in the labs, so we sat and watched their best guesses, until the satellite pictures came through on the internal systems. The first Minuteman IV's payloads – collectively code-named Osterman – took out a city the size of Seattle, only surrounded by deserts and mountains and winds that could carry the cloud it made hundreds of miles. There was a report going around about expected casualties, and the last part, the last couple of sentences, they entirely broke protocol for what those reports had to contain. It said something like, All these numbers are based on the populace being healthy (or even alive to begin with, as we've had no updates from the region about the illnesses), so if everybody is dead we won't be hurting a soul, but if everybody is alive in the country with all their immune systems fucked, we'll be wiping them all out, I'd imagine. I laughed at that, at the tone of the message, but I bet that the Vice President didn't.

Jacques Pasceau, linguistics expert, Marseilles

By the time I got to my sister's house the Americans had launched their missiles, and I had lost a few more teeth. She wasn't there so I went in through their kitchen window, the one that they always left open, and I sat on her sofa and broke off bits of madeleines, chewed them with my back teeth, just because I was so hungry. Eventually I put the television on and saw the reports on the news channels about what had happened. The Americans have attacked a number of Iranian cities, the newsreaders not even bothering to hide their disapproval, all in retaliation for the terror agent – their choice of words, eh? – released on Western soil only days ago. I sat and broke off more bits of the cakes and waited to see what would happen next, like the cliffhanger at the end of a television episode.

Joseph Jessop, farmer, Colorado City

We spent most of the time on the road reassuring Joe, telling him that everything was going to be fine. He was upset by the preacher, and Mark spent a lot of time with him in the back, watching Disney with him, telling him about Disneyland. We were heading to Florida because it was somewhere to go, because Mark said that the others who hadn't heard *The*

Broadcast were going to try to head there. When we get there, he said, we'll try and find out if there's anybody else in the world, I guess. And we'll go to Disneyland, he told him, see that damned mouse. Joe loved that mouse.

As soon as Joe was asleep we sat around the television, watching the news as they showed the first missiles hitting in awful computer graphics, thrown together at the last minute, Mark reckoned, because nobody really saw this coming. Usually there's stock stuff made up in the studios, he said, but they won't have been prepared for this. We spent so many years waiting for an attack, it was like a myth, he said. We had made it to Shreveport, so we spent the night there; we'd be in Florida by the weekend, Mark reckoned, fuel permitting.

Phil Gossard, sales executive, London

When I didn't hear back from Karen after a few hours I went out to tell her in person. My hand was still in that fucking condom, still wrapped up. When I wasn't using it, wasn't moving it, it felt dead, like it wasn't even a part of me any more. Seeing Jess like that was enough, I think, to stop me feeling it. I focused on telling Karen, and I drove there on the quiet streets, because either the curfew was working or people were in church (or, the worst voice in my head said, they're dead). I was feeling sick by that point as well, that taste of vomit permanently at the back of my throat. My hand was so numb I couldn't move it, not even for the handbrake, so I switched the gearbox to automatic and drove with my other hand only. I parked in the ambulance bay, because it was so quiet, and I left the keys in the car. I thought that, one way or another, I wouldn't need them again.

The hospital smelled. There's no other way to put it; the outside, the steps, they smelled of rubber and TCP and rotten fruit. The outer doors, the sturdy ones, were locked; I beat on them until I saw the inner doors open, and a nurse – wearing the hat but not the uniform, her face red and sore, her eyes almost black – came to the glass. Go away, she shouted. I've come to see my wife, I said. We're not letting anybody in, she said, Go away. My wife is a nurse, her name is Karen Gossard. Can you just see if she's alright? I don't know who anybody is, she said. She looked so sad, like she already knew. Please? I asked, and she nodded. I sat against the door, against the glass, to wait, but I already knew as well. It was dark by the time that she came back, alone; and by then I had noticed that the hospital was nearly silent. There wasn't any coughing or arguing coming through the doors, just a quiet dryness. The nurse looked even worse this time. I'm sorry, she mouthed – she might have said the words, but I didn't hear them – and so I left, went round the side of the hospital. I vomited, and I remember thinking, I hope that this is it, that this is the end; then I can join them, wherever they are.

Theodor Fyodorov, unemployed, Moscow

I can't explain the way that the human mind works, and I wouldn't try to even *guess* when it comes to women, but Anastasia decided that she was leaving me. I don't want to end it with you, she said. I'm sorry, but that's the way it is, and then she went back to her parents, to their local church. We didn't have much in the apartment anyway, but she took her stuff in a rucksack and just went. I cannot explain women, especially when there's a crisis.

My mother had already telephoned me – this was just before the lines in and out of Moscow went down – and told me that she and my father were heading toward the town where he grew up, Inta, in the far North. She begged me to go to them. It's colder, they said, as if the cold might somehow protect them from the threat of missiles or from dust blowing in over through Georgia or Kazakh, but then, I suppose, it was as good a logic as any. Maybe the cold would freeze whatever was in the air? Maybe the winds around there might protect them, swirling the dust around and stopping the radiation? Who knew? I was feeling sorry for myself, and we were all going to die.

The streets were pretty heavy, actually, with people just being, getting drunk or fighting or looting the shops. We've seen too many riots! shouted one woman at nobody in particular, and I said, I know, and we shared shots of vodka. I went into a bookshop that was shutting down, where the owner was giving away books. I love translated literature, he said, we have a marvellous section, you should take some, so I did. I took books by authors that I had never heard of, but that Anastasia would have loved, Americans and Spaniards and French people, put them into a bag that he gave me, a leather satchel. I don't even need that, he said. I went to the church, boarded up and built out of smashed windows and fire damage. There were some people milling around out the front – mostly from the Church of the One True God, it looked like, from their boards and leaflets and promises that they could save us all, if we only went to them and prayed properly to our abandoning God, apologized to him – so I went to the back, found some crates, piled them up and climbed in through what had been the most impressive stained glass of the lot, the one of Jesus struggling on his way up the hill to his death. I had to take my shirt off and wrap it around my hand so that the glass didn't cut me up, so I was cold, but that was better than bleeding out like one of those people they showed on television, before the stations all shut off. Inside the church I went to the altar, burned out, now just a table with golden fixtures, charred like used coals; saw the candle-stands, the wax burned down to the core, black with the soot. I saw the Stations burned out of their frames, the paper left in at the edges, the middles, the pictures themselves, burned out. Jesus Is Condemned To His Death. Jesus Meets His Afflicted Mother. Jesus Is Stripped Of His Garments.

I sat in a pew, or what was left of it, and I tried to phone Anastasia but her phone was off, or there was no reception, I forget, and then I went to the fonts, found that there was water still in them, I don't know how, because you would think it would have evaporated in the flames. I blessed myself, headed back the way I came in, and was about to leave when I saw the bodies at the back of the church, piled up, dust and skeletons and burned flesh and robes, all the priests from before, the ones who the city said lied to them. As I got closer I saw that it wasn't a pile; they had been huddled together, and I was so angry at myself that I was even in that crowd the first day.

Ed Meany, research and development scientist, Virginia

They launched a second barrage – we weren't even told on the intranet, so we only found out when the satellites were moved to cover more southern areas of the country. The missiles slammed into cities, with towns, and the damage levels varied depending on conditions that we didn't even know. This was civilian populations, factories, hospitals, schools. We started getting messages from the White House central computers every time a target – so, not the cities, but something that might actually be *worth* bombing – got struck, so when they took out what they *believed* to be a silo we had a blunt message about what was destroyed. They took out a factory, the place that they believed was manufacturing weaponized airborne agents. This might have been where they manufactured the sickness that we've all been suffering, the notes said. Sure, I thought. Sure. There was lots of tech stuff, computer stuff that the engineers needed help with, and the way that we were fractured around on the floors meant that the banks of computers were a couple of floors up, so they called up my team to give them a hand. I know, I said, they should have sorted this out, been prepared, but when you've got a maniac at the controls, who can predict these things? (We were all in agreement that the VP wasn't in his right mind, because this seemed totally unfair, totally unacceptable. But then, you'd occasionally look at the TV and see the hospitals, the people still ill, crying on the steps, or you'd see the reports with the estimated numbers of dead, and you'd almost see where he was coming from.)

I didn't go, because I'm not a computer person; I'm a *things* man. I had my stuff, the bodies and the microscopes and the labs down here, and I had everything from *The Broadcast*, all our sheets of useless paper and reports and stuff that meant nothing, that told us nothing. I had my laptop, and I stayed to work on that. After a few minutes I called for Sam, to see if he was alright, and the girl who answered the phone told me that he had killed himself, hung himself. She didn't sugar-coat it or ask if I knew him well, nothing like that, or even say that she was sorry. I don't know.

Hassan Shah, teacher, Kerman

I remember, we were all terrified. We were, all of us, ready to do anything we could to get out, but that was all but impossible. Before this, in the decades before, when war happened – or when we were caught up in other people's wars, stuck in the middle and made to sign treaties, treated with suspicion for years and years no matter who you actually were – we knew everything that was going on. We knew because we had the news, we had CNN and the BBC coming down through the satellites. It made a huge difference: even on the worst days we would crowd into one of the bars that had paid for the television, and we would watch what was going on, the stuff that we weren't being told. We would be told numbers of how many people were dead, for example. We would be told how they died, and where the next lot were likely to die. It was useful. This time, we were accused because our country once gave birth to a man who decided he liked bombs, and then because people started dying to coincide with his prom-ises of genocide. We didn't know where it came from, the sickness, but it killed our people as well; it was indiscriminate. Terrorists are rarely indiscriminate.

After *The Broadcast*, when people started dying, we had no choice but to pile the bodies up outside the hospitals, in the streets. The hospitals were already full before, because they're never empty. More people just meant even more of a wait to see a doctor, or get a room, and they all died before they even got through the doors, for the most part. I stood back and watched them. I run – ran – a school, which everybody would say was noble. I was one of the few who spoke English, which meant a lot; I translated everything we saw on the news, first, and I spoke to reporters when they came in, second. My school was directly across from the largest hospital in Kerman, which meant we saw it most of all. We shut the school quickly, but I kept going in, because otherwise thieves and looters would move in, take everything we had, destroy the place. The people got out of control easily. I watched my wife die, and then my daughter. My only son had died when he was born, so he was spared seeing the rest of his family grind to their halts. Guita, my wife, died of something, I don't know what, but her throat got sore and her eyes started weeping and her lungs coughed blood before she stopped breathing. Tala, my daughter, fell off a wall weeks before and broke her leg badly, so badly that the bone was through the skin, and it wasn't yet healed. The skin turned black, and the pain was so bad that she passed out, and never woke up. They died within hours of each other, like how a wall crumbles: bricks fall because other bricks have already fallen. I waited to see when it would be my turn, and I waited in the school.

We didn't know about the bombs, the missiles; we didn't have a clue, because the satellites were down, the televisions giving us nothing but static. *Interference.* The first one hit about twenty miles away, and I watched it from the window at the top of the school. It fell as if it were a meteor, just a ball of light fizzing downwards. I remember how, one year when I was younger, somebody had fireworks. We didn't ask how they got them, and we lit them – I was still really just a child, then, so I didn't think anything of it, but we were scared of being caught – we went out into the countryside and lit them and they flew up and exploded, but the best part was watching them as they fell when they were done, the embers of them, the trails. We were so young we didn't think about the people that they might have frightened. That was how the missile fell: it dropped, and it trailed, and it glowed like it had been on fire, but this was the end of the journey. I thought, for a second, that it might have been to do with *The Broadcast*, that maybe it was a sign, a flare: something falls from the sky, from the heavens, maybe this is something for us to think on. But then the bang followed seconds later – like thunder, a clap – and the smoke blossomed up, and I thought, Well, this is the end. I think I even said it aloud, to myself, in that room.

I didn't know exactly how far away the blast was, or how long we had – I didn't know if it was here already, and our fates had been sealed, and the smoke would come to get me, the radiation already having killed me, I just didn't know it yet – so I ran downstairs, out to the front, shouted that if people weren't sick, they could come here, come with me. Nobody did, because everybody that was out on the streets was sick, it seemed, and they all thought that they were going to die. Then I saw it, over the buildings at the back of the city: a cloud of green smoke, like something from a Hollywood film, rising into the air. We all knew that the government had laboratories back there, and we didn't ask what they were working on, but I saw it and it made me feel sick, because I *knew* that it would only make this whole situation worse. I ran to the back of the school – the ground was shaking, like aftershocks, but I don't know if that was real or just my mind playing tricks, or maybe just my legs, my muscles reacting to the stress, to the terror – and I went to the basement. We had a basement put in, before all of this, back when the problem was a threat, not a reality, and a far-fetched threat that we would almost take for granted would never actually be realized, and we filled it with cans of food, a variety of different sources of fuel. It's like a nuclear shelter, somebody had said; they built them in America in the 1950s, when they were scared of Russia, scared that they would be attacked and have to run to their gardens. They're always on television, and in films. I opened it up, saw how much space there was – I had never even been in there since we built it, because there wasn't a reason, so we kept it locked, and I had the only key. It was big enough for thirty, forty people, maybe, cramped, but big enough, and it might save their lives. I went back to the street, but there was nobody around, because they had seen the smoke and run themselves, and they didn't want to come around to the area because of the pile of bodies anyway, even though they were under sheets. The school used to be one of the busiest parts, and then people wouldn't go near it. It was all too much for them, I think, but I didn't want to be in there alone, not when I finally shut the door and waited for the madness to pass.

I could smell it, then, the gas, the way that the air started getting warmer, tasting of cinder, and I thought, I have minutes, less, maybe, so I ran back to the hole, and on the way I passed a dog, a real mutt, on the street, lying down. He looked sick but I couldn't tell, so I grabbed him up, ran with him to the shelter, put him in first then went down the steps, pulling the doors shut behind me. I didn't see anybody else, so I locked them just as the smoke rolled over the tops of the houses just a few roads down, and then I locked the next door, the inside one, and turned the lights on. I sat at the bottom of the steps and listened. The dog didn't really seem to care where he was; he went to one of the beds, climbed up, trod around on the sheet for a few seconds, rubbed his face on the blanket then lay down, curled up. They say that an angel won't enter a home if a dog is there, to which, I thought, the shelter was no home, and the angels had already long abandoned us.

I sat there for hours, hoping that I was wrong about what the gas was, what the falling meteor actually was. I listened as the smoke – I think it was the smoke, the dust, the debris, the green gas, so lurid – beat on the door of the shelter, begging to be let in. It hit on the metal of the outer door, and that was made louder between the two doors, as it echoed, I suppose; and it sounded like fists beating on the doors, trying to wrench them open, to get out of what must have been a horror out on the streets. You can't come in! I shouted, and it took hours for the noise to stop, for the wind to die down, for the people to die, if they were ever there in the first place. I checked the food that we had, counted the tins – there were thousands, maybe, going back, enough food for me and the dog for years – and books on the walls, and fuel, but I didn't have any idea how long that would actually last. That would be, I knew, something I'd learn as I went. Come on Dogmeat, I said – I called him that, as a joke, from a game I used to play as a boy, back when my father imported things we didn't have ourselves – Come on, we have to have dinner now. I opened a tin of meat stew and warmed the tin over the cooking pad, and then split it with him. He seemed even hungrier than I was, if that was possible, and I realized that he wasn't sick, just hungry, and then I started to think about the animals, how I hadn't heard anything about them dying. If God had truly left the world, I said to him, surely you lot would have been dying as well? He ate and didn't answer with anything but a look, a coincidental glance because his mouth was open for another bite of tinned beef.

I realized, as we went to sleep – we were both so tired – that I didn't actually know how long we should stay in there, how long before it might be safe, and I thought, I don't even know if I care about being safe, after all this, but I had the dog to look after, so that made the decision for me, really, that we would stay there until it felt safer, which was going to be much, much longer than just a few days, if we didn't die first.

Phil Gossard, sales executive, London

I decided that it wasn't enough to know; I wanted to see her body, to say goodbye in person. I found a window looking out over a hillock at the back, a raised bit of ground, and I could see that there wasn't anybody on the other side; it was a pharmacy store-room, shelves full of medicine bottles and syringes. I took a rock and smashed the glass over and over, then kept smashing even when it was all gone to crush down the bits around the frame. Eventually I had a hole big enough so I climbed through. I misjudged the height of the window, on the inside, and I fell. I used my hands to brace myself – it's natural, to stick them out, to provide yourself that bumper – and my bad hand . . . I've never felt pain like that. It meant something, I have to say; it had been numb until that point.

I pulled myself up but the door wouldn't budge, locked from the outside. There was a tiny window, only the size of a fist, laced with that wire to stop the glass from breaking, so I took my shoe off, hammered at it. It cracked, just, but the wire was tight and the glass didn't fall through, so I shouted and shouted but nobody came. When my eyes adjusted I noticed the bodies in the corridor, some on gurneys, some on the floor, some with their eyes open, looking at me, and I thought that that was my fate as well, that after Jess and now Karen, I assumed, this was it for me; I would catch whatever was in that hospital and I would die there in that little room, surrounded by nothing but kidney-shaped metal bowls and hundreds of bottles of pills. I shouted out a couple more times, just in case, but there wasn't a sound from the rest of the building, not that I could hear. I didn't want to die like that, so I looked for something to tie my belt to, but the light fittings were all inset. I ended up opening three or four bottles of painkillers, fiddling with those child-proof caps, emptying them into one of the metal dishes, and I drank them down, letting them stick in my dry throat. When I couldn't swallow any more like that I crunched on them as if they were peanuts, fishing out the chunks from my teeth with my tongue to make sure that I got every last bit, and I lay back on the floor and just watched the ceiling and waited for it to come and take me.

Mark Kirkman, unemployed, Boston

We stopped at the side of the road when we passed a car sitting in the middle of the lanes. We were on back roads – Joseph called it The Scenic Route, and he laughed because he had never had the chance to make that particular joke before, I guess – and we had barely seen any other cars, so this one made us slow down, pull over. I want to check they're alright, I told the others; I could see the back of their heads through the rear window, so I knew that they were in the car, that it wasn't abandoned. Besides which, there wasn't anywhere for a couple of miles in either direction, so they wouldn't have walked. Maybe they need help with a tyre or something? Joseph called. I told him to stay put, because I could smell that it was wrong. He was ill, anyway, his throat like grit, and his muscles were aching him; I could tell from the way that he rubbed his arms as he drove, that he kept flexing his knuckles. Jennifer was in the back, asleep; she was worse than Joseph, running a fever, coughing up spots of blood onto a handkerchief. She didn't have long, I guessed, and I didn't want to risk Joseph's last few hours with her, you know? In case.

I walked along the central line of the road, followed the curve of their car, and saw a man glancing at me in the wing mirror, and I thought, Licence and registration, such a callback to stuff I barely remembered. He looked awful, his face yellow, his eyes almost completely red from something, I have no idea what. Next to him was a woman, a wife or a girlfriend, I don't know, and her mouth was red with her blood, and it had all run down her top, over her chest, onto her jeans. I can't think of what hospital is near here, the guy said, can you help us? I didn't go any closer, because I didn't know what was wrong with them, and because I worried that I would catch it. (I'd started wondering, properly, if that was impossible; if, for some reason, not hearing *The Broadcast* meant we weren't susceptible, because Joe was fine, and I was fine, feeling absolutely fine. It was a thought that Ally had had as well, and it seemed, I don't know, plausible, maybe.) I should be dead by now, the man said, and I couldn't argue with him, so I just backed away. I left them there, because there was nothing I could do.

I told Joseph to drive, and didn't say that they were alive, or that maybe just the man was. I didn't tell him because he would have wanted to help, and that wasn't going to happen. We pulled over at a rest stop an hour later, where there was a queue for the three vending machines, each nearly empty. Joseph queued with Joe to get the food and I called Ally from the lot. Jesus, she said, I'm so glad to hear you're alright. Why wouldn't we be? I asked, and she said, Well, we saw about the bombs on the news, wanted to check you were okay. The bombs? Aye, she said; New York's looking pretty much done for, I reckon.

Meredith Lieberstein, retiree, New York City

There was this awful, clichéd second when I woke up where I thought that the shake of the bed was coming from Leonard, that he had never died. He used to get up in the night to pee, and when he came back he always did a little jump onto the bed, a jaunty little move, to wake me up, I don't know. I used to call it his Dick Van Dyke, and the bed would shake when he did it, shift slightly on the floor, sometimes, because the floor was hardwood, and I would tell him off. So when it shook I thought that it was him, and I said his name, even, in my best disapproving voice, and then I remembered through the near-sleep that he was dead. I didn't dwell, because that meant that the apartment was shaking for a different reason, and then the second one came and I didn't even have time to pull myself together. I remember when I was younger I went

314

to Universal Studios, to the rides there, and we went on *Earthquake*. They shake a room that you're in, and books fly off shelves and car alarms start, and you brace yourself, because the gas main, it's about to blow, they shout, so you brace, and the flames roar up, and it's exciting. In the apartment, I could hear the car alarms and the books, all of Leonard's books were flying off the shelves, slamming against the wall, even the antiques, and everything was shaky and blurry, because I didn't have my glasses on, and the sound was fuzzy, as if the ship that you're on is about to capsize and throw you into the waves. Then the dust came in through the window, filled the room, and I heard people screaming on the street, so I got under the desk in case the shaking started again. I really thought that it could be an earthquake, I really did. It would have been better if it was, I suppose.

Tom Gibson, news anchor, New York City

I still don't know how many people were involved in those bombings, how many people were willing to die for whatever it was that they actually died for. We had another video from that terrorist in his cave, and we aired it, but by that point I'm not sure that people were even watching us. He sat in front of the camera, same as before – there weren't any explosions, so he wasn't anywhere near the sites that had been obliterated, assuming that the time-stamp on the film was accurate – and he said that we had proven him right. You will always find what you're looking for, he said, and then he coughed, and I realized that he looked sick, like the illness that everybody was getting, he had it as well. He seemed bemused, almost, about the scale of the attack. We have punished you; this is because you denied us, he said. Rumours went round after it aired: of terrorists in New York hotels wearing gas masks, proving definitively that there was something in the air; of apartments full to the brim with men wrapped in Semtex, their fingers perpetually hovering over triggers and timers; that the bombs that detonated around the US were not even bombs, but were actually God's way of letting the planet go in the same way that illness was Him letting *us* go. We didn't know, for sure. I was singularly failing at my job: reporting what was happening.

The first bomb in the city went off somewhere down toward Brooklyn, and we heard it just before the second, which was at the Islamic Center, down by Ground Zero. The third was at the corner of 23rd and 5th, and that's the one we physically felt, that shook the building. We have to get out, I said to everybody who was left in the studio – four of us? five? – and I grabbed a satchel, some batteries, one of the portable Super-HD cameras, got my producer to switch the live feed to sync with the camera. It would be the only footage worth watching, I knew that, so we owed it to ourselves, to the people, to keep it on the air. I was a runner in high school – had the mile down to four-oh-three, at best – and so I took the camera myself, one of the production staff, and we went down to the streets and headed toward the blast. I don't even think we locked the doors to the studio when we left.

Meredith Lieberstein, retiree, New York City

I stayed under the desk for minutes and minutes, even well after the shaking stopped, because I was too terrified to move. I could just hear the screaming and the car alarms, and I didn't know what was happening.

Ed Meany, research and development scientist, Virginia

They threw their bombs at us to counteract the missiles that we had heading their way. They didn't have warheads, didn't have silos, so they went back to basics, had men on the streets to hammer away with bombs, bringing us to our knees. *We* knew that they couldn't win (if you wanted to think about it in those terms), and they probably knew it as well, so this was about damaging us, which it did. It was tic-tac-toe: you fire what you've got at us, we'll retaliate.

Andrew Brubaker, White House Chief of Staff, Washington, DC

We want power. It's all we care about, as heavy-handed a concept as that is. It's why cities fall, economies collapse, toys get stolen on school playgrounds. We saw that He was gone, if He was ever there in the first place, and we said, I *want* that, so we tried to take it. When we went to the moon we planted a flag and claimed it as ours; not a flag of the world, but a flag of the United States of America. You could bet that, if push came to shove and we were dividing that rock up, we'd claim ownership.

We had a boat on Lake Ontario. It was Livvy's favourite place in the world, she always said, so I took her there and we unmoored, went out a ways into the lake. We had enough food for a few weeks on the water without worrying about coming back – there was a decent-size freezer, and we always kept it stocked with dinners, meat for the barbecue – so we set the anchor down a hundred feet from shore and stood on the deck. Couldn't hear a sound from anything but us and the birds in the trees. They won't get us here, I told Livvy, but she didn't look like she believed me. We both took the medicine Meany gave me, gulped it down with champagne – seemed right, because we were both still there, and we didn't know how long that would last – and we toasted POTUS, toasted our own good health, and crossed our fingers.

Meredith Lieberstein, retiree, New York City

After an hour I could still hear the screams from the street, the apartment grey with all the dust that was flying around, so I decided to go down to the street, to see what was going on. It took me ten minutes to get out from under the desk; I've never been a fraidy cat, but that day . . . We lived on West 81st, only a block over from the Museum of Natural History, and that was where the screams and dust seemed to be coming from, so I ran down the road – I mean, I don't run, but I can walk damned quickly when I need to – and then I saw it, or what *used* to be it. People were screaming and climbing over the rubble, and I say rubble, but we're talking about chunks of the building the size of boulders, of cars, and people scrambling over them. I helped a woman climb down and she started shouting about her daughter, saying she was somewhere under the rubble, pulled away from me, climbed back up the way that she'd come. I walked around to the front and saw that the whole building was gone, along with most of the houses on the front of the block, and as I went another one started to splinter off. Standing on the street was a man with a placard, like one of Leonard's protestor friends, just days and days too late to do any actual protesting. The End Is Nigh, the sign said, so I shouted at him, What did this? Did you see anything? and he replied, It was a bomber, ma'am, and then he stood aside, like a magician pulling back a curtain, to show the hole behind the museum, where the houses had pulled themselves down, splayed themselves across the road, into the park, even. In the park I could see how roofs had smashed into hillocks and had pulled apart one of the bridges, debris over the road that runs through, the courts, a playground, the stage. It was everywhere; I couldn't see where it ended. The man with the sign was standing behind me and I asked him if this was the only bomb that had gone off, and he said, There are another three or four, I think. I heard the bangs, one after another. Like dominos, I said, and he said, Yes, I suppose. We both looked at the museum, looking like it had been crushed by one of those Monty Python feet. My name's Meredith, I said, and he said, Pleasure to meet you, Meredith, but then didn't tell me his name, and I thought that it might be rude to ask, if he didn't want to offer it.

Tom Gibson, news anchor, New York City

Everything looks different from street level, and that's something that you forget when you're up in the studio, talking about everything almost — almost — hypothetically. The people look sparse from the studio, and then you get down there, they're still around, the panic making them run from their hotels and apartments. I'd almost forgotten that the city wasn't just me and the crew for a while. Everybody exists in the microcosm of New York, isn't that what they say? Every type of person? They were all there with me, and none of them had a clue what was happening, and they were all running the way that I wasn't. I went toward the smoke, filming everything, the people running, the cracks in the road, and then I was there when the bomb blew in Trump Tower, and I managed to be there as it collapsed in on itself, this mass of tar-black glass and steel plunging forward. I got it all on digital, every single second: from the moment that it broke, to the moment that the dust threw itself up, to the moment that we were engulfed in it.

Katy Kasher, high school student, Orlando

I told Ally I wanted to give up on the planes, that there wasn't anything going to be leaving any time soon. She already knew that, but she was hanging on for me. There was a man in the airport watching something on his phone, saying that there were bombs going off in NYC, and that more were expected, and that the government had launched missiles or something. It says that we should expect massive casualties, the guy said, they're telling everybody to stay inside, get under doorframes if anything goes off near where you are. That made us worry; five minutes later he said that they were evacuating New York City, and I told Ally that we should leave. Alright, Ally said, we'll go back to the flat, see what we can do, try and phone your mother again. We were halfway back along the road when she said, I've got an idea, and she took an exit, headed toward the freeway, the signs for England. Where are we going? I asked, and she said, Liverpool. What's there? Boats, she said.

Theodor Fyodorov, unemployed, Moscow

The roads to Inta were clogged, all the buses down, and the rail was gone, so I stole a car – which, I am not ashamed to say, was something that I learned to do as a youth, when it seemed like something that was cool to do. I stole one of those big ones with the show grip at the front, and when it was fitted it looked like some sort of tank. I stole it from a car lot. I didn't know how far the petrol would get me, so I stole a few large bottles of that as well – another trick I picked up as a wayward youth, siphoning them off from the other cars with a hose – and kept them on the back seat. The roads were hellish all through Moscow, either with the people still leaving or just from their abandoned cars along the roads, so it was slow, but I made it eventually. The drive to Inta was horrific, because the snow hit as I got further north – this was after maybe a full day of driving – and I had to stop and rest, sleep. I found a garage that was shut in a village, but it had a vending machine, so I had potato chips, four bags, and drank soda, and then I slept in the car, parked next to the petrol pumps, under the roof, even though I had to leave the heating on to stop myself freezing. (That made me worry about the battery in the car, but it was that or freeze to death, so.) In fact, I got so hot that I woke up in the night sweating, dreaming about the people in the church. I didn't go back to sleep, even though it was still dark. The snow made me worry that I wouldn't be able to drive anywhere, but the tank attachment made driving through the snow easy. I knew that it would take me the rest of the day to drive home, so I got on with it.

Simon Dabnall, Member of Parliament, London

Piers and I got a Starbucks from some enterprisingly illustrious – or foolish, such are the blurred lines – young lady who had taken over a branch by herself, using her family as baristas. They didn't run the tills, and cash went straight into pockets. Five pounds, she said when I went to pay, and I gave her a note. She didn't even look up; straight into the apron pocket. Fair enough, I said. We sat in the park and drank them and Piers told me about himself, who he was, what he did; and I did the same, only I didn't tell him about Dotty, that she had died. I didn't want sympathy. We had a brief moment where we both wondered if the other didn't know more about the situation – the bombings, the sickness – than we were letting on, he being a soldier, me being a politician. (Sounds like the fine beginnings of a musical, I joked.) But, of course, neither of us knew anything; why should we have been any different from the rest of the populace?

We walked back along the river, because Piers asked about Westminster, and I said that we should go and have a look. We walked for most of the afternoon, and I said something about how much I had been walking the past few days, back and forth, to and fro, and I said, It's a miracle that I'm still as chubby as I am, and Piers said, completely off the cuff, that I wasn't at all fat, told me not to be stupid, and I thought how absolutely implausible it was that there, then, I might actually meet somebody.

Piers Anderson, private military contractor, the Middle East

When we got to the site Simon flashed his pass, and after some arguing and fuss about having to get something from the far end of the building it still worked. It was empty, totally empty. That building is eerie when it's empty. He took me to the

House of Lords and we sat on the benches and laughed. If there's nobody here, and there's nobody in the Commons, who's running this place? I asked, and Simon said, Well, I suppose we are. He was joking, but it took me a few seconds to get it.

Meredith Lieberstein, retiree, New York City

The man with the placard and I were in Central Park along with the rest of New York City, it seemed; the order had been given to evacuate Manhattan, and people were assembling in the park as if this were the world's biggest fire safety point. Do you think that it's the end of days? asked the man, and I was about to answer when we heard the snap. (It took me back to when Leonard and I had just married; we went on holiday to Greece, and we did walks, walked everywhere. I fell down a slope on the second-to-last day, landed funny, and heard the snap of a stick before I hit the bottom. Leonard raced down, asked me if I was alright, and I said that I was fine, and then I tried to stand and couldn't. Don't look! Leonard said, but it didn't hurt, so I did, I looked, and my bone was right through the skin. That was the noise I heard, the same snap, but louder, coming from the direction of Manhattan, and I realized there and then that most everything would remind me of Leonard from that point onward, I suppose.) Run, the man with the sign said, We have to run, and then we saw the first of the buildings on the edge of the park fall, down by where the Apple Store used to be, the site of the very first attack we had days – weeks? months? it felt like – before. It began with a whimper, not a howl, as Leonard would have said; the building, I couldn't even tell you what it was, some tower block of offices, but it collapsed in on itself, and the smoke began to roar down the streets like this was some awful movie. This wasn't the World Trade Center or the Empire State Building; it was just a faceless office block, and it looked like it had been pulled out of the dirt and daintily tossed aside, toward the park. It happened so slowly. Run, the man said again, and we did. Everyone in the park did, or they just stood there, staring, but you have two choices in that situation, and my logic was, This could be life or death, and I wasn't ready to join Leonard, not yet. We ran back to where my apartment was, because that was the only place that I could think to go.

Do you have a car? the man asked, and I did. It was Leonard's; I hadn't driven in years. Can you drive? I asked, and he shook his head, but, right then, driving was going to be faster than running, so we climbed in and I took the wheel, and we went. Are you scared? I asked the man, and he looked at me, blank, and I smiled. Because of my driving, I said, and I realized that that, then, there, was the first joke that I had made in a long time.

Do you think that God's abandoned you? asked the man as I drove, clinging to the wheel, and I said, Honestly? If He was here in the first place, I don't see how He could give up on us now. The man nodded, as if that placated him.

Jacques Pasceau, linguistics expert, Marseilles

When it became obvious that my sister wasn't coming back, that she wasn't going to make contact or reply to messages I left on her mobile, I tried to call Audrey. I don't know what came over me, what I was going to say, but I dialled the number and she wasn't there, so I tried calling my place, still no answer. I don't know why it mattered to me, to speak to her then, but it did, so I left a message on my own machine telling her to call me, telling her where I was. As I was talking my mouth was full of blood, so I ran my finger along my gumline and my teeth pushed themselves out one by one. It was like they had never been fixed in in the first place. I found mouthwash in my sister's bathroom, swilled to get rid of the taste, counted the teeth that I had left – nearly single digits – and then got on my bike again. I was going down her road when I remember a car coming out of a driveway, and I swerved but I wasn't quick enough, and it thrashed into me, sent me sideways and forwards. I remember – it took hours, it felt like, because I had so many things going through my head – but I remember that I *knew* it was the end, because with the world the way that it was, with people dying from colds, with their bodies not healing from injuries, where I thought that I would die from just the blood in my mouth where my teeth used to be; I knew that a crash like that would be enough to end it all for me.

Mark Kirkman, unemployed, Boston

I woke up, showered, got out and was dressing when my phone buzzed. It was Ally, sending me a picture of her and a girl that I guessed must have been Katy, standing and looking freezing cold in front of a gigantic ship, one of those ocean liners, white and blue. We'll land in a week, said the note with the picture.

I went down the bus to show the Jessops, and I realized that Jennifer wasn't in bed any more: she was at the stove, cooking eggs. You would not believe how much better I feel, she said, and Joseph said the same, that his cough was gone. You think it's over? he asked.

Phil Gossard, sales executive, London

As soon as I woke up I knew that I should have died; that I had taken enough pills to kill me, that I should have been a goner. I was covered in sick – mine, I assumed – and soaking wet from sweat, from where I had pissed myself, but I was alive. I pushed myself up to kneeling, to all fours, and I heaved again, this black-red mess of bile, half-caps of tablet shells drifting in it like buoys. The door was still shut; it was night-time, and I couldn't see anything, no light from anywhere but the emergency exit sign barely visible at the far end of the hall, and it was silent, absolutely silent. That part was too much to deal with, so I started making noises to myself, little grunts as I used the wall to get to my feet, started talking myself through what I was going to do. I'm alive, I said.

I went to the window I had come in through, looked out, put my hands on the sill to help heave myself out of the room and realized that my bad hand, somehow, God knows how, didn't hurt, wasn't even half as swollen as it had been. I pulled the condom off it, unwrapped the bandages and there it was, pink again, still covered in blood and pus, but there, under it all was the beginnings of a scab; thin, new, fragile, but a scab all the same.

ANIMALS IN THE DARK

Ally Weyland, lawyer, Edinburgh

I get seasick something rotten, which I didn't tell Katy, partly because I forgot, partly because I didn't want to make her worry about it, because that makes me even *more* sick. Nobody wanted me to be more sick than I already was, I'll tell you that for nothing. We got onto the boat by using Katy again, getting her to beg with the man on the dock, saying that her family were at home. The boat wasn't charging the passengers, even; it was a mercy run, they called it, to get people back home. Like a hijack, I joked, but I don't think it was that far from the truth. Everybody involved was employed by the company that owned the boats, but still. Even the captain seemed hazy on the legality of taking the boat out like that, but we didn't argue. I'm a lawyer, I said; any problems, I'll fight your case. They packed us all on, nearly four thousand of us – and there was a thing on the wall that said the boat was licensed to carry two and a half thousand, so that made me worry that we were going to just start sinking somewhere in the middle of the Atlantic – and most didn't have a room or anything; Katy and I found a spot in one of the dining halls, set ourselves up in a corner. I'd taken the sleeping bags from the boot of the car, some sandwiches, a positively grotesque amount of digestives we got from a service station that was still, somehow, operating, and we settled in. There was water, there were vending machines, there were people offering to head to the kitchens and cook some meals up; it was all rather chummy, actually. Very World War 2. We were by the loos as well, in case I needed to dash for them, and after I was sick the first time Katy asked me if it was because of the man stationed next to us, this fat, lumbering oaf of a creature, stuffed to the gills with underarm sweat and with only a single pair of socks to his name. That made me laugh so much I nearly chucked again. The captain made announcements and apologized about the lack of entertainment on the ship. I'm sure you understand, he said, which we did, of course, and we weren't even paying, so we were all pretty forgiving. Still, a seven-day trip with chuff-all to do but play cards? This is already dull, Katy said when we weren't even neck-and-neck with Ireland.

After I was sick for the sixth or seventh time that day – which was pretty fucking tiresome, let me tell you – I lay on the floor with my eyes shut and listened as Katy struck up a conversation with fat-and-smelly. I shut my eyes and just listened. He asked her why we were travelling, and she said that she was heading home, because she couldn't get hold of her parents, and she was worried, and he said that he was sorry, that he had somebody die as well. Katy said, No, they're not dead. The sweaty man then told her that if they *were* dead, it was probably because of their lack of faith. He told her about the Church of the One True God, how they thought that, when God left, everybody who didn't believe in him in their heart of hearts died, that was what the illness was. I had a wife, he said, and she didn't believe, not truly. She twisted her ankle, and the next day she didn't wake up. I could smell him as he talked, big fucking sweaty bastard. God works in mysterious ways, young lady, he said. I was worried that Katy would set off, say something, but she just turned to me, leant over and whispered, I'll bet he used to be Catholic, which made me laugh, only because I was, technically, and she just hadn't ever asked.

Ed Meany, research and development scientist, Virginia

I was down by myself in the labs, because everybody else was still helping upstairs. True to form, I wasn't making progress – that whole period of time was the most sterile part of my career in terms of actually being able to do what I was paid to do, what I *loved* doing – but I wasn't going to waste even more time moving satellites and punching numbers. I was getting messages flagged every few minutes on the intranet: possible contagious agents released in Iran; lists of where the bombs were going off; lists of possible targets, places that should up their security; lists of where the US government was going to attack next; and, finally, intel about Israel, of all places, saying that they were gearing up to launch something, and recommending that pre-emptive measures be taken. Brubaker had left, that was common knowledge at that point, and he had been my only contact; I didn't know anybody else that I could phone and ask what the fuck they were doing.

Tom Gibson, news anchor, New York City

We didn't know any of this at the time, because we were on the streets, barely alive; my producer was coughing up her lungs, and I was trying to check that the camera was okay, scrabbling around like animals in the dark. The dust – the smoke, really – was so thick it was everywhere, like sand, but I persevered, and we had it running, though I didn't know if the signal to the broadcasting station was still working. I filmed anyway. But we didn't know about Israel, about what was happening there. If you put together a timeline, it's even hazy as to when we launched against them. Afterwards, it would be claimed that it was a mistake, a huge mistake, a malfunction, but I didn't believe that, because we managed to destroy half of the West Bank, most of Jerusalem. It was targeted, because there was a silo there, the one that they claimed they didn't have but the whole world knew that they did.

Andrew Brubaker, White House Chief of Staff, Washington, DC

When you remove the humanity from government you're left with decisions made behind closed doors, and opportunities grasped with both hands. To this day nobody knows who ordered the attack on Israel, if there *was* an attack ordered; everybody claims it was a mistake, even my most trusted contacts, the ones who have told me everything else that happened. I pushed everybody who ever trusted me, and there's nothing. It was a mistake, they all say. We didn't mean to hit them. What reason could we have had to attack Israel? How about, I say, the fact that we did nothing but worry about their nuclear capabilities since before Obama was in power, even? That we spent *billions* of dollars on intel and spies and research into exactly what they were doing? That every head of every country would have breathed a sigh of relief when they found out that the nukes we *knew* that they had were destroyed?

Sad truth is, it helped in the long run. They were in no position to do anything about it, because the missiles we fired only blew up land that wasn't doing anything – officially, according to Israel – and that, technically, didn't have silos or research factories on it. They admitted that those things *did* exist, we had them over a barrel. It was an opportunity, and somebody seized it. That's the constant, ongoing truth of war, right? They could blame it all on the Vice President, but nobody's saying a word. We didn't find out that he was dead until a few days after it was all over, so he might not have even been in power when the attack was ordered. I don't suppose it matters; somebody was in power, and they made choices. We live with them. Israel had nukes, chemical weapons, biological warfare. They refused to sign treaties, refused to turn over their materials, their research. They were a constant potential threat to pretty much every nation of the globe, so *something* would have had to have been done eventually. Maybe it was pre-emptive; maybe it was the accident they claimed it was. Either way, it was a problem solved with no risk of another war at the other end of it. What would I have done in the same position? No idea. Really, none.

Livvy and I were making the bed, trying to get the boat habitable when we heard the bang, and I screamed at her to get down, a reaction based on years and years of security-awareness training. We watched out of the windows of the bedroom as something – and it was a beautiful, clear day, the sort you get once a year, when everything is just blue – but something was rising, in the distance. Livvy asked if it was DC, but we couldn't see that far, so I guessed it was Pittsburgh, probably, maybe Akron. Livvy said that it was the colour of sunflowers, but . . . I don't know. I don't know, if knowing exactly what the colour really was – the damage it could cause, the numbers of deaths it would bring about, because I had that information on sheets of paper in the drawers of my old office – I don't know if that made it tainted, because to me it was the most rancid fucking yellow I'd ever seen.

Dafni Haza, political speechwriter, Tel Aviv

My mother and I watched the news as Jerusalem was destroyed, as most of the West Bank was set on fire. We didn't know if we were far enough away, and we couldn't get any of the local or national channels, but my mother had a satellite, which was how we knew it was happening. My mother asked why they attacked there, and the Americans said, it was a mistake, but it seemed direct, and we all knew that they never made mistakes, not like that. The Americans spent so many years working on their weapons, they weren't likely to make mistakes like that. And the world had always speculated about the West Bank, about why it was so impor-tant to us, to Israel. That the part we owned should be attacked, then? It was so easy to wonder if the rumours were true. They showed the buildings destroyed, all the Knesset buildings and the government offices, and I remembered Lev, that he was probably there, or would have been when they went down. I put him in the building, got him arrested

332

and trapped there, and then he would have been killed by a missile for no reason at all.

We should leave, I said to my mother, so we got into the car and drove north, toward Beirut, because it was safer. That made my mother laugh, when I told her where we were going. Beirut! Safe! Never in my lifetime did I think I would see that, she said.

Ed Meany, research and development scientist, Virginia

The second law of thermodynamics states that the entropy of a closed system out of equilibrium will constantly increase; in other words, the more you leave something in chaos, the worse that chaos will become, given time.

Six nuclear power plants were hit at roughly the same time: Beaver Valley, Diablo Cyn, Palo Verde, Shoreham, Indian Point, and Calvert Cliffs. It was the last two that mattered most (though they all caused chaos, casualties); Calvert Cliffs was built in the mid-Eighties, it was forty-five miles from DC, and wouldn't have been an issue, were it not for the rebuild ten years back, as a way of making it more efficient, a rebuild that meant it was twice the size, twice as dangerous. When you think about it, forty-five miles isn't far, as the crow flies, and it's even less distance still when there's strong winds coming from the north-east, pushing it toward you. Indian Point was twenty-four miles north of New York City, and that was too close. Now, looking back, I can't even tell why they built it. Chernobyl, when it blew, left a thirty-kilometre zone – that's eighteen miles – where nobody could live, nobody could even enter. It was half the size of Indian Point. They had already ordered evacuations of Manhattan, but this made it the whole of the city, most of the south-easterly part of the state. DC was done as well, evacuated just in case – and it was a good job, because we were hit, it did get to the city. They told us on the intranet, said to make our way to ground level, and there would be buses to take us out of the city. I didn't run, because there was too much stuff there in the basement that I had to take. I started packing up a brown cardboard box, like it was my last day, and I had been told to clear my desk. I didn't think it would be that urgent, for some reason. They didn't even sound the fire alarms.

Simon Dabnall, Member of Parliament, London

When we left Westminster we stood on the side of the river, trying to work out what to do, and we ended up in front of that grotesque screen that they put up for the Olympics, useless ever since, relegated to the occasional football match and episodes of *Eastenders*. The news was on, and the footage of bombs exploding across America, culminating in the smoking remains of one of the power stations, I forget which. The one in New York, I think. The British government had made a statement, a plea to the terror group responsible – we still had no names, of the group or the leader or any of the cells, not a peep – a plea to leave us alone. We want no part of this war, the Deputy PM was saying. Chicken, Piers said. We can't stand with our friends in America at this time, because the legality of their position is in question. The newsreaders seemed scared of what *could* happen. With what had happened in

Israel, I didn't blame him. You want to leave London? Piers asked, and I said, God, yes, please.

Piers Anderson, private military contractor, the Middle East

That night, trying to go to sleep, I told Simon about my parents' house, in Brecon. He listened, and then said that it sounded perfect. Will your parents mind? They're dead, I said, and I told him the story, and we agreed that it sounded like the perfect place. Sometime in the middle of the night, when I couldn't sleep, I went and watched television and drank chamomile, and saw that London was on fire, a home-made bomb – unrelated to the attacks in the US, the press jabbered to tell us, to keep us all calm – having hit Leicester Square, starting a fire on a gas main, gutting outwards on the points from that, up Charing Cross Road, towards Covent Garden, towards Piccadilly Circus. Let's just leave, I said to Simon when I got back to bed, first thing. We've just got to get out of here.

Ally Weyland, lawyer, Edinburgh

They didn't formally tell us about how bad the attacks got for the entire journey. We didn't know about the evacuations until we docked, you believe that? They knew – when we got off, we worked out that they must have known, because they had radios, and were in touch with people at the docks – but we didn't have a clue. We were on a boat in the middle of the sea. None of us had phone reception or internet or anything, and the radios were down. But the crew knew, and gossip started, but none of them would confirm anything. We didn't exactly see much of them anyway – they were pretty conspicuous by their absence for the most part. We sat there for seven days, me being sick, Katy worrying, fucking rocky ship on those fucking waves. What did you do during the war, Mummy? Well, I sat on my arse trying to think about anything other than spewing in my handbag, actually.

Two days in Katy asked me if my being sick might be classed as a symptom of whatever it was that people were dying of, and I suddenly realized that we'd not had a single death on the ship yet. I asked around, but there wasn't a one, so we had a chat about it in the room we were in. This tiny little woman at the back – I mean, honestly, looking at her from behind you would think she was a child, she was so wee – piped up and said, Maybe whatever it was that those terrorists put into our air, maybe it's finally dispersed? Aye, probably, I said, knowing full well that those things weren't exactly a science, that sort of weapon, and then, sweaty man said, Or, what if people were dying because He abandoned us, and now, in His infinite wisdom, He has returned?

And the worst part was, there was no argument for either side of that. Fucking logic.

Meredith Lieberstein, retiree, New York City

I looked back behind me, in the rear-view mirror, just for a second, and I saw the light as it hit out from behind New York, spread like a bloom, like a flower, a halo, and I kept driving. Because I knew, right then, that there wasn't going to be any going back. I don't know how far from New York we were when the plant blew, but far enough, I hoped.

Andrew Brubaker, White House Chief of Staff, Washington, DC

We didn't have body counts of the numbers of dead when I left office; we didn't have estimates, even, because there were so many. Worldwide? We were expecting the results – this was, assuming that we picked ourselves up afterwards, dusted ourselves off, counted the dead, assuming that we were in any shape to do math – but we were expecting the results to be catastrophic. We didn't talk about it, not in these exact terms, but we were expecting the numbers to nod toward what we usually use the Torino scale to measure. We use that scale for asteroid impacts, looking at the numbers of deaths it might cause were a collision to happen. Our best estimate, based on the illnesses we *did* keep track of in the US, was a billion people, accounting for everybody who might have died in countries with less health-care than we had. If you stopped and thought about it for a second, about the implications of that number, it was heart-breaking. We take everything for granted, and then we watch telethons and we see starving people in Africa, or homeless people on our own streets, and we say, Sure, give them $10, because it appeases our conscience, because it makes us think that we've saved our brothers. But when somebody thinks that you might have lost a sixth of the world's population, more, if it was a bad day, that's something else. You can't even compute that.

Livvy and I stayed below decks and watched as the cloud from the ground sat in the sky, the colour of piss and bile, and we held each other. The water shook, little waves coming from the shore even though we were the only people there, and it's always still, as still as anything you've ever seen, but we watched it ripple from the edges, and we felt the boat rock slightly. We sat still and waited and waited, because we didn't know what was happening or when it would stop.

I've never felt so useless, I said to Livvy – I had, at that point, been in service to my country in one form or another for nearly twenty years – and she said, At least you're alive. And that was something, I suppose. At least I was alive.

Simon Dabnall, Member of Parliament, London

In the morning we watched the evacuation of America – alright, of key cities, but it felt like something bigger, I have to say – we watched it as we ate breakfast. This was Piers' version of morning, of course, some revoltingly vulgar hour that I only ever saw on the clock when I was slam in the middle of electioneering; but he made eggs Benedict after bullying me out of bed, so I forgave him. I was thrilled that we were leaving, and I told him that as he packed his bag. He had adopted one of my old hiking rucksacks as his *practical* bag, and was stuffing it with tinned food from the cupboards. I don't want to end it here, like this, I said. He thought that I meant *us* when I said that, and I did; but I meant everything else as well. I meant that I didn't want to end my life sitting in a dingy little house wondering what could have been; it felt like everything was coming to a close, and I wanted to spend my last few days surrounded by beauty instead of chaos and memories.

We hadn't been long out of the house when China played their hand, and Piers drove even faster after that.

Ed Meany, research and development scientist, Virginia

The last bit of news that came through on the intranet that I bothered to pay attention to was about China; that they, in conjunction with the UN, were threatening to step in unless we, America, the brave, the beautiful, stopped all attacks. Israel had been the tipping point. There was half an hour, I reckon, where I watched the intranet feed, waiting for some indication of what was going on. It wasn't an instant reaction, which meant that somebody somewhere was arguing that we should ignore them. They weren't listened to, and eventually it was announced that we had fired our last missile. That was that; the end of it, totally over.

Next thing I knew, a spokesman for the Office of the President was announcing that we could confirm the deaths of the primary leaders of the terrorist cell responsible for the deaths, and that all strikes against Iran would be stopping. It wasn't a surrender, from our point of view: it was a *result*. Afterwards, for years, it would be referred to as the moment when *we* accepted the surrender of Iran for terrorist crimes. What really happened, with China being the hero? Forgotten, or brushed aside.

Mei Hsüeh, professional gamer, Shanghai

They sounded the Public Warning System at ten or eleven in the evening, when I was just falling asleep on Mr and Mrs Ts'ao's comfy chair. It was the first of the month, so we thought – because they sounded it every month, on the first, to make sure that it was working – we thought that it could be a test, or my body did, when I woke up. And then it kept going – usually we get three tones, and they're happy – but this kept going and going. Mr Ts'ao ran from the bedroom in his dressing gown. You have to get up, he shouted, we have to get out of here, but then I heard the shower going. You've got ten minutes! he said, then just took the robe off and went into the bathroom. I got my laptop off the floor, took it off sleep, logged in. The dwarf was playing videos from America and Europe, of smoking cities, and all the characters were standing around and watching. I thought that it might have been a joke at first, so I logged out and used the web – which I never did, because it felt so archaic, so clumsy, like news delivered old-style – but there were so many more videos, all showing the same thing, just from different angles. I wondered why they were all so far away, all taken from miles outside of a city, or from a helicopter circling the plumes – I thought back to that video after September 11, when there was the camera on street level, with the smoke coming toward it as the man ran, you know? – and then I realized that, well, they were all dead. Anybody in the cities who could be filming, they weren't there any more. That was it for them. So I googled about the warning horns here, what they were about, and this pro-Chinese peace site had a news item. We believe that the Chinese government are ready to launch strikes, it said, they have sounded the warning horns to alert the population. Please, stay inside, and try not to panic.

I told Mr and Mrs Ts'ao and they said, Well, why even bother sounding the alarm if they don't want us to panic? And it's true; we looked outside and everybody was in the courtyard, looking around, so Mr Ts'ao said, Get dressed everybody, we're going out there to see what's going on. Half an hour later, nothing had happened, and everything was over. The warning sirens stopped, and I went back inside, checked the internet. We had stepped down; we were the heroes, all of a sudden.

Theodor Fyodorov, unemployed, Moscow

I don't remember very much else about the drive home, because it was all white, all snow. Occasionally I passed another car, but after the first one, seeing the people inside it, I stopped looking. I stopped at telephones if I passed them, tried to call Anastasia again, and call my mother, let her know I was coming home, but every single telephone line seemed to be dead, so I was all by myself. I didn't see anybody else for that whole day, and it felt like a whole lifetime.

When I finally got home, the town seemed quiet. I passed the hospital, and that was silent, cars queued up and abandoned outside it, and I passed my old school, which looked like those pictures of Pripyat that are famous, empty and grey; and then I got to my house, and I wasn't even surprised when nobody answered me when I shouted hello, or when I found them a minute later, in their beds.

Jacques Pasceau, linguistics expert, Marseilles

I woke up as I was being dragged down the road by somebody, and I felt them pick me up, put me across the back seat of a car. There was a woman and a man and a little kid, and I heard the kid crying, and the man was shouting at it to be quiet. We have to move, he kept saying, We have to get out of here. I tried to talk to him – to ask where I was, what was happening – but I couldn't, so I tried to move and my whole body just seized up, it felt like. I couldn't even wriggle a finger. The guy turned the engine on, then looked back at me when he saw that I was moving, and he said, I'm a doctor, I'll help you, just stay there, we have to move, and that was fine, because I immediately trusted him. What else was I going to do?

When I woke up the next time I was on a bed, and the doctor was there, wheeling me down a corridor. I thought all the hospitals were full, but this one looked more like a shop. You know those computer shops, all white and shining? It was like that. The doctor looked at me, didn't say anything, injected me with something, and I went back to sleep. I went back to sleep, and realized that I wasn't dying. All this time I had been slowly dying, and now, when it should have been quick and brutal, I had survived.

Audrey Clave, linguistics postgraduate student, Marseilles

In the church, everything seemed to make so much more sense. We didn't have the television on, didn't have the radio or the internet; all we had was each other, and the peace that we all brought into the situation. We spoke about *The Broadcast* – and reading about everything that was happening afterwards, it seems like people forgot what this was all about, what brought this all on in the first place, that it was the discovery, the validation of God – and we spoke about God, and what He meant to us all. One woman, a lovely older lady, said that she didn't mind if God was truly gone. If He *has* left, she said, if He has decided that we're better off without Him, I think we should honour that wish, eh? I think it's not like He's been hands-on, before; we have worshipped Him for what He *did*, rather than what He was *doing*. We worshipped Him for giving us His son, Jesus Christ; for the moral teachings, for the messages in His heart, that run through each of us, His children. Has that changed? It has not. So, now, if He has left us, we go on as before: spreading His word, because He will return, and we will show Him that He can be proud of us.

We all applauded her, because we all felt the same. I don't know, it's hard to describe. Have you ever felt a real part of something? Because that's how it felt, like we were together. Complicit.

Meredith Lieberstein, retiree, New York City

Because I didn't know where else to go, and because everywhere north of the city was out of bounds, Estelle – Leonard's awful ex-wife – seemed the best option. Her house was this lurid little cottage in a place called Blossberg, one of those forest-filled places halfway between New York and Rochester. Hers was the sort of place sold by realtors as a *Holiday Home*. I used to say to Leonard, Who lives in a holiday home full time? and he would laugh and say, Well, we did. He would always add the proviso – At her insistence, of course – because he knew that I wasn't a fan of that sort of abandon with one's wealth. And she was the sort of woman who would insist, you could tell that from looking at her. I told the man with the sign to wait in the car whilst I went and knocked on the door. Honestly, I didn't know how Estelle would react, or if she would even be there. (And if she wasn't there, I'd decided, we'd spend the night there regardless, jimmying her window and sleeping in her beds and eating all her porridge, and not

343

even washing up after ourselves.) The doorbell rang out a song, an awful jazzy rendition of 'Fur Elise', and she answered a few seconds later, after shouting at me to wait where I was. She was in her dressing gown, her hair swept across her head like a flat cap.

Oh, Meredith, she said, I didn't expect you, not after the last time. Have you seen about the city? I asked, and she said, Yes; Christian (being her new boy, thirty years younger than her, with his manicured nails and glamour-shot white teeth being thrust to the fore in all of her quasi-promotional Christmas card photographs) has gone to check on his family; they live a mile from here, closer to the city. What brings you to this neck of the woods, anyway? she asked, acting as if there was nothing happening more important than doing her damned hair, and I had to summon all the humble I could muster to ask her if we could stay the night. We need somewhere, and we'll move on tomorrow, but we think that this is far enough out of the city. I'll be leaving first thing myself, she said, going to see my father. (That meant that her mother was dead; a casualty of, I assumed, the previous week, but I didn't offer her my condolences.) Fine, I said, we'll leave when you do, if it's no trouble. Oh, I wouldn't say that, she replied, but stood aside to let me through regardless. (Leonard used to say, She has a heart; it's just a very, very small one. Ha!)

She peered at the car as I lied to her, telling her what a lovely home she had. Who is that, Merry? she asked (which made me bite my tongue, because she knew that I hated that name). I knew I couldn't tell her the truth – that he was little more than a hitch-hiker, and that I didn't even know his name, because she would have loved that, to think that it was

344

somehow scandalous. Instead I said, He's an old student of Leonard's, and I gave him a name that I remembered Leonard talking about once, and she nodded. As I was leaving to fetch the bags she tutted. You left your shoes on, she said. We have a rule.

Back at the car I told him about her question. She asked your name, I said, and I told her that it was David, David Walls. He reached out and shook my hand again and laughed. Pleased to meet you, he said, and then lugged his bags into the house. I told her you were my husband's student, I said, so lie to her all you like. You're married? he asked, and I told him that Leonard had died. It wasn't until he was inside that I realized that I was disappointed: I had wanted to tell him about my lie and then he would tell me the truth, and he would tell me that his real name was Jesus or Moses or even God, and he'd ask me why I didn't recognize him, and I would tell him how sorry I was, and then he'd say, I'm here to save you, to rescue you all, like in the last book of the Bible, and then he would mutter something and stop this all, and even, if I asked nicely enough, bring Leonard back to life. I was disappointed that he was just an ordinary man, or as ordinary as a man who preaches the end of the world with a sign can be.

That evening we ate a cremated chicken that Estelle and the toy boy treated as haute cuisine, humming and hawing their way through bite after bite, drizzling idiotically named condiments over every part of the dish, drinking cheap, sweet wine with expensive labels; and then we were shown to a spare bedroom. I thought you could sleep here, Estelle said, and I saw that there was only one double bed. We need another bed,

345

I told her, and she said, Oh, I didn't realize, so ordered Christian to put up a camper in the living room. I'll sleep there, David said, and I ended up in the double on my own, in a stranger's house with the world seemingly ending all around us. And you know, I had the first good night's sleep that I'd had since Leonard passed.

In the morning, of course, we woke up to the sound of the front door banging in the wind, having been left open as Estelle and Christian left in my – in *Leonard's* – car, leaving their own rickety piece of crap in the garage. Damn it! I shouted, but David said, Oh, don't worry. It'll work, I'm sure. The keys were under the sun-visor, and it started first time. It had gas, just about, and it moved, which was something. And it was a stick-shift! I hadn't driven stick in years, since . . . Gosh, since I first learned to drive, I suspect. But then, as I was driving, I remembered that automatics were one of the things that Leonard most bemoaned. I used to love gears, he would say, loved the feel of one clicking into place when you made it, when it needed to. I asked David to look in the glove box for a map, and he had a rummage, pulled out a photograph – a Polaroid, if you remember them, faded and thick-rimmed and slightly out of focus – of Leonard, when he was a much, much younger man, standing next to the truck, proud as punch. That's fate, I said, and David asked what I meant. I can't explain it, I told him, but that, right there, that's fate. This is Leonard's truck, and this is fate.

Piers Anderson, private military contractor, the Middle East

The M4 was a bloody nightmare, all of my bank holiday driving nightmares come true as people tried to leave the cities. I never thought they'd be so willing to run, Simon said, and I said something about how they didn't even know what they were running from. It's amazing, Simon said; all it takes is one pillock, and the roads become *this*. Good job we're not idiots, eh? I said. He made a joke about my car then, and I threatened to throw him out on the side of the road.

Simon Dabnall, Member of Parliament,
London

What I said was, Yes, because you'd have to be anything other than an idiot to drive a 1980s Range Rover in this day and age. It wasn't funny, but it made me laugh. Despite what he might say, it got a smile out of him as well.

Andrew Brubaker, White House Chief of Staff,
Washington, DC

Livvy and I both fell asleep at some point. I have no idea how, because we were both terrified, and I was used to going nights without even a minute of rest. My longest run was three nights, three solid nights without sleeping, because the adrenalin kicks in and you just ride it out, and I had that sort of adrenalin, that rush, as we watched the skies for whatever might happen next. But at some point we slept, and I woke up with the birds, hearing them singing through the trees on the side of the lake. I left Livvy to sleep – she needed it, because she had the worrying about me before we even left DC to contend with – and I went up to the deck and sat there, watched the day start, and I listened to the birds and thought about how I hadn't even contemplated what had happened to the animals

347

when we were dying; that everybody wanted a reason for what was killing people, and nobody thought to look to the animals. It made me cry, which, you know . . . It wasn't just about that, obviously; it was everything. Everything just piled up, and without rhyme or reason, and without the sort of answers that might make it all feel better.

Mark Kirkman, unemployed, Boston

We saw everything that was happening and I made an executive decision. We pulled the RV over in the parking lot of a Target just outside New Orleans. We're here for the next few days, I said, because I have no idea where else we can go. The Jessops seemed fine with that; they were just loving being together again. I think Joseph had been almost resigned to losing Jennifer, and . . . Well, a reprieve makes the world of difference. I thought about Ally and Katy, on their ship, and how we had no way of checking on their progress; and I hoped that they were alright.

Ed Meany, research and development scientist, Virginia

I took an hour gathering my things, making sure that my laptop had all the files I needed, everything I could possibly want for research. Most of the data was on the networks, so I could get to it, but there was some stuff that was handwritten, needed to be scanned; some stuff I just hadn't uploaded to the main server yet. It had been too stressful a time to worry about backing everything up. By the time I went to leave the emergency lights were on, and the power had been shut down to the elevators, so I had to take the stairs, with my box. It wasn't until I got two floors up that I realized how quiet it was, how I was the only one left. The labs were on the bottom floor, and nobody had checked in on me, and I had lost track of time. I didn't know.

The doors were those emergency ones, with the bars behind them, and I pushed my way out and onto the corner of 22nd and H. I had no idea what could be achieved in an hour when your life was at stake, but there it was: empty streets, tumbleweeds (in the form of plastic bags), a complete lack of noise, apart from the hum of the buildings. I didn't have a car, so I thought about stealing one, but realized that I didn't even know where to begin. To walk out of the city was going to take hours, but I didn't really have any other choice, so I went back down into the labs, where we kept the NBC suits – Nuclear, Biological, Chemical, like hazmat but better, designed for the army – and I sealed myself into one. I put some extra supplies in the box I had – Geiger counter, Twinkies, bottles of water – and went back up the stairs. It took twice as long in the suit, and I was sweating before I even hit street level.

Phil Gossard, sales executive, London

I had slept in the car, don't know how long for. Hours. Hours and hours. When I woke up, my hand was nearly back to normal, and I could move it again. The scab was thicker, richer, and I could tap it with the fingernails from my other hand and it didn't give. I remembered Jess, and I remembered Karen, and I ran back to the hospital doors, hoping that, if I was better, they would be too. I tried the doors but they didn't open, and nobody was moving inside. I was better, and they weren't.

Mark Kirkman, unemployed, Boston

On the news – and this was anchors-at-a-desk news, not the frantic stuff that had taken over the days previous – they were talking about the damage caused by bombs at nuclear power plants, how DC and New York had been evacuated because of *temporary exclusion zones*, though nobody was willing to put a time limit on how temporary they actually were. The government isn't making a statement at this time, we were told, and they showed maps with outlined areas where we weren't allowed to go.

We were still parked in the lot, but the Target was shut, along with the Starbucks, the McDonald's, the Jamba Juice, the Subway, the TGI Friday's, the Barnes & Noble. They didn't show any signs of life for the rest of that day, well into the next. We were all waiting for the next load of bombs, I guess, just waiting and waiting, because there's nothing else you can do when it's that far out of your hands. You needed the terrorists' heads to prove it was all over, I suppose. We needed a real enemy, to hate, and to let us know that it was alright to breathe again.

Tom Gibson, news anchor, New York City

I don't know how I got out of the city, I really don't. I remember being there, in the smoke, broadcasting to the end. That was how it started to feel: To the end! I remember thinking, and then my producer dragged me away from it. Run, she shouted, because if you don't run, the footage won't last, won't survive, and that would be it. Your legacy, she said, and I know she was just massaging my ego, but it worked. It worked. We ran . . . I want to say that we ran to the Brooklyn Bridge, but I can't remember if it was that bridge or another entirely. But I filmed and filmed until the drive was full, and by that point we were crossing the bridge, and then we were heading toward New Jersey. New Jersey? I think it was New Jersey. I passed out, and I woke up on the interstate headed toward Philadelphia, my producer driving this van that looked like something out of *The A-Team*. We're going wherever we can, she said, and I said, No, take us back. Take a look out of the window, she said, so I did, and all I could see was the smoke, nothing but.

She drove straight down 95 until we got to Philly, and the offices there. They let me take a shower, gave me a change of clothes – wasn't in a position to argue, but the shirt . . . Jesus, I would *never* have picked that shirt – and they let me on air, to tell people that I was alright, to do the update. Being Senior Anchor on the network gets you certain privileges, even in other broadcast areas. There hadn't been a report of a bomb in hours; no more threats, either. The terrorists? No idea why they stopped. We had a call-in, and the woman said, It's because they knew that they had lost. You try saying that God isn't real, that He doesn't exist, you're going to lose that argument pretty damn hard, you hear me? You hear what I'm saying? We hear you, I told her.

Simon Dabnall, Member of Parliament, London

Piers drove most of the way, because he told me that I drove like an old woman. (His words; I have nothing against elderly women. They were my primary constituents at one point.) We chugged along until, I don't know, Newbury or Swindon, and then we were in a jam and some people in the car next to us put their window down, leant out, shouted to us. It was a woman, her entire family seemingly crammed into this two-door matchbox, eight of them, maybe, on laps, total disregard for seat-belt laws. (I joked about that to Piers, but he didn't get that I was joking. Tough sense of humour on that one.) Where are you going? she asked, and we said, Wales. Right, she said, we're going to Manchester. If they could do that to New York, imagine what they could do to London! I smiled and nodded; I didn't fancy telling her that Manchester would be the second target, if there was such a thing. Twenty miles down the road – and that was hours of travelling – there was a man on the hard shoulder, just him and his kids. We didn't ask where his wife was, because we knew, I think. His engine was gone, and Piers offered his services, set to work, shirt rolled up to the elbows. We left London because the kids were scared, he said. Where do we go? asked the man whilst Piers tinkered, and I said that I didn't know. I don't know very much, I'm afraid, I told him. Piers got the engine working, of course, and as we were leaving the man asked us about God, and I swear, I had almost forgotten. Do you think that, if we had prayed, He might not have gone, and then none of this would have happened? Isn't this all our fault, that we let Him go? And I said, I think it's our fault anyway, and I don't think it's got anything to do with God. Whether He was here in the first place; whether *The Broadcast* was Him or not; whether He left us; whether He came back; does any of that really matter now? He looked like he was going to argue with us about it, or make a case for something, so I stopped him. I'm not going to argue this point, I said. We don't know. We just don't know, and, chances are, we never will. Either way, we did this, and we've made our beds, and now we really have to just damn well lie in them. We started driving again, but he sat there, engine running.

Five minutes later, on the radio, a very-tired sounding lady announced that there was – her words – reason to believe that the sickness that had plagued the world in recent days was ended. Wonder if they found out what it was? Piers said, and I hummed and hawed along, all the time thinking about my pills, and about how lucky I was. I hadn't died, and, really, if God had anything to do with it, I probably should have.

Peter Johns, biologist, Auckland

I felt like we were forgotten about here. We had a funeral for Trig, days after he kicked it, and people came from all over. We didn't have the curfew, because we weren't scared of anybody doing anything against us. Stay out of the way, that was our motto. Even when you got over the Ditch, they kept their noses clean just as well as us. We had the service, some of the people from the Church of the One True God dealing with it, and it was just like the old service, essentially, a few different words, but the same sort of thing. Trig would've liked it, I reckon.

Afterwards we went to the pub, and we sat and we drank him under, and we got into this whole thing about why we were left alone. We don't interfere, they forget about us, I said.

Nah, nah, said Trig's brother, it's because we're in Godzone, eh? (We called it that sometimes, because of God's Own Country.) Fucking Godzone, I said, and we drank to that.

María Marcos Callas, housewife, Barcelona

The Church of the One True God said, We need more priests, and we need to decide who can become a priest. I stepped forward, and I told them that I would like to offer my services. One of the criteria, I said, is that the priests should *know* that our Lord never left us; that this is another of His tests. I quoted the Bible at them, the King James version, because I had learned the English: this is a trial of our faith, I said, being much more precious than gold that perisheth, and though it be tried with fire, it will only help us praise and honour and glory at the appearing of Jesus Christ. Amen, they all said, and Amen, I said.

I went home after that for the first time in days. Roberto, my husband, was on the kitchen table, lying on it like he passed out from eating his soup. He was dead, but that would be because he had not gone to church when called, because he had continued as he wanted. They spoke about this for years, years and years: what saved those people who were saved? And I maintain, it was: and always will be, their faith.

Simon Dabnall, Member of Parliament, London

We ran out of petrol somewhere near Bristol, just after we saw the sign suggesting that we visit Bath for the day. Rather not, Piers said. We ran on fumes until we got to the mouth of the Severn Bridge, and then – at Piers' suggestion, I hasten to add – we walked – *trudged*, in hindsight – along the side-path of the bridge. Luckily, Piers was quite willing to carry the majority of the things we'd brought with us, so I let him. At the other side we saw the signpost – Welcome to Wales! it said – and I faux-kissed it. Piers rolled his eyes. I rested against a hillock, and he sat next to me. You know it's about another thirty miles, right? he asked, and I lay back. I didn't even know Wales was that big, I joked.

It must have been something that he picked up in the army, but Piers' ability to stay awake was *formidable*. The walk took us all the way through the night and well into the early hours, and I was, honestly, at the point of no return from about the five-miles-in mark. My eyes were sagging and tired, even with my glasses off that they might get rested a tad; Piers' were prodded wide open as if they had those old cartoon match-sticks underneath the lids. I couldn't tell you how many times I nearly nodded off as we walked up those ghastly little roads, and even off-road, on trails and paths. I know a short-cut, Piers kept saying, which invariably meant hills and shrubbery and a distinct lack of light other than that from the moon. I'll catch up, I said at one point, lying flat on a short wall. If we don't do it together, we won't get there in one piece, he said. He was right; I persevered (mostly because he threatened to walk off on his own, and I realized that I didn't have a damn bloody clue where on Earth I was).

When we reached the house it was morning, and we were halfway up a mountain without a proper road on it, just a tarmac path between two hedges. I looked down at Wales, the clearest day I could remember, the most beautiful view out over the sea, the hills, the city – Cardiff? Newport? I couldn't tell which – twinkling away in the distance. Piers' parents' house was at the top of the hill, so we ploughed on. It was quaint, but better than that word suggests; all the luxuries of the modern age, along with some older touches. And an Aga! It was quiet in there, and cold, so Piers went and fetched logs and set the fire going, and we turned the Aga on, sat in front of it, boiled water to add to the tea bags that Piers decided were one of the emergency provisions we had needed to bring with us. How long has it been since you've been here? I asked him, and he said, Too long.

In the garden there was a hutch, for chickens, and a bit of cornered-off soil for veg. Nothing growing there, of course, but, in time. And, an hour after we turned up, a cat appeared on the doorstep, so Piers fed her some of the tuna we'd brought along. Really, I couldn't believe my luck.

Meredith Lieberstein, retiree, New York City

We drove up to Rochester, because it was away from any danger. The town was next-to-normal, apart from the people in the streets. We still, even though we all have a TV, we *still* do that thing of standing around the outside of shops and watching their sets, as a community. What's happened? I asked a group of girls, and they said, It's all over, we guess. What is? Everything, they said. The bombs have stopped, the war is over, the illness has stopped. David didn't react, but I started crying, because it felt so *solid*. We had a drink in a diner, opened (the owner told us) for the first time in days. I bought David a Coke, and we watched the news, that awful anchor from Fox that Leonard used to hate having uprooted to

Pittsburgh or Pennsylvania, another city, same awful, arrogant man; but he had the best news. He spoke about how there were six or seven places across the US that were designated as *exclusion zones*, said that nobody could go near them. One of them was New York City, one of them Washington, DC. He spoke about how many people were estimated as having died, but clarified the numbers with provisos – There are numbers still coming in, especially from abroad, and many of those people were sick prior to the sickness – and he spoke about landmarks that were destroyed. He showed the last video from the terrorists then, saying that it just arrived in the studio. He looked so scared before they played it that I even believed him.

Tom Gibson, news anchor, New York City

The DVD arrived, hand-delivered. Security here was nothing like it was in New York, so nobody saw who dropped it off, and they didn't have cameras on the drop-box out front, so it was anybody's guess. It was that same terrorist, same cave, same camera, and he spoke slowly. We have been told to stop attacking you, he said. We have punished you for your sins, and you have learned your lesson. The next time you parade false Gods to the world with your science, your tricks, we will strike you from the face of the earth. He looked serious, but scared, as scared as we were, and ill; his eyes were almost black, and not in an *evil man* way. In a tired, not sleeping, pained way.

Ladies and gentlemen, I said, we have clarification that it's over. It didn't matter that the video didn't mesh with what the government had said, that they had killed everybody, or captured them; it didn't matter that the video didn't say who had told them to stop attacking us, their government or their terror cell or, you know, *The Broadcast*, maybe; what mattered was that it was all *done*. We had that relief then, across the country, both that it was over, and that he was definitely confessing to the sickness, to whatever was causing it. Because, it ended when he said that it was over, so that made sense; they caused it. You need a confession, because it's as good as proof, right?

Meredith Lieberstein, retiree, New York City

When we had finished the drinks – and watched nearly an hour of interviews with people on the streets around the country, all so happy, so glad that this was all over – we left the café. We should just drive for a while, I said to David, and so we set off out of the town. I asked him questions as we went, but he wouldn't answer them properly, darting around them. Do you have a family? I asked, and he said, Yes, but then didn't offer any more. I didn't want to push him.

After a fashion we were at the edge of the lake, and I said that I wanted to see it. It feels like a new start, I said, and David smiled. I'll be along, he said, so I went to the shoreline. There was a boat out, bobbing on the waves; some people on the deck. Hello! I shouted, Hello! It's over, I yelled, because I thought that they might want to know. They waved back, and I saw the woman beckon me aboard. The man climbed into a little rower that they had tied to the back, started to come toward the shore, so I shouted for him to hang on, ran back to fetch David. But David was gone; his bag, his placard, everything. I don't know where he went. I locked the car, took my bag with me, went back to the shoreline, and the man introduced himself. I'm Andrew, he said, and you have no idea how good it is to see you.

Andrew Brubaker, White House Chief of Staff, Washington, DC

Livvy and I sat on the deck and watched the cloud mingle with other clouds that had started to form around it, and we listened as an automated voice – like something from the Second World War, sometime back then – as the voice told us where we could and couldn't go. Six areas across the US had been declared as uninhabitable for the foreseeable, including New York City and DC. What's that they say? Livvy said, You can't go home again? Well, we *really* can't. I know, I said, this is it, I think. This is where we're staying.

Then we saw Meredith, on the shore, and she told us that it was all over, that it had ended, and we were safe again. Didn't change anything: we weren't going anywhere.

RECONCILIATIONS

Mark Kirkman, unemployed, Boston

When they knew there was no way they were going to land in New York, all ships – there were four of them on the Atlantic, making their way over from Europe – were told to dock down the coast, in Norfolk, Virginia. We arrived there a few hours before the ship did, and Joseph and I waited on the dock, watched the waves. The supervisor there said that it hadn't been used for ships as big as ocean-liners for years, because everybody used to go in through New York. They wanted to see her as they arrived, he told us. We used to be US-only, schooners mostly, so we're undermanned. And we lost some of the crew as well. I didn't say anything to that, because everybody had lost somebody. It had become this thing where we all knew that everybody else was grieving, but moving on; the usual stuff you said when people had relatives or family that were dead. No more, Sorry for your loss; it was just taken as a given. When the ship appeared – amazing day, because we'd had a run of them, a run where there weren't clouds in the sky, where you could see for miles and miles – we watched as the crew ran around to get everything ready. We both helped, along with a few others who were waiting for the ship. The crowd of relatives and loved ones went back to the diner, just off the road, and they all cheered when the ship pulled in. They lowered the cargo entrance, because that was the easiest way to dock it, and we watched as the passengers slid off, thousands of them, but none of them pushing, probably because of tiredness, hunger. Joseph said something about how dirty they looked – I didn't know they could look that awful after only a week! he said – but I barely noticed. I was trying to find Ally and Katy, and I knew I'd be mostly relying on them to recognize me, because all I'd ever seen of them was that small picture Ally sent me before they got on the ship. Katy saw me first, and I caught her waving as she walked toward me, and then Ally, who looked horrified that we were there. I haven't got any make-up on, and look at me! Jesus Christ! She kept hiding her face away and making this, like, this growling noise, embarrassed, because, I don't know, she was nervous. We hadn't met, and we'd only spoken a few times, but there was . . . I don't want to call it an expectation, but that's what it was, I think. That we would get on? That we'd connect?

Ally Weyland, lawyer, Edinburgh

I looked like absolute shit. Actually, no, I looked worse. Shit would have been a step up. You have no idea. No make-up, the remnants of week-old vomit caked on my shirt, in my hair, and the last thing I wanted to do was meet Mark there and then. I wanted to have a shower first, at the very least.

On the ship Katy had asked me if I liked him – You know, she said, *like* like – and I said that he seemed nice, but I didn't know. I wasn't going to give her anything like gossip, because it was one thing to chat on the phone, but it was quite another to actually meet somebody, aye? But, he seemed nice.

Katy Kasher, high school student, Orlando

They were so fucking cute together it was disgusting.

Mark Kirkman, unemployed, Boston

First thing they asked was why they hadn't been allowed to dock at New York, because they didn't know. The captain hadn't told them (presumably because it would have caused too many problems on the ship, too many upset people), so it was left to us. From the looks of the dock, that's what everybody was doing, and there were whole families crying when they heard the news, sobbing, being comforted. It was strange; it felt normal, like, that was how we *should* have all been feeling. We told them everything else, then. Formal estimations of the numbers of dead; about the Vice President being found, dead, when everything ended; where was uninhabitable. How did it all end? Ally asked, and Joseph fielded that one. We woke up and it was over, he said. Did they cure the sickness thing, then? We don't know, I said. What about *The Broadcast*? she asked, and I said, Shh!, as a joke, and she asked what I meant. Nobody's really talking about it, I told her, because they weren't. Then Katy asked if we had spoken to her parents.

Katy Kasher, high school student, Orlando

I swear, I was so happy to be on land, to be back, but all I wanted to do was talk to my mom, check she was okay. Mark said that we were going to get to the van and then we'd drive south, find them, and I said that was fine, but wanted to try and call first. Sure, he said, there's a cell in the RV. When we got there my mom and dad were on the couch, playing with Joe. Holy shit, I said, and my mom looked really angry at the cursing, but she didn't really seem to care. You're home, she kept saying.

Phil Gossard, sales executive, London

I didn't move Jess for a couple of days. I didn't go back to the house, in fact, because there she was, there she would be. I can't remember what I did, exactly; I called my mum, who was alive, and fine, and I drove to see her. We had a reconciliation. I told her about Karen, about Jess, and she made me spaghetti, and I slept. I slept for hours and hours. When I went home, finally, she went with me, and we called the people from the funeral home to pick her – to pick Jess – up. They said it would take them until much later that day, so we sat in the kitchen and waited. Neither of us went up to look in on her, because it wouldn't have helped. When they finally came – dressed in jeans and T-shirts, none of the formality you expect, with one of those collapsible trolley things, and a black sheet – they bundled Jess out of the house so fast I barely even noticed that they were there. It helps, the man said as I paid him, that they've let us cut the hospitals out of the equation. That would only slow the process down. He only took cash.

Karen was a different matter. We had to identify the bodies, because they needed to know who was dead and who was just missing, so I was asked to go and stand on the steps of her hospital with everybody else who had a loved one inside. They asked us to not cross the white line at the top the steps until instructed, because they wanted to keep us all in control, stop any histrionics. It made it feel like sports day. The doors to the hospital were open, those tarpaulin curtains put up on the inside, so that we couldn't just see in, see what it was like in there, but we could smell. It reminded me of a rabbit hutch, almost, but more bitter. Sharper. They made us wait whilst they brought some people out – those easily identifiable, I assume – carrying them on gurneys, lining the bodies up against the ambulances at the far side, behind a cordoned-off area. One by one we were called forward, and then there was a pattern: through the barricade, policeman's arm across shoulder, tears, furious nodding, sometimes struggling, escorted behind the barricade, body tagged. They called me up after I had been there a few hours, led me over. I didn't even need to look at her, because her ID was pinned to her shirt, and she looked like the same woman in that picture. She hated that picture, I told the policeman, but then, doesn't everybody? Is this your wife, Mr Gossard? he asked, and I said, Yes, but I didn't look at her face. I just focused on the picture, because it still looked like her, exactly like she did before.

Andrew Brubaker, White House Chief of Staff, Washington, DC

After we had welcomed Meredith on board she told us about what had happened to her, what had happened to the cities.

It's all over, though, she said. Nobody seems to be saying *how*, but it's over. The terrorists have given up, she said. They gave up? I asked, and she nodded. (She wouldn't look at me, not directly, so I worried that something – something related to me – had been an issue. It wasn't, though.) Yep, she said, the main one, on the videos? He said that they had heard from God that they had punished us enough. God spoke to them? Livvy asked, and Meredith said, That's what he told us. There was another *Broadcast*? Livvy asked – she was scared, I think – and Meredith laughed. Oh, no, she said, not as far as I know, no.

Meredith Lieberstein, retiree, New York City

I recognized him; of course I recognized him. How could I not? Leonard *hated* Brubaker, hated him with a passion. I remember, close to the end of the previous administration, when he'd been press officer – I think – Leonard had a picture of him up on his desktop as the wallpaper, with a horse's *ass* put onto the picture where his lips should have been. I kept saying how distasteful it was, but Leonard loved it. I couldn't do something like that myself, he said; I found it on a forum. Funny, eh? So, every time I looked at the man for my first few hours on the boat I kept seeing that damned ass on his face, and it was all I could do to stop myself from laughing.

They asked me to stay the night. It's a two-berth, Livvy said, and we've got all this wine. Seems a shame to waste it. She was *lovely*. We got on so well, which was nice, and it made a change. We . . . I don't want to say that we *forgot* what had happened, but we ignored it, I suppose, for the evening. We spoke about who we were, rather than what was happening. It was nice.

The next morning I decided to leave, because I had Leonard's truck. Their boat ran off diesel, same as the truck, so they gave me a can. We won't need it, Brubaker said, and I reckon you're going to have a hell of a time finding a station with working pumps, at least for the next few weeks. I got back to the truck, put the fuel on the passenger seat, had a last look around for Leonard – I thought I could see his sign through the trees, if he was still around, but he wasn't – and then I left. Did I say Leonard? I meant to say David. I had one last look for David.

Jacques Pasceau, linguistics expert, Marseilles

I woke up alone, at some point. I don't know how many days it had been. A few. Many. My mouth was swollen, and I tried to talk, to shout, but I couldn't. I didn't have my teeth, I felt that much, and my arm – my left arm – I couldn't see it. I was strapped to a bed, thin, I could tell, so I tried to shout out again, but all I could get was wind or dust on my throat. There was nobody around me, no noise, nothing; just that pristine white room, posters on the walls showing stomachs with dotted lines across them, noses with different gradients applied. My doctor, the one who saved my life, was nowhere to be found.

As the pain got worse I got more desperate, realizing that the painkillers were wearing off, and I started wriggling to get free. I managed it eventually, rocking the bed – it was a gurney – until it tipped over, and the back snapped and I made it out. I couldn't walk, and I didn't know why, but I pulled myself to the cabinets in the far corner, raided them for pills. There was stuff with names that I recognized, for pain; I swallowed them down, and I passed out again. When I woke up I saw that the pain was as bad as it was because my left arm was all but gone, up to the elbow, wrapped off in bandages, howlingly painful when I so much as prodded it. But, I was alive. I passed out again, from the pain.

After that, when I woke up next, I pulled myself to the reception area, raided the vending machines, because I was so hungry, smashing the glass with one of the chairs, eating crisps and old pies and sandwiches and chocolate bars, drinking fizzy drinks, taking my pain medication. I found a wheelchair and I pushed myself outside with just one arm, using my leg to try to make myself move in a straight enough line, to try and find some people, or make it to a phone, maybe even to find Audrey, tell her I was sorry.

The next time I woke up it was to receptionists. One of them, in a pink smock, screamed when she saw me. Who's this? she kept asking, and I tried to speak, to tell her – My name is Jacques Pasceau, I am a translator, I work at the University of Aix-Marseilles, that, damn it, is who I am – but I could only mumble the words out, because of the teeth, because of the painkillers, which made me sluggish, like I was speaking through tar. Eventually another receptionist appeared, and a doctor (though not the same one as before), and they pulled me to a room, put me back onto a bed. They asked me if I broke the vending machine, if I stole the medicine, but I couldn't explain properly what had happened. They locked the door and called the police, and it was left to them to piece it together when they arrived. That I had been operated on was obvious. My arm, I heard them saying, was still in the medical waste disposal.

Ed Meany, research and development scientist, Virginia

You get a half-hour, max, from a hazmat suit. You get protected for longer, in terms of the suit's capabilities, but your air runs out at the thirty-minute mark, because it comes from a tank, like you get in scuba suits. I ran out of that before I was even at Reagan Airport, and I still hadn't seen anybody, no army transports, nothing. I had to make the decision there and then about what to do, so I took the mouthpiece out and kept walking, taking in the air from the suit first, then cracking the seal every few minutes, let more air in. It slowed me down, but I kept checking with the Geiger, and by the time I made it to Alexandria, a few hours later, the readings weren't so bad. I called the emergency services from down there, because I felt alright taking off the mask for a few minutes, told them who I was, and they told me to stay where I was, that they'd send somebody to pick me up. It took them hours, and when it arrived it was an ambulance, only unmarked. The EMTs were all in hazmats as well, and they asked if I was alright, looked at my eyes, that sort of thing. They told me not to take off the suit. It's still so dangerous, sir, they said.

When we got to the hospital – one that I had never been to, and that I didn't recognize, with no signs up to tell me the name of it, and no patients other than government employees – they put me in a decontamination room, sprayed me, checked me all over, bloods, skin samples, the works. We need to check to see if you're alright, they said. Three days later they let me leave, telling me that I needed to have monthly check-ups, to make sure that nothing changed. I'll get myself checked, I said.

María Marcos Callas, housewife, Barcelona

We spent three or four glorious days with our churches full of the people, brimming with joy and wonder. We didn't talk about *The Broadcast*, because it was gone and, whilst not forgotten, consigned away. It was merely God's way of testing our faith, and we would write about it in our new Gospel, and it would be a sign. The church had found an author who wanted to write the Gospel, one of those big literary types from America, and he was taking suggestions from all over the world as to the content. My suggestion? It should be always true to the ways that the Lord tested His people in the past. He sent plagues to them, as He did to us; He tested their faith, as He did to us; He blessed and forgave them, as He did to us. This was merely a new Gospel, I said, and it would be foolish to mark it as anything else.

Piers Anderson, private military contractor, the Middle East

Simon was rattling on and on about how we could help pick ourselves back up, how we could try to make something new out of all of this. He seemed almost desperate to claw some sense of normality together, so I humoured him. We shopped in the local supermarket, where people still remembered me as the son of David and Angharad, and they were all very nice. We didn't tell them how we came to be there, or what our relationship was, exactly; we let them assume. Let them have their gossip, Simon said. Truthfully? I think he quite liked it. He was used to people taking it for granted back in London, and I think he liked being slightly different, for once. The villagers had set up a Church of the One True God in the old Christian church, and they asked us to go along. It's really lovely, one of the women who ran the post office told us. I'm sure that it is, Simon said.

We got chickens that week, from one of my father's old associates. You're going to be staying in that house, you'll need to get the coops back up and running, he said, and he gave us three. I offered to pay him, but he turned me down. Favour to the son of a friend, he said. Couple of days after that, we were taking a walk on the hills when we found a dog, a black lab, stray. I said it was stupid to think it was just a stray, because it was as healthy as any dog I'd ever seen, so we took it home, put up a poster on lampposts and in some of the local shop windows. We put up the posters, nobody came to collect him, so then we had a dog.

According to the newspapers, there were over eighty MPs who did what Simon did, just upped and ran away from their seats, and the newspapers put out a plea a few days later, asking for them to come back. Your country needs you! they said, and Simon pulled a face. He didn't go, but he did think about it. You could see that he thought about it.

Tom Gibson, news anchor, New York City

I spent the week in Philadelphia, but they were annoyed. I was treading on their toes. I told them that I'd get out onto the streets, do field reporting, head to the towns around New York, see if they had anything to say for themselves. I decided to start at the top and work my way down.

Meredith Lieberstein, retiree, New York City

I stayed in Rochester for a week. That town had never been so busy, because people were coming from New York City, looking for places to stay. What you had was an unparalleled situation where all these businesses, reliant on the city, were suddenly uprooted. Some of them had other branches, but many of them didn't. Nobody knew what would happen to them all, when law firms had to run themselves out of people's living rooms, and entire generations of family restaurants, grocery stores, department stores, when they were all lost in a second. I decided to move on, because the hotels needed the rooms – frequently, it was to cram whole families into one room, like we were a Third World country – and because I had no reason to stay there. I ran into that reporter as I was leaving, as I was packing up the car, that awful reporter that Leonard hated so very, very much. He was very polite, asking me what I was doing. You're leaving Rochester, he said, can I ask why? My husband passed, I said, and I don't have a reason to stay here. There's a lot of this country I could go to, I suppose. I could see the cogs turning – older lady, dead husband, chance for a story – and he pounced, asked what Leonard was like. He was stubborn, belligerent, argumentative and kind, I said, and he absolutely *hated* you.

Peter Johns, biologist, Auckland

We were all back at work by the Monday, and by the Wednesday, we'd found somebody to take over Trig's job.

The Tieke bird that bit him survived, and the others hatched not long after, all healthy. We called one of them after Trig, which I didn't want to do – wasn't my idea – but that's the way people do things.

REVELATIONS

Audrey Clave, linguistics postgraduate student, Marseilles

Life abides, that's what they say, isn't it? Life abides, we move on. I moved up here, back in with my parents, pretended that the last few years – that my work, my career, my relationships – never happened. It wasn't easy to forget about Jacques, of course, not at first, and especially not after he ended up being on the television as much as he was. We're all really into the Church of the One True God, and we go to church every day, sometimes twice, occasionally more. I sleep in my old bedroom.

Jacques Pasceau, linguistics expert, Marseilles

It wasn't for days and days that they managed to get an ambulance to take me to a proper hospital, in Lyon. The place that I had been in? It was a plastic surgeon's, the man that operated on me was a specialist in nips and tucks. I laughed when they told me! Eventually they got one of the nurses to drive me to Lyon, to the hospital there, to get me checked out properly, and they poked and prodded me, ran tests, checked I wasn't infected. I was fine, they said, physically. Psychologically? You've been through a lot, the doctor told me. You need to take it easy, relax, go through rehabilitation. It's a hard time for us all, but for you? It will be doubly hard.

I was walking the grounds a couple of mornings later, as they tried to track down my sister, to ask her to come and pick me up, when I got talking to a journalist, mentioned what I had gone through – mentioned it, in passing, like, How is the weather, or, Oh, God abandoned us and then I nearly *died* – and she asked me if she could write a story about me. She wanted case studies, of survivors, she said. We're all post-9/11, or post-Katrina; we should all tell our tales, and yours is a good one. Sure, I said, sure, and I told her it all. I left Audrey out of the story completely. I didn't think it was fair to drag her into this.

Audrey Clave, linguistics postgraduate student, Marseilles

Every time he tells his little story about this – about how *he* tried to work out where the signal was coming from with his linguistic skills, about how *he* saw his friends kill themselves, about how he *went to find* his sister – not ran away, like a fucking coward, but *went to find* her, like it was an adventure – every time I see him tell that story, which is a lot, because we French people are still not bored of it, apparently, not bored of talking about it; every time I hear it, it makes me want to vomit. He has his new false teeth and his fucking plastic arm, and I hate him, so, so much.

My mum and dad ask me why I don't go and visit him, see if we can't work things out, and I just say that I don't want to. I sit instead and read on the internet. People think that He came back. Suddenly they stopped being ill, and people stopped dying, so they think that He came back, and if He did, He'll let us know. Or, you know, they argue that it was a biological weapon, and it just blew away, on the breeze, but when have you ever heard of that happening? So, I sit and I wait for another one, for *The Broadcast* to happen again; because, if He did come back, if He is here, you'd think that He would let us know, right?

Elijah Said, prisoner on Death Row, Chicago

I lay there on the floor of the prison for hours or days, I don't know, shaking and passing out, shaking and passing out; until finally the doors at the far end of the corridor opened, and I heard soldiers – or police, maybe – with their guns, come to see what had happened. They took me away in a van, not cuffed, along with five other prisoners that they had found, all of whom had chosen to stay. The warden had thrown the doors open, they told me, and you guys didn't run. This'll count for something; I'd expect retrials, even. One of the soldiers looked at me, I think, his helmet covering his eyes, but I'm sure he was looking at me. Might even get you a stay of whatever they were going to do to you in there, he said. that's what happens for good behaviour, right? His accent was southern, relaxing. We'll see; either way, gonna be weeks before we're back anywhere even close to normalcy.

We drove past a church; the sign outside read, *We are at the end of days.* I ground my fist in my palm, and wondered if Janelle and Clarice were alright.

Ed Meany, research and development scientist, Virginia

When everything ended, there wasn't a reason for it. I wish I could say that somebody found a cure for the sickness in a lab, that they had a sample of something and then, all of a sudden they watched that sample heal itself, or start to rebuild, or kill off the *bad* cells that mingled around with the tissue; but it wasn't. Nobody knew that it was getting better until it was, until reports started coming in that people weren't staying ill, that there were people having heart attacks and not dying. Within days everybody was healthy again. There were people who had diseases who were plunging toward death, and those diseases went into remission; people who had flu that *would* have killed them, and they woke up the day after it ended right as rain. When it was all over, and nobody was sick any more, there wasn't even anything to test, so the press started talking about it in terms that we – the public – could understand. Remember Swine Flu? Remember Bird Flu? It was another of those, the worst that we ever saw. Governments are starting plans to provide everybody with jabs to help prevent future outbreaks, they said, but, of course, the jabs never came. We forgot about it. We forgot about the sickness – not the dead, never forgot the dead, but forgot that we never knew *why* they died – just as we forgot about *The Broadcast*. It became another thing, something that got taught in Religious Study classes, the word of God if you were religious, an anomaly if you weren't.

What do I think *The Broadcast* was? I had this theory way back, that it was television or radio, stuff we sent into space or back from space during the Apollo missions, maybe. I still maintain that's the most likely. Because, it makes no sense. I mean, nothing that happened makes sense, not really, but especially that. I know – I *know* – that it wasn't anything unexplainable, because *everything* is explainable. You just have to know what you're looking for.

Dhruv Rawat, doctor, Bankipore

I knew that it was over when the television – which had been on a screen telling me that there was a problem, but that they were working on it – came back on, and they started telling us everything that had happened. It was the local reporters, and they were talking about everything happening around the rest of India, all the problems, all the people dead. The reporters were so quiet I had to turn my volume up on the television; I was still so hot that my fingers dripped sweat onto the buttons of the remote control. The worst seems to have passed, they said; I put my air conditioning on, tore the sheets off the bed and lay on the mattress to cool down.

After a while they said they were showing a reporter in Bangalore, so I watched again. They were at the hospital where I had left the man, and they were bringing bodies out on stretchers. There's still so much work to be done with clearing this all, putting our lives back to normal; that starts with healing those who are still sick. They didn't mention God, or Brahma, or whatever you want to call what we heard. There were no answers. That was when I saw him, the man without his foot. I wish I could say that he was sitting up, but he wasn't. It was a body, under a sheet, and I only recognized him because of the way the sheet lay flat across his whole body, peaked and troughed like a mountain range, before falling away in the space where his leg should have been, leaving absolutely nothing there to see, nothing to fill the hole in the sheet.

María Marcos Callas, housewife, Barcelona

What was *The Broadcast*? In the Church of the One True God we don't even call it that, not any more. We just call it what it was: the voice of God.

Dominick Volker, drug dealer, Johannesburg

If one thing never fucking changes it's an addict. I did that whole thing, you know: I'm out, I've lost my wife and kid, all that, but that didn't stick, because it was there, waiting for me. Everybody was in pain, and they wanted medication. I had a garage full of stuff to sell. I didn't hear from most of the dealers, so I sold it myself. I sold the house, bought an apartment in Yeoville, started selling from there. You hear all these stories on the news, about mompies turning their lives around after *The Broadcast*, but nobody ever actually does, nobody changes. It's not in our nature, I don't reckon.

Theodor Fyodorov, unemployed, Moscow

I joined the army when it was all over. The Russian army wasn't what it had once been, because there was no need for it. The time after *The Broadcast* proved that, I think; nothing was on the ground, everything was over almost before it began. But it gave me a place to be, a place to spend my time. I didn't want to go back to Moscow, or to even think about the place, and I couldn't stay in Inta. Too many memories, and they said that the army is good for forgetting. It was, I suppose; although, how much of something so big *can* you forget?

Dafni Haza, political speechwriter, Tel Aviv

My mother and I managed to get a boat to Cyprus from Beirut, and from there we got to the mainland. There was no heading back to Israel; they told us the areas that were out of bounds. My job was gone; the Prime Minister was dead, and the Knesset had assigned somebody else to the position, a man who was with the army before, and would offer stability. A year after we arrived in Greece my mother was diagnosed with cancer, blood cancer. She had radio-therapy, which I paid for, because I wanted her to have the best possible treatment. She's still alive, but still sick. I work for the government. I've learned Greek, and I have Greek blood, and they love a strong woman. They call me The Bull, because I don't take their shit. I tell them how to act. I am going to run for office, just local office at first, an economic stance. I am studying economics at night, after my Greek classes. I take every Wednesday night off in order to take my mother to the hospital, and when she has her treatments I sometimes take a full day, and we sit in the apartment together while she rests. My mother eventually asked about Lev, and I told her that he left me, and she consoles me, like I'm sad about it. I have to act slightly sad about it, but she's proud. You're such a strong woman, she says. My mother tells me that everything happens for a reason; that I was there for reasons that I cannot compre-hend, maybe, but that it had a purpose, and had *meaning*.

Hameed Yusuf Ahmed, imam, Leeds

Months after it all ended, I went back to the Jamea Masjid for the first time. It was sometime after four in the morning, and I hadn't been able to sleep properly since Samia died. That one night I lay in bed, totally lost, and I realized that *I* had lost, that it was me that had given up. I got dressed, made my hot lemon – that space where Samia had lain, that stayed empty, her side of the blanket tucked in under the mattress, so that I couldn't disturb it – and I went to the mosque. The door was locked with a padlock that I didn't have the key to – the actual lock was melted away, the door splintering and charred – so I climbed the little wall at the side, let myself into the door at the back that was still intact, let myself into the library-office. The books were still whole; the room was fine, exactly how I left it. All those teachings, bigger than me, more important, were still fine, somehow survived the fire. I went into the main room, all alone, and I started to pray.

Meredith Lieberstein, retiree, New York City

I met a man. Not like when I met the man with the placard, when I met David, but a *man*. His name was Byron. Byron! I met him after I left Rochester, when I decided that I wanted to head to parts I loved from my youth. I used to love skiing holidays with my parents in Vermont. There was a little town called Killington – I remember it as a town, but, of course, it was more a resort, when push came to shove – but I decided that I'd go there, for want of anything better to do. I got there, took a room in a hotel – it was off-season, so most places were quieter, because they shifted from skiing to walking, adventure pursuits, they called it – and I was wandering around the town when I met Byron. He owned a health food store there, like a Whole Foods but, you know, without the branding, and I stopped in there for apples. He served me, asked where I'd journeyed from, I told him, we chewed the cud, as he would say, and then he asked if I wanted to have a drink with him. I said that I would love to, and he apologized, said that the bar across the road was still shut – the owners don't open for off-season, he told me, though I suspect that they were dead, from the way that he said it – so we went to the back of the shop, fetched a foldable picnic chair set from the shelves, made ourselves cosy in the wine aisle, and we had a drink, like we might have done before all of this happened.

I had to remind myself about Leonard, of course, because it actually wasn't that much time since he had passed, but it felt longer. It felt like years, somehow. So, I told Byron, we have to take this slowly, and he agreed. I lost my wife myself, he said, and that was that. We became – and, gosh, I am loath to use the word, but – we became *companions*. He wanted to leave the shop. There are people that need far more help than I do, he said, and he had a lot of money in the bank, he said. So did I, for that matter. We packed up his car with food and provisions and we left at the end of the week, not knowing where we were going. We found it as we headed closer toward New York, we went through Springfield, and it was like nothing I had ever seen outside of my television, people set up in little huts along the side of the roads, in the parking lots of the outlet malls. They were all from the city, we discovered, all those people just having to get as far away from what used to be their home as possible. Some of them were whole families, but a lot weren't. A lot of them had lost people, in the plague before. There were graves, as well. They didn't talk about them on the news much, but they existed. Most of the cemeteries were full, or couldn't cope with the amount of bodies that there were. So behind a lot of these villages – that's what you could call them, even though they were much closer to towns or cities, the amount of people living in them – behind a lot of them there were graves, fields that were dug up for the bodies. For a while, we tried to help some of those people out. Many of them got services, burials – done by the Church of the One God people, or other religions, or just families remembering their loved ones (and those broke my heart, they really did, because I never had the chance to do the same for Leonard). Some of them had nobody; they were just bodies, no names, or no family, the homeless and afflicted who passed away. Those that weren't cremated were buried by us, and we tried to give them the best we could. Some people wouldn't touch them, because they were worried that the plague would come back. That never even crossed our minds. It felt less important.

(They called it the plague, not me. I still don't know what it was, and I don't suppose that I ever will. I don't suppose that it matters, not really, but they all thought of it as a plague. That's what will be written in the history books now: that there was a terrorist attack, and a plague, and it killed hundreds of millions of people, then the world was bombed as part of what we now call World War 3, a name that still feels presumptive, even, calling it a war. Almost everybody knew somebody who had died, and we all grieved, knowing that, in time, we'd heal. Part of that healing would be attributing blame, and so we all decided, by proxy, seemingly, that we'd put that blame firmly on the terrorists, because they were real, tangible. If we didn't blame them, we blamed the government, or ourselves, and those were harder to deal with. But terrorists? We could hunt them and put them on trial, and punish them – even kill them, for the bloodthirsty few among us – if we caught them. The alternative was . . . it was unthinkable, for most.)

Byron and I decided to stay, to help them all out. There were initiatives to get houses built, to get proper shelter sorted – and worse jobs, like organizing the landfills, but we stayed away from those, because I'm not sure that I would have been able to cope. We worked on projects to build some housing at the back of a Walmart, on their spare land that they donated, if you can believe that, and then Byron said, There must be other places that need this, so we went to some other towns in the area, found the same thing, only on a smaller scale, and we offered our help. We set up a company – Residence, we called it, and I say that we set it up as a company, but we just named it and started it, no paperwork, no fuss – and we started helping out families who were sleeping on floors, or worse. We run it, now, for people who need help, mostly; we organize the housing, run it. I don't know, Byron says that it's like guest-houses. We have a field and we grow vegetables, and we share that out. Byron jokes that we're like the Amish.

Mei Hsüeh, professional gamer, Shanghai

Mr Ts'ao died a few weeks after everything finished, after life went back to normal. We don't know why – and Mrs Ts'ao worried that it was the plague again, come back, because she kept saying, He was so healthy, he was so healthy! but he really wasn't. He ate fried shrimp for almost every meal, and fried chicken when there wasn't the shrimp to be had. And he drank so much milk! He's got a taste for it, Mrs Ts'ao used to say. We both have, but after he died I never saw her with a glass of the stuff. We stuck together as well, and she asked me to go with her back to where she grew up, in Fuzhou, down the coast. She had a daughter, apparently, but they hadn't spoken to her in years – an argument, they would not say what about – and she wanted to find her. We didn't. I remember sitting in the offices of the police, reporting her as missing, but even the police didn't seem optimistic. She's probably dead, one of them told me when she was out of earshot, you should prepare her for that. I don't think we'll find the girl. I helped Mrs Ts'ao look for her for a few months, and finally we ended up going to her sister's house, which is where I left her. I'm sorry, Mrs Ts'ao, I said, but I can't stay here. It's not for me. So I got a boat to Bali, of all places. I had always wanted to travel, and I went around all the countries I could that didn't involve flying (which has always scared me too much). I didn't see the cities, because, for the most part, I couldn't; I saw the countrysides.

When that was done – when I got bored, as awful as that is to say – I went to Tokyo. Tokyo seemed exactly the same, like they were pretending that *The Broadcast* never happened. They were the least involved country out of us all, I think! The Japanese kept their noses clean, out of everybody's business, and nobody shot at them. Whatever, Japan was fine, and thriving. After that I went back home, back to Shanghai. My apartment was gone, re-let, and I didn't have any money, so I went to stay with some friends I knew from a forum. We had five of us in a three-bedroom apartment, but it was awesome. We put up fake walls with food boxes, fixed them in, had mattresses from bunk-beds on the floors. They had faster internet than my old connection, and I got back online. My character was still going, and my guild. They still hadn't finished the game. We still haven't.

Phil Gossard, sales executive, London

I go and visit their grave every month. It's like a ritual: flowers for them both, tell them what's been happening. Sooner or later it'll become a yearly thing, I know, or when I feel like it, and that'll be fine, because it'll have to be. I don't have a house yet, and I don't know when I will. My mother and I are living together; I'm back in my old bedroom, which they had decorated into a spare room, but I've got some things in there to make it feel more like mine. My age, and back home. Jesus. My hand still twinges, and it still makes me think of Karen and Jess, every single time.

I don't believe in God now, and if I ever did before all this, before *The Broadcast*, I can't remember that either. Some bloke in a pub once said to me, when I was drunk, crying over everything I had lost, that God abandoned us and then came back. We're His children, they told me, and no parent can every truly abandon their child. Could you? they asked, and I just fucking decked them.

Katy Kasher, high school student, Orlando

My mom and dad were still totally into God, and I wasn't – my mom, when she thought I couldn't hear, kept saying that it was Ally's influence, that I had my faith until I met her or something, but she didn't know. And we didn't speak about why I didn't hear *The Broadcast*, because I think she was worried about what it might mean. I wasn't worried; Mark had a theory.

Mark Kirkman, unemployed, Boston

I think there were more than just us. I think that – I'm tempted to say that I know, but I don't, and I never will – but I think – I'm sure – that *The Broadcast* wasn't God, that it was something else, voices bouncing around off satellites, something else. How did people hear it in their heads? Maybe everybody became psychic for a second. Maybe it was some government experiment, and it worked, and they can't own up to it, because it's a weapon, and everything now is some great secret. Could have been anything. Aliens, that was a popular theory when it happened, and, you know, I'd totally buy that over it being God. As for why we didn't hear it, I told Ally and Katy and Joe that I didn't think it mattered. Why didn't we get sick? Katy asked, and I said, Well, no idea. Maybe it was related to *The Broadcast*, maybe it wasn't. Plenty of other people didn't get sick either, and they all heard it. It didn't seem worth worrying about.

Katy Kasher, high school student, Orlando

Mom and Dad decided that they wanted to go back home, because it was still okay, still standing, and well away from anywhere that had been affected by whatever. Life went back to normal, pretty much. School started back that fall, and pretty much nobody remembered that I didn't hear anything, or if they did, nobody said anything. I got a boyfriend. I did my SATs, and my scores were okay. It was like it never happened.

Then, last weekend, my boyfriend and I went to The Holy Land theme park, for fun. It had been shut down since everything that happened, nobody to run it, I guess, so we jumped the fence. Everybody did it; it was a well-known party spot, because it had a pool, because the cops never went near it. We were the only ones there – that we saw, at least – and we found a bit on this hill and watched the stars, and then we started kissing and stuff, and I realized that that was the spot where they used to crucify the actor playing Christ, where they would put him on the cross and throw stuff at him as he sang, and I thought about how fucked up that was. We stopped, and I said I had to go, and when I got home I felt terrible, so I called Ally. It was the first time we'd spoken in ages, but it felt just like it did before, and she gave me some advice. My Mom asked who I was speaking to, and I lied, because I knew how she'd feel, but then I went with her to church, to one of the One True God services, and that made her so happy I thought she'd pass out.

Joseph Jessop, farmer, Colorado City

We left Mark and Ally and Katy a few months back, headed back toward home. We could have stayed – they asked us to stay with them, to see if we couldn't all find more people like they were, like Joe was – but we knew we had to go back. We had to see what it was like there, because you never know. We got back into the RV and back onto the road, and it was alright, honestly.

We were fine, and we knew that we could always return to Mark. Mark said as much; he said, There's always a place here for you, and I believed him, I truly did.

When we got back to Colorado City everything was different. All the things that they had believed seemed to be gone, really. It was all Church of the One True God this, Church of the One True God that. Ervil Smith was dead, apparently; died in the plague, which didn't surprise me, because he did *not* have a strong heart. There was a new leader, his son, named Joseph, like me, and that Joseph was the one responsible for pushing the group toward the newer church. We went to see him straight away, and he embraced me, welcomed us back. We worried you were dead, he said, and then he apologized for his father's actions. We all watched you on television, he told me, and I asked how, because we didn't have televisions there, and he said, I bought a computer, and you're on this website, and he showed me YouTube. We can't be stuck as we were, he said. No, we cannot, I said.

He explained that they adopted the new church because of *The Broadcast*, only he called it *The Testimony*. Used to be, with our religion, that your testimony was what you got when God spoke to you in some indirect or direct way, guiding your life toward Him, to let you know that you were on the right path. When we asked somebody to marry us they received their testimony, to let them know that they were right to marry; *The Broadcast* was, Joseph Smith said, a testimony for everybody. Apparently, he said – and he was proud of this – they're taking the phrase across the whole church, across the entire thing. We won't be credited or anything, but we'll know, and isn't that the important thing?

They hadn't touched our house; I asked what happened to Eleanor, because I had decided that I only wanted my family to be myself, Jennifer and Joe. She's gone, he said, she left, but we're speaking about dissolving some of the marriages for everybody; we're trying to make this right, he said, conform. (Truth be told, they had no legality to them anyhow, so dissolving most of them was just a case of saying that they never happened. I didn't say that, of course; he reached that point eventually by himself.) I asked him if abandoning the old ways was the right thing to do; he said that it wasn't abandoning. It's adapting, he said. It's very different. Besides, he said, everybody heard *The Testimony*, so they must have been doing something right. (He took me to one side as well, away from everybody else. We want to make it up to you, he said, so we've got some money that my father left. He was a rich man. I didn't ask how much, but the cheque, when he dropped it off a few days later, made me near-hysterical with laughter.)

We took back the old house, and moved our stuff in from the RV. A few weeks later I drove out into Colorado state, to look for schools for Joe, to get him out from under our wing. Every day now I drive him in, and I've taken a job at a restaurant, as a short-order cook, working the grill, that sort of thing. And Jennifer is pregnant, now, with child number two, and we live together in the house on the compound, and we're very happy.

Ally Weyland, lawyer, Edinburgh

We hadn't been together a month when Joseph and Joe and Jennifer left, and then Katy said that she was going, and that just left Mark and myself. I tried to call my aunt a few times, to let her know I was okay, but she never answered. A few weeks after I started trying to call, the line went dead one day, and . . . God, that's an awful term. That's an awful way to think of it, I suppose.

So, I didn't want to go home, anyway. Nobody there to go home *to*. Mark said, Well, why not stay here, with me? And it's a fucking good job he did ask, because I was up the duff.

Mark Kirkman, unemployed, Boston

When she told me I panicked, because I didn't see it coming, because we'd barely been together for any time, and I didn't know what it meant. I asked her to marry me. Did she tell you what she said?

Ally Weyland, lawyer, Edinburgh

I told him to fuck off, is what I said.

Mark Kirkman, unemployed, Boston

She said Yes about a month after that, when I fetched her something from the shop, I can't remember what, but it was the middle of the night and I just did it, didn't even question her. I got back, I gave her the food, whatever it was, and I was going back to sleep when she kicked me in the shin to wake me up. Alright, she said, I'll marry you.

We've got a house in Atlanta, or just outside it, in a place called Peachtree City. Ally chose it, because of the name. I couldn't believe it, but she's quite the romantic. She always wanted one of those big places you saw in *Gone With The*

Wind – she called them Plantation houses – and we found one, run down, ruined, pretty much. I sold my bike, used my savings, and we got the place, and I spend my days decorating, tearing down walls, working on the floors (to stop them caving in, replacing the rotten boards with fresh ones). Ally sits on the porch and drinks lemonade (that I've made) and tells me that I'm doing it all wrong. We've started a group, mostly through the internet, but we've met in person, like a small convention; none of us heard *The Broadcast*, and none of us got ill during those weeks afterwards. None of us know what it means, either, and I don't think we want to. Either we don't care, or we really, really do, but there are no answers, and there won't be. It's like God, Ally says: you didn't know if He was there before, and so much was unanswered – life, the universe, everything – so why should it matter now? We lived through it, and that's what counts. There are thirty-five of us, with a few more who have emailed, asking for details about who we are and what we do. What do we do? We just talk, I guess. Nothing more than that, because there's nothing more we *can* do.

This morning I was in the yard, raking leaves, keeping it neat. Ally wouldn't do anything around the place if she had the chance, so it all falls to me. She goes to work – she's got a job at a law firm here – and I do the gardening, to get the place into shape before the baby comes. This morning I was raking, and then I heard it, static. It was faint and tinny, and distant, and I couldn't tell where it was from. I thought . . . I heard it, and then it disappeared. I sat on the couch, put the TV on and went through every single channel, but nobody was talking about it. It can't be just me, I said, so I switched the set off and called Ally, to ask her if she heard it – like, maybe we were catching up, finally? – and she had only just answered when I heard it again. I turned around and the TV set – one of those old ones, enormous and boxy, left here when we moved in – had switched itself on, but to no particular channel. There was that wash of white and grey and black fuzz, and the hiss that accompanied it, and then, all of a sudden it switched itself off again.

What's wrong? Ally asked, and I said, I think we need a new television. I didn't tell her why.

Simon Dabnall, Member of Parliament, London

Piers and I decided that we'd write our own set of rules for living here. We get up when we want to, and we don't tell the other off for not moving if they want a few more hours' sleep. We keep any pets or animals that we find wandering the hillside that might want a home. We help anybody we see that needs help. In the cities, the deaths that happened get brushed over, I think, treated as something that just occurred; I mean, they're never forgotten, gosh no, but they happened, and they remember them, but life abides, as they say. It's a phrase I've heard a lot since *The Broadcast*. Here, the plague decimated villages, families. We found a cow wandering the hillside a week after we moved in and now we have milk, after a lot of huffing and puffing and Piers getting himself covered in the stuff almost every morning. We need to find a bull now, and then we can hopefully get them to mate, and we'll have even more milk. Don't think I could eat them – we're practically gone veggie since we started naming the damn animals, so we collect them as if they're household pets. Makes sense; we've got the land for it (as soon as Piers finishes building his fence).

We spend our days walking, or taking trips to the library a few villages over. It's up and running again, and we get books that we would never otherwise have had the time to read, and we light a fire and sit there and eat something that we've grown out the back and we read. I never think about government now, and I haven't missed it yet, not even for a second.

I ran out of my pills a few weeks ago, and I went to the chemist to ask for more, but they didn't have them. We think that's special order, she said, bless her. It's a chemist that works out of the back half of a post office, can you believe that? I don't know why I was surprised. Can you order some for me? I asked, and she said that she would, but weeks passed. Supply is slow, she said when I went back, and I said that it was fine. Are they urgent? she asked, and I realized that she can't have even been the real chemist, because she didn't know what they were for. No, they're not, I told her. I didn't tell Piers that I'd run out, and he didn't ask, which either means that he didn't notice that I wasn't taking them, or he just didn't want to say. After a few weeks without them I didn't feel ill, and then, months passed, and I *still* didn't feel ill. I made an appointment at a doctor's surgery, one down in Cardiff. I'm heading there for the day, I told Piers – this was close to Christmas (which survived, thank heavens for commercialism!), so he didn't question it, because I said that I wanted to do some shopping for him, secret stuff – and I caught the bus in, and waited like everybody else, like every other patient. He made me do the customary ahhs and coughs, and then said that I looked to be in fine health. We'll test your bloods, but it looks like your body's doing a fine job. He wrote me a new prescription, which I collected from the Boots in the centre, but kept unopened.

A week later he phoned, and cleared his throat. Can you come in? he asked. We need another sample, so I duly obliged, and, a week after that, he sat down opposite me and told me that he was very sorry, but the doctors that gave me my initial diagnosis must have been mistaken. We've run the tests multiple times, now, and the margin of error on this many tests . . . Well, it's non-existent. First time, he said, in his built-for-singing voice, must have been a false-positive. On the bus back I remembered that virus that I had in the mid-Nineties, like the flu but so much worse, how much it took out of me, how I felt as if I were dying. I remember the doctors doing their tests, and I remember them making their prognoses, and me forcing them to re-test, because I was so scared. I remember how I had to start living with it, and what that took, and I remember how it changed me. And I knew – I *knew* – that these things didn't just heal, or disappear, or fade, not like that.

When I got back, Piers was making lunch. I didn't say anything, because there didn't seem to be that much point, not really. I spent every day after that wondering if I would catch something, if, finally, this doctor's opinion would be proven wrong. I didn't take my medicine, and nothing's happened, not yet. Nothing bad, at least.

Ed Meany, research and development scientist, Virginia

I didn't go back to the government, to their labs. They offered me a job in Rockville, doing what I was doing but with more money, a car, an apartment. I turned them down. We need somebody to tell us what the biological agent was, to solve that, they said. They sent agents, men in suits to my front door, and they begged me. I didn't go with them, because they just wanted something that they could weaponize, that they could do something with. They didn't want the time post-*Broadcast* to be all for nothing. I turned them down. Fine, they said, work on *The Broadcast*, tell us what that was, and I turned that down as well. That's a lost cause, I said; there's no way to track it unless we get another one. Well, maybe we will, they said. I don't want to study it anyway, I said. That was a lie. Let's just leave it at, We had a few good years, and I'll see you when it's time for my pension. They didn't like it, but they stopped pestering me after I shut the door on them for the tenth, eleventh time.

I moved to Portland a few months later. It's a nice enough place, mostly, busy. Much busier after *The Broadcast*, the locals say. I had some friends who did independent R and D here, and they gave me a corner of their labs for research stuff. I can't pay them, because what I'm working on doesn't pay. I had all the test results either on the laptop or on USB drives or on paper, the physical reports. Nobody ever noticed that they were missing because nobody ever knew that they should be there in the first place, and the teams searching the labs in DC aren't scientists, or clued in, from what I've heard. I wanted to try and work out what happened, both of the things that the US government asked me to do, but not for them. This was something else, a puzzle. People used to ask me why I wanted to be a scientist, and I would tell them that, when I was a kid, I loved puzzles. Science – or *discovery*, that's a better word for it – was what drove me, what made me want to learn. There are things that happen, I would say, and I want to know how, why. It's the same reason that people read crime novels: there's a murder, and they want to know who did it. I want to know who did it. I've worked on *The Broadcast*, and on the plague, the sickness, whatever you want to call it, for months now. There are no answers. I have a cough and I hack up blood and something that, I swear, looks like ash, black and powdery, like nothing my body should be able to create, but I don't go back for my check-ups, because I know what they'll tell me. I come into work and I get on with it, because I have the test results and no way to thread them together.

Last week I got a delivery, a UPS van outside the offices. According to the note inside – which I think came from Andrew Brubaker, based on the handwriting, but I can't be sure, because it wasn't signed – I was a hard man to track down. I didn't give the government a forwarding address, and I wasn't listed as living here. I had been paying for everything in cash. I don't know why I wanted to stay under the radar, but I did. Anyway, the delivery. It was files and files, bound with elastic bands, then hard drive backups of those files. Nothing really made all that much sense – most of it was plans for deployment of weapons, nuclear weapons, statistics, weapon casings – but there was one file on the hard drive that I couldn't open properly, corrupted – don't know what by. I got it open in a hex-editor in the end, which meant all the pictures were gone, but the words were mostly there. It was a file about the US's involvement with biological warfare testing, a list of dates and cases and trials and the names of the people doing the tests. The last entry in the file, the last bit of text, was for a test codenamed *Orpheus*, a test spearheaded by Sam Tate, out of the Nevada office; something about biological agents that carried on the winds, that put a stop to people's immune systems. I threw the box out with the garbage and tried as hard as I could to forget about it, and I concentrated on working out how we all heard *The Broadcast* at exactly the same time, because *that*, that was the real puzzle.

Andrew Brubaker, White House Chief of Staff, Washington, DC

Livvy and I lived out on the boat until she died, which was nearly three years after we moved onto it. It wasn't until she was gone that I went back to DC – or, close to DC, to Front Royal, which was where the majority of the government were set up in those days. (They tried putting themselves in Bethesda, but the levels seemed to change with the wind, and it was deemed too unsafe, so they had to move even further out.) They asked me to go in and chat with the new President, who was a nice guy, really nice guy. I knew him from when he was a senator, because he supported us on a lot of issues. They asked me to take a post, and I – gratefully – declined. They didn't push the matter; I was glad. I didn't want to tell them that it was guilt-related, because that would have soured things. They seemed to think I was some sort of hero, though God knows how they got to that point. It's amazing how, when your name isn't on documents, and when you have plausible deniability, you can get away with anything. They let me spend some time cleaning out my stuff, which I did. Everything that they had managed to salvage from the White House was stored in a warehouse just off 88. I didn't even look through it; all the weapons reports that ended up on desks, all the stats, the facts and figures, most of it gone through with black marker, making sure anything important or secretive was erased from history. What could I do with them? I picked out a few, anything important – stuff I knew about but ignored, mostly – and decided that I'd send them to Meany, wherever he was. If I knew him, he wouldn't be giving up on his research.

Livvy had cancer, which wasn't related to anything we'd seen before, not to the missiles or anything. It can just happen, the surgeon said, these things can just appear. That's part of being human, he said; sometimes we just stop, and there's nobody else – nothing else – to blame. How long? we asked, and he said that he didn't know. It depends, he said. Hopefully we can get to it in time. He was being nice, but we knew it was going to be fatal from the second we got the diagnosis, because he said that they had to rush, but there wasn't actually any sense of urgency to it. Livvy seemed okay with it; she let them try to cut it out, telling them it was fine as long as it wouldn't hamper her last few days, as long as it didn't affect her motor functions or her memories, anything like that, but they couldn't get it all, and it would be too much to hit with chemo. We can try, they said, but she turned them down. It's better if I just deal with it, she said. We were on the boat for a year after that, and then she didn't wake up, one day. I think I knew it was going to happen the night before it did, because I lay in bed and couldn't sleep, and I watched her sleeping, which I never did; but that night, it seemed like something I should do. I finally slept sometime around four, and when I woke up, before six, she was gone – as if she didn't want to leave with me watching.

After her funeral – a Church of the One True God service, for the sake of the family, not me, or her – I was at a loss, so I went back into the city. Nobody had been in DC apart from government people, soldiers, that documentary crew who did the *Ghost Towns* film that got the Oscar, and I wanted to see it for myself. It was fenced off, because when you crossed that line and went into the heart of the city the radiation was bad enough to cause sickness, sickness that would only get worse the longer you stayed, and would be fatal in most cases, but that didn't stop me. I probably could have gone any time of day, with a team, wearing suits to protect us, but that seemed to almost defeat the point. I went at night, in through one of the safe houses just outside the city, the tunnels that stretched for miles, with their golf carts to drive you through. It took me hours to get to the city itself. It was amazing, completely empty in a way that I had never seen it, absolutely dark. None of the street lights were on; just the moon to light it. As I got there it was turning to dawn, and I watched it coming up. I didn't take a Geiger with me, because I knew what it would say, that the clicking as it warned me would spoil this. It was nearly midday when I got to the White House, and I found my old office, sat in my old chair. They hadn't painted, yet; it was customary for the new staff to paint every room completely when they moved in, to put their own stamp on the building. But the guys who took over from us for those few days? They hadn't even removed my name from the door. The team outside spotted me on the security cameras – they were up all around the city, to prevent intruders like me, I suppose – and they swarmed the White House, bundled me into the back of a van lined with thick tarpaulin, drove me out of the city, sprayed me down, stripped me. Doctors examined me, where my skin had blistered along the line of my clothes. We're going to have to run some tests, they said, but they had that same look in their eyes as when the doctor diagnosed Livvy, so I told them I wasn't submitting to it. They kept me locked in a room for a few hours, but I pulled some strings and got myself released, and I went back to the boat and lay on the deck.

The doctors warned me that the drugs they had given me might make me see things, hear things; so when I was lying there, and I could swear that I started hearing the static again, I wasn't even close to surprised. I started talking to Livvy instead, in case she could hear me, and I stared at the sun and waited to see if anything would happen to us all before I died.

ACKNOWLEDGMENTS

This novel was, with its multitude of voices and synchronous events, a bit of a devil to write. Thanks to my invaluable readers and idea-thrower-arounders for helping beat it into shape: Holly Howitt, Sam Barlow, Tim Glister, John Smythe and Vikki Chandler.

And, even after those early beatings, the incredible editorial team at Blue Door helped me see that it still needed another ten rounds in the ring: the wonderful Laura Deacon, the insightful Emad Akhtar, and the estimable Patrick Janson-Smith. They saw everything that the novel could be, and they tirelessly helped to make it better. Thanks to them, along with the rest of the gang at HarperCollins UK.

Thanks then to Sam Copeland, my fantastic agent, who helped shape both this book, and the many others soon to come. He passionately goes above and beyond, and I'm incredibly grateful to him.

Special gratitude to early teachers, who had faith in writing (and whose names might well be misspelled here, thanks to the passage of time and the failings of memory): Mrs Ogley, Mr Moretta and Mrs Babuta.

And lastly, thanks to my family, every single one of you. Without you, I wouldn't have had the chance to write the book, let alone these acknowledgments.

Here's an exclusive extract from

THE MACHINE

by James Smythe

Coming soon

blue door

There are hundreds of files inside, all date-stamped, and all under an umbrella of his name. She presses the first one, which she can barely remember being recorded because it was so long ago, and waits as it loads. A bar appears on the screen and an icon of a play button. She presses it and the Machine starts thrumming. The file starts loading. The technology isn't there with the size of these files: the pristine nature of exactly what they've recorded, and how long they are. The amount of data that they contained inside the packets of the audio files themselves . . . Everything important. The audio is essentially worthless. It's wrapping paper. But the files are enormous, and streaming them all is impractical. It would take far too long; too much waiting for them to load. She should be using the hard drive of the Machine itself, but she wants to check it works first. That, and she wants to hear him. She's too eager.

Then the first file is done queuing itself up, and it plays automatically, and she hears somebody clearing their throat in the background, the click of something. Somebody sitting down. She doesn't know where the speakers are in the casement, but they're somewhere, or it uses the metal itself as a speaker. Maybe that's where the vibrations come from: internal sound channelled outwards. She saw that once, when she was a teenager: something you could plug your iPod into and it would turn any glass table or window into a speaker. She remembers being impressed by it: as the boys that she knew ran around her parents' house plugging it into everything they could find, dancing in their room full of art pieces as the glass covering a statue that her father described as priceless vibrated with the sounds of trilling keyboards and squawked singing.

They danced on the rugs, because of the novelty of not being able to hear their own footfalls.

The first voice she hears is that of a stranger. It must be one of the doctors who had worked with him.

We're ready? Can you say your name for us? it asks.

Victor McAdams. His voice is suddenly full in the room. She can't remember exactly how long it's been since she heard his voice talking properly, saying sentences. Long enough that it's become a memory, rather than something tangible. She's forgotten how deep it was. How it cracks at the higher end. The trepidation as he says their surname, and the pause that hangs in the air afterwards. She can hear him breathing.

And could you state your rank and ID number, for the record?

Captain. Two-five-two-three-two-three-oh-two.

Great. Don't be nervous, the voice says to him. You know why you're here?

Yes sir.

Don't call me sir. My name's Robert. First-name terms here, Victor.

Vic.

Vic it is. Beth hears the smile. Shall we begin? Beth stops the recording. The voices hang in the air, like the dust. It works. The files are intact. Her first worry dealt with. She presses the screen and goes back a few stages, back to the central menu, and ticks the box to copy the contents of the drive to the Machine itself. The vibrations start as it accesses its drives. It's older than her tiny hard drive by a couple of years, and she thinks about the information – about the recordings of Vic's voice, pages and pages of entries where he sat in a room and spoke about the things that he didn't want to remember any more – she thinks about it all expanding as it fills the drive of the Machine. It gives her a time-bar for the download, of hours rather than minutes. The slowest crawl. She goes to the main room of her flat and thinks about how she should tidy more. It's become worse since she got invested in this project, stealing both her time and her energy. The kids have suffered most: mountains of marking sit by the front door, and she knows that they need to have most of it done before the summer holidays. Her deadlines are theirs. She has six weeks coming up, and she's planned how she'll break it down by the day. She's begun stockpiling food and provisions: the kitchen is brimming with canned foods, and the bathroom has toilet-roll packets stacked behind the door. The plan involves her not leaving the flat for the first week because Vic will most likely need her. He won't be able to be left alone for more than a couple of hours, not for at least that time, and probably much longer. The schedule of how those six weeks will work is punishing, she knows, but needs must. She has printed them out, a week per sheet of A4 paper, and she's put them on the fridge under a large magnet that Vic got given by his parents when he was a child, that he hung onto. She's kept it as well, like a trophy. Proof that he was once real. She can tell that people don't believe her, when she talks about him. It's like he's a ghost. She says, He used to be a soldier, and they smile, and they ask where he is now. She tells them that he's away, serving still. They look at her – or, if she's let them past that barrier, at her flat – and they know that it's a lie. Nobody's away serving any more. Everything where they were is rubble. So she has to tidy, and she has to make sure that she knows exactly how the Machine works. Two weeks before the end of term.

She has videos on the computer, kept on the desktop. They're taken from a forum about these things, where she's nothing more than a username that bears no relation to who she is. Numbers and letters chosen at random, on purpose. She doesn't know if the forums are monitored – or who would be monitoring them – but just in case. She grabbed the videos over one long weekend, determined in case the site ever suddenly disappeared. She's renamed the videos with numbers, so that she knows what order she's learning them in, and she's already watched them tens of times, but never with anything to practice on. It's different when there's a practical application. Plus, there's a difference in the firmware in the Machines, and she needs to know exactly what she's playing with. She thinks that she should check it, so she goes back to the bedroom. It's the first time she's been surprised: before, she pulled the paper off, and exposed it piece by piece. Now she sees how big it is for the first time, and the mass of blackness seems to make its own negative light, casting the rest of the room in a shadow of its own making. And it seems so tall to her. Impossibly tall. The ceilings are high, ten foot, and this wasn't much taller than the first removal man, but it seems to fill almost every bit of the space. She tries to see on top of it but can't, so she idles in front of it. The screen is still active but on standby, the colour and brightness dampened. She presses it and the whole Machine whirs into life. The noise – she hadn't noticed it before, but it must have been there – is like gears, as if this were some nineteenth-century apparatus. Something almost industrial. She knows that this is a computer, and that what's inside is fans and microchips and cables to carry processes from one part to another; and the hard drive, never forget the hard drive, the brain and heart of the Machine both – but the noise is unlike any that she's heard. She supposes that she's forgotten: that things have changed since this was cutting edge. She thinks about the newer models of the Machine, the ones after this. How much one of them would have cost her, even if it could be hacked and updated like this one has been. That she would have been here in a decade still, forming her plan, slowly losing herself, alone for so long, with Vic's body rotting more and more. Less her husband with each passing day, week, month, year.

The screen gets lighter, and she sees the button labelled ABOUT. She presses it, and there, a year and a firmware number. She reasons that this must have been one of the first commercial models, before even her mother started on the programme, and well before Vic was using one. She pulls the Crown down from the dock and the screen changes, updates. PURGE, it invokes, or REPLENISH. Like this is some sort of advertisement. She's seen the language on beauty products and bleaches both. She doesn't put the Crown on her head, because she dare not.

She's thought about it, sometimes: as she's tried to get to sleep, lying in bed, thinking about how easy it would be to wear a Crown, to press the buttons and to talk about Vic and herself, and their old life together. To talk her way through everything that she's lost. To press the PURGE button and feel it all drift away. Vic used to say that it felt like when you take painkillers for a wound. He said that they gave him heavy stuff after the IED went off and put its shrapnel in his shoulder and his neck, and once he'd popped them there was a sense that it had once hurt, but that it was like an echo of the pain was all that was left, or the memory of the pain. Like it's been rubbed hard and then left alone. That's what the Machine did. He rarely spoke about it as time went on, but in the early days, before Beth was allowed anywhere near the process, when Vic still knew what he was doing and why he was doing it, he frequently used to describe it to Beth when he got home. They said it would be two weeks before he'd start to lose what it was he was running from, and it was, almost to the day. After that, Beth didn't like to say anything more. He knew that it was time for his treatments and he didn't question them. Beth looks at the bar for copying Vic's files over, and it's barely gone down.

Come on, she says, though it's not like she can do anything with it here and now. She lies on the bed next to the Machine, a bed that she's never actually slept in because it felt wrong, somehow, ever since she decorated the room. She watches the bar and shuts her eyes, and thinks about Vic and what he could be.